DOWN BELOW BEYOND

T.A. BRUNO

First published by Feathersong, LLC, 2023
Copyright © 2023 by Thomas Bruno. All Rights Reserved.

No part of this publication may be reproduced, stored, or transmitted in any form or by any means, electronic, mechanical, photocopying, recording, scanning, or otherwise, without written permission from the publisher. It is illegal to copy this book, post it to a website, or distribute it by any other means without permission.

This novel is entirely a work of fiction. The names, characters, and incidents portrayed in it are the work of the author's imagination. Any resemblance to actual persons, living or dead, events, or localities is entirely coincidental.

Cover Illustration © Tom Edwards, TomEdwardsDesign.com
Interior artwork by T. A. Bruno

Second edition: January 27th, 2025

OTHER BOOKS BY T. A. BRUNO

The Song of Kamaria Trilogy:

In the Orbit of Sirens
On the Winds of Quasars
At the Threshold of the Universe

AUTHOR'S NOTE

Down Below Beyond is a standalone novel. It shares some elements with the Song of Kamaria Trilogy, but readers are not required to have any knowledge of those novels to understand this one. For reference, there is a spoiler-free glossary containing information about alien races, planets, and the main characters in the back of the book.

Prepare to sail out into the wild, vast void.
—*T.A.*

For those who create curiosity.

ALIEN GLOSSARY
THE CITIZENS OF LODESPACE

ALBERRYAN	DINTUPPAN	ERUNIAN
FLUCTAN	HUMAN	KURIKOID

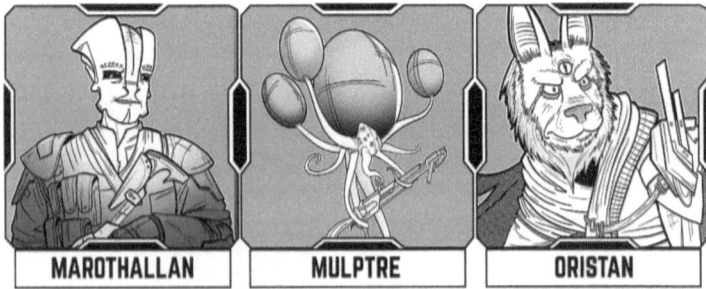

| MAROTHALLAN | MULPTRE | ORISTAN |

| RESLUNI | TAYOXAN | XIKOLING |

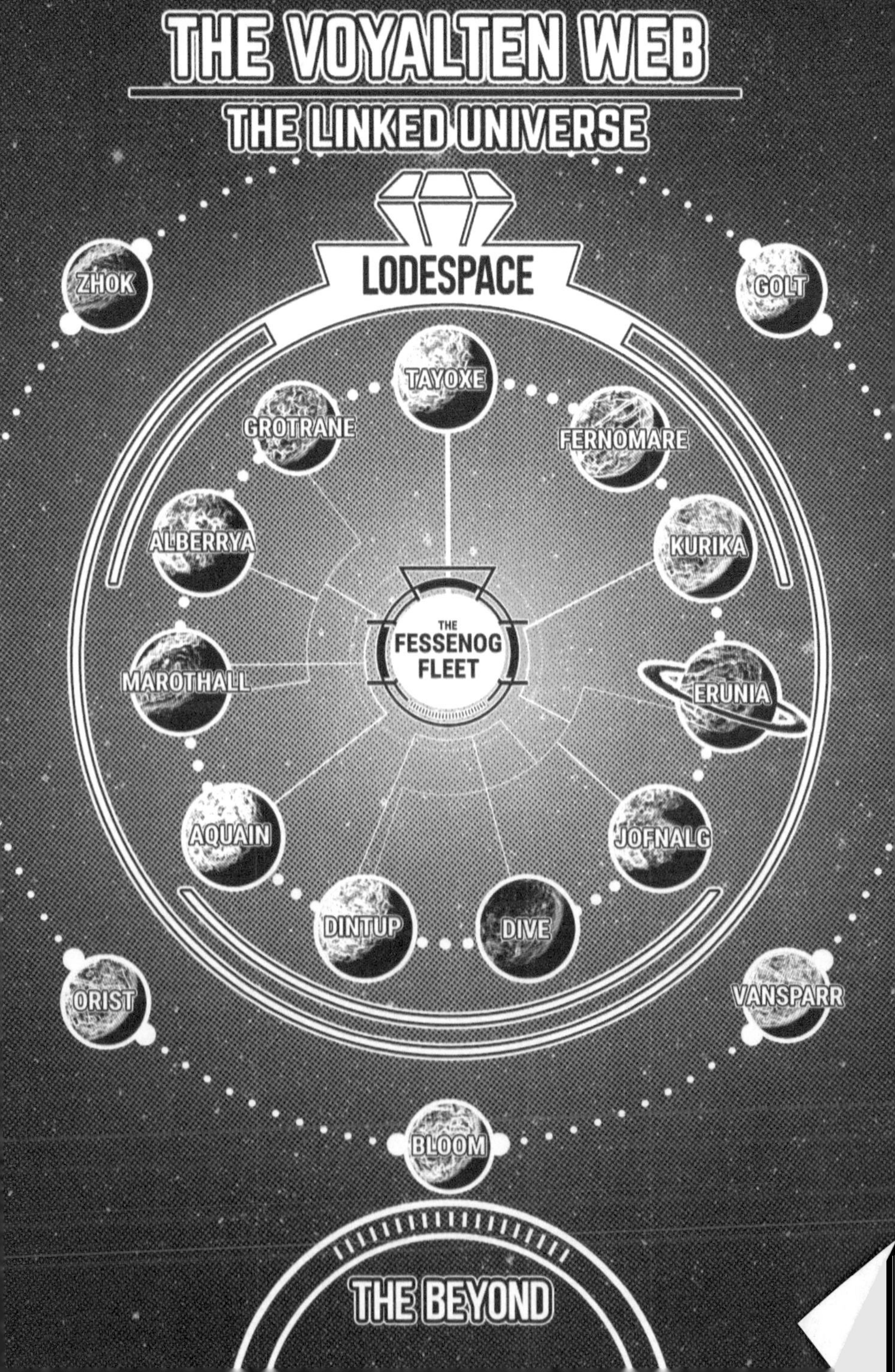
THE VOYALTEN WEB
THE LINKED UNIVERSE
LODESPACE
ZHOK
GOLT
TAYOXE
GROTRANE
FERNOMARE
ALBERRYA
KURIKA
THE FESSENOG FLEET
MAROTHALL
ERUNIA
AQUAIN
JOFNALG
DINTUP
DIVE
ORIST
VANSPARR
BLOOM
THE BEYOND

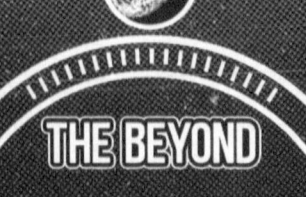

PART 01
A Prospector Stakes a Claim

ONE

"Pretty sure we just walked in a circle," Bayfo Niall grunted. Sweat coated his blond hair, and his ivory-white enforcer suit weighed him down as he trudged along. "How long are we gonna wander around?"

Levort Aatra huffed. "We're coming up on something big. I can feel it." He checked the datapad infused within the sleeve of his prospecting cloak. Strands of his long, ebony hair dangled in front of his bearded face. His gear jingled and clattered, and his HAMMER model salvager hung loosely in its sling on his lower back.

"I'm not in the mood for hunches, Lev. Have you found something or not?" Bayfo asked as he slumped down onto a low stone fence wall. His enforcer gear landed with him with a resounding thunk.

The world of Tayoxe had once been a thriving planet, inhabited by a highly technological race of beings that had already vanished before the Fessenog Fleet bought it and turned it into a prospector playground. Tall towers of mostly stripped buildings loomed over piles of scrap metal ripped apart, misunderstood things that could be traded for hapron credits. The Fleet paid handsomely for unique trinkets found on Tayoxe's surface, but valuable salvage was becoming rarer every day. To find even enough to make the effort worthwhile was becoming an impossible task. The planet was mostly stripped down to its rotting bones, leaving the scavengers from above starving for a meal.

Bayfo pushed a gauntleted hand through his hair. "You're not gonna suddenly die if I take a little rest, right?"

Levort looked over his shoulder at Bayfo and smiled. "A thousand things can go terribly wrong."

"So don't do any of those things," Bayfo huffed.

"You're no fun."

"Not my job to be fun." Bayfo waved a lazy hand at Levort and said, "Go do your thing. Just come back when you're done. Shuttles are leaving in forty."

"Forty?" Levort asked. "I thought we had more time."

Bayfo jerked his head toward the horizon. Beyond the vast wastes of ruins and stripped metal was a deep dark cloud that choked out the setting sun. Tayoxe often had acid rain showers throughout this part of the cycle, but the brewing storm looked extra vicious. It swirled with green lightning and void-dark clouds. The air underneath was a vast curtain of brownish-green haze, as rust and pollution coughed from the surface with every acidic raindrop. It burned Tayoxe with its anger.

"*Drit!*" Levort cursed and hustled up the ruined street toward a cluster of collapsed buildings.

Bayfo called after him, "If anyone asks, I was with you the whole time!"

Levort continued up the street for a few more blocks until he was surrounded by tilted behemoths, once used to house Tayoxans. Buildings that had collapsed in some sort of seismic event. No one knew the answers to the questions Tayoxe posed. It was a ghost world, and its secrets were held tightly.

The tingle raced up Levort's spine. It tickled the back of his neck and tugged him toward an alleyway. Compelled, he allowed it to guide him. Prospectors were highly intuitive people, much like gamblers—often, they were both. Feelings, hunches, gut instincts, trick knees, trick *anything* would be considered a prospecting sense. Science dictated it was all in their heads, but prospectors would never believe it was dumb luck anytime they struck a big score. It was the skill of reading their senses.

The tingle pulled Levort down the alley. He scrambled over debris through a hole in a wall until he was inside a tower that had two other buildings collapsed on top of it. Levort slapped the sleeve of his jacket, and the fabric glowed with a bright blue ambiance, faintly illuminating the dark place enough to see. For more directed light, Levort reached for his salvager.

The salvager was a two-handed tool; one hand gripped a handle like a rifle, and the other gripped a throttle on the top. It was an all-in-one kit for a prospector. Levort had saved up enough hapron to get a HAMMER model, which was capable of more intense carving than the standard Srengor models. The HAMMER's long barrel could do many things with projected ultra-heated plasma. Levort could cut through anything—scrap metal, the side of a building—or even mine raw minerals with it. It was worth the missed meals it cost him.

In the dim azure light rested a spaceship covered in the rubble of multiple centuries in the ravaged city. Its design was unfamiliar, almost insectoid, like the flatland hoppers he had seen in vid-docs. It had a green incandescence on its hull, and although it had been trapped in this tomb, it looked brand new.

"Where did you come from?" Levort whispered to the mysterious ship.

Perhaps it came from outside Lodespace. Thousands of worlds were linked by the Voyalten Portal Web, but only hundreds were considered part of the Fessenog Fleet's trade empire, locally known as Lodespace. Levort's experience was restricted to Tayoxe, and he had many blind spots in his knowledge.

To leave the confines of Tayoxe, Levort would need an S-Class license. With an S-Class license, Levort could prospect on worlds all over Lodespace. His blind spots would become his new adventures beyond the small husk he mined tirelessly. Levort's mouth salivated at the sight of the ship—at the idea of the score he was about to crack open. His tingle morphed into an electric shock of cold bumps all over his skin.

Levort activated the plasma saw on the end of his salvager and plunged it into the ship's hull. With practiced movement, he carved a circle wide enough to move through but small enough so he could weld it back together for a more significant profit. Shifting the throttle on the top of the salvager and pulling the trigger on the grip created a burst of energy that punched the circular-cut hull away, making an entry point. He stepped through.

The inside of the ship was just as unusual as the outside. It was pristine, with curved edges at every angle and a soft reflection on every surface. Besides the mess Levort had made walking in, the place still looked fully operational. Lights dotted various machinery of mysterious purposes, and canisters lined the walls. An odd language was scrawled on some of the surfaces. Usually, Levort's fluency node in his jacket would have translated the text for him as he looked at it, but nothing came. *Maybe it's art?*

The time on Lev's datapad sleeve said he only had minutes to spare. He wouldn't be able to salvage the whole ship in that time. Still, with Bayfo present, he could lay a claim and return to haul the rest next time. It cost more to do so. The Fleet charged a fee to protect a claim that roughed out to about twenty percent of the overall haul that came from it, on top of their other fees for extracting and protecting the prospector. Still, it was Levort's only choice. Claim it, or hope for the best. This was too good a find to simply hope.

A small hazy light emitted from a console nearby. It had not been on when Levort walked in. He was unsure if it was some long-dead security module that had activated in his presence. Colored lights that changed hue grew as Levort approached the console. More of the obscure lettering appeared within the lights. They shifted and curled within themselves like writhing creatures. He tapped his finger against the console, and there was no reaction. Determining the console wasn't somehow dangerous, Lev inspected it further and found a latch. He pressed his thumb against the small latch and worked it upward. The console spat out a small palm-sized device, and Levort caught it.

It was curved on top and flat on the bottom. A dot of light hovered above the top surface, and as Levort waved it around, the dot moved toward him. It reminded him of an electronic compass. But this didn't seem to be pointing toward Tayoxe's magnetic North.

Bayfo's voice crackled through Levort's communication channel. "Time's up. Gotta get moving unless you want an acid bath."

"On my way out. Staking a claim." Levort said, pocketing the strange, curved device.

"Wait, you actually found something?" Bayfo asked with excitement in his voice.

"Starting to think you're my bad luck charm, Bayfo." Levort laughed, his uncontained smile pulling his face apart.

"I'll leave you alone more often if it makes us rich." Bayfo accepted the dig with a practiced sincerity obtained from cycles of friendship. "I'm coming by. Ping me your position."

Levort tapped at his datapad sleeve, sending Bayfo the data he requested. He exited through the hole he'd cut in the ship's hull and dropped back into the ruined building. He made his way back to the street, but stopped when he noticed a shadow in the ambient glow ahead. "You got here quick. See what I—" Levort squinted and realized the shadow wasn't Bayfo. It was too large and didn't have the distinct silhouette of the enforcer suit.

Bayfo's voice crackled over the comm, "Man, didn't I tell you to stay close? You wandered halfway across Tayoxe!"

The shadow before Levort was quiet, proving his fears correct. After a moment of stillness, the shadow spoke with a deep raspy voice, "You better get gone. Don't worry. I'll take good care of that ship for you."

Lev had never been accosted by a fellow prospector before but had heard of the cheaters who had stolen claims. Sometimes they shirked their enforcer escorts and spent time on Tayoxe between shuttles, cutting a deal with their guard to sign them in and out. This prospector must have come into the alley looking for shelter from the incoming storm and stumbled on the same find Levort had.

"Time's wasting." The cheating prospector hissed the words.

Levort reached for an emergency button on his cloak, and the cheater lifted a smitegun. The large handheld blaster looked like a toy in the cheater's monster-sized fist. The huge prospector stepped closer to Levort and revealed himself in Levort's cloak light.

The cheater wasn't human, which wasn't a surprise to Levort—humans were rare in Lodespace. Tufts of hair peeked out between plates of crustacean exoskeleton. His mouth clicked as he talked, salivating bubbles as he anticipated a fight. He wore a dingy cloak like Levort's, but clearly tattered from extended stays on Tayoxe. This was a Dintuppan, one of the many alien races in Lodespace.

"Where's your enforcer?" Levort asked, his hand hanging over the emergency button on his cloak. The Dintuppan didn't respond, and he got close enough to Levort to push the smitegun against his chest.

"Going to be hard to miss from this—" The Dintuppan was interrupted as scuffling came from the rubble near the corner on the right. Another shadow moved from behind some debris and up to a hole in the ceiling. Levort had assumed it was a friend of the cheater, but the surprise on his crustacean face said otherwise. The shadow vanished into the hole in the ceiling corner.

Levort was smaller but quicker than the Dintuppan. He swung his salvager with one hand, using the broad side of it like a club. It struck the Dintuppan in the head, and his smitegun fired into the ground near Levort's foot. Levort's other hand jabbed the emergency button on his cloak. A bright red light pulsed through his clothing, creating a confusing strobe effect in the dimly lit place. This setting on his cloak also immediately informed Bayfo that he was in danger.

Blinded by the light, the Dintuppan swung his burly arms wildly, catching Levort in the shoulder and throwing him sideways toward the entrance. The air was knocked out of his lungs, and his vision blurred.

"You *konndan drit*!" the cheating Dintuppan cursed, shooting in Levort's direction with his smitegun. Levort rolled to the side just quickly enough to avoid being hit. The Dintuppan rushed toward Levort to get a better shot. His stalked eyes were no good in the strobing red light. Levort throttled the top of his salvager and pulled the trigger. As the cheater approached, a blast of hot plasma punched the Dintuppan back so hard he hit the opposite wall of the building's interior. Debris loosened and fell on top of the Dintuppan.

Levort scrambled to his feet and moved toward the cheating prospector, unsure if he had killed the Dintuppan. With a burst of stone and rubble, the Dintuppan launched at Levort and bashed him into the ground. Levort was pinned by the Dintuppan's immense weight and could only watch as he raised his fists, preparing to smash down on Levort's head.

A white-hot bolt of lightning exploded into the room and struck the Dintuppan. The electricity shocked both the cheating prospector and Levort. Pain flushed through Levort's veins, bouncing around his skeleton. The Dintuppan slumped to the side, freeing Levort, but both were too stunned to do anything except seize up.

Bayfo Niall entered the room, his white suit shining with bright light. He put his foot on the Dintuppan's chest and trained his enforcer rifle on his crustacean head. Bayfo looked from the Dintuppan to Levort and asked, "You good? Sorry you got a piece of that stun too." He lifted Levort onto his feet.

"Thanks," Levort coughed.

"Bad luck charm, my ass." Bayfo pulled a detainer from the sleeve on his thigh and pushed it onto the Dintuppan's chest. It wrapped itself around the cheating prospector, inflated into a balloon, and then levitated off the ground. "Come on, we're late now. Put your hood up and hope we get back before the storm overtakes us."

"Don't forget. Claim." Levort struggled to speak, still half stunned.

"Sure. Move," Bayfo said. With a few clicks of his gauntlet, the position was registered with the Fessenog Fleet as rightfully Levort Aatra's claim.

They had no time to waste. Levort and Bayfo worked their way back to the street and down the hill toward the prospecting outpost. Bayfo pulled the cheating prospector along like a child holding a balloon while Levort nursed the pain in his shoulder. His teeth felt weird after the stun, and his tongue searched his mouth. They approached the prospector's outpost as it began to drizzle acid from the sky. The shuttle had already gone through its preflight check.

The shuttlemaster, a Kurikoid, rolled her bulbous eyes at Bayfo. "What-what is that? You-you can't bring that here. No-no room!" she croaked, pointing at the ballooned Dintuppan under arrest.

"This one's out past curfew. His enforcer escort isn't here. We should bring him back to see who's long-terming," Bayfo shouted over the shuttle's roaring engines.

The Kurikoid shuttlemaster shook her horned amphibian head. "No-no room, I said!"

"Stick him in baggage, then. I don't care!" Bayfo shouted,

handing the balloon to the shuttlemaster. She reflexively grabbed it and tried to protest as Bayfo passed by her. It was her problem now. Levort quietly apologized as he moved past the Kurikoid.

Levort entered the shuttle behind Bayfo and took a seat next to him. The window on the opposite wall gave them a full panoramic view. The shuttle lifted off, and Tayoxe dropped away. There was some chop as they pushed through the acid storm clouds and rushed into orbit.

Levort thumbed the small, curved trinket he'd found inside the ship on his claim. He didn't dare bring it into the light where other prospectors could see it. That could tempt another cheater's unscheduled visit to his claim in the future. Instead, he smiled and thought of the S-Class license he would purchase and what worlds he might see.

He noticed the faces of the other prospectors. Though a few had thick cloaks stuffed with various goodies from Tayoxe, others looked empty-eyed out into space. The mask of desperation wore heavily on the prospectors who had taken multiple trips down to Tayoxe and found nothing. There were more of these cases on every trip. Staking a claim to find nothing was an easy way to fall into inescapable debt with the Fleet. It was too easy to lose what little you had. Too easy to slip. That was what made prospecting a gamble. When you won, you won big. When you lost, you lost everything.

Levort was one bad trip away from losing it all.

The shuttle pivoted, and the panoramic window was filled with ships of all shapes and sizes. The Fessenog Fleet was a conglomerate of starships from the various alien worlds of Lodespace. Each vessel's design was unique to its homeworld. Some were curved, and some were hard-edged. There were colorful ships and dull gray hulls. Some were built horizontally, others vertically, and others like wheels or orbs. Each starship had drones shipping to and from its docks constantly, like insects entering and exiting hives. It was a bustling, crowded place in space, more alive than the surface of Tayoxe might have ever been.

Consonance Hub was in the center of the ships, a space station shaped like a giant egg. It was filled with low-rent housing and various shopping and entertainment districts, all designed to relieve hapron from anyone wandering through it. Levort lived on the hub with all the other prospectors. It was the only option available to them. Without an S-Class license, they would be forced to remain in Consonance Hub until they could afford one.

Hovering above it all was the largest starship, the *Ultimatrion*, where Gulna Kii Fessenog resided over his trade empire. The Fessenog Fleet was named after him. Even though the naming convention implied it was a tightly ruled monarchy, the only things governing this collection of ships were hapron credits and trade. The masters of each vessel could do as they pleased, but netting hapron kept them tightly bound to the Fleet. It was too lucrative to go elsewhere and irresponsible to start fresh anywhere new.

The shuttle clunked to a stop.

Bayfo stood and checked the datapad on his gauntlet. "It's good to be home."

TWO

Levort shouldered his salvager and followed Bayfo off the shuttle. The Kurikoid shuttlemaster croaked, "Don't-don't forget your cargo!"

Bayfo mumbled, "Almost forgot about that guy." He went to the back of the shuttle to collect the detainee while Levort stretched his arms and rubbed his sore muscles. The Dintuppan was dazed inside the balloon. The cheating prospector had suffered a rough ride from Tayoxe to Consonance Hub. "Just need a second, Lev," Bayfo said as he carried the balloon over to the counter on the far side of the dock.

Consonance Hub had many docks on its shell, and it was the same on every port—crowded, cramped, and smelly with its inhabitants' various alien body odors. Levort kept his hand on the trinket in his pocket and a tight grip on his HAMMER model salvager.

Bayfo handed the balloon over to a large Resluni, a bipedal reptilian species with hard scales and long tentacle-like whiskers that protruded from its short-snouted face. He wore an enforcer combat mech-suit unit—an EMU—adding to his imposing stature. Dock security was always overly prepared for a pirate raid.

Bayfo smiled and said, "Here you go, happy birthday." The Resluni grunted and took the balloon, somehow looking smaller while holding it. After a short inspection and tagging the balloon for transport, the Resluni attached the tether to a drone nearby and watched it sail off toward the nearest enforcer station for processing. "I appreciate it," Bayfo thanked the Resluni, who grunted back in reply.

Bayfo walked across the dock toward Levort and said, "Well, we're back early, thanks to the storm. What do you want to do?"

"I gotta drop my kit off back at home. Want to meet up later?"

Bayfo cocked an eyebrow. "Winder's? We got stuff to celebrate."

Levort answered by bumping forearms with Bayfo and nodding. They said their goodbyes and parted ways. Navigating Consonance Hub was a routine annoyance for Levort. He had a room on the void side of the station with a window that gave him an excellent view of nothing-at-all. Most people dreaded staring into the void, but after a long day prospecting in a junk world and swimming through crowds, gazing at sheer darkness was a treat.

He stepped on and off automatic platforms and walked through two districts before returning home. It was a cramped one-room escape pod that had been refurbished into a living space two generations ago. One wall had a circular window with a hammock under it, the pillows constantly drifting into the pit that formed when Levort wasn't laying in it. The walls were functional, with many compartments and locks for storage. They were repurposed from the survival creches they used to be into *plenty of closet space!* The bathroom contained a vacuum toilet with two hoses and a stand-up shower that was barely functional enough to clean him off. He gave it his best effort.

Clean enough for Winder's, he took two half steps from the shower to the small pull-out tray table, where he'd put the curved trinket from the strange ship. For the first time since leaving Tayoxe, he noticed no shifting lights or glowing green dot. "Ah, *drit*!" He picked up the trinket and shook it, hoping it would reactivate. The device offered no response.

"Might still be worth something," he mumbled. Levort put on his casual station clothes and jacket and shoved the trinket in his pocket before taking the four steps from the hammock to the door to exit his home.

A Fessenog Collection Center was a short walk and a public

shuttle ride from Levort's home. He stopped and waited in line behind other prospectors he had seen around before but never conversed with. Prospecting was a selfishly kept job. Revealing your score could lead to a robbery. There was only one place where prospectors shared their adventures, which involved much more alcohol.

All Fessenog facilities were pristine, making the prospectors who had come straight there after a haul look more decrepit. Levort believed that taking a quick moment to bathe between work and trade led to a better deal. There was no proof of this, but it hadn't hurt anyone to try. Levort figured some would call it hygienically superstitious.

"Next!" an Erunian called, beckoning Levort to its counter window. It was a lumbering six-legged giant parasite with a thin snout and big round black eyes. Erunians lived in four phases, and this late-phase broker looked freshly molted. Its exoskeleton still showed some pale markings from shedding through its previous phase-body. The Erunian fiddled with a datapad in its long palps and looked up at Levort as he approached.

"Good to see you again, Lev," the Erunian's antenna patted against the glass window in genuine friendliness.

"Yeah, Glott, been a while since I had something to trade. Hope it's worth something," Levort slid the trinket under the glass. Glott inspected it in its palps, turning it over and touching it with its antenna for extra sense.

"Hmmm. Very interesting. Not much here, though. Looks like rare tech but not much doing. Hmmm…" Glott analyzed. A notification pinged his datapad, and the Erunian stopped inspecting the trinket. Levort watched as Glott read the silent message. This was a little unusual. Glott looked up from the datapad and asked, "A claim is also on your account now. Yes, very interesting. Is it true, yes?"

"Yeah, made a stake today. Had to fight for it too." Unsure of the trinket's worth, Levort decided to bluff. "Plenty more of that where it came from."

Glott looked at the trinket, then back to Levort, "Ah, yes. Good, and yes." Levort waited for the total as Glott looked to the curiosity and back to its datapad. Finally: "Eighty thousand hapron. Yes. Eighty thousand."

Levort frowned. Eighty thousand credits might cover his tab at Winder's tonight. Still, it was a little disappointing after the show Glott put on about it. Levort signed the digidoc that transferred the hapron credits to his account.

"Fessenog thanks you for your service." Glott bowed its long snout and spread its palps outward.

"I'll be back with more." Levort winked, rhythmically tapped the counter, and exited the facility. Outside, Levort checked his data sleeve for messages from Bayfo. The lights in the station had shifted from pinks to darker blues, imitating a night sky on Tayoxe. The station even added the interior temperature drop to simulate nightfall.

"Excuse me." A thin human wearing ragged clothing tugged at Levort's jacket. "I have things worth many hapron. Would you like to trade for them, prospector?" The thin human showed Levort scraps of jagged metal before he could answer.

Levort's heart sank in his chest. "No luck on Tayoxe?" Levort asked.

The thin beggar looked down and covered the wares they'd meant to barter. "No. I lost my partner a few cycles back. Haven't had much luck since. The Fleet takes more in fees every day."

Levort had never had a partner. Not that he didn't want one. It just always seemed like too much work to keep two mouths fed. Bayfo was the closest thing to a partner he'd ever had, but as an enforcer, he still got paid even if Levort found nothing but dust.

A few more beggars shaded the corners of the street outside the trading facility. Levort sighed. It didn't matter if you had the biggest score on the best claim, every prospector was only a few bad trips away from the state these people were in. Levort knew his claim would pay out, and that was a blessing not many could afford. His heart told him what to do.

"Keep your stuff. Trade it in for whatever it's worth." Levort tapped the sleeve on his jacket, illuminating a panel of the fabric with a data screen. He gently held the beggar's sleeve and did the same. With a few flicks, Levort transferred forty thousand hapron to the beggar's account. The beggar's eyes grew wet. Levort winked and whispered, "I hope this helps."

The beggar wiped at the tears staining their cheeks and thanked Levort. Levort patted the beggar on the shoulder and said, "I hope Tayoxe is kinder to you."

"Y-you too," the beggar said as they collected their scrap and entered the collection center. Levort walked toward Winder's with half the hapron he'd earned, but he didn't care. The thought of his claim gave him a lift to his steps. Maybe some of his luck had transferred to the beggar with the hapron, and Tayoxe would shine brighter for them both.

Winder's was on the far end of a large plaza filled with neon lights and artificial fog. Restaurants outlined the plaza, with people from all over the station enjoying meals in the ample open space. An ornate fountain sprayed digital neon-colored water into a basin filled with light. Tucked into the corner was the tiny bar with a sign in big, bold letters: WINDER'S.

A whistle alerted Levort as he stepped through the doors. Bayfo was already inside, sitting at the bar near the long window that lined the far wall. Levort crossed the room toward him, passing by the regular patrons. Prospectors frequented this bar to brag about their scores and cut loose after long days on Tayoxe. Some of the more distressed prospectors would try and link up with people who had good claims planetside, attempting to get a small cut of their perceived wins.

This night, the bar was pretty quiet. The claims were shrinking, the bragging smaller, the tension hotter. A game of asteroid jousting was playing on the vid-screen that hung behind the bartender, but no one seemed to care, despite the number of eyes staring at the display.

"Sorry for the wait. I got held up at the collection center for a minute," Levort said as he sat next to Bayfo.

"Just in time for the show." Bayfo pointed toward the long window. Outside, many other Fleet trade ships drifted amicably, as always. Their small drones zipped in and out from Consonance Hub as exchanges constantly took place. Bayfo took a sip of his drink and tapped the bar, requesting another one for Levort from the bartender. "Keep watching," Bayfo said as he caught the glass that slid across the bar and handed it to Levort.

Three ships sprang into view, pulling full throttle. The lead was a ramshackle thing, made of junk from Tayoxe and whatever else could be cobbled together to create something spaceworthy. The pursuers were enforcer gunships. They fired at the fleeing junk ship as it swerved through a crowd of drones and smaller trade ships. Bayfo explained, "Some prospectors, trying to take an unscheduled visit to Tayoxe. Our Dintuppan friend from earlier vented the info."

There was a flash of light but no sound. The junk ship was struck by a plasma blast and crumpled apart before smashing into one of the trade drones. The gunships moved in and sucked up the debris, making the trade lane viable again for the drones. No one except Bayfo and Levort noticed. The other patrons' eyes remained sullenly glued to the vid-screens in the bar. Bayfo turned toward Levort and clinked his glass against his. "Congrats on the claim today."

Levort took a moment to regain himself. He wasn't so quick to forget the junk ship explosion. His thoughts remained on the prospectors who had just died outside the window. He coughed, "Yeah, uh, thanks. I think it'll be a big one."

"What was in there? I only saw the Dintuppan and some rubble. Didn't have time to look around with the storm comin' in." Bayfo took another sip of his drink.

"Looked like a starship to me, but it was different than anything I'd seen before." Levort peered into his drink as his mind thought of the strange find. "Inside was all new looking, but it must have been trapped under those collapsed buildings for centuries. Looked pre-Fleet to me."

"Pre-Fleet? *Drit*, I don't think I'd ever heard of a prospector finding a ship that old in good shape. You might be setting a record," Bayfo said. "What's your plan for your jackpot?"

"S-Class license. I want to travel all of Lodespace." Levort smiled and drank heartily at the thought.

Bayfo laughed. "Oh, you mean Tayoxe doesn't have pretty enough vistas for you? What about the sunrise from Mount Crap? Or how the hills of junk roll gently into the acid lakes? Ah, and that early morning rust smog. How could it be any better?"

"Yeah, I know. Hard to believe," Levort added, echoing his friend's sarcasm.

"I've been to a few worlds since I graduated from the academy." Bayfo spun his chair to face the rest of the bar, his elbows leaning back. "They are something, that's for sure. The Fleet trades for exotics on a bunch of interesting worlds. But you know, you could save that hapron if I got to crew my own ship. One day I'll be a commander, and I'd take you along. You could be my crew's official prospector."

It wasn't the first time Bayfo had mentioned wanting his own ship. As much as Levort wanted to believe Bayfo would rank up enough in the enforcers to become a commander and crew his own starship, it still seemed like it would take too long. Bayfo had graduated from the academy three cycles ago and had a long way to climb to become a commander. Prospectors were short-game people, and enforcers were deep planners. It was one of the aspects of their friendship that wedged them apart.

"Sounds like a good deal," Levort said, not wanting to disagree with his friend. He'd rather beat Bayfo to the chase and absolve their aspirations before waiting cycles for Bayfo to fulfill it. It was a race to happiness.

"Maybe they'll bump me up after you strip this claim clean." Bayfo smiled.

"Hey, maybe *I'll* buy us a ship with this claim money," Levort offered.

Bayfo squinted at him and shook his head. "Never heard of a prospector striking it that rich. You'd have to find a new fleet down there on Tayoxe to buy one portal hopper. Sorry, friend."

Levort was slapped by the reality of Bayfo's words. He heard the unspoken thing Bayfo hadn't said: *Prospectors don't leave Tayoxe.*

Bayfo ordered another round and caught the glasses that slid down the bar. He went to hand one to Levort, forcing Levort to finish his current drink and accept the next one. "Cheer up, Lev. You got a good claim. We'll get you that S-Class license and hitch a ride somewhere. It's all up from now on. Let's drink like we own this station!"

Levort accepted the next drink and clinked his mug with Bayfo's. "Damn right!"

THREE

Levort felt the whole station spinning around him. The dance of artificial gravity on his bones, the stale scent of oxygen pumped into the pressurized air, the cold press of the metal wall against his palm as he spat onto the floor in the alley outside the bar. "I think I'm gonna be—" He was cut off as he violently expelled his stomach's contents into the alley behind Winder's. Suddenly the stale air was preferable to the new scent he had created.

Bayfo shook his head. "We might have overdone ourselves. Take your time. We got all night."

Levort pressed his forehead against the wall and groaned.

Bayfo rolled his eyes. "Come on. It's a good night. Let's not cut this off early."

"Early?" Levort glared at Bayfo. "We've been drinking for what feels like a whole cycle!"

"It's been four hours. Grow up." Bayfo smirked playfully.

Levort pushed himself away from the wall, wobbling on his feet. "I think I'm ready to go back home." He stumbled toward the front of the alley. Bayfo caught up with him quickly.

"Just follow me for a minute," Bayfo insisted. "I got an idea."

Levort shook his head, and his double vision reduced back to singular momentarily. "What?"

"Follow me. This way. It'll be fun." Bayfo walked to the corner as a public shuttle pulled up. Levort took a few deep breaths and summoned his fortitude, warding off his drunk stupor just enough to walk in a relatively straight line. He made it onto the shuttle next to Bayfo and flopped into a seat. Bayfo stood, holding the bar that stretched floor to ceiling for stability. Levort saw him as he always did, as his protector, friend, and the older brother he never had. The jolting of the shuttle seemed to have no effect on Bayfo Niall's stoic posture.

"Let's get off here." Bayfo tapped his hand against Levort's shoulder. Levort nodded. The drinks left in his stomach were releasing their grip on his body. He could stand and follow Bayfo out into the street with only minor corrections in his movement.

Levort blinked a few times as his eyes adjusted. "Wait, this is…"

"Just look at the state of it." Bayfo walked toward a worn-down building welded into an outlet in the metal walls. It was hidden away from the shuttle stop, down an alley, and lit only by a flickering light that would one day die out and cast this sector into forgotten darkness. Window panels lining its outer walls were mostly broken and smashed, and a failed attempt had been made to weld the front door shut to keep out intruders.

Levort's veins were coated in ice, and sobriety quickly engulfed him. He had no words for this place. "Home" was incorrect, yet he had spent his childhood here. Scrap metal and other rusted junk lined the path to the front door, and although it wasn't always abandoned, it always felt haunted to Levort.

"Why are we here?" Levort asked.

Bayfo picked up a heavy metal plate and waved it around, testing its weight. "It's where we met! You recognize it, don't—"

"How could I forget?" Levort whispered. "Let's get going."

Bayfo eyed Levort with slight disappointment. "Oh, come on. I thought you'd be more sentimental. You're on the verge of making a big score! Your life's looking up for the first time in a long time. I thought it might be fun to come back here and bury some ghosts."

"Bury ghosts?"

Bayfo gripped the heavy metal plate and hurled it through one of the less broken windows, shattering it and casting the loud echo of broken glass through the abandoned space. Levort covered his ears until the noise stopped.

"Your turn," Bayfo invited him. "Go ahead."

Levort looked in the immediate area around his feet until he found a suitable pipe. He snatched it, ripping it free of the junk it was submerged inside. All the windows had been smashed, but a panel hung loose from the front wall. Levort hurled the pipe, watching it twirl through the air until it collided with the panel. It cracked against it, sending it all crashing to the ground in a loud explosion of dust and rust.

"*Drit* yeah! How did that feel?" Bayfo smiled.

Levort didn't feel anything. Hurting this building didn't remove the pain it had given him long ago. The memory of his parents selling him to this place was still breathing in these walls.

The Aatras—Levort's biological parents—had sold Levort to the Fleet to cover expenses when he was only eight cycles old. Shortly afterward, they were both killed in an accident on Tayoxe. Levort was old enough to remember the betrayal and still angry enough to hate them for dying. Levort worked in the Fleet's sorting facility for his entire childhood, organizing garbage into the right machines until sorting facilities were made illegal.

Junk was all he knew, so he became a prospector. Just like mom and dad.

"Let's go inside," Bayfo suggested. He moved up to the front door and gave the bent metal that blocked their entry a strong pull, bending it further. Bayfo pushed himself inside and slapped his hand against his chest, activating an ambient light in the fabric of his clothing.

Bayfo vanished from view before Levort could will himself to follow. After a few deep breaths, Levort stepped toward the building and through the door. Suddenly he was a scared little boy again.

The interior of the sorting facility was dark, only dimly lit by the glow from Bayfo's clothes. Machinery had been stripped down to its frames, and the walls and floors were mostly bare except for rusted metal. A mound of useless scrap was piled against the back wall, and a staircase traveled to an upper floor. Holes in the ceiling implied the upstairs had been harvested as much as the first-floor area.

"It looks so different now," Bayfo said, his words echoing off the empty walls.

"Not to me," Levort whispered.

Bayfo walked over to the frame of an old sorting machine and smiled. "Remember when we used to have scrap wars?"

Levort approached his friend and nodded. "Still got some scars." He pointed to a nick in his hand, long healed but never forgotten.

"Benny got the worst of it."

"You sent him to the hospital," Levort reminded him.

"He came back fine! I saw what he was going to throw your way. Glad I stopped him when I did. You junk kids really didn't know when you were going too far."

"Yeah, I remember." It had been an old saw blade. As kids, they had gotten caught up in the moment, but it would have been much worse for Levort if Bayfo hadn't stepped in.

"I bet I can still hit that back wall from here." Bayfo ripped a piece off the metal frame of the sorting machine.

"I'm sure you could. If you could do it as a kid, I imagine it would be easier now."

Bayfo ignored him and launched the broken frame across the room like a javelin. It plunged into the far wall, easily implanting itself in the rusted metal paneling. Bayfo pumped his fist. "Still got it."

Levort shook his head and looked toward the stairs. He stepped away from Bayfo, who was preparing to see if he could hurl another improvised javelin at the far wall, and ascended into the shadows above. He tapped a panel of fabric on his chest, and it released an ambient glow, giving him enough light to see into the abandoned place. The hallway was familiar to him, and it was easy to retrace the steps he took as a kid to his old room.

He shouldered open the door, and his light illuminated the place he used to restlessly lay. Dreams were eaten by walls like these. A row of bed frames and rotten mattresses flanked the room on each side. Long ago, an orb on the opposite wall provided light, but it had long since needed a new bulb. Three beds from the back, he saw it. The frame was rusted, and the mattress was ripped to shreds, a home for various insects that crept their way onto the station.

Something clawed at Levort's heart as he stood at the base of the bed. Memories of loneliness, sorrow, never-ending dread. It was all still resting here, in this room. Places remembered what people often forgot—or what people would strive to forget.

Still, there was one secret known only to Levort Aatra.

He knelt next to the wall and pushed his hand against a small panel roughly the size of his fist. It clicked and fell into his hand, revealing a hidden pocket in the metal. His light revealed an artifact that a child once held dear. He grabbed it and held the small thing in his hand.

A toy, something soft in a world filled with jagged metal and rust. It was dusty and a little rotten from time, but warmth still radiated from within its stitched cloth skin.

"Oh wow! I didn't realize you kept that thing." Bayfo said. Levort hadn't noticed him come into the room. "I remember when I gave you that. It was just a baby thing I used to like that I didn't need anymore."

Levort rubbed the stuffed figure, its button eyes and stitched grin still intact. It had long ears and floppy arms and legs. It was once a vibrant green, but now wore a pale brown hue. The stuffed toy did not resemble any animal or creature Levort was familiar with. Yet, its shape was a comfort to him. Levort turned toward Bayfo and said, "Just having this thing with me helped me calm down on the bad days. Thank you for letting me keep it."

Bayfo nodded. "My dad got pissed at me when he found out I 'lost' it." Bayfo pumped his fingers. "He wanted to give it to a coworker's kid or something. Eh, whatever. Glad it helped you instead."

Bayfo had never lived in the sorting facility. His father was an enforcer, just like him. He was in charge of the owners' security and was assigned to help keep order among the junk kids that lived here. Sometimes Bayfo would tag along, and that was how they became friends. Bayfo was only a little older than Levort and bigger than the sorting facility kids, making him Levort's perfect protector. Their friendship often stirred the ire of the other junk kids, but they knew better than to upset the friend of the enforcer's kid. It didn't stop them every time, though.

"They should tear this place down." Bayfo spat on the floor.

"I thought they did," Levort said. Sorting facilities and the use of orphans as junk organizers had been outlawed when Levort had almost finished his teenage cycles. The facilities had originally been designed to help stray children learn how to become engineers and give them a home when they had none to return to. But they had become workhouses, abused in their purpose to sort junk to scrape hapron out of the refuse that prospectors brought back from Tayoxe. Anything they couldn't use was melted into ingots and sold cheaply.

Levort was happy this place didn't somehow find further use after he was freed.

The stuffed animal bounced against the ripped-up mattress as Levort tossed it.

"Don't you want to take that home?" Bayfo asked.

"Don't need him anymore." Levort patted Bayfo on the shoulder. "Let's get out of here. We got a big day tomorrow."

Bayfo nodded and followed Levort out of the old dusty room. The stuffed figure rested on the bed, soothing the ghost of Levort's past as the lights faded and the shadows engulfed it.

FOUR

The shuttle settled onto the Tayoxe dirt. Prospectors and their enforcer escorts stepped off and inhaled the scorching air. Levort tightened the straps on his cloak and adjusted his HAMMER salvager's position on his hip. The Kurikoid shuttlemaster barked at them from the ship, "Wear-wear breathers! Acid-acid rain kicked up lots of *drit*. Don't-don't be stupid!"

Levort removed the breathing mask from the pouch on his shoulder and strapped it to his face. Bayfo stepped off the shuttle and clicked a button on his collar that forced a mask over his mouth and nose automatically. "Time to get rich." He bumped forearms with Levort.

"Let's get that hapron," Levort said, his voice slightly muffled through his breather.

The atmosphere that followed acid storms gave Tayoxe a sense of beauty in a dreary way. The rain had burned off the top layer of rust on everything, leaving reflective puddles in the dirty streets. The smog was beaten down temporarily, and visibility was higher across the area. As Levort and Bayfo walked uphill, they could see the white reflection of the enormous portal floating in space, looming like an extra moon.

The space portal was the main trade route outside Tayoxe, built long ago by a race of aliens known as the Voyalten. These aliens linked the universe like a web with their network of portals. Worlds that would have never met before were now only a threshold away.

The Voyalten never forced any world to partake in the web if they didn't want to. Instead, they gave every world a choice—open their portal, shut it off, or make it a one-way stream. Voyalten portals were gigantic, big enough to fit multiple starships through. Many of these thresholds were planetside, but some were constructed in orbit, like Tayoxe's. After linking the worlds, the Voyalten would leave the planet alone and move on to the next one, their journeys taking eons. The Voyalten were immortal creatures, so time was no issue for them. Not many people had ever seen a Voyalten in person.

Around Lodespace, the Voyalten were treated as a simple fact and pushed to the back of the useless trivia pile—despite the fact that there would be no Lodespace without the Voyalten Portal Web.

Tayoxe's orbital portal might be the most frequently used threshold in the web. From planetside, it was impossible to see the ships that constantly passed in and out of it, but all Fleet citizens knew of the legendary traffic jams it generated.

Levort smiled as he looked at the portal. He thought of the worlds beyond its threshold and what might be out there. All it took was an S-Class license, and he was going to get one. His claim was up ahead.

They came to where Bayfo had rested the day before and stopped their hike.

The blood drained from Levort's face, and a cold chill lanced through his veins. His hands felt numb, and his breather felt like it was malfunctioning, because he had difficulty inhaling anything. "No. No-no-no-no," Levort mumbled as he observed the crater where his claim had been the day before. "What happened? Where is it!"

Bayfo didn't say anything. Words almost crackled out of his throat, but he couldn't produce them. Levort felt crazy. He began to doubt yesterday's events momentarily before rage slapped him out of it. "They fragged it! They fragged my claim!"

"It... It looks that way..." Bayfo whispered, his eyes never leaving the crater.

Levort slumped to his knees. "It's gone. The whole thing is gone."

"Why would they do this? They must have had some sort of

reason." Bayfo looked up into the sky. The only thing that could have vaporized the entire block was one of the Fessenog Fleet warships. They would have blasted it from orbit, which took an immense amount of calculation from the mainframe on Consonance Hub to get correct. Although, the wide radius of the crater implied they gave themselves plenty of room for error. "What did you say you found here again?"

Levort shook his head. "It doesn't matter what I found."

"Hard disagree, Lev. Whatever you found was worth stabbing from space."

"I told you. There was a starship. Weird one. Worth a lot of hapron. Worth *nothing* now, though." Levort slowly brought himself back to his feet. "I'm gonna check out the crater, see if anything survived that we can trade."

Bayfo patted a heavy hand on Levort's shoulder. "Take your time. Weather's good today, so we have until nightfall. Sorry about this, Lev. I know it meant a lot. Let me know if I can help."

"Thanks." Levort slung his salvager into his hands and worked his way down the crater. He was an insect in a canyon. All around him were smooth rock surfaces and sheered flat metal. Levort looked back up at Bayfo, another insect high above this range. Bayfo must have known as well as Levort that there'd be nothing left worth salvaging, but he was kind enough to let Levort futilely search in privacy.

No salvage, no scrap, no payday, no S-Class license.

The crater was devoid of anything, an empty husk of dead promise. Levort looked up at the Voyalten portal in orbit; it felt farther away than ever before. He'd be stuck below it. With no money from the claim, he'd have to sell his room on Consonance Hub and live in the public hostel. It was a spiral down the drain. Fees would incur late fees, which would incur more debt. Levort Aatra would be another funnel for the Fessenog Fleet to siphon hapron through until he was too old and weak to move.

Why did this happen? Maybe the ship managed to activate thrusters? Did its reactor—or whatever it used for propulsion—explode? But then there'd be something left. Levort thought back on the night before. Parts were a little hazy thanks to his celebration with Bayfo. Still, he remembered everything before and after Winder's pretty well. He came home, showered, went to the collection center, and helped that beggar. *Was this the beggar's doing somehow? No, impossible.* But there was something else.

Glott, the Erunian collection center broker, acted strange when Levort turned in the trinket. He even mentioned the log file of Levort's claim during the brokering. Glott would have been the only one other than Bayfo with knowledge of the claim, except for the data pushers who filed away the claim digidocs. *Why would Glott have scheduled a fragging of this spot?* It still didn't make sense. Maybe it wasn't Glott, but something about the curved trinket he sold had forced the Fleet's hand.

It didn't matter much. Levort's fate was sealed. The sun was setting, and Bayfo asked over the comm, "Hey, Lev. I know this vents, but we gotta start gettin' back to the shuttle. You need any help down there?"

Levort sighed. He took one last look around before responding. As he was about to say, "No, I'm coming back," something caught his eye. There was another shadow in the dimming sunlight of the crater with him, not far off.

Someone else was down here.

"Just let me check one last thing, and I'll be up," Levort replied to Bayfo as he started moving toward the shadow. Whatever it was, it was tearing through something on the crater's floor. *Salvaging!* Levort rushed toward the other person, ready to tackle them to the ground and beat the *drit* out of them for molesting his claim this way. Destroyed as it was, this was the only thing he had left. Rage propelled him like a starship.

The shadow turned toward Levort and tensed up. It had four long arms and a thin body. *Good! Easier to take you down!* Levort thought and he continued his rush. Mere feet away from the stranger, Levort launched himself into a tackle.

The stranger pivoted away from Levort, produced what appeared to be a smitegun, and fired.

Before Levort had time to wonder how badly he messed up, a bright swirling blue and yellow light appeared out of nowhere, silhouetting the stranger and engulfing them. Levort's dive launched him straight into the light.

When it instantly evaporated a blink later, all Levort could see was red.

FIVE

Levort tumbled down a hill, unable to stop himself from the mad roll. The world was spinning around him when he finally hit a flat surface. Everything was a dark crimson hue. The dust on the ground, the fog in the air, and thorned vines wrapped around everything near him—all crimson. The sound of racing footsteps trailed off into the distance.

"*Wait!* Come back!" Levort realized the stranger was making a break for it.

Then he realized he wasn't on Tayoxe anymore.

Dread gripped Levort's soul, and his eyes darted around, searching for anything familiar. He looked up the slope he had come from. The circle of light he had entered through was gone. "How the…" Levort had a million questions. He tapped the comm button on his cloak and shouted, "Bayfo! Bayfo, you hear me? Anything! Bayfo!"

No response.

The sky was so thick with fog that only a dim red bulb above implied a star nearby. The terrain was uneven, sloped, and cragged, with blood-red vines everywhere. It reminded him of paintings of Zhok, the place bad people went after they died.

Levort suddenly wanted very much to go back to Tayoxe.

With nowhere to go and no one to answer his questions, Levort had no choice but to walk in the direction he'd heard the stranger's footsteps go. He gripped his HAMMER salvager in his hands and moved forward.

As he worked through the terrain, his mind raced to catch up to his situation. He had chased down the stranger. *What sort of thing were they anyway?* With four arms and a thin body, he could only equate it to a skinny Marothallan. But it had too many arms—Marothallans only had two.

What about that light?

As impossible as it seemed, that light could have only been one thing. If he hadn't been killed by a smitegun blast, which he hoped was the case, Levort had to assume the stranger somehow made a pocket portal. But technology like that didn't exist. Period. It was impossible to just up and create a personal portal. Only the Voyalten made the portals, and that was centuries ago. Also, the Voyalten portals were massive. This one had been only a little taller than Levort.

So, a mysterious stranger and an impossible portal.

Levort had never seen this Zhok-like planet on any datadocs. If the general populace knew about it, more people would have pointed out a nightmarish world like this. *Is there a Voyalten portal here? Am I even in Lodespace? Does the Fessenog Fleet know anything about this planet?*

Levort grunted, noticing the pain he felt all over his body. It was due to more than the tumble. Traveling through the light felt like it had ripped him apart atomically and rebuilt him. His skin was buzzing and itchy, and his muscles were a forest fire. Giving up the chase, Levort sank to the ground and lay on his back. He kept his salvager gripped tightly in his hands and stared straight up at the dim bulb of a star, not even bright enough to hurt his eyes. He was thankful he was still wearing his breather, unsure of what the atmosphere of this place was made of.

Thoughts of Bayfo came. *What is he doing now? Did he see the light?* He hoped Bayfo would be all right. Levort's mind was so busy fluttering with questions and concerns that he didn't notice himself slip into sleep.

Levort awoke with a start, unclear how long he'd slept.

Fist-sized creatures with dark exoskeletons were crawling all over his body. He screamed as he pulled them off. They released themselves with little resistance, and Levort stood and throttled the salvager. He pulled the trigger a couple times, blasting pulses of plasma at the offending creatures until they scurried into the thick tangles of vines.

Heaving with anxiety, Levort checked to see if they had eaten parts of him, expecting to be missing a few fingers. Thankfully, his body was intact. The only thing missing was the thin layer of dirt and dust he had accumulated from exploring Tayoxe and falling downhill in this Zhokish place. The creatures had picked him clean, but not in the way he'd feared.

Levort slung his salvager behind him and looked around. He had lost his direction after waking up in a panic. The world was still coated in the same dark crimson fog, and even the potential hours he had been asleep had not changed anything. Levort roared into his breathing mask, venting his anger at his situation and uncaring for who might hear him.

A whistle responded.

Levort searched, his eyes darting over the thick mist and vines. It took him a moment to notice the dim blue dot in the fog. His brain had combined it with the hazy red star that never seemed to move throughout his stay on Zhok—he was officially calling it that now. The blue bulb shifted, reverberating with yellow hues as it swirled.

"Another portal?" Levort said aloud to himself. Wasting no time, he cut into a sprint. The plasma saw on Levort's salvager slashed through his obstacles. The portal grew more prominent as he approached, confirming his hopeful suspicions. Unsure how long it would remain open, he scrambled his way up the side of a cliff until he found a small tunnel within.

Although Zhok was blood-hued, the cave swirled with azure and gold. It was a wild thing to behold. Levort had not gotten a good look at the portal that brought him to Zhok, but this time, aware of the impossible thing's presence, he took it in full. He could not see to the other end of it; his reflection was mirrored on its vibrating surface. When Levort placed his finger against the portal's surface, his reflection inhaled, becoming a thin swirl of darkness against an ivory sea of glass shards.

Levort pulled his hand back but noticed the sensation that came with it. Every pore in his skin stung, and his muscles felt like they had been pinching a pen for a season. The strain of going forward and retreating was worse than the first time he had come through the portal. Levort took one more look over his shoulder at the hazy expanse of Zhok and decided the pain was worth the venture.

He inhaled a deep breath and stepped through the portal.

SIX

Levort's feet sank into something soft. Every atom in his body burned with the strain of the portal walk. He opened his eyes—he had clamped them shut as he pushed through the gateway. The world revealed to him couldn't have been more different from Zhok's eerie landscape.

Outside the cave were waterfalls and thin green trees with fluffy blue leaves clustered near the trunk. The sky above was a gentle peach color, and the grass that lined a nearby gurgling creek shifted from green to a darker teal as a breeze pushed through it. The squish he felt under his boots was a thick layer of moss that coated the cave tunnel.

The stranger who created the portals was nowhere to be seen. Curiously, this portal had not shut off. The reflective oval of light remained in the back of the tunnel, casting dancing light against the rock and moss. The portal that took him to Zhok had shut off before Levort was even done rolling down a hill. Yet, this one showed no sign of evaporating.

Tired from the stress of teleporting, Levort walked down to the edge of the creek and stuck his hand in the cool water. The fluency node in his prospector cloak caught the taste of the water and informed Levort that it was potable when boiled. "Interesting," Levort mumbled to himself. Zhok had given his node no data during his entire stay on its nightmarish surface. But here, data was freely available within minutes of exposure to this new landscape.

Maybe this is a Fleet world? It was possible. *The stranger had been to Tayoxe. Why not other Lodespace worlds?* If this were the case, then Levort potentially had a way home. *With my claim laid to waste, lanced from orbit for some unknown reason, how can I call the Fleet my home?*

Levort sighed and brought up his datapad on his cloak's sleeve. If it had data about this planet's water, it probably had data on its air too. After processing, his fluency node detected a breathable atmosphere with no harmful contaminants.

"Thank the nova," Levort whispered as he removed his breathing mask and sealed it back into his prospecting cloak's shoulder pouch. He sucked in a deep breath. This planet had a sweet taste to the air, and the smell of moisture was thick in his nostrils.

He listened to the gentle creek's babble and the trees swaying in the light breeze. Alien birds sang their joyous tunes in the distance, and insects buzzed in the grass nearby. For a moment, his mind was clear. It was a special peace he was unaccustomed to. Levort Aatra had never felt such simple pleasures on his skin, and it became overwhelming. He gripped his hands tightly into fists, becoming accustomed to this beautiful world around him. He thought how much Bayfo would like it here.

"Bayfo!" Levort said aloud. He raised his data sleeve and tapped at it, begging it to operate faster. He swiped through various menus, looking to send a message to his friend, hoping to tell the enforcer how to find him. If the fluency node in the cloak worked, that must mean—

OUT OF SERVICE AREA.

"Piece of *drit*!" Levort cursed. His data sleeve could detect simple things like potable water and breathable air, but beyond that, he was off the grid. He kicked a nearby rock, and as he watched it tumble into the creek, his breathing slowed. It was difficult to be angry in this place.

A shriek came from the forest. Levort's fluency node pinged it as a recognized language, having heard it prior to his arrival. Two terrified phase-one Erunians splashed through the water down the creek, heading in his direction. The youngsters were faster than their older-phase elders, with three long legs and two clawed arms accompanying their palps and thin snouts. They screeched and clamored over the rocks and moss as something huge bounded behind them in full chase.

It was an arachnoid beast with eight legs and a sizeable snapping jaw full of saw-edged teeth. An array of eyes littered its forehead, and dark hair exploded from every part of its core. It roared and snapped at the young Erunians, coming extremely close to gobbling one up as it gained ground against them. Many tongues protruded from its long maw, like the tentacles of some sea monster attempting to pull in its prey.

"Hurry! This way!" Levort shouted before he had any sort of a plan.

The Erunians did not stop to question. They diverted their chase toward him. The arachnoid crashed through one of the tall green stalk trees and sent it hurtling downward, almost on top of one of the Erunian youths.

Levort started toward them, throttling his HAMMER model salvager and preparing a blast. "Keep running!" Levort urged the children as they came close. They rushed past him, the monster not far behind. As it approached, Levort blasted it with a punch of hot plasma. The beast was thrown backward into a tree stalk, but it rebounded with a speed that Levort wasn't ready for.

Tentacles from the beast's mouth wrapped around Levort's arm. Tiny barbs ripped into his skin, adding to the fire he felt from teleporting. Levort pulled the saw trigger on his salvager, and the plasma blade emerged from the end. He swung the blade at the monster, hacking off the closest of its eight legs and slicing a deep gash in the beast's face. It shrieked and ejected a creature from its mouth before collapsing into the creek.

Levort screamed as the tentacles wrapped around his arm again, revealing the creature that had freed itself from its larger body. A mess of teeth and claws climbed toward Levort with exceptional speed. It tangled him in its strong tentacles and pulled itself toward Levort's face, embracing him and exhaling putrid breath into his nostrils.

The salvager was pinned between Levort and the mess of tentacles. Levort squeezed the trigger, and it activated. The plasma blade sliced the creature in half with a hiss and a shriek. Levort stood and shook off the remnants, unsure if the arachnoid would eject another, smaller version of itself at him once more. But the larger husk lay still, the creek's water curling around it.

Cheering erupted from up the creek. The two Erunian youths came back toward Levort, cheering and honking. "Thank you, enforcer! We had never seen anyone fight off a karrori before! Especially not after a phase change!"

Levort fell to the ground next to the creek and tried to catch his breath. "Enforcer?" He huffed. "I am not an enforcer. I'm a prospector."

The Erunians looked at each other in confusion. The older youth, identifiable by the number of markings on its exoskeleton and the size of the blood sac on its back, asked, "Is the Fleet not here with you?"

"No." Levort wasn't sure how to explain. He felt hot all over. "I came here on my own. Is this Erunia?"

"Yes, yes, this is Erunia. Are you all right, prospector?" the younger of the two asked. It pointed one of its palps at Levort's wounded arm. A bubbling fizz was spitting from his wounds.

Levort looked at his injury, but before he could respond, his eyes rolled back in his head, and he fell back onto the moss.

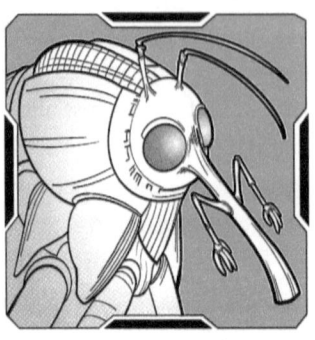

SEVEN

The lights were blurry at first. Levort could see the hazy forms of many-armed things working around him. He felt a sting in his neck, and everything shot into focus. A few Erunians stood beside him, and Levort recognized the young ones he had saved from the karrori.

He was inside a home made of stalked tree siding. Large glass containers lined the walls from floor to ceiling, and a few Fleet amenities were placed around the house—small useful objects like replicators and cleaners.

"Easy now, prospector," a late-stage Erunian said as she pulled a needle from Levort's neck. "The serum will nullify the karrori venom, but you should not move too much while it does its work."

Levort felt the burn on his arm under the bandage. The pain crescendoed, then went cold as ice as the serum batted away the venom from the horrible beast. Levort caught his breath and said, "Thank you."

"Nonsense. Thank *you*, prospector. You saved my offspring from the karrori. We owe you so much," the doctor said. "But we must ask, how are you here? The Fleet is not due back for another season. What is your name? Why have you come ahead of schedule?"

Levort hoisted himself into a sitting position and said, "I wish I had good answers for you, but I'm not clear on how I got here myself.

My name is Levort Aatra. A little while ago, I was on Tayoxe, then, somehow, I ended up in a place that looked like Zhok. Now I'm here with you. The best answer I can give is that a stranger was making portals, and I was moving through them. Sounds crazy when I say it out loud, though."

The doctor looked at her offspring and waved a palp toward the door. The youngsters thanked Levort one more time before exiting the humble home. The doctor used her palps to check Levort's head and said, "My name is Cythemi, and this village is called Eukotall. I have never heard of a stranger who can make portals. Your story *does* sound crazy, Levort Aatra."

"I get how it sounds, trust me," Levort said. "But it's the truth."

The doctor took a step back. "I believe the venom hasn't worked itself out of your system. That was the last of our Fleet medicine. I hope it is enough. Take some rest, and we will discuss your situation when ready."

"I need to get back home—to Consonance Hub," Levort urged as the doctor pushed him back onto the bed.

"You will have to wait until they return next season. They make their trade at that time, and our harvest is not ready to initiate the process early for one strange human, no matter how thankful I am to you. But do not worry. I don't intend to throw you back into the wilderness. We can make arrangements. But for now. Rest," Cythemi ordered.

The strain of the day washed back over Levort. He agreed and closed his eyes, allowing himself to recover.

***

The next day, Levort awoke as the sun was rising on Erunia. His muscles still burned, and he couldn't tell if it was from the karrori sting or the portal walk, but he was recovering well enough.

The Erunians in the village of Eukotall mumbled about in their predawn routines, each noticing the human walking amongst them and staring. The grass was black until the sun rose above the nearby mountains on the horizon. As the light caressed their ebony-bladed bodies, the grass would shift in hue to green and dark teal, reacting to the gentle morning whispering to them to awaken.

A spot near the stalk-sided house provided an expansive view. Levort had never seen something so beautiful and so simple as a sunrise. His trips to Tayoxe were often well after morning began, and even when the light reached the junk world, it was still a *junk* world. Erunia was raw, untamed, and unbeaten by prospectors. The town was surrounded by waving grass meadows, and the tall mountains and foothills lay beyond. There was a sharp-edged allure to the crags in the hills, covered in the flowing calm greens of the valley, yet strong and wild as the cliffs dropped off into deep crevasses.

Inhaling the fresh morning air filled Levort's lungs with a coldness that gave him bumps all along the skin on his arms. Dew wetted his boots, and the slowly peeking sun warmed him gradually as the morning progressed.

Cythemi approached. "Good morning, Levort Aatra. How did you sleep?"

Levort had barely noticed the sleep. He had slept on a flat surface in a wide-open room. The bed was something Cythemi had cobbled together out of some soft material and a worktable surface. Still, it was much better than the worn hammock Levort was used to on Consonance Hub. It felt as if he had blinked, and time rushed by. Yet, it might have been the best sleep he'd ever had. "I slept great. Thank you again," Levort said.

"Follow me. We will learn from each other as we tend to the animals." Cythemi lumbered off toward the field beyond the stalk houses.

A herd of strange beasts covered in long fur grazed in the expansive meadow on the outskirts of Eukotall. They were plump with six long legs, making them taller than the village's tiny houses. Levort watched as a mid-stage Erunian nudged one to get it to move, and the beast raised itself upright on its hind legs and flopped forward with a loud thud. A dirt patch remained in the spot where it had been resting before.

Cythemi made a noise that Levort's fluency node picked up as laughter. "The look on your face was all I needed to see to know you are not an enforcer in disguise."

Levort shook his head and huffed, "Nope, just a prospector." He looked away from the beasts and asked, "Enforcer in disguise? Why would they do that?"

"I wouldn't know, but it was a more plausible explanation than a man who fell through two portals to get here." Cythemi lumbered closer to the herd. "I have long wondered when the Fessenog Fleet's waning desire for our ulncha would slacken their desire to trade with us. They keep us distant, denying requests for our spaceships to use the portal in orbit. They only allow so many of us to leave Erunia."

They passed another Erunian farmer who had stuck a long syringe-like tool into the side of one of the ulncha. A sack attached to the syringe began to slowly fill with blood. The beast didn't seem to mind as it munched on a leafy plant the ranch hand had provided.

"Does the Fleet need lots of blood from these…uh, ulncha?" Levort asked.

"No, the blood is for Eukotall. We provide milk from the ulncha to the Fleet, which they find a luxurious delicacy. The ulncha also reverse-phase, and the husk they leave behind we recycle down into carbon to help in our own phase process. The ulncha grows again, and we harvest the milk and blood from it as it grows. They eat for free and live protected in this valley as they see fit, and we benefit from their laziness."

"Sounds like everyone wins," Levort noted. The rancher finished drawing blood from the nearby ulncha and scrubbed their palp behind the beast's eyes. It let out a long mew in appreciation for the leafy greens to munch on.

"It should be so. But the Fleet has been trading less and less. We rely on the Fleet for tech we can't create independently. Things we need to warm our homes in the cold seasons and medical supplies for our late-phase Eukotall citizens." Cythemi looked toward the mountains. "They demand more from our harvests in exchange for less. But we need their supplies. Unless they were to give us ships of our own—we could trade more outside the Fleet and on our own terms. I believe they found some new delicacy to crave, and the ulncha milk has moved out of favor."

"Why won't they provide ships? The Fleet has plenty."

"They lose control of Erunia the moment we can go where we please," Cythemi stated.

Erunia's raw beauty demonstrated the allure of leaving Lodespace to see what other beautiful worlds existed in the Voyalten web. Gulna Kii Fessenog, master of the Fleet, must have also known this as well. It explained the high cost of prospecting outside of Tayoxe. Levort was beginning to wonder if S-Class licenses were ever actually given out, or simply used as a treat to dangle in front of desperate prospectors to keep them hopeful for more. Keep them scraping Tayoxe clean.

For what purpose? Levort wondered.

"If you wish to stay until the enforcers return, you will need to help us with our harvest," Cythemi said. "There is much to do. You can aid the young ones with grooming the ulncha and cleaning their nesting areas. Do this, and we will provide you with food and shelter until the winter comes, and then you can go with the enforcers back to the Fleet."

Levort wasn't sure he wanted to go back to the Fleet. The portal in the forest called to him, singing to his heart. He felt that old prospector's tingle just thinking about the possibilities the portals brought. His curiosity about the stranger made it grow hotter in his mind. "Cythemi, what if there was a secret way you could move off of Erunia?"

Cythemi turned her lumbering body toward Levort and tilted her big-eyed head. He elaborated, "The portal I arrived in was still in the cave last time I checked. If we could figure out how it works, maybe you could use it to help your people."

Cythemi looked out toward the field of ulncha, munching and mooing, knowing their use among the Fleet was dwindling at best. Levort could tell the late-phase Erunian didn't believe his story about the portals. Still, the allure of a secret passage to another world was too tantalizing to ignore. Cythemi said, "How about this, prospector. Take Yrelg, the older of my offspring, and bring him to the portal. We will decide how to proceed if Yrelg verifies what you are saying. But when you return, there is work to be done regardless of the outcome. Our people cannot sacrifice too many resources for the sake of the harvest."

"Deal," Levort said.

***

An hour later, Levort and Yrelg hiked down a path into the stalk-tree forest. Levort kept his salvager handy, and Yrelg held a weapon in his two clawed hands. Yrelg pointed off the beaten path and said, "The karrori chased my sibling and me off here, and we fled toward the creek. We eventually spun around and tried to come back this way when we found you. I did think it was strange we didn't see you on the way into the woods."

They came upon the cave near the creek. Mossy growths had already started to dangle over the cave entrance, proliferating in the healthy forest. Yrelg shook, his palps twitching. The cave was too deep and mysterious for his limited bravery. "Can you go in first?"

"Yeah, follow me. It's not far in." Levort tapped his cloak, and an ambient blue light engulfed the fabric on it, filling the cave with enough light to see clearly.

"Wonderous!" Yrelg's palps flittered in awe.

They took careful steps through the cave, unsure if another karrori had made its den within between visits. Ahead, a flickering light licked at the cave walls. Levort smiled, "Thank the nova."

"It is true then!" Yrelg said as he saw the mysterious anomaly for himself.

The portal looked back at the two hikers like it had been waiting. Yrelg reached one of his clawed arms toward the shimmering mirrored surface when Levort put an arm in the way. Yrelg's shocked expression made him look like he'd been slapped, and Levort knelt down to his level, keeping his tone soothing. "I need you to tell Cythemi about this. If you were to enter and not return, your village would think the worst of me. We should head back and discuss this with everyone, and then maybe your people can use this unique resource."

Yrelg's antennae and eyes shifted back and forth from the portal to Levort, "Yes, you are right. We should tell the others."

"We'll head back right away," Levort said.

Yrelg stared back at his spiraling reflection on the portal's shimmering surface. His palps twitched eagerly, and he said, "When we start to use it, I want to be the first to walk through."

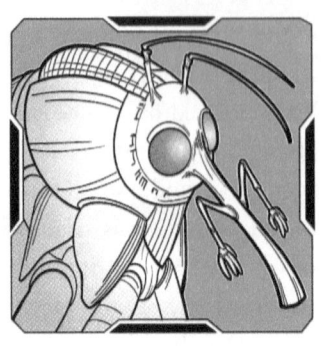

EIGHT

The days after Eukotall discovered the pocket portal were filled with movement. Cythemi put Yrelg in command of a small expeditionary force that went to Zhok daily. Levort explained the dangers—how the portal could collapse at any moment and the scouts could be trapped on Zhok indefinitely. Yrelg didn't care. The idea of stepping off Erunia was too addictive.

Yrelg's team brought back many of the tiny black-shelled creatures that inhabited the eerie planet. Soon, they had thousands of the little buggers and had created conditions in which they could breed them in Eukotall. Erunian chefs were already finding ways to make them into exotic foods, another thing to entice the Fleet to trade with them more often. They had Levort test their delicacies often, and each was more delicious than the last. He was their target audience, being from the Fleet and knowing the Fleet's tastes.

Unlike Yrelg, Levort found Zhok too eerie to return to. He stayed in Eukotall with the herd, grooming and caring for the ulncha, and processing their phase molts for the upcoming harvest. It was hard work, but he found it peaceful.

A season came and went faster than time had ever moved for Levort before.

***

"Wake up, prospector," Cythemi shook Levort with one of her palps.

Levort rubbed his face and squinted in the early dawn light of the stalk-sided home. "What is it? Little early for the ulncha."

"The Fessenog Fleet has arrived," Cythemi said.

A wave of cold water filled Levort's veins. Last season he would have halfheartedly welcomed a ticket home, but time away had worn his homesickness thin. Cythemi continued as Levort got out of his makeshift bed and got dressed. "I told them about you, and they sent for a different shuttle. Very strange. The captain of the new shuttle requests to see you."

"Thank you, Cythemi." Levort slung his HAMMER salvager onto his waist and gathered his things. "Can you take me to them?"

Outside the house, a Fleet ship hung high above the clouds. A shuttle was parked in the grassy meadow at the edge of the town of Eukotall. Crates of supplies were exchanged between Erunians and Fleet enforcers. An enforcer, a Kurikoid wearing ivory white combat armor, bartered with Yrelg about the new delicacy.

The shuttle's captain stepped off the ramp and said, "You must be Levort Aatra." She was a tall Dintuppan with white hair braided under a rose-colored crustacean-shelled exoskeleton. Her combat suit had long sleeves and a body vest.

"Yeah, that's me," Levort answered with guarded concern, unsure if he was in trouble.

"I am Captain Tegarl Myrs. I understand the Erunians found you in the forest. We have a few questions for you," the Dintuppan captain said smoothly, her voice official.

"I'll answer anything I can."

Captain Myrs eyed Levort suspiciously, assessing him for trustworthiness. "Good to hear it. One thing before we start." Captain Myrs turned and blew a high-pitched whistle through her mandible. "Niall!"

"Niall?" Levort whispered. A smile grew on his face.

Bayfo Niall dropped a crate and rushed out from behind the shuttle. "Where have you been!" He embraced his friend roughly, the white enforcer suit bashing against Levort's chest. "You vanished off the face of Tayoxe!"

"It's hard to explain," Levort offered. "It's been *something*."

Levort noticed Cythemi eyeing him from across the trading area. The Erunian's antennae dropped low. Seeing the friendliness with an enforcer must have been a blow to Cythemi's hospitality. In the season Levort had stayed in Eukotall, he'd neglected to mention Bayfo to her.

Captain Myrs said, "You two go catch up. The Fessenogs are very interested in Mr. Aatra's story. We'll handle the trade negotiations here. I want a full report later."

"Yes, sir," Bayfo said with a military tone that Levort had never heard come out of his friend. He turned to Levort and whispered, "Let's walk and talk."

The friends walked through Eukotall. Erunians moved about, preparing everything they could to deliver for the harvest. VIPs from the Fessenog Fleet, tourists, renowned chefs, and others visited the Erunian marketplace, buying exotic items to bring back to Consonance Hub. They bustled about, finding trinkets to take back to the Fleet to upsell.

"I thought you were dead," Bayfo said, his tone serious. "I turned my back for only a minute, and you were gone when I looked back down into the crater. I searched for hours until the shuttlemaster forced me to return." Bayfo shook his head and looked Levort in the eye. "I didn't know what to do. People don't just pop out of existence. No one believed me."

"I'm so sorry, Bayfo. Trust me, I didn't intend for any of this to happen," Levort said. "I was about to come back up when I saw someone else in the crater."

Bayfo cocked his eyebrow. "We were there for hours. I didn't see anyone from above."

"I believe you. It gets weirder. I thought this stranger found something salvageable, so I tried to tackle them." Levort pushed his hands together.

"Bad idea. You never were much of a fighter," Bayfo scoffed. "So what? Did they pull you underground or something?"

"No, not that. It's…" Levort stopped walking near an alley between two stalk-sided houses. He looked around and pulled Bayfo into the shadows before explaining. "Listen, this is going to sound insane. But it's the truth," Levort continued. "The stranger made a portal. I don't know how they did it, but one minute I was on Tayoxe, and in a flash, I was somewhere else. Somewhere awful."

Bayfo shook his head. "What? A portal? You mean a *ship*?" Bayfo kept his voice to a whisper to not expose his friend's lunacy.

Levort whispered back, "No, a *portal*. Just like the Voyalten portals, but smaller. A little pocket portal of some kind. I didn't believe it the first time. I thought maybe the stranger shot and killed me, and I went to Zhok."

"Come on, you're not that bad of a guy," Bayfo said, then added, "Wait, *the first time?* You mean this happened more than once?"

Levort nodded. "Well, I thought I was going to die on Zhok until I found a *second* portal. It brought me here to Erunia. Since no one here could bring me back to the Fleet, I was stuck here for a season."

Bayfo was quiet for a minute. He looked around the alley, trying to make sense of Levort's story. "We can't tell Myrs this. I've been on a short tether ever since…"

Levort noticed Bayfo's drop in attitude. "What happened?"

Bayfo was heavy with his words. "I was demoted after you vanished. I'm an errand boy again. First, they stuck me on Aquain, then Kurika, then Dintup, and now I'm here on Erunia. Been pushing crates back and forth from shuttles for a quarter now. Pretty sure they were gonna keep me here forever too." Bayfo looked back to Levort. His eyes widened, and a smile formed. "Wait. Hold on. Can you prove this portal exists? It might be my way back on track to rising in the enforcers. Maybe a find like this will net us a ship of our own!"

Levort knew he could bring Bayfo to the portal, but for a moment, he hesitated. He watched as Bayfo's hopes flared up and slowly faded in the heartbeat it took for Levort to say, "Y-yeah. I can take you to one. It's about an hour's hike from here."

Bayfo's eyebrows launched upward. "You can *show* me one? That's a lot better than I was expecting. This will be big." Bayfo looked out from the alley and whispered, "Ok, here's the deal, though. I don't know Captain Myrs that well, and I need this to rebuild my rep with the enforcers. Let's go on our own tonight, and I can get footage of the portal to present to Gulna Kii Fessenog himself."

Levort's bones rattled at this suggestion. He wasn't sure about showing the portal the Erunians frequented to an enforcer. Still, Bayfo was a long-time friend. He knew Bayfo wouldn't bring harm to the Erunians. Plus, going at night ensured the Erunians wouldn't be scouting Zhok. "Yes, we can do that. We'll meet at the southern edge of Eukotall tonight."

"Ok, see you there." Bayfo smiled a big toothy grin. "It's good to see you again, buddy."

"You too, Bayfo." Levort tapped his forearm against Bayfo's. They both walked back toward the trading area to perform their duties and await nightfall.

NINE

The sun sank, and the flowing grass faded to black along with the pink-hued sky. The ulncha mewed and yawned as they began to slumber for the night. Their strange figures turned into heaps of fur and spindled legs, morphing into soft lumps in the dark grass.

Levort checked his HAMMER salvager one more time as Bayfo approached from the center of town. He looked over his shoulder to ensure no one was following him. Bayfo had on his ivory body armor and a smitegun sidearm, but he lacked the rifle enforcers typically carried. He whispered, "You ready?"

"All set. Follow me." Levort nodded and led the way into the forest of stalked trees. In his season on Erunia, Levort had never gone into the woods at night. Three moons shined through the stalks, and the ring that encircled the planet cut through the sky in a long green arch. They followed the trail along the creek, its babbling constant and welcoming.

Bayfo asked, "So what do you think of the Erunians? You've had plenty of time with them now. You didn't fall in love with a young Erunian mid-phase maiden, did you?"

"Oh, I had to bat them off of me. It was awful," Levort joked. He continued earnestly, "The Erunians have a peaceful way of life. They helped me, and I helped them in return. I consider many of them my friends now."

Bayfo grunted. "Aren't many of them in the Fleet."

Levort answered reflexively, "Gulna Kii Fessenog keeps it that way."

"What'd you say?" Bayfo asked with a sharpness in his voice.

Levort stopped walking and looked over his shoulder at his enforcer friend. He had been away from the Fleet for so long that he forgot Bayfo was still loyal to it. Faithful in a way Levort may have never been. "Nothing. Not important."

Bayfo shook his head. "You keep that *drit* to yourself. Got it?"

Levort nodded. They continued their hike in silence until Levort eventually asked, "So, Captain Tegarl Myrs. You been working for her for long?"

Bayfo sighed and said, "No, she's new to me. I got transferred to her unit recently. She seems like a good enough Dintuppan, though. Gave me leave tonight so I could hang out with you." He playfully shoved Levort's shoulder from behind.

"Oh, that takes the fun out of it. I thought we were sneaking out." Levort smiled.

"Probably way easier to sneak around here in Erunia than when we were kids." Bayfo looked up into the trees.

"I didn't have much trouble doing it," Levort admitted.

"No *drit*! You didn't have enforcer parents to worry—" Bayfo caught himself.

Levort felt the familiar sting in his heart at the mention of his parents. He had few memories of them, overshadowed by the vivid image of them selling him to the sorting facility. Bayfo never seemed to realize how much remembering something like that felt like a plasma bolt to the chest. Bayfo was the son of enforcers. Although he had been there for Levort since they were only little ones, slips like this reminded them both that they came from different circles.

"Eh, sorry, Lev," Bayfo said quietly.

"We're getting close," Levort offered, changing the subject. "Keep your guard up. The first time I was here, I had to fight off a karrori beast."

Bayfo looked over his shoulder and said, "*Drit, now* you tell me."

They walked through the creek and up the incline toward the mouth of the cave. The vegetation that had been concealing the entrance had been pushed to the side by Yrelg and his team of scouts. Levort led the way into the cave tunnel, tapping his prospector jacket to create the ambient glow. The blue light washed the walls, illuminating their path. They walked into the tunnel, their feet squishing through the thick coat of moss on the floor.

After walking deep into the cave, Levort began to second-guess himself. He slowed his pace until he came to a standstill.

"What's wrong?" Bayfo asked.

"We should have run into it by now," Levort whispered, unsure of what was happening.

"You sure it's not deeper in?"

"Positive," Levort said. "I think it's gone."

There was a silent moment, then Bayfo spun Levort around with a rough pull and pushed him against the cave wall. "What do you mean, *it's gone?*"

"Look around!" Levort pushed Bayfo. "You see a bright light? Any mirrored surfaces in this cave? It's gone!"

Bayfo lifted a finger and looked away from Levort's eyes. "You... You *konndan* lied to me. I *believed* you, and you lied!"

"I'm not lying!" Levort thought for a moment, then snapped his finger. "The stranger! They must have come back and disabled the portal."

"Oh, shut up," Bayfo said. "Show me the ship you found."

"What are you talking about?" Levort asked.

"You told me before we went to your claim that a ship was there. Let me guess—you somehow found it in that crater and flew it through the Voyalten Portal to Erunia. Right?" Bayfo put his hand on his sidearm's holster. A movement that usually was a casual shift in weight suddenly felt like a vague threat to Levort.

"You saw the crater. You know there wasn't a ship there," Levort said.

"You got here somehow. I should have known not to believe your ridiculous story about pocket portals. I needed a bandage for my reputation and would have believed anything." Bayfo shook his head. "So *stupid*."

"Bayfo, listen to me! I—" Levort was cut off.

From the cave entrance, another voice echoed off the walls. "Niall. Aatra. Get out here."

Bayfo's blood drained from his face, looking bluer in the dim ambient glow of Levort's cloak. "Captain Myrs…" he whispered.

Captain Tegarl Myrs shouted, "Not gonna ask twice."

Levort shook his head, his eyes wide. Bayfo's face fell into a defeated frown. The enforcer grabbed Levort by the shoulder, escorting him outside with the smitegun pressed to his back.

They walked down the tunnel silently, seeing three figures in the triple moonlight at the entrance. The imposing silhouette of Captain Myrs in the center and two other enforcers flanking her sides, both Kurikoids. Their slick skin and bulbous eyes glinted in the moonlight.

"Captain!" Bayfo pushed Levort toward her and tried to explain. "Aatra made a wild claim that I thought to investigate further. I didn't want to waste your—"

"Cut the *drit*, Niall," Captain Myrs said. She stepped closer to Levort and said, "Your girlfriend went that way, Aatra. We've been ordered to track her."

Levort and Bayfo looked at each other in confusion.

"The stranger!" Levort whispered to himself loud enough that Bayfo heard him. "Wait, girlfriend? It—she's not… Whatever." Levort had only seen the silhouette of the portal maker, and the four arms were the most of what he noticed. Captain Myrs must have gotten a much better view of the stranger.

"So you were telling the truth." Bayfo smiled, ignoring the relationship statement entirely. Levort frowned at Bayfo for doubting him. He could tell Bayfo was slapped by the stern look because he looked away.

Good, Levort thought.

Captain Myrs clicked her crustacean mandible and said, "We followed you here from Eukotall and noticed someone else observing you from the trees across the creek. Pretty sure half the planet heard you tromping through the forest. We were quiet, though. She didn't see us. She went off that way a moment before I called you out of the cave. If we hurry, we can catch up with her." Captain Tegarl Myrs jerked her head toward the forest. "Let's move."

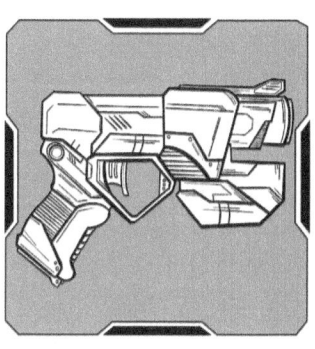

TEN

The forest grew thicker the farther they hiked, the sky concealed behind the dense canopy. The creek joined a roaring river as the water cut a deep wound into the sloping mountainside. Erunian wildlife watched them from the trees, their strange forms cloaked in shadow.

Captain Myrs held up her large arm, her fist tight. She pointed a finger forward, through some foliage toward a waterfall. Levort, Bayfo, Captain Myrs, and her two Kurikoid enforcers peered through the bushes to see their target ahead.

"What in Zhok is that?" Bayfo whispered. His voice was hidden by the roar of the waterfall. Ahead was the stranger, her silhouette draped in the forest's darkness. She looked around, then activated an orb of light, revealing herself in full to the audience she was unaware of. Her skin was slick and deep purple, her body slender and tall. Four long arms removed a container from her harness and searched its contents. Her pants were made of plated fabric tiles, each hexagon interlinked tightly with something that shimmered. She wore no shirt; only belts with mysterious devices crisscrossed her thin torso. On her upper left arm was a hefty gauntlet and shoulder pauldron. Panels on the gauntlet shimmered with strange symbols that she manipulated and studied.

"Told you." Levort nudged Bayfo.

"Eyes on target," Captain Myrs spoke into her comm. The Kurikoids gripped their rifles in their hands. "Waiting for confirmation."

"Wait, what?" Levort whispered. His eyes darted between the stranger near the waterfall and the team of enforcers. Bayfo appeared just as confused as Levort.

The stranger pulled out an object shaped like a smitegun, only smaller in profile. With the orb of light illuminating the object, Levort could see it was no weapon. It was a tool. It was curved in the front and had intricate gold lining intersecting its ivory exterior. Lights activated on its shell.

"Identified. Copy," Captain Myrs mumbled again into some shared comm device. She nodded to her team, and the Kurikoids aimed their rifles. Bayfo—with a look of confusion—unholstered his smitegun and aimed it forward, blindly following orders.

"What are you doing?" Levort hissed frantically. "Put your weapons away!" His heart raced, and his eyes flicked back and forth from the stranger to the enforcers.

"Aatra!" Captain Myrs barked in a hushed tone, her eyes not leaving her rifle's sight. The shout was a slip. The stranger heard Myrs and spun on her heels, looking directly at the bushes.

Her eyes found Levort's: deep black pools of stars. He felt his breath rush from his lungs. The moment hung still. He looked to the aimed rifles, then back to the portal maker. His voice exploded from his lips before he could consider the repercussions. "*Run!*" Levort shouted.

"*Lev!*" Bayfo tried to shut him up, but everything happened too quickly.

Instantly, the stranger activated something on one of her belts. The enforcers had been focusing on the tool in her two main hands—they had neglected to track the other two hands entirely. A bright flash blew up the night, and everyone was blinded.

"Damn it, Aatra!" Captain Myrs shouted. "Open fire!"

In their blindness, gunfire erupted. Levort stumbled forward toward the stranger. He blinked away the confusing mess of light and saw her open a new portal. Steam vented from the hovering gate's mirrored surface. Before the stranger could leap through the portal, she was struck with a blast from one of the enforcers. She tumbled, bleeding, through the portal.

Levort ducked, narrowly missing being struck by gunfire, and scrambled toward her. He heard shouts from the bushes and the sound of foliage being trampled mixed with more gunfire. Captain Myrs barked more orders, "After them! Shoot to kill!"

Bayfo shouted his pleas, "Lev! Get back here! *Stop!*"

Levort didn't look back. With a great heave, he hurled himself through the portal.

The waterfall and forest burned away as his atoms reorganized and delivered him to the other side. It was a bright sunny day, with a crystal-clear blue sky tinted green near the horizon. Steam was everywhere, and the world was a sauna.

Levort fell. The portal was elevated above a surface of boiling water.

Levort splashed down. His face burned in the bubbling cauldron, but his clothing protected the rest of him. He emerged as quickly as possible, feeling the water reddening his skin. He struggled to keep his head above the surface, his HAMMER model salvager weighing him down. Prospecting gear was built for extreme conditions, but it had its limits.

Ahead, he saw an orb of light moving toward a nearby shore, becoming only a dot in the distance. Levort swam after it and heard screams coming from above.

Four enforcers had jumped through the portal after Levort and crashed into the water. Only three came back up. Bubbles boiled as one of the Kurikoids drowned in the superheated lake. Although unsure of Bayfo's condition, Levort had to move forward. He swam for the shore and emerged from the lake, steam venting from his body. The screams of the enforcers were loud behind him, and one came through clearer than the rest. "Lev! Wait!"

Levort took one look over his shoulder. The previous order Captain Myrs had given echoed in his mind: *Shoot to kill!* It didn't matter if Bayfo wasn't involved—Myrs and her remaining Kurikoid were dangerous enough. He knew if he waited, the enforcers would kill him. *Wait and die, or flee and live.* Easy choice. Levort scrambled to his feet and chased after the orb of light in the distance. He ran across cragged surfaces, dodging bursting steam geysers. Crystals of sulfur gleamed bright yellow in the daylight. Pools of pink and green water boiled around him. The thick air, with its dank smell of minerals, made it hard to breathe.

A plasma blast zipped past Levort's shoulder. He spun as he ran, tripping over himself. His HAMMER model salvager, acting as a counterweight, whipped Levort into a pit in the rocks. He tumbled down a smooth tunnel carved out by hot thermal water. His tumble became a slide, and Levort covered his face as superheated steam rushed up to meet him. The fabric on his arms burned through, and the technology interwoven within it popped in the stress. The heat cut into the parts of his face he couldn't cover fast enough. As quickly as the steam vented, it halted, spitting Levort out into a cavernous underground world.

He rolled out of the way of another blast of thermal ventilation and laid on his back. Levort groaned in pain as he caught his breath. His labored breaths echoed off the expansive underground cavern. Daylight from aboveground shined into the various crystals that lined the cave walls and created a spectrum of color that engulfed the world. Sweat dripped off the ceiling, but it was cool to the touch. Levort welcomed the drip of it on his face.

Slowly, Levort got to his feet. He had a few deep cuts, and his face felt raw with burns. The stress of teleporting had also taken its toll, adding to the ache he felt all over. He looked around and found no sign of the stranger or the enforcers. He was alone, deep underground, on a world that appeared to have nothing edible nearby. Minerals and crystals offered no nutrients, but there was a chance he could tend to his wounds.

Levort stumbled through the cavern until he found a glowing blue pool in the refracted crystal light. Underground was much colder than the thermal surface, and Levort wondered if these pools would be similar. He removed his glove and gently caressed the pool's surface with the back of his hand, fearing it might be scalding. To his relief, the pool was nearly ice cold. Levort weakly rolled himself into it fully. He left his HAMMER salvager outside his mineral bath, unsure if the thing still worked.

The cool mineral water soothed his burns, and Levort's fluency node—its data crackled and glitchy—noted that the water was potable. He could drink it without purification, and he did so greedily. He worked his hand into his jacket and opened it up, clearing a path for more refreshing water to engulf him. He relaxed into his bath, allowing it to heal him from his pain.

Nova, what do I do now? Levort wondered after some time. *Captain Myrs and the others will either kill me or detain me. Bayfo will also probably be in trouble when they press on him. I'm a fugitive suddenly. For what?*

Levort had no answers. *Whoever this stranger is, the Fessenog Fleet doesn't want her around. Captain Myrs was given orders to shoot and kill the stranger. Enforcers can be harsh, but not so quick to the trigger. Why was it so important to kill her?*

The portal tool. Levort sat up. *The Fleet doesn't like people to move around freely, and what's freer than a device that could spit you out on any world you wanted?*

"They know about the pocket portals," Levort whispered to himself. "And they want to keep them a secret at all costs."

Another voice answered Levort's whispers: "Precisely."

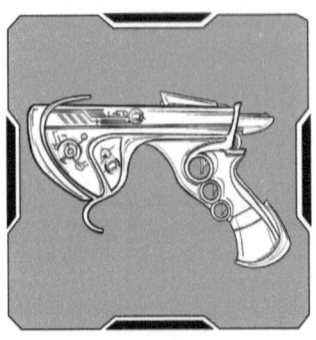

ELEVEN

The stranger lowered herself into the cool water across from Levort. The prospector didn't know what to say, so he remained in stunned silence. She clutched at a deep wound on her lower left shoulder, in the space between where her two left arms met. Green blood oozed between her four long fingers, and her face jolted with a wince as she submerged herself.

"You're hurt," Levort pointed out the obvious.

"I am," the stranger kindly confirmed. "My name is Wolil. I have been keeping an eye on you, Levort Aatra."

Levort pushed himself out of the water and sat on the edge of the bath with his clothed legs still dangling in its coolness. Somehow, it felt rude to be in the bath with her, even though she had entered without his permission. He observed the alien before him, unlike any race he had seen in the Consonance Hub. "Keeping an eye on *me*? Why watch me? I'm just a prospector. And how can you speak my language?"

"Anyone can be more than they are, Levort. No one is *only one* thing. Don't lock yourself with a label." Wolil nursed her wound in the cool water and let the minerals work. "First off, my people invented the Lodespeech you speak. And second, I wasn't sent to find you, but you have entered my life regardless. I feel a little responsible for you."

Levort huffed. "Great. I'm a pet now?"

"Hardly," Wolil sighed. Her eyes flicked from the pool to Levort and she nodded. "If you're willing, I'd like to see you as an ally." Wolil reached her long, unbloodied hand toward Levort. For a moment, he stared at her hand, the long fingers missing nails, outstretched and waiting to embrace his hand. A human gesture, and yet this alien knew it. Confused, Levort gently shook her hand, noticing it had more physical power than he'd imagined it would.

Levort smiled. "Ally. Sure, I could use some friends right about now." His mind went to Bayfo, and what their friendship had endured in this jaunt across portals. "Well, friends tend to know a lot about each other. I don't know anything about you."

"But you are very curious." Wolil smiled. "Curiosity is the most important thing someone can have," she mused. "You know more than you may realize. That was my Curio starship you found on Tayoxe."

"Really?" Levort asked.

Wolil nodded. "My existence, and what I represent, is a threat to the Fessenog Fleet. Upon returning to Tayoxe, I was chased down by some gunships. In an attempt to flee, I tried to locally portal away. That was my downfall." She winced and pushed more water onto her shoulder wound. "Upon activating the portal, I was automatically targeted by the Fleet laser cannons. I was struck as I passed through the portal I created, burying my Curio ship in the rubble of those collapsed buildings you were exploring. The ship was stuck and remained there for some time—until a certain lucky prospector found it."

"I don't believe in luck," Levort stated, showing his prospector side.

Wolil smiled. "You put a claim on my ship. I had been moving around from that location for about a quarter of a cycle before you discovered it. I'm delighted you found me right before that mean-looking Dintuppan did. I watched you fight with him."

Levort remembered the shadow that had distracted the cheating prospector long enough to allow him to strike the Dintuppan. "That was you!"

"Yes," Wolil admitted. "Needed to give you a chance, or that Dintuppan would have blown a hole in your chest. I was hoping you'd run away after that, but you stuck around and fought him. That was very brave of you, considering his size."

"Bayfo had my back," Levort said.

Wolil winced again. "Well, I assume when you filed your claim, it alerted the Fleet to my ship's hidden location, and they fragged it from space. I ran into you again in the crater where it once was. You managed to sneak up on me before I could wide-range teleport, and together we went to Zhok."

"So it *is* called Zhok! The real Zhok?" Levort asked.

"It didn't have a name," she confessed, "but I heard you use it once, and I thought it worked well." Wolil removed her hand from her wound. It was already sealing shut. "At first, I didn't realize you had followed me to Zhok. I had deactivated the portal as I moved through it, but you slipped right through. When I noticed you were traveling with me, I gave you an exit. I created the portal to Erunia for you."

"I appreciate that. Zhok was creepy." Levort shuddered thinking about it.

"I think so too. I love all worlds, but it's not uncommon to love something that can make you shiver. Even derelict space stations have their charms," Wolil said. "I had stepped away from the portal on Erunia, and when I returned, you showed the Erunians how to use it. That told me you're a good person. I only shut the portal off when the enforcers arrived to trade with the Erunians. I had hoped to return after they left to reactivate it. But I wasn't quick enough. Now we are here on Vansparr, treating our wounds. My mission remains uncertain."

"Vansparr?" Levort asked. "Wait, mission?"

"Vansparr. This planet's name." Wolil lifted herself out of the pool, allowing her long legs to dangle in the water from the rim like Levort. "My mission is to search and rescue. Originally, I am a native of Tayoxe, the world Gulna Kii Fessenog has people like you picking apart for scraps."

Levort was stunned to be in the presence of a Tayoxan native. "But now?"

Wolil locked eyes with him. "Now, I am from a place we lovingly call the Beyond. It is a sector in space that transcends this one. Not another dimension, but a place that exists outside the reach of your current understanding and technological capabilities. But only because Fessenog made it that way."

Levort leaned in closer. He wasn't sure if he believed what Wolil was saying, but his curiosity overwhelmed him.

"The Voyalten Portal Web, as you know it, connects millions of worlds. To some, that is all there is. It is enough. But to others—like the people of Tayoxe—we noticed this connection represented an opportunity. We were all linked. All we had to do was work together to accomplish even greater things. The Voyalten Web linked worlds that had grown so wildly different that something extraordinary was bound to spring from pooling together resources."

Wolil leaned back on her lower set of arms and lifted her leg out of the mineral water. She caressed a bruise on her knee with her free upper hand. "We were correct," she continued. "We built the Curio starships that could travel farther than anything. We created technology like the gateslingers, things that could achieve what we thought impossible, and we raised everyone upward together. There was only one thing standing in our way."

"Gulna Kii Fessenog," Levort guessed.

"Not Gulna personally, but someone much like him. Opponents with egos and power that prevent transcendence to the Beyond. They know the Beyond is the great equalizer when it comes to opportunity. They cannot cheat, manipulate, and kill their way to lofty positions there. In the Beyond, we still have people who stand out, but they are genuine heroes. They help those in need, create exciting inventions, and find new opportunities for ascension. They don't have to horde resources for attention."

"So every time people seek out the Beyond, they have to get past someone like Gulna," Levort said. "That's a little disappointing."

"Not always so," Wolil reassured him. "After we established the Beyond, various travelers of Lodespace would journey to meet us. We had spread the schematics for Curio ships to every planet in Lodespace. We were always open to those who could make it—those with the right mindset. Those who lived inside of curiosity. But around three hundred cycles ago, the travelers stopped coming entirely."

Three hundred cycles would have been long before Levort's time. Humans were cursed with the second shortest lifespan of all the alien races of Lodespace. Kurikoids lived the shortest lives of all.

Levort asked, "Why did they stop?"

"We didn't know. I sent a group of Beyonders back to Lodespace to investigate. We weren't sure if an extinction event or some other natural phenomenon prevented visitors from seeking the Beyond. That group never returned." Wolil looked into the pool. "I felt responsible for their disappearance, so I set out to save the people I sent back here. I came alone, not wanting to risk anyone else's life. I am the last attempt to save the missing Tayoxans and relink the Beyond to Lodespace. If I fail, the Beyond becomes hidden again, known only to those living within it. That was never its intended purpose."

"Sounds like you found out what happened to the others," Levort said.

Wolil's face contorted with grief. "The hard way. Yes. And you have, as well. Gulna Kii Fessenog fragged your claim specifically to censor the Beyond. He has created an empire unrivaled in my experience, and it is because of his stranglehold on hiding the Beyond. I'm sure he destroyed all the data tablets we shared. I am uncertain of the fate of the group of Beyonders I sent back here, but I now know Gulna Kii Fessenog was responsible for whatever happened to them."

"Does Gulna have Beyonder technology?" Levort asked.

Wolil leaned over herself with one of her four arms. "He does. When seeking the Beyond, all the various worlds of the Voyalten Web were combined in one place. On one planet."

Levort's breath almost didn't push the word through his voicebox. "Tayoxe."

Wolil nodded. "Yes, Tayoxe. My homeworld. Gulna Kii Fessenog was a leftover from when we transcended, someone who worked for the opponents we leaped over back then. When we left, the Fleet had not been stationed in Tayoxe orbit, and Lodespace wasn't this organized. Imagine my surprise when I returned to begin my mission.

Gulna uses prospectors like you to pick Tayoxe clean of all Beyonder tech and sells you lies about its worth. The centuries Tayoxe remained abandoned and left to waste under Gulna's rule has turned my beautiful home planet into a profitable junkyard."

Levort sat quietly as he let all the pieces slide together. His muscles weakened, unable to fight anymore. He had been beaten down his whole life by the Fleet. Forced to strip a beautiful world into something rotten and dead. Gulna Kii Fessenog had won the fight before anyone knew they were fighting.

"So that's it then." Levort sighed. "That's my life. Work to ensure Gulna stays rich and powerful. It never meant anything real. There's nothing else. S-Class licenses are a lie."

"If only there was some sort of zone in outer space that you could build a better life in," Wolil suggested, smiling as she stirred the water of their shared pool with her leg.

Levort cocked an eyebrow at Wolil.

"I am not against bringing you back to the Beyond with me." Wolil smiled. "Maybe we can help each other. I want to find out what happened to the other Tayoxan Beyonders I sent before me, and you want to start over somewhere better."

"You want my help?" Levort asked. "What could I do?"

Wolil nodded. "Help me investigate. I'll replicate a gateslinger for you and teach you how to use it. We will stop Gulna Kii Fessenog from keeping Lodespace choked out of the Beyond."

Levort considered his options. He wasn't sure what to say. The offer sounded incredible, impossible even. He wasn't sure what a gateslinger could be, but he guessed it was the portal device Wolil had been using to whisk them across the universe.

Wolil added, "We will have to build a new Curio ship, though. It takes one hundred cycles to travel from the edge of the Voyalten Web to the Beyond. Curio ships are designed to endure that journey and pass through the Barrier. Without one, we can't get in."

Levort Aatra stood and paced back and forth on his side of the bath. He considered the time debt involved in traveling to the Beyond. One hundred cycles was roughly the same amount of time as the average human life expectancy in Lodespace. Even in stasis, your age and body would be preserved as when you went in, but whatever you left behind wouldn't be the same when you woke up. Travel complexities aside, Levort inspected Wolil's kit with a prospector's eye and organized his thoughts as he considered the stranger from Beyond.

"You don't believe me, do you?" Wolil looked down at the pool.

Levort answered quickly. "Oh, I believe you. How could I not? I have already traveled through multiple impossible portals that I was told couldn't exist. I'm talking to an alien of a species I have never seen before, and I spent a season on Erunia after having spent my entire life up to this point going no farther than Tayoxe. What you're saying makes all of that make sense."

Wolil smiled.

Levort nodded. "Okay. I'll work with you."

Wolil patted some of the trinkets on her belts and said, "Excellent! A pleasure to have you as an ally, Levort Aatra. Now Let's make you that gateslinger I promised." Wolil pointed at Levort's HAMMER salvager and asked, "Does that thing still work?"

TWELVE

Captain Tegarl Myrs slammed Bayfo Niall against a crag as thermal vents exploded around them. "When I give an order, you follow it! Understood?" Myrs shouted over the roar of high-powered steam.

"Understood!" Bayfo barked back. She released her hold on him, and it felt like a crate filled with starship parts had been lifted off his chest. Bayfo struggled to catch his breath on the strange new world. The sky was bright blue, and the planet's star was beaming down with an intense heat. It must have been midday wherever this was. Crags and crystals of sulfur jutted out from weird angles through the rocky surface, and pools of steaming hot water sizzled in small puddles.

Captain Myrs, Bayfo, and the Kurikoid named Kedd had survived their dive through the portal. Kedd's spawnling, Togg, had drowned in the boiling water. If Kedd was sad about it, he wasn't showing it. Kurikoids often seemed one-note as far as emotions. It made them good enforcers—and card players.

The Dintuppan captain turned one of her stalked eyes to Bayfo. "Is there something you want to say, Niall?" Her tone was frustrated, furious even.

"Captain, what's going on?" Bayfo asked as the thermal vents quieted their incessant roaring. "I wasn't briefed on any of this."

Myrs shook her crustacean head and asked, "What did Aatra tell you?"

"Nothing, really."

"He told you about the portals, right? You knew about them."

Bayfo looked between Myrs and Kedd. *Lev, what kind of trouble are you in?* He wondered before responding. "Yeah. I thought he was lying, so he was going to show me one. but you found me in that cave with him. There was nothing there."

"You certainly saw the one we jumped through to get here. Did Aatra tell you about the Beyonders?" Captain Myrs asked.

"Beyonders?" Bayfo asked. His confusion must have seemed as genuine as it was, because Captain Myrs believed in his ignorance.

The large Dintuppan captain kept her stalk-like eyes scanning their surroundings. "We're dealing with an advanced and dangerous cult." She gestured to Kedd, commanding the Kurikoid to search the area. "The Fessenog Fleet has been dealing with Beyonders for hundreds of cycles, doing a good job keeping them out of Lodespace. But every now and then, some slip through. Looks like they may have gotten their claws into your friend. They can be very persuasive, but it's all tricks."

"A cult?" Bayfo scoffed. "How come I've never heard of this?"

Captain Myrs glanced over her hulking shoulder for only a moment. "The Fleet's whole position is to not spread their influence. Sorry, Niall, you didn't make the clearance cut to be briefed on them. Need-to-know only. I was briefed when reports of Aatra's presence on Erunia came in. Gulna Kii Fessenog was on our command ship in orbit around Erunia and personally asked me to investigate. It's why we followed you when you left at night with Aatra."

Bayfo's skin felt heavier, as if all the weight in his body had doubled. Not being deemed important enough to know about the Beyonders ahead of time was a shot to the guts. Kedd and Togg were fully informed and had no more clearance than he did. *Is this because I was Lev's enforcer escort to his claim?* Bayfo wondered. "Ok, the Beyonders are a cult. Fine. But how do the portals work? I thought that was impossible."

"It's just some tech they dug up on Tayoxe that they refuse to turn in to the Fleet. It's dangerous equipment. Spits you out randomly anywhere in the universe. Before Lodespace was established, there was a violent rebellion involving these pocket portals. Many people died. Gulna Kii Fessenog was one of the heroes who battled off the cultists and organized the Fleet as a safe haven for all," Myrs explained. "It's why he's driven to stop the Beyonder cult from ever getting a foothold in Lodespace again. He's seen what they could do firsthand."

The history of the violent revolution before the Fleet was formed was common knowledge, but the news of Beyonders and pocket portal tech had been omitted. If what Captain Myrs was saying was true, even history had been altered to stop the spread of this cult. Bayfo shivered at the thought of something so persuasive and dangerous that even history needed to be changed to hide it. "What do the cultists want?" Bayfo asked.

Captain Myrs answered, "They use those gateslinger devices to bring people to far-off worlds and force them to work in their compounds. Once they are outside Lodespace and on whatever planet they choose, the victims can't leave. They become enslaved by the Beyonders. We don't know their endgame, and they won't share the tech they have. We've been ordered to shoot on sight if we confirm a Beyonder presence."

Bayfo's muscles sank into his chest, collapsing his very core. "I'm sorry, captain. I can't do that."

"Want to repeat that, Niall?" Captain Myrs asked with a harsh menace to her voice. Kedd looked to Bayfo and gripped his rifle tightly.

Bayfo looked between the Dintuppan and the Kurikoid and held his ground. He gripped the smitegun in his palm, his muscles preparing to raise the weapon if necessary. Bayfo continued, "Levort Aatra is my friend. I can't be expected to kill him based on a briefing on cultists I never heard of until a minute ago."

Tegarl Myrs's stalked eyes flicked from Bayfo's face to his smitegun. For a moment, Bayfo thought she would order Kedd to shoot him. After a few extended heartbeats, Captain Myrs nodded her crustacean head. "I hear you, Niall. This news of Beyonders and portals is pretty new to me too. We have orders to shoot the Beyonder on sight, but Aatra is an unknown. Technically not a Beyonder *yet*. Maybe if we can subdue him and bring him in, we can still save him. I give you permission to stun him if necessary. But if he's gone full cultist, we must put him down."

Bayfo tightened his grip on his smitegun as he considered the possibility of Captain Myrs killing his friend. His blood rushed through his veins, and his eyes brimmed with moisture. His gaze locked onto the captain's eyes. It was all happening too quickly. Bayfo had reunited with the friend he thought he had lost—vanished, possibly dead. Now he was pursuing Levort through impossible portals, and he might have to make a hard call too quickly to process.

Still, Captain Myrs's offer was the best he would get for saving Levort. Bayfo inhaled sharply through his nostrils and looked away from the captain as he said, "Understood."

Myrs continued, "Good then. We need to find that Beyonder and get their gateslinger, or we're never leaving this *drit* planet. Search the area. Find them."

Bayfo obeyed like a good enforcer should. For hours they wandered the thermal venting planes of the new world with no signs of tracks. The air was dense with moisture, and the geysers of hot steam sprayed incessantly. Bayfo noticed some of the small holes in the craggy rocks were blowing cool air outward. Although the surface of this world was a sauna, the interior caverns were significantly cooler. Bayfo hoped to find an entrance large enough to escape the surface. All the holes he had seen so far were venting too much steam to safely enter.

"Captain-Captain!" Kedd croaked. "I-I hear something!"

Captain Myrs and Bayfo hustled across the thermal puddles toward Kedd's position. The Kurikoid pointed to a smooth-walled tunnel that led down into the depths of the planet. A sound unlike the roar of the thermals emitted from within.

"What is that?" Captain Myrs mumbled. The sound bounced around the caverns deep within the planet and echoed toward them.

"I know that sound," Bayfo said. "It's a HAMMER model salvager."

THIRTEEN

Levort's salvager sliced through another chunk of crystal, allowing it to drop to the floor with a resounding crash. Wolil put one of her four hands up, and Levort shut his salvager off.

"Yes, this will do," Wolil said. "Here, let me show you something." She hauled the large chunk of crystal over her shoulder, her strength surprising Levort. The Beyonder carried it to the pool they had previously used as a bath and dropped it in. Wolil's entire Beyonder kit was working at once. One device had turned the bath into a bubbling cauldron while another machine buzzed and printed out nanochips and other things Levort didn't fully understand. A few items lay cooling in an adjacent pool, finished and resting.

The crystal vaporized in the smelting pool when Wolil dropped it in. The water changed from hot red to swirling blue and yellow. Wolil dipped various canisters into the brew and twisted on caps. She fed these canisters into her other machines, and they continued to spit out advanced technology.

"This might feel like magic," Wolil said, "but in the Beyond, this is child stuff. We can only bring so much back here, because the Below hasn't been locusformed like the Beyond."

"Do you mean terraformed?" Levort asked, his tone quiet as he watched the machines print out a kit.

"You terraform *planets*." Wolil tapped a thin canister against her forehead, adding, "We locusformed *space*. It allows us to do all sorts of things in the Beyond: self-teleportation, flying, and more. We enjoy breaking the laws of physics before we've even had breakfast."

"Incredible." Levort's mind ran with the possibilities of such a place.

"Incredible things can happen when you transcend with millions of unique brilliant minds. Although locusforming allows us to use technology that we can't down here, it's also why the Barrier exists. It was never intended to be a gate to keep people out, just a side effect of our work there. We tried to counteract it by spreading the data tablets around to show people how to pass through the Barrier. It worked for a while until Gulna ended it."

"I'll believe that when I see it," Levort said, shaking his head.

"That implies *you do* intend to see it," Wolil said. "I'll hold you to that." She used a device on the tip of her gauntleted finger to weld the final piece of a tool together. She twirled it in her hand and swung it toward Levort. "Here you go, prospector. A gateslinger."

The gateslinger was a smooth-edged device with various symbols glowing above its shell. Three triggers lined the smitegun-shaped grip with a rectangular barrel that gave it a tall shape. Levort had seen this tool before. It was a portal maker. It was a ticket out of Lodespace. It was magic. It was impossible.

"It is yours," Wolil said.

Levort took the gateslinger in his hand. It was heavier than he had expected. He pointed it at the far cave wall and looked down the barrel. The symbols on the surface of the gateslinger still perplexed him.

Levort asked, "What do the symbols mean?"

"You can't read them?" Wolil asked.

Levort shook his head.

"Great, what a wonderful way to discover another dirty trick by Fessenog. You're still using the fluency nodes we made, right?"

"I have a…"

"Let me guess. A Fleet issued fluency node?" Wolil interrupted him.

Levort nodded.

"Looks like Gulna has censored the Tayoxan alphabet from the node's database. Sadly, I don't have an easy fix for that. But regardless, the gateslinger is simple to use," Wolil explained. "As I said, we let kids use these until they learn to teleport without them. Can't self-teleport outside the Beyond, though." She stood up, glancing at the other machines still busy rattling off new pieces for the rest of Levort's kit.

She pointed at her own gateslinger as she gave instructions. "Notice the three triggers. They stand for Local, Wide, and Random. Go ahead and try the local trigger. Point it over there." Wolil gestured toward the cave expanse.

Levort pulled the first trigger, and his hand recoiled backward as a bright light burst ahead of him. A few feet away, hanging in the air, a mirrored oval flattened out. Levort could see Wolil smiling in the reflection. "Look past it."

Levort leaned to the side to see around the portal and noticed a second portal deeper into the cavern. Wolil said, "We use that to get around obstacles. You can even curve it if you follow through with your arm movement as you launch it. It's the same setting I used on my ship when I was shot down on Tayoxe. But you have to be really careful with that one. You saw what happened to my ship when I localed blindly. My ship was built to withstand a jump like that, but our bodies would be crushed if we exited inside a wall."

"Amazing." Levort was stunned by his new device.

"Let's deactivate that one. Shoot it again. Any trigger will do. It neutralizes the portal."

Levort let out another shot, and a bright light slapped the portal. Upon impact, the hovering mirror fluctuated, shrunk down to a pinpoint, then burst into tiny particles of light. A moment later, the second portal that hovered beyond the first did the same. The cavern was empty once more.

Wolil pointed at the second trigger. "The Wide setting is complicated, so we'll save it for last. Instead, let's try the third trigger,

Random. That's the best one because you'll never know what you'll get."

Levort straightened his arm, now prepared for the recoil. He squeezed the third trigger, and another portal flung out into existence. It looked similar to the last one—mirrored. "It looks the same," Levort mentioned.

Wolil said, "But *you* know it's not. Portals aren't usually for a group. They're for a singular user. The way it connects points in space is very complex and specific. There is no way to customize the experience to be more aesthetically pleasing. But you know that portal will take you somewhere random."

"In Lodespace?" Levort asked.

"*Maybe*. Maybe not," Wolil answered. "Sometimes you'll get a world that no one's ever seen before, but it will *always* put you within an atmosphere you can survive in—comfort may vary. You don't need to worry about jumping into open vacuum. Normally, these tools are for children to use in the Beyond, and they work very differently there. Down here, it operates this way. It's not like we have our kids accidentally gate-walking to mysterious worlds. They make that choice when they are ready."

"Should we try Wide?" Levort asked, already aiming his gateslinger.

Wolil put one of her hands on his and lowered the gateslinger to the floor. "We'll get there. Let me clean up my kit, and we'll jump somewhere safer."

Wolil moved back toward the clean bath with the finished tools cooling within. Levort looked down at the gateslinger in his hands. Although Wolil wanted to go elsewhere, Levort knew Bayfo was here on Vansparr. He knew he had to convince his old friend to join them. This was the thing they had both dreamed of. It wasn't an S-Class license, nor a starship, but something better than both. He knew Bayfo would come around, but he needed a chance to explain everything.

A boom slapped the cavern's walls. Wolil cried out and crashed into the bath with a splash. Blood splattered the floor and began to tint the cold pool green.

Levort's eyes widened.

He stumbled toward the pool and landed on his knees next to Wolil's body. He turned to see where the shot had come from, and his view was filled with the barrel of a smitegun. "Easy now, Lev!" Bayfo shouted. His friend was eyeing the gateslinger in Levort's hand.

Levort looked at the bath and saw Wolil face down in the water. His horror surged up his stomach and into his esophagus, where it choked him. Levort looked back to Bayfo and pleaded, "What have you done?"

Bayfo stretched a hand toward Levort. "I'm trying to help you. Hand me that device." Bayfo's eyebrows knitted upward. Two more shadows moved toward their position in the cavern behind him. No doubt the other enforcers Bayfo had come through the portal with. "We don't have time, Lev! *Now!*"

Levort kept the gateslinger on the floor and pulled the third trigger.

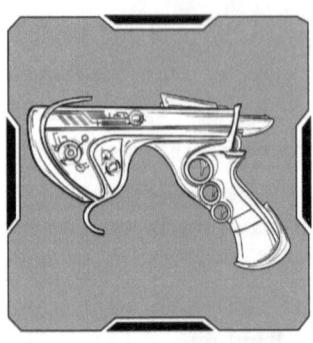

FOURTEEN

Levort screamed his lungs out.
    Random—the third trigger on the gateslinger could shoot a portal *anywhere*.

Levort just pointed it at the floor and squeezed it.

It was as if a rug had been yanked out from underneath him, and he went from sitting on Vansparr into freefall on an entirely different planet.

The wind rushed past him, forcing his prospecting cloak and HAMMER salvager to wrap and flail around him as he tumbled through the open sky. He could only take in vague details of the planet he fell toward. Levort was too distracted at the sight of the ground rushing up to meet him.

Levort hurtled toward a rocky beach cliffside. Ruby red waves crashed against the black-sanded shore. He rushed past some sort of enormous bird, its squawk announcing that it was just as shocked as he was.

It was at that point he noticed that he had not come through the portal alone. Past the startled bird, Bayfo tried to correct his tumble as he rushed toward Levort. Wolil's body had also made the trip, flailing limply through the sky as liquid trailed off her like jet streamers.

No time to think.

The crimson seashore was coming up too fast. Levort closed his eyes and pulled the third trigger again. Another portal launched ahead, and he fell through, feeling his body deconstruct and reconstruct. Bayfo and Wolil sailed in right after him.

Still falling.

This world was covered in swampy algae. The water underneath swirled and boiled as tentacled monsters started to notice the strange morsel that had burst into existence in the sky. Levort was quick to pull the trigger this time. Again, the group fell through.

Still falling.

Skyscrapers erupted all around Levort as he zipped through the portal. A street wasn't far below, and with every jump, it seemed like the ground of the new world was closer to impact. He was losing time. He pointed his gateslinger down to attempt to jump again, but felt something grab his leg.

Bayfo yanked Levort toward him and tried to grab the gateslinger out of his hand. Levort struggled to retain it. Thinking quickly, Levort grabbed his HAMMER salvager and crashed the blunt end of it into Bayfo's face. Blood burst from the enforcer's nose, and Bayfo recoiled in pain.

Levort pulled the third trigger again, and they fell through.

Still falling.

Bayfo collided with Levort again, this time striking him in the ribs and face. Bayfo's strong fists crashed into Levort repeatedly. The prospector didn't have time to notice the world he was diving through as fists crashed against his body and head. He could only feel the heat in the air and the splatter of insects that weren't fast enough to move out of his way.

Bayfo's arm seized the hand that Levort kept the gateslinger in. In desperation, Levort pushed his HAMMER model salvager into Bayfo's body and pulled the trigger. A burst of hot plasma exploded between them. Levort was flung sideways, away from Bayfo and Wolil.

Bayfo flipped around in his freefall, completely unable to steady himself. Levort recovered and shot another portal into Bayfo's trajectory. Bayfo and Wolil's body vanished into the unknown.

Levort was still falling.

He felt something bash into his back, sending him into a wild spin as he was struck from all sides. He bashed through a dense jungle canopy, hitting many branches as he fell toward the ground.

With a thud, Levort Aatra collided with the mud.

No longer falling.

Levort groaned in pain and struggled to push himself to his knees. Everything on his body felt like it had been resubmerged in Vansparr's boiling water. The constant portal hopping had re-atomized him so many times that he couldn't tell whether what hurt was from the portals or Bayfo's strikes.

"Wolil…" Levort whispered as he looked up into the jungle canopy. "Bayfo… What have I done?"

FIFTEEN

Bayfo felt the hot jungle air shift into a deep cold so fast his body almost went into shock. Had it not been for his enforcer suit, he might have been paralyzed. He fought to keep his senses about him in the frigid night air. Only seconds before hitting the ground, Bayfo noticed Levort was not falling alongside him anymore.

After tumbling for a few feet, Bayfo came to a stop face down in the cold white powder. Blood streamed from the wound on his face, and he was sure his nose had broken when Levort swiped at him with his salvager. Bayfo spat blood into the snow and pushed himself to his knees. His body shifted between burning and freezing as his atoms tried to figure out what the Zhok was happening. He remembered his deep pain from the first portal jump onto the boiling world, but after several jumps, his body felt like every limb was trying to leap free from his skeleton.

He looked up into the clear night sky, and a billion stars looked back at him. He roared with his heart until he thought he might pass out. "*FINE!*" Bayfo shouted into the alien void. "Have it your way!" He slumped over himself and took a few deep breaths. "Damn it, Lev. I was trying to *help* you. You went and messed it all up."

A groan cut through the silent winter air.

Bayfo searched the area around him and saw a shadow in the snow, a figure lying flat. He struggled to his feet and pushed through the high powder toward the shadow. "You don't know how screwed we are now!" Bayfo shouted as he approached the figure he assumed was Levort Aatra. "Do you know what they are gonna—"

He stopped when he realized who the figure was.

"Oh, it's you." Bayfo sneered.

The Beyonder lay groaning in the snow. Somehow she had survived both the shooting and the fall. How long she would remain alive was a mystery. Bayfo used his boot to shift the strange being over onto her back. Her eyes squinted up at him, and she didn't have the strength to lift any of her four arms. The Beyonder had taken a shot in the collarbone area, but it already appeared to be healing.

Bayfo stood over the Beyonder, allowing some of his blood to drip freely near her face. "I thought I killed you."

"You'll have to try harder than that, Fessenog thug," the Beyonder coughed.

Bayfo watched her struggle for a moment. Without saying a word, he placed his boot on her thin neck. He remembered the orders Captain Myrs had given him. *Kill on sight.* His boot was following orders, but his heart wasn't. The Beyonder weakly attempted to swat at Bayfo's boot with one of her four hands, but she didn't have enough strength to even dust the snow from him. Her eyes closed, and she began to gasp.

Bayfo removed his foot, and the Beyonder sucked in a deep breath. He slumped down in the snow next to her and looked off into the white hills as she caught her breath. Off in the distance was the skyline of a large industrial city, with towers venting smoke from chimneys and bright lights creating a greenish haze on the horizon. Black rock mountains licked by deep blue glaciers surrounded the wilderness.

"Where are we?" Bayfo asked the Beyonder after her breathing settled.

She answered, "The planet Golt."

Bayfo touched his gloved hand against his face and felt the sticky blood. He winced at the pain that shot through his face and looked down at the Beyonder's tools littering the snow. One object looked familiar. Bayfo stood and walked over to it. The Beyonder pushed herself into a leaning position when she realized what he was after.

"Wait!" she coughed.

Bayfo pulled the gateslinger from the snow and held it in his hand. Such a small thing, such a huge problem. This was technology that Gulna Kii Fessenog could never allow into the hands of the public. Yet, Bayfo was turning it over in his bloody glove. "This is what has been causing all this trouble," he whispered.

"You got what you wanted," the Beyonder sighed.

"You have no idea what I want," Bayfo snapped. "I didn't ask for any of this."

The Beyonder eyed Bayfo more carefully. "You're Levort Aatra's friend, aren't you?" she asked. "I recognize you from the fight in front of my ship."

Bayfo considered the question as carefully as it was asked. He looked past the gateslinger in his hand, his eyes focusing on nothing. He shook his head in a tiny movement. His frown said much more, and his injury gave the most convincing response.

"Levort wants to go to the Beyond. How about you?" the Beyonder asked.

"Levort's an idiot," Bayfo stated curtly. He pulled out his smitegun and pointed it at the Beyonder. "You say another word, and you're dead. I'm not one of your marks. You can't say anything that would convince me to join your cult."

The Beyonder looked slapped by Bayfo's words. She opened her mouth as if to retort, but her eyes caught sight of the smitegun, and she thought twice. She sneered at Bayfo.

"Get up. Let's get moving." Bayfo waved the smitegun at her. The Beyonder strained to get back to her feet. She was less dressed than Bayfo, yet she looked more comfortable in the frigid Golt temperature. He had her lead the way, his gun trained on her back as she shuffled through the snow. Although Bayfo had the gateslinger, he'd had enough portal jumping for one day. What he needed was time to think, and Golt was a remote enough planet to suit his current needs.

After shuffling through the snow for half an hour, the enforcer and the Beyonder came across a small hut nestled deep in the woods. Firelight flickered from cracks in the window, and smoke plumed out of a humble chimney.

Bayfo knocked on the door of the small cabin. He heard shuffling inside, but no one came to open the door. After waiting, Bayfo grunted. "Nothing's ever easy." He thrust his foot into the door and knocked it off its hinges, toppling it inward.

The creature that lived inside was half plant, half feline. It had a large mushroom cap on the top of its scalp that overlapped its body and four long hairy legs. Its large eyes were locked on Bayfo with concern, and it let out a loud hiss. It wore warm clothing and had a long fire poker in its paw. Bayfo shot his smitegun into the sky twice, and the mushroomed feline's hair stood on ends.

"Get out," Bayfo commanded, aiming the smitegun at the feline. Its eyes darted between Bayfo and the Beyonder, then scrambled past them, bumping into the Beyonder in its haste. With the resident gone, Bayfo grabbed the Beyonder's arm and pushed her into the cabin. He put the door back into place, where it hung crippled against its hinges, then sat near the fire.

"Great first contact with the Xikoling, enforcer. I'm sure the Fleet will do great business here one day," the Beyonder mocked.

"What did I say about talking?" Bayfo asked. He was too tired and too hurt to get more aggressive with her. He kept his smitegun palmed in his right hand and inspected the gateslinger in his left. Strange symbols lit up on its surface, glowing against the firelight. He wondered what Gulna would do for this unique tool.

What will Gulna do to me if he finds out I have it? Bayfo wondered. Gulna was too smart to let Bayfo walk freely with a Beyonder and their technology. *Somehow, I have to convince Gulna Kii Fessenog to let me keep this tool so I can track down Lev.* Bayfo's mind began churning out strategies as he gazed into the firelight. The Beyonder remained silent next to him. She studied him.

Bayfo nodded. *I'll have to make Gulna Kii Fessenog a deal.*

SIXTEEN

Floem Zeu Uubog meditated in the grass outside her starship, the *Tumbleweed*. The morning dew was still burning off, and she enjoyed every morsel she could absorb through the bright green and yellow cuticle of her epidermis. She wore a modified flight suit that kept her shins, feet, and forearms bare. She wore it with the zipper down to her belly, with a thin black shirt underneath designed to absorb sunlight and slowly feed it to her throughout the moments when the sun wasn't visible. Broad leaves and petals lined Floem's scalp, which she patted and arranged the way mammals groomed their hairstyles. Her eyes were dark pits of black with tiny dots of bright green.

Although she didn't have nostrils like most alien races, Floem inhaled the carbon dioxide surrounding her and exhaled pure oxygen through her cuticle. Floem drank in the sunlight cast off by Jofnalg's star, which rejuvenated her better than any caffeinated liquid ever could.

"Beautiful day, eh Skipper?" Floem smiled at her silent companion, a weed she had found on a previous tourist trip to the junk world Tayoxe. It had grown hard and thorny, and she'd fallen in love with its iron-clad determination. It sat in a small flowerpot, joining her in the morning meal of sunlight.

The *Tumbleweed* was parked in a rare clearing in one of Jofnalg's expansive jungles. The canopy was bare above, allowing the grass to grow fluffy and long. Floem sent out energy pulses into their blades, and they tickled her back. It was a unique joy that Alberryans could share with plants on any world.

"Floem!" the voice of her friend Vobsii Essaurntii called from inside the *Tumbleweed* through the open hatch that faced her. Floem's eyebrow twitched, and she tried to ignore him for a moment longer. Inevitably, Vobsii shouted once more, "Floem! The thing!"

"Couldn't stay quiet forever," Floem sighed and looked to Skipper. She shouted back to Vobsii, "Eh, what thing?"

"The *thing*, Floem!" Vobsii burst from the *Tumbleweed*'s hatch, waving a small, curved device, his steps making the ship groan and shaking dust free from the exterior hull. The large Resluni was heavy enough to almost tip the tourist-class ship as he leaned outward. His blue and orange scaled skin and long tentacle-like whiskers glistened in the sunlight. He wore a brown leather jacket and a knitted sweater with padded overalls. His boots were bulky, like the rest of him.

"Use more words! What thi—" Floem began to ask when she noticed the device in Vobsii's large hand. "Oh, *that* thing."

"It's glowing!" Vobsii elaborated. "What do you think it means?"

Floem stood up, dusted off her clothes, then walked over to the ship. She looked up at Vobsii with her large dark eyes. "That depends on what we think *the thing* actually is. I still think it's a kid's toy."

"I told you, it's much more than that," Vobsii said. He turned it in his hand and added, "It's no kid's toy. It's ancient Tayoxe technology, and I think it found something."

"*It* found something?" Floem tilted her head. "*It* can find? What was it searching for? Like a good deal at the starship outlet?"

"Observe." Vobsii tilted the device toward Floem, showing her the green dot on its curved surface. The dot maintained its original positioning when he tilted his hand, defying the device's orientation. "It's pointing off that way."

"Well, that's strange," Floem admitted.

Vobsii closed the hatch and leaped down to the grass next to Floem. The ship shook as it was released from his weight. Floem winced as he smashed the grass but knew the blades didn't mind such things. If they did, they would have revolted long ago.

"Let's follow it," Vobsii smiled, his snout crinkling.

"Follow it? Are you whacked?" Floem scoffed. "You're out of food, and you want to go for a hike. We need to get moving on and find ourselves a supply depot."

"Go on without me." Vobsii stepped around Skipper and wandered into the jungle, his eyes locked to the device and his hands holding it steady.

"Without you? Vobb, I eat *light!* I'll be fine! I don't need anything from the... Ugh, all right!" Floem conceded defeat. She turned to her potted friend and said, "Skipper, keep an eye on the *Tumbleweed*. We'll be back in a little bit." Then she hurried off after Vobsii.

Floem and Vobsii moved through the jungle, allowing the strange device to guide them. The jungle canopy only allowed narrow spears of light to pierce its thick leaves, which led to Floem's energy decreasing. She turned a knob on the collar of her flight suit, and a UV light emitted from it, soaking her head and neck in false sunshine. It was nothing like the real thing, but it was the best she could do in dark places.

"How far do you thi—" Floem started.

"Look! It started blinkin'!" Vobsii stamped his feet like an excited child.

"Oh wow. Blinkin'. You don't say?" Floem mocked his enthusiasm. "Maybe it'll start—"

"It's beeping now too!"

The device emitted a gentle tone that matched the same pace as the light blinking. It wasn't annoying... Yet.

The farther they traveled, the closer the blinks and beeps became until they entered a part of the jungle where the canopy had a hole.

"Oh, thank the Nova." Floem smiled and bounced her way into the sunlight. She flopped onto her back and closed her eyes, allowing as much of her cuticle to absorb the light as possible.

"Hmmm..." Vobsii noted the sustained beep and pocketed the device. It halted its tone upon entering his pocket. The Resluni scanned the area around them and grunted. "There's nothing here."

"Maybe that thingy is just an old pedometer." Floem opened her eyes and screamed with terror.

Vobsii jolted into an attack stance. "What? What did you see?"

"Vobsii, look!" Floem sprung to her feet and grabbed the Resluni's big head, twisting it straight up.

He opened his mouth in awe. "Guess it's not a pedometer…"

A translucent oval-shaped mirror hung midair in the hole of the canopy. The object glistened like a rippling pond, as if it wasn't completely solid. It remained motionless, unaffected by wind or gravity.

Vobsii brought the curved device out one more time and did some stretches with it to watch the green dot of light jolt its way back in the direction of the strange mirror above. "I guess it's made to find whatever that thing is."

"Is it dangerous?" Floem asked. She was latched onto Vobsii's arm, attempting to use him as a big scaley meat shield if necessary.

"I have no way of knowing that. Wait, maybe I can find out," Vobsii said.

"Find *out*? Why in Zhok would you want to find out?" Floem asked.

Vobsii grabbed a nearby rock, about the size of his large fist, and hurled it straight upward. His strength propelled the stone right into the mirror high above. To their surprise, it didn't shatter. Instead, the mirror ate the rock, swallowing it within its surface. After a moment, the rock came back down. Vobsii wasn't quick enough, and the stone crashed into his boot. He yelped and slumped to the ground to hold his injured foot.

Floem laughed explosively.

Vobsii stood back up and frowned at the mirror.

"I think it's like a window," Floem said as she finished her chuckle. "It's not making a shadow, and it's letting the sunlight through."

Vobsii grunted. "Maybe. But a window to what?"

"Yeah. Got me wondering, though…" Floem took her gaze off the mirror and inspected her surroundings. Broken branches and smashed grass littered the area. If she had to guess, maybe up to three other creatures had been here. "Wait, you don't think that thing's a ship, do you?"

"Ship?" Vobsii grunted. "A little small for a ship. What's your thinkin'?"

"I think something fell out of that window and came through the canopy, then went marchin' off that way." Floem pointed toward the jungle, where some more broken foliage was visible.

Vobsii looked up at the strange object in the sky, then back toward the rustled tree line, and stroked one of his long whiskers. He nodded and said, "Worth a try. Let's find the thing responsible for that thing."

Floem led the way into the wilderness. Her connection with the plant life of the jungle gave her an unmatched tracking sense. She sensed that the jungle was confused. Which was odd, because jungles were known know-it-alls. Plants were usually the first colonizers of any world and, therefore, the wisest, given their observational prowess. Something about the strange object in the sky made no sense to them.

I'm as stumped as you are, Floem communed with them in her unique way. The vines that heard Floem had more theories, and the stump nearby appreciated her pun.

Ahead, ferns rustled. Something was slowly moving through them and trying to stay quiet. Whatever it was, it was failing miserably. Floem approached the cluster of plants and whistled. "Oi! We can see you."

"*Drit!*" a voice cursed from the plants. After some more rustling, a human lifted himself onto his knees and raised his hands in surrender. "Unarmed." He coughed. His long black hair was messy, and he wore a ripped and ragged prospecting cloak. A salvager was strapped to his lower back, and he was entirely covered in a thin layer of dirt. "I'm harmless."

"Mostly harmless. At best," Vobsii grunted. "What about that salvager you got there?"

The human grunted and shook his head. "Don't think I could lift it even if I wanted to. Hurt myself pretty bad."

Floem looked around the sloping jungle and noticed more tracks leading away from the human's position. She squinted at the man and said, "Got a lot of questions for you, humie."

"*Watch out!*" Vobsii barked and grabbed the human by the arm, lifting him into the air. Vobsii jabbed his hand at the human's waist and pulled away a small smitegun-shaped device. Vobsii snarled, "You said *unarmed!*"

The human waved his free hand and shook his head. "It's not a weapon! Prospector's honor!"

Floem scoffed. "Long way from Tayoxe, aren't you?"

"Yes? Maybe? I don't know where I am," the human said, still dangling from one arm in Vobsii's grip.

"Great, a stupid liar." Vobsii dropped the human but kept the smitegun object. The human fell onto his back and almost rolled back into more vines. Vobsii answered, "You're on Jofnalg."

"Jofnalg?" The human held his ribs and flinched. "So we're in Lodespace?"

Vobsii and Floem shared a look, then cocked their heads toward the man. Floem asked, "Course we are. How'd you get here? You got an S-Class license on you?"

The human shook his head and looked down at the grass.

Vobsii answered him while inspecting the not-smitegun. "Yes, we're in Lodespace. My friend's name is Floem, and I'm Vobsii. We're...uhh...tourists."

Floem scoffed. "Tourists?"

Vobsii nudged her with his elbow.

The human cocked his head. "Well, thank you for finding me. I think. Still not sure if you're robbing me or helping me. Name's Levort Aatra either way."

Floem looked at Vobsii and cracked a smile. "Now that you mention it. We haven't decided if we're robbing you or helping you yet, either. Let's give it a moment and see what happens."

Vobsii huffed. He brought Levort's strange device closer to his eyes and whispered, "This sort of looks like..." The Resluni brought out the curved tracker they'd used to find the weird mirror object and held it next to the human's device.

"Where did you get one of those?" Levort asked when he saw the tracker-thingy.

"You're familiar with it?" Vobsii asked. "I feel like these two objects are part of the same kit. Do you know what it does?"

Levort said, "I'm not exactly sure what your device does, but I had one before. The device you took off of me is called a gateslinger. It can make pocket portals."

"*Fungus!*" Floem scoffed. "Now we know you're stupid!"

Vobsii didn't react immediately, his eyes studying the weird tools.

Floem scrunched her face. "Wait, you think he's telling the truth?"

Vobsii raised one eyebrow. "Tayoxe technology is very advanced and mostly unknown. In all my research, there's so little we know about the Tayoxans and their civilization that I deem it *suspiciously mysterious.*"

Levort nodded as if he knew something he wasn't saying.

Vobsii turned to Floem and said, "It explains that thing we found floating above the canopy. This tracker led us right to it too. I bet it sniffs out—you called them pocket portals?"

"Yes." Levort nodded.

Floem gave the human a puzzled look. "Pocket portals... Well, who else came through with you?"

"Enforcers. I heard them coming through the jungle after me, and I hid in some dense bushes." Levort winced in pain. "Not sure where they went from here. They want my gateslinger."

"Damn." Floem searched the jungle for signs of the human's pursuers. "Hear that, Vobb? *Enforcers.*"

Vobsii reached down to help the human up. "Right, let's get back to the *Tumbleweed* where it's safe. You can tell us everything you know, and then we'll decide if we want to help you or rob you."

Levort's eyes widened. "Wait, you're *still* not sure?"

Vobsii grabbed the injured human and pulled him onto his large shoulder. The man let out a weak sigh but could do nothing to stop the Resluni from carrying him. They marched back toward the *Tumbleweed.*

SEVENTEEN

Levort couldn't do anything except go along for the ride on Vobsii's shoulder. He hoped the Resluni and his Alberryan friend would decide to help him, but either way, he was their captive. Levort's injuries from falling from several worlds away had made him too weak to do otherwise.

As they hiked through the wilderness, Levort explained everything he knew about the gateslinger and the Beyond. The Resluni—Vobsii—and the Alberryan—Floem—listened and said nothing for a long time, probably processing the weird and unbelievable story Levort spewed out.

"Ok, I think I get it," Vobsii said. His voice was gruff, and his words short.

"Really?" Levort asked.

"Yeah, really?" Floem echoed.

"Sure. We saw the portal. We knew people fell out of it, although we thought it was a ship. But yeah, I believe it. I've been studying Tayoxe for some time. A mass pilgrimage to somewhere unknown makes a lotta sense—considering what they left behind. Not sure I'm buying *the Beyond* just yet, but his story and this advanced tech he's got are checking some boxes for me."

Floem leaned closer to Levort and whispered, "He's a bit of a history buff."

"A bit?" Vobsii scoffed. "The only reason we even found the portal tracker thingy was because I suggested we do a prospecting expedition on Tayoxe. Sort of a thing I've wanted to do for a long time."

"Tourist prospecting? I never thought they actually let you keep anything you found." Levort was aware that sometimes the wealthy, their offspring, or people from off-world who had enough hapron could volunteer to do a little prospecting excursion on Tayoxe. To them, it was a thing to do on vacation to *experience the culture of Tayoxe*. To Levort, it was his food and housing.

Floem elaborated, "They don't let you keep *drit*! We felt offended by that, so we delicately smuggled it away." She smiled.

Levort nodded. "You stole it."

"Stole it? From who? Gulna Kii Fessenog?" Vobsii scoffed. "I'd say we repurposed it. I knew it had some use, but I couldn't tell what. The thing remained a little trinket of our tour of Tayoxe until earlier this morning when I noticed the green dot on it."

"Fine, you didn't steal it. Since you're not thieves, does this mean you won't rob me?" Levort asked.

Vobsii glanced over his shoulder at Floem. She sighed and admitted, "No, probably not."

Vobsii laughed. "We'll get you patched up back at our ship, and then maybe we'll chat more about finding this Beyond."

"You want to go there too?" Levort's smile widened.

Vobsii nodded. "I'd love to find out what happened on Tayoxe. Sounds like my little hobby has been heavily censored by the Fessenog Fleet, and I want the real story."

Floem nodded. "While Vobb looks to the past, I like to check out the future. The Beyond is both! I wonder what kind of starlight I could drink up in a place that's locusformed."

"Why do you want to find it, Levort?" Vobsii asked.

Levort thought about it for a moment. "When Wolil told me about it, I was mostly curious about her technology. The Beyond was interesting, but it was still something I wasn't sure I could believe. The technology was tangible, and I had even accidentally been involved in its use for some time."

Floem asked, "And now, why do you want to find it?"

Levort thought of Bayfo. He thought of his tiny home on Consonance Hub and the debt he had racked up before he became a portal-hopping fugitive. With his claim zapped from orbit and his friend now pursuing him—assuming Bayfo survived their tumble across the planets—going back to the Fleet was an easy way to get killed. Whether Levort liked it or not, the Beyond was a chance to survive. It was the only road left that didn't involve hiding forever.

Levort answered, "It's complicated."

Vobsii nodded his big whiskered face and said, "Complicated is right. We still need to find the place. Without your Beyonder friend…"

"Wolil." Levort had just met her, but he knew she could do impossible things. Wolil didn't even get the chance to fully explain how the gateslinger worked before Bayfo shot her. The second trigger—Wide—was still a complete mystery, and the language used on the Beyonder tech was indecipherable.

"I don't know how we'd even get there." Levort sighed.

Vobsii stopped walking, and Floem bumped into him. "Oi! What's the—"

Vobsii shushed her and lowered himself to the jungle floor. He slid Levort into a sitting position against a tree and motioned for him to keep quiet. He whispered, "Found your pursuers."

Vobsii pointed into the clearing ahead. A medium-sized dirty ship sat atop its landing gear, gathering dust under the late afternoon sunlight. Moving around the landing struts were two shadows, one large and the other wide.

"Captain Tegarl Myrs and one of her Kurikoid enforcers." Levort peered at them through the ferns and vines.

"*Drit*! Enforcers," Floem whispered. "I told Skipper to watch the ship!" She gestured to a weed sitting uselessly in the flowerpot in the middle of the grassy clearing. The enforcers ignored it entirely. Floem sighed. "I take it they probably don't want us knowing about your gateslinger."

Levort whispered back, "They shot Wolil without even a warning. Without Bayfo around, I don't think they'll hesitate to kill us."

"Guess we're involved now," Vobsii grunted. "They got rifles."

"We got…" Floem patted her flight suit and looked at her general surroundings. "Some rocks, and Levort's salvager… And…"

"The gateslinger," Levort suggested.

Vobsii and Floem looked at Levort with wide eyes.

***

Captain Tegarl Myrs pointed at the hatch on the upper part of the junk ship they were investigating. "Check inside."

Her Kurikoid enforcer, Kedd, croaked in agreement and moved toward the ladder while Myrs scanned the tree line. It had been a long morning. After watching Levort, the Beyonder, and Bayfo fall through a portal on the floor of the thermal cave, Captain Myrs had to make a judgment call. It was foolish to blindly jump into the portal. At first, she had lowered Kedd into the portal with an emergency rope they each had built into their enforcer suits. Kedd reported a new world with ruby red waves and no sight of Bayfo and the others.

They couldn't stay on the thermal world, so the next choice was to follow the portals downward. Captain Myrs remembered an old trick from survival training. They used the detaining balloon as a parachute and drifted down through the portals. Kedd was temporarily detained, and Myrs held on tight. Their speed was still quick and hard to control, but Myrs—with her hard crustacean exoskeleton and dense bone structure—had a better chance of surviving a high fall than Kedd.

Down, down, down they drifted, following the path of portals in a relatively straight line until they hit Jofnalg, a familiar planet. Although there was another portal in their flight path, Myrs opted for safety. She had no idea how many worlds they'd have to float through or if they'd end up on a Lodespace planet at all.

Myrs maneuvered around the other portal for known ground. On Jofnalg, they could call reinforcements and investigate the other portal when prepared. A hole in the canopy provided a safer landing, and upon doing so, they noticed the debris. It was either Levort or Bayfo—or both if Bayfo betrayed them.

Either way, it was time to rein them in.

In front of the tourist-class ship, Captain Myrs heard a whistle from the tree line and turned her attention to the jungle. As she did, Kedd fell from the ladder and landed on his head with a crunch. Myrs spun to watch the enforcer fall, her rifle aimed and ready. There was a sound behind her, and suddenly, a mirror popped into existence only a few feet away.

A Resluni roared as he came through the portal fist first. He swiped the rifle out of Myrs's hands and followed up with a brutal left hook, striking the captain in the maw. Myrs stumbled backward and regained her footing. She shoulder-rushed the Resluni, knocking him off balance.

The Resluni was shoved back a few paces, and Myrs pulled her smitegun out of its holster. Another portal appeared on her right flank. Before she could register it, Levort Aatra stepped out of the portal and blasted her with a punch of super-heated plasma from his HAMMER model salvager. The blast threw Levort back through the portal and launched Myrs sideways. She dropped her smitegun in the chaos of the roll.

Captain Myrs finally stopped rolling and swung herself to a crouching position. The Resluni rushed toward her. She braced to lunge at him but was interrupted as she heard a voice shout from behind.

"Stop!"

Captain Tegarl Myrs rotated one of her stalked eyes to see her own smitegun in the hands of a young Alberryan. *How many of them are there?* Myrs wondered. Knowing she was beaten, Captain Myrs raised her hulkish arms upward.

Kedd croaked and wobbled to his feet, his rifle shaking in his hands. The Resluni had retrieved Myrs's rifle and aimed it at the Kurkoid's chest. Myrs turned her head toward her partner and said, "It's over, Kedd. Drop your weapon."

The Kurkoid shook with dizziness and fell onto his butt. He dropped his weapon in the grass beside him and croaked a long, distressed ribbit.

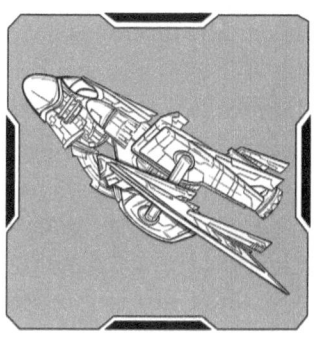

EIGHTEEN

Before the sunset on Jofnalg, Captain Myrs and the enforcer Kedd were stripped down and tied up. Vobsii kept the rifle he'd stolen from Myrs trained on her and Kedd while Floem bundled everything else they had into a pile next to Skipper. Levort, still bruised and weak from the strenuous day, sat down in front of the enforcer prisoners with his legs crossed.

"So, what now?" Captain Myrs asked, staring knives into Levort's eyes. "Can't let us live. We'll hunt you down and eradicate you and every other Beyonder in Lodespace."

Levort looked back and forth between Myrs and Kedd. Myrs didn't look away, but Kedd kept glancing at his captain. His amphibian skin looked slimier than before. Levort glanced over his shoulder at Vobsii, who nodded back to him. Floem shoved the big pile of enforcer gear into an exterior hatch on the *Tumbleweed* and walked over to join them, keeping Myrs's smitegun in her hand.

Levort shook his head. "We're not going to kill you. I don't even know why you're trying to kill me."

Myrs shifted her stare to her other captors, then back to Levort. "You spoke with the Beyonder. You have been converted to their cult. It's too dangerous to let you wander around with that damn portal device, snatching up people and vanishing them."

"Cult?" Levort asked. His shock was genuine. Wolil had never mentioned anything about a cult, but now that the word was out in the open... *Is there a chance she was lying to me?* He looked down at the gateslinger in his hand. *Why would she give me my own gateslinger and teach me to use it? And I saw her Curio starship. If this is the cult recruitment process, it relies too heavily on coincidences.*

"You don't even know. Do you?" Myrs huffed. "The Beyonders were behind the violent revolt that took place before the Fleet was formed. They killed many civilians and took off with the tech you are waving around there."

Vobsii grunted. "She's talking about ancient history."

Levort nodded and asked, "You hear that from Gulna Kii Fessenog?"

"He was there!" Myrs shouted. "He saw what those cultists did! It's too dangerous."

Levort sighed. "Gulna was there, yes. But he was part of the problem. Everyone was going to the Beyond, and people like him were trying to stop it. When the ships sailed, they were cast out. Left behind. And Gulna made a new problem for everyone who remained."

"Shut your mouth, human!" Myrs struggled in her restraints. "How dare you call the Fessenog Fleet a *problem!* After everything Gulna has done for you! I knew it. You went full Beyonder."

The Kurikoid, Kedd, squinted at his captors and croaked.

Levort didn't respond for a moment. He inhaled the fresh jungle air and felt the temperature dipping lower as the sun slowly fell behind the canopy. He felt the fresh grass underneath him and squished some soft, moist soil into his hand. The Fleet didn't give him any of this—the Fleet was actively trying to stop him from ever experiencing this.

Wolil gave me this.

Levort slowly got to his feet and dusted himself off. "We're going to leave. You won't be able to follow us, so call for help and get yourselves back home. We'll leave you a communicator to call whoever you need to." Levort looked at the captain and the Kurikoid once more. "Captain Myrs. If we ever meet again, I hope it is on friendlier terms."

"Levort," Captain Myrs shouted as he began to walk with Vobsii and Floem to their ship. Levort turned as the others continued on. The Dintuppan captain looked deep into his eyes and said, "Be careful out there. Don't trust everything you hear. I hope you learn the truth about the Beyonder cult before it's too late."

Levort nodded. He placed the communicator near his feet, out of reach of the restrained Myrs and Kedd, then he climbed up the ladder toward the hatch and entered Vobsii and Floem's ship.

Floem shut the hatch behind Levort. "They'll be out of those restraints soon. We better get moving." She moved across the living room and into the pilot's seat of the rickety old tourist ship. Ships of this class were built like houses, designed for touring the galaxy in comfort and style. It had all the accommodations of an average planet-based home, but it could sail across Lodespace.

Vobsii placed Skipper's flowerpot on a shelf and sat beside Floem in the copilot seat. "Already pre-prepped the engines. We can take off as soon as you're ready. Levort, strap yourself into the couch in the living room."

Dust kicked up as Levort sat on a long couch near a bolted-down, oval-shaped table. Seatbelts lined the couch, enough for four travelers. The main room was dirty like the rest of the ship, but in a raw, natural way. Plants lined the walls, hanging in pots. Piles of dirt traced paths on the floor, with footprints visible around the tiny mounds. It smelled fresh inside the *Tumbleweed*, unlike the overly recycled air Consonance Hub generated. The air inside the ship was almost as fresh as the Jofnalg wilderness.

Trinkets from the various planets of Lodespace were strapped into a display across the room from the couch. Levort recognized a few objects that originated from Tayoxe, but the rest were new and exciting. One of the more prominent objects looked like a hook with jewels adorning its handle.

Everything in the room jolted as the ship lifted off the ground. The *Tumbleweed* hovered straight up through the canopy, then kicked on the thrust to exit Jofnalg's atmosphere. The rumbling calmed down as they broke into high orbit. In the distance, Fleet ships surrounded the curve of Jofnalg, culminating near where the giant Voyalten portal was stationed planetside. Shuttles dipped in and out of the atmosphere, trading with whatever city Jofnalg offered to the Fleet. By the time they cut thrust, Jofnalg was only a green ball in the window about the size of a quasar peach.

Vobsii and Floem entered the living room as Levort took off his seatbelt and checked his HAMMER model salvager. Floem crashed onto the couch and put her leafy feet on the table while Vobsii leaned against the display case.

"What a day!" Floem shouted as she stretched. She slapped a button on the wall behind her, and a UV lamp shone down on her. She sighed deeply as the light nourished her.

"Welcome to the *Tumbleweed*." Vobsii waved a big hand at the interior of their ship. "I hope you have a plan. The second those enforcers get ahold of their communicator, the Fleet gunships will be on top of us. *Tumbleweed*'s a runner, but she isn't that fast."

Levort nodded. "I can't thank you enough for all the help you've given me already."

"Thank us by getting us out of here," Floem smiled.

"Uh, right." Levort stood and pulled out the gateslinger. "Wolil said she used the gateslinger to teleport her whole ship. I'm not much of a mechanic, but do either of you know of a way we can attach the gateslinger to the *Tumbleweed* and amplify the portal so it's large enough to move through?"

"Can I see it?" Floem asked. Levort handed the gateslinger over to her, and she inspected it closer. She hummed as she twisted the object in her hands. Her large dark eyes widened, and she waddled over to Vobsii. They whispered something to each other, and Vobsii cocked his head. He took the gateslinger from her, looked it over himself, and nodded.

Vobsii said, "Maybe we can rig this up to the particle projector and have it cast out a wider portal. It's worth a shot and has a low risk of harming the gateslinger. More of a risk to not try it and let the Fleet take us."

Floem was already scrambling down a hatch. "I'll get the projector."

"And I'll get my suit on," Vobsii sighed. "Someone will have to go outside and turn it on."

"I could do it. I owe you that much. Plus, I know how the gateslinger works," Levort offered.

Vobsii grunted. "All right. You can use the spare suit in the back—we'll make it fit you."

***

Fifteen minutes later, Levort stood strapped to the roof of the *Tumbleweed* with tension cables. He wore an atmospheric suit designed for Vobsii that they used adhesive tape to force to fit Levort's body. The helmet was too long, intended for a snout with whiskers. Still, his prospecting gloves were good enough for extravehicular activity in space.

The rigged-up particle projector was mounted on a thin tripod with a half-orb-shaped lens on its front. Floem had welded a quick harness where the gateslinger would sit upside down, making the triggers accessible.

Floem and Vobsii were visible through the windshield near Levort's feet. Floem's voice crackled from inside his helmet comm. "Ok. We're ready on our end."

Levort acknowledged, then took a deep breath. "Man, I hope this works." He squeezed the third trigger—Random. A light flung out from the gateslinger, hit the orbed lens of the projector, and spread out before slapping itself into a sizeable oval-shaped mirror sustained in space. It was a vast portal, big enough for three *Tumbleweeds* to fit through.

A plasma shot zipped past Levort.

Vobsii spoke over the comm: "Fleet's on us. Hold on tight!"

More plasma bolted by, nearly hitting Levort and crashing into the portal. The *Tumbleweed* jolted as thrusters engaged. The ship took a hit and bounced, snapping one of the tension ropes that kept Levort pinned to the roof. He slipped from his position until he was facing backward, one hand on the particle projector's tripod.

"Almost there!" Floem shouted over the comm.

A Fleet enforcer wearing an EMU suit rushed toward the *Tumbleweed*, jets blazing on their back. They shot again, striking part of the roof near Levort and breaking the tripod. Levort snatched the gateslinger as it snapped free of the harness Floem had made for it.

"Bomb's away!" Floem shouted. A hatch near Levort jolted open, and a ball of sludge launched from inside, striking the EMU nearing the *Tumbleweed*. The sludge clogged their engines and blacked out their visors. Levort pulled the first trigger on the gateslinger, creating two local portals behind the *Tumbleweed*. The EMU passed into the closer one and emerged farther back, crashing into a Fleet gunship with an explosive bang.

The world changed as the *Tumbleweed* rocketed through the projected portal. Levort was punched with sudden gravity. Where there had been a void and stars, now there was a bright pink and yellow sky. Smoke trailed from behind the *Tumbleweed*, and more particle blasts came through the portal behind them.

Thinking fast, Levort aimed the gateslinger and pulled the third trigger again. Light flung out from the gateslinger and crashed into the projected portal, causing it to shrink and burst. The mirrored portal vanished, leaving behind only sky.

"We're cutting too fast! Lev, hold on!" Vobsii shouted.

Levort turned his head and saw the world below. It was a vast expanse of hills and flowers. Beautiful orange, white, purple, and green filled every inch of the landscape. As the *Tumbleweed* lurched, Levort swung sideways. He pulled the strained tension cord tightly as the ship smacked the meadow below. Levort bounced off the roof once, feeling its hard metal surface jab him. The ship skidded through the flowers, sending a plume of dust, smoke, and pollen in its wake.

Eventually, it slowed, then came to a halt against the side of a hill. The *Tumbleweed* rocked back into a settling position, and then all was quiet. Levort rolled onto his back and pulled the long helmet off his head. He laughed and sucked in the fresh wildflower air. Floem and Vobsii burst out of the hatch and scrambled toward Levort.

When they saw him laughing, they sighed. Levort sat up and turned toward Floem. "That ball of sludge you launched at the EMU... That wasn't..."

Vobsii rubbed the back of his neck and mumbled, "Sort of wish you hadn't seen that..."

Floem smiled. "Can't have a good garden without fertilizer, and Vobsii makes the best stuff!"

NINETEEN

Wolil collapsed to her knees, her arms tied behind her back. Bayfo Niall stepped through the portal behind her, aimed smitegun in his right hand and the gateslinger in his left. His face had partially healed from the bashing he took from Levort's salvager. The blood was cleaned, and now only a large bruise and a purple discoloration under his left eye showed the damage. He took in a deep breath and smiled. "Told you I could figure it out on my own," Bayfo mocked his prisoner as he dissolved the portal behind him.

"You got lucky, human," Wolil mumbled through her sneer. The world of Tayoxe was spread out before them. Junk and abandoned city streets of a long-forgotten civilization lay crumbling deeper into dust every moment. The air was clear with no storm in sight. To Bayfo, it might have been the most beautiful day he'd ever spent on Tayoxe.

"Time for you to keep your mouth shut." Bayfo slipped the gateslinger into a holster on his belt and removed a silencing patch from his pocket.

"Wait. What are you—" Wolil attempted to ask but was cut off as Bayfo slapped the silencing patch on her face. The patch wrapped around her head, from just under her nostrils to the point of her chin, gagging her mouth shut. Wolil attempted to bite through the silencer but couldn't move her jaw.

"Heard enough from you already." Bayfo tapped the button on his gauntlet and fired his detainer balloon. Before Wolil could protest, she was encased in a floating orb six feet off the ground. "I won't have you messing up my meeting with Gulna." Bayfo adjusted the dial on his gauntlet to make the balloon opaque, typically used in case celebrities or politicians needed to be detained without ruining their careers. Not an option afforded to many others.

Balloon in tow, Bayfo began his hike. He had wandered Tayoxe for cycles with Levort, but this zone was one of the less frequented areas.

The squeak of a flitskipper alerted Bayfo to another's presence. He hurried over a mound of junk, causing mild landslides of metal and scrap in his wake as he mounted the hill. Over the other side, in an outlet of dirt surrounded by hills of garbage, Bayfo saw a Fluctan prospector. Fluctans weren't often prospectors. Their bodies needed to stay slick and wet. They could only scoot around on their tummies and flippers without a flitskipper to act as mechanical legs. The Fluctan had a long snout, a flat nose and whiskers, and sleek dark-gray skin with white and orange spots. He adjusted knobs and buttons on his flitskipper, allowing him to manipulate a salvager in the robotic hands of the vehicle.

Bayfo waved his hand and shouted, "Hey, down there!"

The Fluctan stopped his salvager's plasma laser and raised the goggles off his large dark eyes. He cocked an eyebrow.

"State your business, enforcer," another voice came from the mound of junk off to Bayfo's right flank. He had not noticed the Fluctan's enforcer escort sitting in the stack. The other enforcer's ivory suit was stained with neglect and had almost blended into the garbage around him. He was a Marothallan, with a long face and two large dark eyes. His blue and white skin was flecked with green, and his body was tall and lanky. He stood and thumbed at the grip of his rifle slung across his torso.

Bayfo pointed at the balloon. "It's complicated. Not here to cause any trouble. Just need directions to the closest prospecting outpost to catch a ride back up."

The Marothallan and the Fluctan eyed Bayfo carefully, sizing him up. The Marothallan asked, "Who's in the balloon?"

Bayfo shook his head and sighed. "Listen, I don't have time to answer all your questions. Are you gonna direct me or not? I'll be leaving either way."

The Fluctan looked at his escort, and the Marothallan looked back at him. After a few more glances, the Marothallan gave the slightest head shake to the Fluctan and put a hand out flat as if to "stand down." The prospector barked, shook his snout, and flipped the goggles back to his eyes to get back to salvaging. The Marothallan jerked his head over his shoulder and offered, "Outpost is about an hour that way. I'll let them know yer coming."

Bayfo nodded. "Thanks. Good luck, you two."

"Aye," the Marothallan said.

Bayfo scrambled past the duo and finally found a road to walk on. He could see the outpost on the horizon, nestled in the crib of a few downed buildings. Not long after, he reached the shuttle and hitched a ride back to the Fleet.

***

"What-what is the meaning of this? How-how did you get in here?" Malxu, a Kurikoid member of the Fessenog Directors, shouted, his voice tinged with fear.

Bayfo had made an entrance. After arriving in Consonance Hub, he carried Wolil's balloon to the Director's boardroom and teleported locally through the door—without an appointment. The Directors had their daily meetings, and Bayfo had theatrically interrupted them.

He had never been in a room with these people before. None of the directors were human, each a different species from the Fleet worlds. They sat at a table shaped like a ring. It had an open space in the middle so someone could stand in the center of all the directors. In the center seat of the table sat a prominent Marothallan with red-flecked dark gray and white skin. If Gulna Kii Fessenog was surprised, he hid it very well.

"Gulna Kii Fessenog," Bayfo addressed the calm Marothallan, "I have a proposition for you." He deactivated Wolil's retainer and let her drop to the floor in the center of the room. She looked up at them, her mouth bound with the silencing patch, her eyes lit with fury. The directors gasped and looked to Gulna.

Bayfo's theory was validated. He'd suspected the whole boardroom knew about Beyonders. Now he knew they trusted Gulna to save them from the dangerous cult.

Gulna Kii Fessenog stood from his chair and adjusted his expensive-looking suit. He had the bearing of a military general, stoic and formidable. He locked eyes with Wolil and smiled, keeping one of his long hands on the table as he spoke. "This is certainly a surprise."

Wolil launched toward Gulna, but Bayfo yanked her back with the tight cord wrapped around her wrists. Gulna didn't flinch. Instead, he laughed. "It is good you have sealed her mouth shut. Beyonders cannot be allowed to speak, this one especially." He looked to Bayfo and said, "I'd like to know who is granting me this gift. If we are to make a deal, it is only fair." His voice was low and calm, with only a hint of slyness.

"I'm enforcer Bayfo Niall. I've come to help you with this problem," Bayfo stated, pointing his smitegun at Wolil. Gulna's face went serious.

Malxu laughed. "He-he is an errand-runner. I-I have his file right here."

Bayfo winced. The directors wasted no time putting him in his place. Yet Bayfo was the only one with a weapon. He wielded a power different from theirs, although his smitegun was less effective in the long game. Bayfo kept his eyes on Gulna and raised the gateslinger out of his holster and into view of the directors. "You know what this is."

Gulna sighed. "Of course. What do you intend to do with it?"

Bayfo had been preparing this for a few days, although he couldn't be sure how many Fleet standard orbits had passed. He had stayed on Golt until he started experimenting with the gateslinger. Then he and Wolil traveled to over a hundred different worlds before landing on Tayoxe by accident. Wolil was useful as a meat shield. Bayfo shoved her through and yanked her back before testing each portal. He learned a lot quickly, and his advanced education gave him the insight to rapidly pick up the gateslinger's tricks. He understood the first and third triggers but didn't know what the second trigger did or what the symbols on the slinger's curved surface meant.

"This Beyonder duplicated her gateslinger before I could detain her. I know the person she gave it to: a prospector named Levort Aatra. I want to offer you my services to track him down and bring him back here with the gateslinger," Bayfo said.

"In exchange for what?" Gulna asked, a smile forming on his sinister face.

"I want to be the commander of my own ship."

Gulna's eyes widened, and he looked at his directors before saying, "You'd do this for a promotion? Is that all?" He offered Bayfo a chance to sweeten the pot.

"I have a few stipulations." Bayfo was already getting what he wanted, it seemed. Still, he didn't want to sound foolish. Bayfo needed to ensure they knew he wasn't easy to push around.

"Name them, Mr. Niall." Gulna put his hands behind his back. He gestured to Malxu, who began swiping away at his data sleeve.

"As I said, I want to bring Levort Aatra in, but I don't want him harmed. He's an old friend, and I want to stop him from making a fatal mistake."

Gulna frowned. "Anything else?"

"I want to work alone. I can move much faster that way."

Gulna looked to his directors. They mumbled and nodded. He looked back at Bayfo and said, "We are willing to accept your terms, but we have conditions that must be met before we trust you. We need an act of loyalty."

Malxu stood and said, "Bring them in."

Two shadows were escorted into the room from a side hallway by elite Marothallan enforcers. They had restraints on their wrists and were worn down, wearing only prison jumpsuits. One was a tall Dintuppan, the other a Kurikoid.

"Captain Myrs? Kedd?" Bayfo asked in a hushed tone. They didn't respond. They moved to the space before Bayfo and were forced down to their knees. Wolil inspected them both, then looked over her shoulder to Bayfo. Her eyes were firm, her head shaking. The elite Marothallan escorts left the room, leaving Bayfo standing in front of the prisoners.

Gulna continued, "Yes. I had personally sent the Captain and her team to investigate the very same Levort Aatra you mentioned. We agreed to let you tag along because you knew him, but it seems Mr. Aatra has slipped the leash. We found Captain Myrs and officer Kedd on Jofnalg, embarrassing the Fleet." Gulna paused for a moment and added, "These two have failed. Not *only* failed but alerted more members of the Fleet to the existence of Beyonders. This is a crime too harsh to ignore."

Wolil's eyes sank deep with worry. Bayfo returned her gaze, and a brief understanding came between them. He knew what was coming.

"Captain Myrs is loyal. We understand that mistakes happen. She will be transferred to active duty in the Yawning Lock for this transgression," Gulna explained, referencing the deepest prison the Fleet had to offer. "Her rank affords her such comfort."

For all the cycles Bayfo had been an enforcer, none of the people he had arrested had gone to the Yawning Lock. It was a secret prison located inside Tayoxe's sister planet, Fernomare. The planet orbited close enough to the star it was uninhabitable on its surface. This seemed like too high a sentence for slipping up. It was also one of two possible fates if Bayfo failed his mission. The second possible fate was about to reveal itself, and Bayfo's blood raced through his body.

Gulna Kii Fessenog continued, "Officer Kedd, on the other hand, can't be granted the same kindness."

"Please-please!" Kedd begged. "I-I will not tell anyone!"

Gulna clicked his tongue against the roof of his mouth and smiled. He looked at Bayfo and said, "Shoot the Kurikoid. Prove to us you can do what needs to be done."

Bayfo blinked a few times. He tried to plea, "Why not shoot the Beyonder—?"

"Do *not*!" Gulna lost his composure for a moment.

Wolil sneered at Gulna, unshaken by Bayfo's proposal to execute her. Gulna straightened his suit once again. "I asked you to shoot the Kurikoid. If I wanted this Beyonder dead, I would have had both of you shot the moment you appeared in this boardroom."

Bayfo looked at Kedd. The Kurikoid's bulbous eyes darted around the room, locking eyes with Malxu in hopes of having shared Kurikoid sympathy. Malxu shook his head and smiled. Bayfo knew he couldn't hesitate long.

"Sorry, Kedd," Bayfo said. The Kurikoid croaked one last time before Bayfo raised his smitegun and fired twice. Kedd slumped over to the floor with two new holes in his chest.

Gulna nodded. "That seals our contract."

Captain Myrs let her head droop. She looked away from her ex-squadmate.

Malxu shouted, "Guards! Take these three away. Vent the Kurikoid."

The Marothallan enforcers returned to the room, silently removing Captain Myrs, Wolil, and Kedd's corpse. Bayfo watched them leave. Wolil gave him one last look of concern. He could tell she wanted to shout something, but the silencing patch on her face prevented her. The Marothallan enforcers pushed her into the adjacent room.

Bayfo's hand holding the smitegun rattled, and his blood rushed through his body like a rapid river. He shuddered in uneven spurts.

"Here, a token of our appreciation." Gulna produced a device from under his chair and slid it across the table. It was a small thing with a curved edge on the top and a flat base on the bottom. A green dot pointed toward the portal in the room behind Bayfo. "This will help you on your mission. It's a portal tracker. As long as Levort Aatra keeps a portal open on the world he's on, this will lead you to it. Jump to a world and check the tracker. If the light is green, investigate. If it's not, jump again. I keep my promises and will not require you to kill Levort Aatra. But if you discover anyone besides Levort Aatra with Beyonder technology, you will execute them without hesitation."

Bayfo looked back up at Gulna and noticed how shallow his breaths were for the first time. Gulna leaned forward and asked, "Is that clear, *Commander* Niall?"

Bayfo's brain took a moment to analyze what Gulna had called him. His promotion was already effective, but only effective as long as he brought Levort in. The adrenaline response of killing Kedd washed away, and he felt his muscles tighten with purpose. Bayfo straightened and said, "I'll get started immediately."

TWENTY

Levort plunged his HAMMER model salvager into the cave wall. He had been mining every day since they landed on the planet Floem nicknamed Bloom. The *Tumbleweed* had been critically damaged in the plummet out of Jofnalg space, and the three travelers worked tirelessly to get it operational again. Vobsii broke down the raw materials Levort gave him to make the necessary repairs, while Floem welded the parts Vobsii forged. Together, the three made an efficient team, but repairs were slow.

Bloom was a small planet with soft sloping hills and underground tunnels. Everything on the surface was blanketed in wildflowers, and the most prominent native lifeform was only a fist-sized insect that resembled a Tayoxe strider. This was a world untouched by civilization—unharmed by the Fessenog Fleet. A lazy moon hung in the air, close enough to see the details in its craggy exterior.

The days on Bloom were short. The sun rose and fell twice in a twenty-four-hour period, allowing for a lovely lunchtime sunset. The day flowers would close their petals in the evenings, leaving the dusk to the night blooms. The grass glistened with tiny glowing gnats and flower petals that reflected starlight like thousands of mirrors.

Levort entered the *Tumbleweed* and hung his salvager on the wall in the living room. Vobsii plunked himself onto the couch—which doubled as Levort's bed—and Floem sat in the corner, meditating under a UV light. They had finished their work for the day.

"It's been a little over a quarter, Fleet Standard time at least. Do you think the Fleet is still looking for us?" Vobsii asked, translating Bloom's days into Fleet Standard time.

Levort shook his head. "Doesn't matter. They could be looking until the end of time and never find us. We are fully off the grid here."

"Speaking of being *off the grid*." Floem opened one of her eyes. "We're running out of rations. We were already low before you showed up, Levort, but now that we're spreading Vobsii's vittles out, there's even less to go around. We'll need to swing out and buy something."

Vobsii shook his snout. "Where? You see a shipping depot nearby?"

"We need to do something." Floem looked at the gateslinger.

Levort picked the gateslinger up and studied it in his hand. The glowing letters were still a mystery to him—the Beyonder alphabet had been removed purposefully from his fluency node's understanding. Levort shrugged. "Maybe we should teleport somewhere quick and grab something to eat."

"Too risky. If the Fleet spots us, they'll kill us," Vobsii said.

"We can be quick about it," Levort said. "Peek in, make sure it's safe, then investigate. If it's not, we just shut the portal off."

Vobsii grunted and stroked one of his whiskers. "I suppose even if we end up on a world with only raw material as food, we could have the *Tumbleweed* scan it to make sure it won't kill us. Or worse, kill our stomachs."

Floem nodded. "We could make a garden here if you find any seeds, so we don't have to jump out so often."

Vobsii shifted in his seat to stare at Floem. "Sounds like you're planning on rooting here."

Floem smiled and bobbed her head. "I mean, we can still be tourists. We barely need the *Tumbleweed* now that we have that gateslinger. Why not make a little home here? It's safe, beautiful, and welcoming."

Vobsii grunted and sank back into the chair. "I still wanna fix the

Tumbleweed in case of an emergency or something. We owe her that much. She's been a good ship."

"Fair," Floem said. "But if we're gonna fix her, we need to feed you boys first. Question is, who goes out shopping? I wouldn't know much about what's good. How about you two?"

Levort and Vobsii looked at each other. Levort said, "That could work. What do you think?"

Vobsii stood up from the couch, and the *Tumbleweed* lurched a little. "Yeah. Let's give it a shot. But we'll be quick about it."

The trio stepped outside into the evening air. The stars drifted at a medium stride across the sky, and the flowers glistened in the speckled voidlight. Levort put his hood and breathing mask on to conceal as much of his face as possible. Vobsii grabbed a satchel and a hooded cape, primarily for warmth and in case it was raining on whatever planet they ended up on. Floem sat atop the *Tumbleweed's* wing with Skipper resting in its pot by her side.

Levort brought the gateslinger into his hand. "Okay, in and out."

"I'm ready," Vobsii said. "Floem, make sure no one comes through after we leave, okay?"

"No problem. Skipper's here to help me keep watch." Floem patted the side of the potted weed. She whispered to it, "You're on first watch, old pal."

Levort aimed the gateslinger away from the ship and pulled the third trigger—Random. A bright light flicked out and slapped an oval-shaped mirror into the air. Levort holstered the gateslinger, stepped closer to the portal, and pushed his head through.

On the other side of the portal was a world covered in moss and algae. Thousands of small ponds pocked the surface of the green world, with forests made of tall, bulbous green fungi. Through the fungi, Levort could see the lights of civilization.

Levort pulled his head back into Bloom. "There's a town not far from the portal. Looks like a promising start." The effect of moving through portals was wearing off. His individual atoms were growing accustomed to the strain of running, falling, jumping, and sliding through worlds. Levort wondered if soon he'd stop feeling the effects entirely, and it'd be no different than stepping into an adjacent room.

"Let me see." Vobsii approached the portal and stuck his head through. He pulled back and said, "Ah, that's Kurika. Lodespace world. We've been there before."

"Should we risk it?" Levort asked.

Vobsii stroked his whiskers for a moment and bobbed his head. "It being Lodespace has its pros and cons. On the plus side, no one will think we're aliens."

"But if they recognize us, we're in trouble," Levort pointed out.

Vobsii nodded. "The portal looks concealed well enough in this fungi forest. We'll keep our heads low and try not to cause a ruckus. I got some hapron, so we don't have to steal anything this time." He turned toward Floem. "Aye! Keep a smitegun on you. Scare off anything that comes through. Kurika has a lot of weird beasties we don't want coming to Bloom."

Floem called, "Looking at a weird beastie right now."

"Very funny," Vobsii said sarcastically. "Be back in a few."

Floem waved goodbye as Levort and Vobsii stepped through the mirror.

It was humid on the other side of the portal. The night air felt like a wet blanket, and Levort immediately began to feel damp as he walked through the mossy swamp with Vobsii. The Resluni didn't seem to mind. His scales liked the moisture.

Resluni and Kurikoids were not too different in their biology. Kurikoids were amphibious, and Resluni were aquatic reptiles. Hot and moist was their favorite flavor of world. Humans, on the other hand, preferred something a little less sticky.

They walked out of a tall fungi forest into a flat area with many small ponds spread over a vast clearing. Far off in the distance, an enormous bird stepped through the area on long stalk-like legs. It had a sharp beak and frills waving off its neck and spine. The giant bird jammed its beak into one of the pools and pulled up a slimy beast to gobble down quickly.

"Should we be worried?" Levort asked. He knew nothing about Kurika, despite having plenty of experience with Kurikoids.

"Oh, the shadolgra only eats the pests in the spawn pools. The Kurikoids got lucky that way. It doesn't eat them or their offspring. Probably because they taste gross," Vobsii said. Levort noticed for the first time that the surface of each pool that surrounded them lapped and wiggled. Large tadpoles swam in each pool, future citizens of whatever village they were about to enter.

"There's too many, aren't there?" Levort asked. "Wouldn't this little village be overwhelmed with citizens?"

Vobsii shook his head. "Luck again. As adults, Kurikoids have a very short lifespan. Even shorter than you humans. They spend most of their time in these pools before evolving into the adults you see outside this world. Every village is more like an old folk's pen. It's also why their planet is stuck at a primitive tech production level. Stone castles, thatch villages, that sort of stuff. All the smartest Kurikoids leave the planet while the young ones take over what's already around. They don't innovate much on their own."

Vobsii stopped for a moment and adjusted the satchel slung over his midsection. "Hey, listen," he started. "I know you don't get out much, so I'll let you know. None of the Kurikoids in the village ahead are children. Some might be smaller because they may have emerged from the spawning ponds more recently, but within a quarter-orbit, they'll shed their tails and be as tall as us. I'm only telling you so you don't treat them like kids."

"Good to know," Levort said.

The shadolgra snapped up another pest from the spawning pond in the distance and gobbled it down. It looked at Levort and Vobsii momentarily, then turned its attention back to the ponds. Levort asked, "You said you've been here before?"

Vobsii continued the hike toward the village ahead. "Yeah, of course. Me and Floem have been all over Lodespace. Kurika is nice when it's dark like this. In the daytime, it feels like the sun spit on you."

"How'd you start being a tourist?" Levort asked. It was a lifestyle he'd never obtain, only observe. He had no clue how someone could *begin* something like that.

"Uhh, well…" Vobsii patted the back of his neck with his large hand. "Funny thing about that word." He looked around suspiciously. "Since we're friends now, I'll level with you. We only call ourselves tourists, but really, we've stolen everything we have. The people who owned the *Tumbleweed* before us were tourists, so we sort of adopted their vocation."

"So you *are* thieves?" Levort asked.

"*Opportunists*! Not thieves." Vobsii pointed a finger into the sky. "We just find opportunities often. For instance, those *opportunities* that owned the *Tumbleweed* before us. They were trying to rip us off. We had been moving around via shuttles before that. Everyone loves having an Alberryan on their crew, and Floem always makes them take me with as part of her sign-on requirements. These tourists wanted some guides on Dintup to take them up the tall mountains, so they hired us. Then they decided they weren't gonna pay us, so we took what we were owed. It's hard hiking on Dintup. Gravity's harsher."

"Why weren't they going to pay you?"

"Because the *view isn't as pretty as the data doc made it look.*" Vobsii made his voice whiney as he mocked the previous owners of the *Tumbleweed*. He waved his hand off. "Total *drits*. Not worried about them. They had plenty of hapron. I'm sure they bought a nice cruiser to replace the *Tumbleweed* and continued to rip off honest opportunists like ourselves... Once they got down from the mountain on their own..."

"You left them on the peak?" Levort asked. "Remind me not to cross you guys."

Vobsii laughed.

They came to the edge of town and heard strange music playing. The only way Levort could describe the tune was *lumpy*, which felt more accurate than it sounded. The mossy path they walked continued into the village, a medium-sized place with homes built of stone and moss stacked on each other. Lights and other Fleet tech speckled the town, giving it only a hint of a modern aesthetic. It was comfortable, in a cozy, wild sort of way. The townsfolk cocked their heads and blinked their bulbous eyes, croaking questions to each other as the aliens walked by.

Levort leaned over to Vobsii and whispered, "I thought you said we wouldn't stand out here."

Vobsii whispered back, "It's Lodespace. They at least know about humans and Resluni, but none live in this village. We just look like strangers. Which, I'll remind you, we *are*."

A small Kurikoid leaped off the side of a nearby home and landed in their path. She was short, fresh out of the spawning ponds, with a long tail complete with a fin. She croaked, "Don't-don't see aliens here often. Why-why are you here in Phiburb?"

"Uhh…" Levort mumbled.

"Supplies. We're travelers. Just passing through." Vobsii fielded the question in a way that sounded practiced. He had clearly done this sort of thing many times throughout his various *opportunities* with Floem.

"Supplies-supplies…" The Kurikoid turned her head to inspect the strangers better with her large amphibian eye. "Then-then, follow me. I-I am called Darbles." The short Kurikoid waddled down an alley. Levort and Vobsii shared a glance, then followed their host.

They walked down a mossy, stone-cobbled alley until they entered a small pocket lit by a singular streetlight featuring a humble supply store. Inside, the walls were lined with smooth slate, and devices sucked in excess moisture to keep the off-world products from molding too quickly. A few other Kurikoids mumbled around the store, eyeing the strangers as they came in.

Darbles hopped up onto a counter and rummaged through some things. "What-what sort of supplies?"

Vobsii looked around. "Food mostly. But we'll take some Mubb and ship repair tools if you got it."

Darbles nodded and croaked to one of the nearby Kurikoids. They came shuffling over, bumping into Levort as they scrambled by. "Buwwi-Buwwi! Watch-watch the customers!" Darbles straightened Levort out.

"It's fine," Levort said.

"Buwwi-Buwwi will help you find your supplies. You-you have hapron, yes?" Darbles asked.

Vobsii nodded and followed Buwwi around the store. They provided a three-wheeled crate to stuff things into. Levort looked around the store while Vobsii picked up the things they needed. It was a deeper building than it appeared from the outside. A staircase went upward, and behind the counter was a trap door that led to a cellar. Items were inside various barrels and pots that hung from the ceiling. More lumpy-sounding music played from a small music box hanging near the window as insects whizzed around the plants nearby.

Wherever Levort walked, he noticed Darbles watching. No doubt, the Kurikoid was suspicious of the strangers, and in return, Levort was wary of the Kurikoid. They had barely explored the town of Phiburb before being corraled into Darbles's shop. No chance to see if their supplies could be found elsewhere.

After some time, more short Kurikoids entered the store and croaked greetings to Darbles. They were so similar in spots and speckles that they could have shared the same spawn pool. Levort reminded himself that these were not children, but also wondered who owned the shop. If these Kurikoids had recently left their spawn pools, someone else must have been operating the store before. Unsure of Kurikoid laws and store ownership policies, he dropped his wonder and focused his curiosity elsewhere.

After some time, Vobsii and Buwwi returned to the front of the store. "All set. This should keep us going for a few quarters at least." Vobsii patted the top of the sealed crate. "We'll take the container too."

Darbles smiled and rang up their total on a crude mechanical device. Vobsii pulled a data chip from his jacket pocket and flashed it over the counter instead of using his sleeve for the transaction. Darbles croaked, "Thank-thank you. Safe-safe journies."

Vobsii nodded and pushed the cart out the door. Levort followed. They left Phiburb the way they entered, not daring to explore more than they needed to. As they left the mossy village and traveled up the path to the portal, Levort asked, "They seemed nice. Right?"

"Sure," Vobsii agreed. "But I'll be happy to get back to Bloom. I feel like I'm starting to molt."

It wasn't long before they came to the small clearing in the fungi forest with the portal. Vobsii shoved the crate through, with Levort behind him. Vobsii whistled and patted the top of the container. "Floem! Got some Mubb for you!"

"Mubb!" Floem shouted and sat up straight, jostling Skipper's flowerpot a little. She hadn't moved much since they left. "Toss me some of that sweet-sweet Mubb!"

Vobsii opened the crate and searched its contents for the

fermented mud and algae concoction popular in the Fleet. At the same time, Levort reached for his gateslinger to shut down the portal to Kurika.

Levort's soul spilled from his body when his hand patted his hip. He searched himself, slapping his hands all over his prospector cloak and turning to check every angle. Vobsii's smile shifted to a frown.

"Don't even say it…" Vobsii shook his head.

Levort sputtered the words. "The gateslinger is gone!"

TWENTY-ONE

"When did you see it last?" Vobsii asked.

Levort hustled behind him as they hurried back to Phiburb to find the missing gateslinger. "I put it back in my holster right after we made the portal." Levort remembered, but even his memories felt false given the current circumstance.

"Had to be that Darbles kid!" Vobsii pounded a fist into his palm.

Levort didn't bother saying something like, *"You insisted they aren't kids!"* and kept his mouth shut.

They returned to the streets of Phiburb and noticed the distinct lack of Kurikoids. They had just been here barely a half hour ago, yet the town felt suddenly abandoned. Levort's suspicion escalated, and he wished he had brought a weapon. He knew if they stalled too long, the Kurikoids could accidentally make new portals and potentially cut themselves off from Kurika, stranding the gateslinger somewhere in the cosmos and leaving a doorway to Bloom wide open forever.

A croak from above alerted Levort and Vobsii. They snapped their attention up to a nearby rooftop in time to see a small shadow dip out of view. Levort whispered, "Is the whole town in on this?"

"Not gonna stop me!" Vobsii shouted and marched down the alley toward Darbles's store. The Resluni kicked open the front door, knocking it off its hinges and sending it crashing into a barrel full of canned Mubb. The trap door behind the counter slapped shut. "You can't hide, Darbles!" Vobsii shouted.

As Vobsii ripped open the trap door, he was struck with a stun bolt from across the room. The Resluni shook violently, then slumped into the open trap door, falling out of view. Levort spun around to see Darbles swinging toward him, feet first. Levort didn't have time to dodge and was drop-kicked in the chest. He fell through the trap door and smashed into Vobsii.

"Ugh... Get off a me!" Vobsii grunted, recovering from the stun. He shoved Levort off, sending him splashing into dark, dirty liquid. The cellar was submerged in three-foot-deep stagnant water.

"What is this?" Levort asked.

"Looks like an indoor spawning pool..." Vobsii whispered.

A light flashed on, and they found themselves surrounded by short Kurikoids. Darbles flopped into the water and hopped back toward the far wall to sit on a large throne positioned atop a pile of loot. The mound of stolen objects was piled up to the cellar's ceiling. Levort's uneven footing implied more treasure lay below the water. Levort recognized many Fleet trinkets and tools, but something else caught his eye.

Behind the throne was a flat data tablet with strange lettering. Levort recognized some of the symbols, having seen them before on the shell of the gateslinger. He couldn't read them but knew them when he saw them. Levort assumed the tablet must be some sort of Beyonder technology—yet, that was not a gateslinger or a tracker. He remembered Wolil mentioning important data tablets that Gulna had destroyed to censor the Beyond. Whatever was on that thing was important enough for him to wipe it from Lodespace.

"You-you should not have come back, Fleet tourists!" Darbles twirled the gateslinger in her hand and smiled. "We-we sent you on your way. Phiburb-Phiburb has nothing else for you now."

Vobsii stood, bumping his head on the low ceiling. He shook off the pain and grunted, "You stole our...our..."

"What-what did we steal, exactly?" Darbles apparently didn't know what the gateslinger was. Levort remembered that the Kurikoids were technologically stuck in a primitive age. They had Fleet tools given to them, but they had not built nor understood much else.

Thinking fast, Levort tried, "Our magic shooter!"

Darbles huffed. "Try-try a little harder."

Vobsii shook his head. "Doesn't matter. That's our thing, and we want it back."

The Kurikoids that lined the room hopped closer, enclosing Levort and Vobsii tighter. Levort tried again. "Let's make a deal. We have more hapron. We'll pay for it."

Vobsii whispered, "We *don't* have more hapron."

Darbles looked at the two strangers and said, "You-you don't do this often. Do-do you?"

Levort looked at Vobsii and shrugged. Vobsii rolled his eyes and said, "Here we go." The Resluni grabbed the nearest Kurikoid thug in one hand and hurled him at Darbles. Darbles was struck by her fellow thug and smashed against the throne.

The gang lunged at Levort and Vobsii. They had strength in numbers, but Levort and Vobsii had reach and physical power. They batted off Kurikoid thugs left and right. Vobsii, covered in small Kurikoids, rushed the nearby wall and crashed into it headfirst, smashing three of the thugs at once against it. Above, the store creaked, and dust blew out from the basement made of stone and moss.

Levort pushed one Kurikoid off and kicked another in the face as it rushed him. He spun and struck another on his side, giving himself an opening. A light flashed as the stun gun Darbles used before went off. The blast missed Levort by an inch and struck another Kurikoid behind him. Darbles roared in anger, her composure ruffled.

Darbles lined up another shot, and Levort grabbed the nearest thug and pushed him into the line of fire. The Kurikoid was zapped and fell below the water, splashing and thrashing about. "Stop-stop that!" Darbles shouted in frustration.

Another Kurikoid came sailing over Levort from behind, thrown by Vobsii. Darbles leaped from her throne and landed on Levort's head, smashing his face down into the dirty water. He pushed upward, lifting his head above water and throwing Darbles into the air. She landed on Vobsii's arm and clamped her jaw down on it. Vobsii roared in pain and tried to pry her loose, but she held on tight.

Levort punched another thug out of the way and snatched the Beyonder data tablet behind the throne. It was large and heavy, and Levort needed two hands to hold it. He rushed over to Vobsii and brought the tablet down on Darbles's head with a loud, wet thud.

Darbles went crosseyed and unclamped from Vobsii's arm. Levort swung the tablet in an uppercut at the last remaining Kurikoid thug, knocking them hard into the wall, not noticing it was Buwwi until they slunk down against the stones.

Vobsii reached down and grabbed the gateslinger from Darbles's limp hand. Groans and croaking could be heard all over the room as Kurikoid thugs struggled to regain their footing. Their croaking got more organized; it wouldn't be long until the thugs were ready to attack again.

"Move it!" Vobsii shouted. The Resluni grabbed Levort by the back of his prospector cloak and heaved him through the trap door above. He tossed Levort the gateslinger, and Levort caught it, bobbling both Beyonder tools in his hands as he struggled to hold onto them.

A Kurikoid thug sprung up from the trap door, only to be yanked back down by Vobsii. There was a splash, then Vobsii jumped up from the cellar, scrambling to get through the trap door. Levort put the tablet and gateslinger on the counter and helped Vobsii up as Kurikoid thugs attempted to drag him back down. With a great heave, Vobsii tumbled into the room on top of Levort.

They scrambled to their feet. Vobsii grabbed the tablet and gave it a quick look of confusion while Levort holstered the gateslinger. He saw Vobsii's eyes go wide as the Resluni figured out the importance of the strange device. "You don't think—?"

"I do! Let's run!" Levort shouted, shoving Vobsii from behind. They vaulted over the counter and rushed out of the store as Kurikoids burst from the cellar and scrambled close behind. Outside, windows opened their shutters, and older Kurikoids assaulted them with various thrown household objects.

"It never ends!" Levort shouted, guarding his head as a cooking pot clanged off him. Finally, they made it to the edge of town. The Kurikoids kept a furious pace, only a few hops behind Levort and Vobsii. They raced up the hill at the edge of the spawning pool valley and found the portal waiting for them.

Vobsii dove through the portal, with Levort following behind him. Levort crashed into a bed of flowers on Bloom, the sounds of furious croaks echoing through the portal. He rolled onto his back, grabbed the gateslinger, and pulled the third trigger. Light flashed from the device and slapped the mirrored gate, causing it to shrink and burst.

Then, it was quiet.

The early sunrise breeze whistled through the blossoming morning flowers. Levort unclenched his muscles and flopped back into the flowers. He felt the pain of various kicks and punches, but he didn't care. He tried to settle his rapid breathing.

"So... How did it go?" Floem asked from her perch on the *Tumbleweed*.

Levort and Vobsii didn't respond.

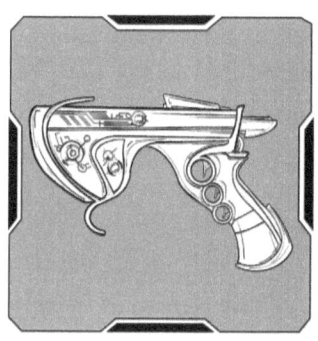

TWENTY-TWO

"What'd you bring me this time?" Floem lifted the strange Beyonder tablet out of the flowers. Levort sat up with his elbows on his knees. Vobsii hadn't bothered to get up at all. The Resluni remained on his back.

Levort said, "I think it might be one of the lost data tablets the Beyonders used to pass around Lodespace. We got trapped by some Kurikoid thugs, and I noticed it in their pile of loot. Pretty sure they stole it off of someone else. Either way, it's something Gulna Kii Fessenog missed."

Floem rotated the tablet and said, "You might be right. Sure has a lot of that Beyonder language all over it, but it does us no good if we can't decipher it with our fluency nodes."

Levort sighed. "Well, at least we learned a lot going to Kurika. The first lesson; don't bring the gateslinger through the portals. I think it's best we leave one of us here with the device in case things get messy on the other side. I should have left it with you, Floem."

"I was telling Skipper the same thing." Floem threw a thumb over her shoulder to the weed sitting in the flowerpot on the wing of the *Tumbleweed*. "I think we should try and find someone who can read this tablet. It should have information on how to reach the Beyond."

Levort thought of Wolil and the short time he'd spent with her.

If Bayfo hadn't stepped in, these mysteries would be answers. He had no knowledge of either of their conditions after separating in the fall from Vansparr. They might both be dead somewhere, on some distant world. *Damn it, Bayfo. Why did you do it?*

Vobsii finally sat up. "If we're going to find someone who can decipher that thing, we will need to be more efficient. There are millions of worlds out there. What if we launch a bunch of random portals here in the meadow? We can have whoever is on portal-watching duty keep an eye on them out here so they can shut them off in case someone tries to come through."

"You want to make a spread when only *one* almost got you two killed?" Floem scoffed.

"We have to play the odds," Levort said. His prospector's gambling habit outweighed his worry. "If we keep playing small, we're only going to win small. This is a long shot. We need to bring it closer with more chances for success."

"How about we start with two portals and work our way up?" Floem reasoned.

Levort and Vobsii looked at each other and nodded. "Yeah, probably for the best," Levort agreed.

Vobsii elaborated, "We can also shut off any portals with no noticeable civilization nearby. Some of these will lead to empty worlds like Bloom, which are fun, but we have an objective, and worlds like that won't do." Vobsii groaned and lifted himself into a standing position. He rubbed at some of the injuries he'd sustained from the thugs and shook his head. "I'll take the first watch. You two have fun jumping around the universe."

Floem smiled. "Before we do any of this, let's have some of that Mubb and eat breakfast."

* * *

After a few hours and a few Mubbs, Levort, Vobsii, and Floem got busy preparing for another portal scout. Levort had removed his prospector's cloak and was busy scrubbing it in the wash basin near the bathroom. Vobsii lay on the couch in the main room and listened to music, recovering from the previous grocery shopping adventure. Floem was making a lot of noise welding something together.

"Maybe if I..." Floem mumbled to herself as she worked.

"What are you making over there?" Levort asked, scrubbing out a particularly persistent stain on his sleeve.

"Well, these portals we're making can go anywhere, right? And we can't see or talk through them, so what happens if we get in trouble?" Floem asked rhetorically, then answered her own question. "That's where *this* comes in. I call it a jump-phone!" She held up two egg-shaped machines linked by a small cable. "Nova knows if it will actually work, but I figured it was worth a shot. We put one of these eggs on each side of the portal, like doorstops. They function like data antennas. The small cable between them will link them back to Bloom. That way, we use Bloom as a hub, and these egg antennas will let us chat remotely on our normal comm devices no matter where we go. I figure if we always come through in one piece, data should too, right?"

Levort shrugged. "Sounds right to me. Good thinking. We'll use Bloom as a communication hub between worlds." Levort finished cleaning and threw on his cloak. Floem finished her tinkering. Vobsii finished the song he was listening to.

It was time to jump.

Outside the *Tumbleweed*, Levort shot two portals with the Random trigger and let them hang in the meadow. Vobsii plunked down in a rickety chair and sat with the rifle he'd stolen from Captain Myrs resting in his lap.

Levort stretched, still sore from the last jaunt but too excited to sit this one out. This method of scouting scratched his prospecting itch. It was a gamble for what was on the other side. Because he didn't intend to sell anything to the Fessenog Fleet again, the score was all for his personal enjoyment.

Floem took one of her jump-phones and walked over to the portal on the right. She twisted the bottom of one of the egg-shaped antennas, and a spike sprang out, allowing her to insert it into the ground at the portal's base. The short cable that connected the antennas was long enough to go through the gateway and allow the other antenna to be planted on the opposite side—on whatever planet that side might be. Floem stepped through the portal; the short cable wiggled, then went taught.

"Testing—testing. Hello?" A voice came crackling over Levort and Vobsii's comm channel. "This is Floem coming to you live from…somewhere in the universe!"

Levort smiled and answered, "All good on this end. You're a genius, Floem!"

"No *drit*!" Floem responded. "Just set it up the way I showed you and try it on your end, Levort. I'm not sure where I am, but there's light in a canyon up ahead. I'll see you boys in a little bit. I have some exploring to do."

"Stay safe out there," Levort responded. He unholstered the gateslinger from his hip and handed it over to Vobsii.

Vobsii took it and nodded. "You get in trouble, you call me. I'll get you out." Vobsii said in a tone more serious than Levort had ever heard the Resluni use.

Levort shook his head. "I've gotten you in enough trouble. I'll be fine. You keep things sealed on this end."

Vobsii grunted and put the gateslinger in a holster on his belt. Once more, Levort donned his breather mask and hood and grabbed a satchel. He planted one end of the jump-phone antennas in the ground and stepped through the mirror to another unknown world.

TWENTY-THREE

Floem Zeu Uubog sang loudly into the rain that sprinkled her leaves. The portal had delivered her from Bloom to a cliffside on some unknown planet during a night rain shower. She could see the hazy lights of a city in the distance, not too far from her current position. Floem looked around for a way down and discovered a trail that zig-zagged into the flat valley below. She skipped down the path, drinking up the rain and enjoying the free nourishment it provided.

Levort's voice crackled over the comm, "Hey Floem. Can you still hear me?"

"Loud and clear, *Vort!*" Floem responded.

She grinned at Levort's groan at the nickname. "Great job on the jump-phone," he said. "It's strange talking to you like you're right next to me even though we're worlds apart. Zhok, we could be on opposite ends of the Voyalten Web for all we know."

"I better start selling these before the Fleet finds out. I think the fastest they can communicate between worlds still has about a half-hour delay." Floem laughed. She slipped a little on the muddy path and caught herself. "It's raining where I'm at. How's your planet looking?"

Levort said, "This place is weird. Very craggy and hot. A little like Dintup mixed with Vansparr."

"Vansparr?" Floem asked.

"Oh, right. Where I met Wolil. It's not in Lodespace. It's uncharted, like Bloom."

"Look at you, Mr. Tourist. I knew you were like us." Floem laughed.

"I was chatting with Vobsii during our grocery shopping adventure, and he mentioned that you two aren't actually real tourists."

Floem snorted. "Well, we are *now*. Aren't we? Who cares how we got started... What did he say exactly?"

"The word he used was *opportunist*." Levort huffed while he spoke, possibly climbing over some obstacle in the world he was hiking on.

"Opportunists could be right. Sounds good, at least. We've been a lot of things."

"Like what?" Levort asked. "You two seemed to have been together for a long time. I bet you have all sorts of stories. How did you become friends?"

"Funny you ask." Floem smiled. "I never told anyone the real story. We always came up with some charming lie to tell our marks. But you're no mark." Floem had made it to the flat part of her hike to the city. "Us Alberryans are highly sought after for space travel. Basically, if we want to be on a ship, we only have to point, and we always get a yes. We cut costs on oxygen by providing it naturally, sucking up all your funky gases and all that." It was a crude way of explaining how her race of female plant people inhaled carbon dioxide and then exhaled breathable oxygen, but she figured Levort would follow it better than deep science. "I could have gone anywhere, with anyone. Pilots came to Alberrya all the time, usually to pick up a passenger. But one day, a ship came to drop someone off."

"Vobsii?" Levort asked.

"Yeah. He was just this little Resluni kid when we met. The people who dropped him off were not his parents. They were friends of theirs, though. They had no idea how to take care of a kid and were doing some dangerous stuff in Lodespace. They never said what...

Zhok, they could have been seeking the Beyond like us for all I know. I was young then, too, just a few cycles older than Vobsii. I knew I could be like his big sister. So, I took him in, and we've been welded together ever since."

"That's very kind," Levort said.

"I had some self-interest, too. We started thieve'n right away. He was the distraction, and I was the hands. We'd hop from ship to ship for a while. Like I said, I had the pick of the lot. My condition was always that Vobsii came with too. We ransacked so many marks." Floem sighed. "The good old days. Now we're too old. Can't use our *Cutes* anymore, so we had to use our super-smart brains. Eventually, that *drit* gets tiring, so we stole the *Tumbleweed*, changed all the licenses, and painted it to make it ours."

"That's all a lot less kind," Levort admitted.

"Why thank you." Floem tilted her head to the sky, proud of herself.

"Well, for what it's worth, I'm glad to be part of your crew. I am lucky you guys found me on Jofnalg. I really had nowhere else to go after…" Levort trailed off.

"*Junior* crew member," Floem joked. "You don't get full privileges until you can keep down your Mubb."

Levort laughed through the comm. After a moment, he asked, "Why did you guys bring me along anyway? You could have just taken my gateslinger and traveled around the universe."

Floem shook her head. "That's no way to make new friends."

Levort was quiet.

"Don't you have friends back on Consonance Hub?" Floem asked.

"Not really. It was just Bayfo and me for as long as I can remember. He was like a big brother to me, after my parents…" Levort hesitated, but Floem let him take time to find his words. "I grew up in a sorting facility, one of the junk kids. My parents sold me to the Fleet to cover costs to prospect on Tayoxe."

Floem winced. She'd never had true parents. Alberryans simply dropped off the tree they came from and continued on as seedlings until they sprouted leaves and got picked for various ship crews. But she had Vobsii, and he, too, was given away by his guardians. "I'm sorry to hear that."

"Yeah, it's ok. I don't remember them. I raised myself and became a prospector, and Bayfo was with me the whole way. We were trying to get out of Tayoxe and travel to other worlds. He was working toward becoming a commander, and I was going to get an S-Class license. He never thought I could do it…"

Floem offered her advice. "If there's one thing I've learned in my cycles hopping around Lodespace, it's that friends need to be there to lift each other up. I know Bayfo has been with you a long time, but the fact you knew he didn't believe in you tells me everything I need to know about him. Friends don't keep you small."

Levort thought about her words, then said, "Maybe you're right. It doesn't matter anymore, anyway. After what happened, I don't think he's on my side anymore."

"Me and Vobsii are on team Levort! We believe in you and want to find the Beyond with you. And I know for a fact we're gonna do it too." Floem smiled, hoping he could feel her optimism through the comm.

After a quiet moment, Levort said, "Thanks for talking with me, Floem."

"Anytime, any world." Floem was approaching the city. "Hey, Levort, how exactly will we ask if people can read the Beyonder tablet? I can't just walk up to people and ask. The Fleet could overhear."

Levort laughed. "I haven't figured that out myself. We'll have to improvise."

"I'll see what I can do. Getting close to my location, talk to you in a little bit."

"Good luck!" Levort said.

"You too, Vort." Floem cut the comm before Levort could protest that specific abbreviation of his name. She needed to find someone who could decipher the Beyonder tablet but had little to go on. As much as it seemed like Gulna Kii Fessenog and his big scary Fleet were trying to conceal the Beyond, they seemed to have a lot of blind spots. Floem was looking for a mark, but not the kind you steal from—the kind you befriend.

A sign boasting "Welcome to Gracefall: The Most Stunning City on Planet Dive" stood outside the city limits. Floem noticed some other Lodespace races walking and felt relieved she wouldn't freak anyone out by showing up as an alien.

The buildings in Gracefall were short, covered in colorful orange and blue lights, and connected by bridges. The misty rain obscured most objects more than a few blocks away. Under the bridges, the world seemed to drop off. Cities on Dive had been built into the sides of deep canyons in the mountain valleys. Although the buildings only went up a few floors on the surface, each shared an edge that plummeted dozens of stories down. Where the buildings stopped, a river rushed.

"Dive sounds right," Floem whispered as she looked down. She scanned the area, curious about where to begin her quest. Having no solid answer, she chose to wander. *Sometimes the only way to find what you're looking for is to roam.* She took a staircase on the side of the bridge that linked up to the layer below the surface. Underneath the cliff hang, it was dry. Water created a thin curtain to the outside, and the lights became hazy across the bridge.

Floem spent a few hours wandering around Gracefall, admiring the city's beauty. The lower she went, the louder the river got. Citizens fished off the sides of the lowest bridges, often pulling up river creatures. Floem watched from a layer above, leaning against the railing to rest.

A human woman's voice quietly rose over the sound of the river. "What am I supposed to do now, Thea?"

Floem turned to see a person shrouded in a hooded jacket, wet with rain. Floem listened in, her nosey instincts propelling her to snoop. The woman floated a holographic image of another smiling human. The stranger brought a hand to her eye and sniffled.

Floem reflexively asked, "Is everything all right?"

The stranger spun to face Floem, her eyes wet with tears despite having cover from the rain in her hood. She slapped the holographic image shut. The stranger looked at Floem and began to walk away.

"I'm sorry," Floem said. "I didn't mean to spy on you."

The woman stopped and turned to face Floem. "What do you

want?" Her words were laced with frustration, but not at Floem's intrusion. Instead, Floem caught the plea for help hidden away in the woman's words.

Floem didn't see her expedition going this way; this was hardly the person she'd ask about Beyonder technology. She put her mission on hold. "I don't want anything. I'm new around here, and I overheard you. I thought I'd maybe lend you a shoulder."

"A shoulder?" The woman looked Floem up and down, analyzing if she was a threat. "And nothing else?"

"No. I don't need anything." Floem smiled sincerely.

"Why help me?" the stranger asked.

Floem wasn't sure what to say. She had built a lifestyle out of thievery, but that had not made her so cold. When she heard the woman ask her question, the memory of when she first met Vobsii surfaced. A deep loneliness had filled the air that day, one that had also filled Floem's own heart until the small Resluni entered her life. She never wanted to feel that way again and hated seeing it in the universe around her. This stranger was just as lost as Floem used to be, and she wouldn't let it stand. She could have been anywhere in the universe, yet she was here.

Floem simply stated, "Because I'm here with you."

The stranger hesitated momentarily, then took a few steps closer to Floem. She weakly said, "My name's Piper. Piper Cridhe."

"I'm Floem Zeu Uubog."

"I don't think I've ever actually met an Alberryan before," Piper admitted.

"I'm the coolest one, honestly." Floem laughed.

Piper laughed—a small huff, but a laugh. She sighed. "It's my sister. She—I can't believe I have to say it out loud."

Floem waited patiently.

"She died. Just a few hours ago." Piper's face contorted into sadness.

Floem stepped closer and put her arms up for a hug, not wanting to presume Piper wanted one. Piper threw herself into Floem's embrace and let go of her emotions. Floem held her gently and allowed Piper to do whatever she needed. She whispered, "I'm very sorry for your loss."

Piper wiped her face and eventually took a step back. "I wish it was the same for us humans as it is for you Alberryans. You turn into trees instead of dying, right?"

"It's not really instead of death, at least not how you think. In a way, it's the same for you as it is for all of us," Floem said, carefully choosing her words. "My people root down and phase into our tree form, but we shed ourselves completely into that form before we drop off more seedlings like me. Yeah, the tree is still me, but it's a different me. The version of me I recognize dies, but I live on still. Humans are similar. They die, but they live on as memories. Sure, it's not as visible as a tree, but it's warmer."

Piper sniffled and looked away from Floem. "I don't know what to do. She always looked out for me. When she got sick, I did everything I could to return the favor… But…"

Floem locked eyes with Piper and said, "You did great."

Piper's eyes widened and grew wet. "She still…"

"But she did so with your love to guide her to the end."

Piper huffed and nodded. She took a moment for herself, then added, "Damn. What a day. I could use a drink."

"Me too," Floem said with a smile. "I have some hapron. That's good here, right?"

"Of course, it is," Piper laughed. "Where isn't it good?"

"Maybe I'll tell you all about it. But for now, let's celebrate a life and honor a death," Floem suggested. They walked across the bridge to a small building with green glowing signs on its outer doors and a few empty seats inside. Once inside, Piper Cridhe removed her hood and raincoat. She was a middle-aged human woman with short reddish-blond hair and deep brown eyes. Floem found a seat near the window, and they ordered something more elegant than Mubb to drink.

The drinks came, a wine from some local Gracefall winery, and they clinked glasses together. Piper looked out the window and said, "Thea liked this place. It feels right to send her off like this."

"I can see why. It has good wine." Floem took another sip. Drinking red wines temporarily changed the colors of Floem's leaves as her plant biology absorbed the liquids.

"We did a lot of traveling together," Piper reminisced. "Even to here, Dive. We were still traveling. Thea didn't want to die in a space station or locked in some hospital. So we went on this one last adventure together. We did all sorts of things she wanted to do. Zhok, we even took some stunt flying courses." She laughed as she reminisced. "Turns out I'm pretty good at it too." Piper sighed. "We didn't have a planned destination. We wanted to world hop until… Until the lights shut off."

"That's the way I'd want to go. I'm a world hopper myself, with a few close friends of mine. Looks like you and I crossed paths just in time," Floem said. The two spoke for some time, finishing off a glass each and getting a refill.

Piper spoke of Thea and the good times, as well as some of the bad times—a much shorter list. She described many of the worlds she visited with her sister. "We were always seeking challenges in our travels. Before Thea got sick, we would go rock climbing on Dintup and sailing on the rough seas of Aquain. We even got to pilot one of those rocket racers once, like the ones you see on datastreams. Thea was great at finding adventures. Ah, those days were the best."

Floem listened to all of Piper's stories with great interest. For a little while, she felt like she was sitting with two people. The way Piper spoke of her sister made her presence in the room tangible.

For a little while, Piper smiled.

After some time, Piper said, "Thank you for talking with me. I really needed a friend."

"I'm happy to be here," Floem said with a sincere smile.

Piper looked down at her drink and summoned the strength to take another sip. "I suppose I could keep traveling until the hapron runs out, and I have to return to Marothall."

Floem took another sip of wine and thought for a moment. She looked out the window, then back to Piper. "Hey. I have this crazy idea."

TWENTY-FOUR

"You too, Vort!" Floem said before abruptly clicking off the comm.

"Please don't call me—ah, you're already gone," Levort mumbled. He shook his head and scrambled over more crags until he reached the top of an uneven plateau. Ahead, the world was filled with mountains, dark clouds, fire, lava, and industrial lights. Something was moving around in the glow, and the world was filled with loud clangs, thuds, and bangs. Sparks flew from various dark shapes as thunder rumbled in the sky above. In the silhouette, Levort thought he could make out scaffolds or frames of some sort.

Another figure was standing on the plateau's rim. Levort recognized the ivory of a Fessenog Fleet enforcer uniform. He panicked, hopped off the plateau's edge to another layer below, and tucked himself against the cliff wall. After a few heartbeats, he dared to stick his head above the lip of the plateau. The enforcer kept an eye on the trenches below. She didn't seem to notice Levort's presence.

This enforcer was a big Resluni, larger than Vobsii, with a longer snout and some tusks instead of whiskers. She huffed and patrolled away from Levort's position.

I better get off this world, Levort thought. He attempted to scramble back up onto the plateau and slink back the way he came, but his jump wasn't high enough, and he only crashed his hands against the upper ledge. Levort tried to pull himself up, but his angle was wrong, and he slipped back to the lower shelf. He hit the ridge with a thud and felt it give away underneath him, sending him tumbling with the dirt and rocks into the trench below.

Levort free-fell briefly before landing on something soft. He heard a strange sound, like air squeezing from an elastic balloon. It continued for a prolonged moment as Levort recovered from his dizziness. Around him were strange floating creatures with thin tentacled appendages. Some of the creatures were only one balloon, while others were a series of two or three balloons strung together by tentacles. In each of their center masses were a grouping of eyeballs. They carried tools and wore safety equipment.

Levort realized he was crushing one of these ballooned creatures under his butt and quickly shuffled sideways to get off of it. As feared, smashed into the dirt was another of the balloon creatures, but this one wore different equipment. If Levort didn't know any better, he'd say it wore an ivory enforcer kit.

"Uhh..." Levort looked at the creatures floating around him. They stared down at the crushed enforcer balloon. There was a sharp squeal, and the crushed enforcer balloon began to wiggle and reinflate. Levort sighed with relief and watched as the worker balloons drifted toward their enforcer. One carrying a pickaxe in its tentacles got close and hovered over the enforcer, watching it inflate with gas.

"I didn't mean to—" Levort started to beg for forgiveness. He was cut off when the worker slammed their pickaxe down on the enforcer balloon, causing it to burst and spray goo everywhere. "Woah!" Levort shouted in surprise as he was coated with the innards of the popped balloon.

The worker turned toward the other balloons and raised their tool above their inflated sacks. They shouted, "It is time!" The rest seemed to garble back in excitement. They turned back to Levort and repeated, "Now is the time!"

"Ti... Time?" Levort mumbled in confusion.

The creature and their fellow workers floated closer to Levort as the leader explained, "For too long, Mulptre have been forced to work in these trenches for the Fessenog Fleet. We build their starships but are never invited to sail among them. No longer! We will go with you!"

Levort put his hands out and explained, "I'm just looking for someone who can read Beyonder language."

The Mulptre looked at their fellows and then back to Levort, "We can read."

"Really?" Levort put a hand on his head. *What luck!* "And you want to come with me?"

"You must take all of us," the leader Mulptre said.

"Take you…all…" Levort counted only three in total. "I think I can manage that." In the time it took Levort to look back up the cliff, assess their escape route, and turn around, the little outlet in the trench was filled with fifteen ballooned Mulptre.

"Oh," Levort stammered. He pushed his hood off his head and ran his hand through his long black hair. He thought of Vobsii and Floem and considered using the jump-phone to discuss with them.

"What's going on down there!" The Resluni enforcer from the upper plateau had discovered them. "Who is that?"

"*Drit*! Out of time," Levort gasped.

"Revolution!" the leader Mulptre shouted and floated upward toward the Resluni enforcer.

"Wait!" Levort pleaded, but the balloons paid him no mind. He managed to grab onto one of the last Mulptre's tentacles and hitch a ride back up to the higher ledge as they sprang their attack.

The Resluni pulled out a stun stick and swung it into the first Mulptre that came at her. It made a bouncy, hollow noise on impact, and the Mulptre was batted to the side. Before the Resluni could swing again, the other balloons engulfed her. Levort heard her screams as the Mulptre curled themselves around the enforcer and took her weapons. They then tossed her down into the trenches.

Plasma blasts zipped by, and the Mulptre, now armed with the Resluni's enforcer kit, fired back. Levort ducked as a shot came close to his head. The leader Mulptre came to Levort's side and asked, "Where is your starship?"

"It's not a—" Levort thought to mention the portal but decided it was a bad idea to explain it during a gunfight. He opted for, "Follow me."

The Mulptre followed Levort through the crags and canyons, returning fire to the enforcers that pursued. Chunks of canyon wall were blasted loose, and dust was everywhere. A plasma blast popped one of the Mulptre near Levort, dropping the enforcer rifle it was holding. Levort picked up the rifle and returned fire. "Keep moving forward! You'll find a floating mirror. Move through it, and you'll be safe!"

Levort took a few more shots, mostly for effect. He tapped the comm device on his cloak's collar. "Vobsii! I have some friends coming through the portal. Don't shoot!"

"You have some *what?*" Vobsii's voice crackled.

"No time to explain! I'll come through last. Get ready to shut down the portal!" Levort shouted and fired a few more shots while walking backward. He could see the light of the portal reflecting off the crags around him, and he bumped into one of the Mulptre as he walked backward.

It was the leader, pickaxe still gripped in their tentacles. "What is this strangeness?"

"It's Beyonder technology," Levort explained. "Wait, I thought you said you could read Beyonder?"

The Mulptre leader garbled in response.

"Wait, *can* you or *can't* you read Beyonder?" Levort asked, firing off another shot.

"I said we can read," the Mulptre said vaguely. "Schematics, mostly."

Levort grunted and kicked the jump-phone antenna back through the portal. "We'll figure it out later. Get moving!"

The Mulptre moved through the portal. Levort scanned the area to ensure all the Mulptre had made it through and was glad to see no more balloons floating around. Before stepping through the portal, something caught Levort's eye.

Off in the distance, a portal exploded into existence. The silhouette of a human stepped through, wearing a long cloak. The portal walker noticed Levort and stopped moving for a moment. Levort was lucky to not be hit by stray plasma fire from the pursuing enforcers as he became paralyzed by the site of the other portal walker.

Levort whispered, "Bayfo?"

Bayfo Niall cut into a run, rushing toward Levort. Levort noticed the crackle of a stun bolt as it exploded against a nearby rock, and he knew that Bayfo was not here to rekindle their friendship. Levort felt a knot in his throat and tears come to his eyes. This validated what Floem had said before. Bayfo wasn't here to join him. He was here to stop him.

Friends don't keep you small.

Levort stepped back through the portal.

He got one last look at his old friend before he slipped back to Bloom. Bayfo's face had been injured, and his eyes were dark with fury. He wasn't the same person Levort grew up with. Vobsii quickly collapsed the portal, and the line to the Mulptre's homeworld was severed.

Levort remained stunned, staring into the space where the portal had been. His thoughts were caught in a vortex of sadness and confusion. Although he wasn't struck with a plasma bolt or stun shot, Levort was wounded just as severely.

Bayfo was with Gulna Kii Fessenog now.

Bayfo was a threat.

TWENTY-FIVE

Bayfo stumbled to a stop, his hand outreached. He stood motionless for a moment, then tightened his hand into a fist. His luck that his portal had delivered him so closely to Levort made him wonder if it was more than a fluke.

Enforcers shot at Bayfo, forcing him to shoot back. His smitegun lashed out another stun bolt, striking a pursuing Resluni enforcer. The Resluni twitched and fell on his face in the dirt. More were around the corner. To them, he was the stranger they were after.

"Amateurs." Bayfo shook his head. He knew he needed to hide the existence of his gateslinger, and he shot out a portal with the third trigger. It slapped into existence, and Bayfo stepped through, deactivating it as the other enforcers rounded the bend to discover only their stunned comrade.

***

"What happened? You were only gone for fifteen minutes?" Vobsii asked, spinning in circles to watch all the Mulptre that had come through the portal. "Who are these guys?"

Levort didn't hear Vobsii at first, still paralyzed by Bayfo's brief presence. The leader Mulptre broke Levort's trance by saying, "We owe you a great debt." They reached out the tentacle that wasn't wrapped around the pickaxe to shake Levort's hand.

Levort shook off his worry. "Uh… Yeah. No problem." Then he got ahold of the situation. "Wait, yeah! *Some* problem! You told me you could read Beyonder? Now you're saying you can't?"

The leader Mulptre looked to the left and right. "We misunderstood the question. Everything happened so fast. We needed to escape before the enforcers got to us."

Levort couldn't argue the speed at which everything had happened. He realized he hadn't even introduced himself. "Well, we're friends now. My name's Levort Aatra. That guy over there is Vobsii Essaurntii, and we have one more who's still off-world named Floem Zeu Uubog. She's—" Levort stopped himself and turned to Vobsii, still spinning in circles, tracking the balloon creatures that had come through with Levort. "Vobsii!"

"Yeah, what?" Vobsii said, holding his head to cull his dizziness.

"Did Floem check in?"

Vobsii nodded. "She was making it to a city when she called in a bit ago. She's fine."

"That's good," Levort whispered. He thought of Bayfo. Having an enforcer tracking them made every jump dangerous. Levort had seen what Bayfo was capable of over the cycles and was always glad to have him on his side. Now, they were the focus of his ire.

Captain Myrs had called the Beyonders cultists, but Levort couldn't help but think it might be the other way around. The operation Gulna Kii Fessenog was running—gaslighting all of Lodespace into thinking the Beyonders were dangerous—felt more like cult behavior to him. An old phrase from his childhood surfaced: *He who smelt it dealt it.*

"We are named Sevodan. We are Mulptre," Sevodan introduced themself. "We are one and many." The balloon creatures flittered around in unison, creating a large orbit of gas-filled sacks and tentacles.

"Hive mind." Vobsii nodded. "Pretty cool. Don't think I've ever heard of your people before, Sevodan."

"We Mulptre are the Fleet's darkest secret. Gulna Kii Fessenog has used us to supply off-worlders with luxury starships to secure trade routes. He works the Mulptre to death in the shipyards of our homeworld, Grotrane. Mining and forging. We are builders, and Fessenog took advantage of our strength."

Levort admitted, "Well, the door to Grotrane is closed off. I didn't mean to kidnap you. We can try to find a way back to—"

"Grotrane was our homeworld, but it does not resemble a home anymore," Sevodan said. "You have not kidnapped us. We are much happier on this world."

"We call this place Bloom," Vobsii said. "You are welcome to it. We don't have much, but you're welcome to what we got."

Sevodan and their legion twirled with delight. "Thank you, kind Levort and Vobsii. In return, we will build for you."

"We couldn't ask you to do that," Levort said. "We won't make you do anything you don't want to. You have been through enough."

"We Mulptre are builders. It is our delight. Fessenog had forced us before, but now, building for ourselves would be a great satisfaction. We know many schematics, and our memory is image-perfect. We will begin with shelter." Sevodan moved in many directions, then moved back into a huddle. "Can we harvest materials on this world?"

Levort looked at Vobsii and shrugged. "If that's what you want to do. I had been carving out a little mine to try and fix the ship. You're free to use it however you like."

Sevodan checked their many bodies to see what had made it through the portal. "We have a full maker's kit. This is good. Only missing a salvager. Lost when one fell during the escape."

Levort offered, "Use mine. I bet you're better with it than me."

"That would be excellent." Sevodan fluttered with glee.

Levort retrieved his HAMMER model salvager for the Mulptre. Sevodan admired the salvager with trained eyes. "This is the finest piece of equipment we have ever held. We will build such excellent things."

"Thank you." Levort smiled.

Levort and Vobsii sat for a few hours and watched the portal for Floem's return. Sevodan worked quickly, refining raw minerals into flat pieces of metal and building the scaffold for a shelter. With so many tentacles and tools, the home was nearly finished when Floem finally stepped through the portal.

"Woah," Floem whispered.

Another figure stepped through the portal behind Floem. Levort noticed it was a human, one of the only others he had seen besides Bayfo in a long time. She emerged from the portal and threw back her reddish hair.

Floem opened her hand toward the newcomer and said, "Everyone, meet Piper Cridhe."

***

"It's nice to meet you all," Piper said with a smile. She took in the sights and whispered, "I don't believe all this." A world covered from horizon to horizon in beautiful flowers. Creatures shaped like balloons with tentacles welded away at structures. A rusty old tourist ship rested behind a Resluni and a human. Floem had been upfront about all of this, but it still felt impossible to Piper.

The portal to Dive was still active. Floem had been clear she wouldn't force Piper to stay if she didn't want to. The mirror hung, vibrating in place. Floem's human friend pulled up two chairs so they could watch Sevodan work. Piper thanked him and took a seat.

Floem introduced her friends and sat with them. "I know it's a lot, but it's been interesting. We can leave the portal to Dive open if you change your mind, but if you want to stay, you are welcome to. Even if you decide to leave later, we can always find a different Lodespace world to bring you to so you can return to your life. No obligations to stay."

Piper wondered, *What would Thea think of this? Personal portals. Worlds only a skip away. We spent so much time traveling by ship that suddenly, it feels old-fashioned to keep that up.* Piper knew what Thea would recommend. She felt her sister's warmth in her heart, and it brought her a smile to know she was carrying her with her across the universe.

"Shut the portal off. I'll stay for a while if that's all right," Piper said resolutely.

"Why not try it yourself?" Vobsii asked. He held the gateslinger out in front of her. Piper looked down at the weird thing in the Resluni's hand. It was curved and covered in strange letters. Three triggers lined its grip. She picked it up and held it like a smitegun.

Levort added, "Point it at the portal and squeeze any trigger. It'll collapse it."

Piper turned to the portal and held the device forward. For a moment, she held still, allowing the situation to sink in. This was a leap—longer than any portal could throw her. It felt like the early days of traveling with Thea, hopping rides on ships, and meeting new friends. Adventure awaited. *Goodbye, Thea. I will have so many stories to tell you when we meet again.*

A light flashed from the device and slapped the portal. It burst, and only the flower-filled horizon glistened in the setting sun beyond it. Piper took a deep breath and turned back toward the others. She held the device out for Vobsii, and he slung it into his holster.

"One of us!" Floem squealed with joy. "About time we had another lady around here. Skipper's not much of a conversationalist, and I've been hanging out with these two fart-boys for too long."

Piper laughed.

Levort waved Floem off. "It's good to have you with us!"

Piper thanked them. "Floem mentioned the Beyond language. I'm sorry, but I wouldn't be able to read the tablet. Wish I could be more useful."

Levort shook his head. "That's no problem. It's not about usefulness with us. We're on the hunt for someone who can read the tablet. It might hold some keys to reaching the Beyond. The more of us who can portal walk, the more worlds we can cover." Levort stopped for a moment and looked away. He added, "But we have to be careful. The Fessenog Fleet wants to hide the Beyond at all costs. There is another portal walker, but he's…"

"We need to be careful to avoid him," Vobsii interjected. "Luckily, he wouldn't know you, so as long as we keep the portal out of sight, you're as safe as can be."

Piper nodded. "I'm aware of the risks."

Floem spread her arms out. "She's a tourist! She gets the drill. Space is dangerous, strangers are bad, and don't eat the Yolmit. All that."

Vobsii said, "A tourist. Great!"

Piper mentioned, "I had been traveling with my sister. I picked up a lot of skills along the way. Maybe I can put some to use." She looked at the rusty tourist ship. "I'm a pretty good pilot. But I don't know…"

Levort looked over his shoulder at the ship and laughed. "Yeah, the *Tumbleweed* is a work in progress. But we'll get her flight capable again someday."

Sevodan floated over to the group with their entourage of themself. The Mulptre said, "The shelter is complete. Would you like to see our work?"

Levort stood from his chair. "Lead the way."

Piper followed the human, the Resluni, the Alberryan, and the Mulptre toward the shelter. It was perfectly built, a structure that would be considered luxury-class in most worlds. It was curved on one side, resembling an elongated half-moon, with windows facing the setting sun. The interior had multiple rooms but no furniture. "We will build anything requested. Bloom only has so much. We will need to portal walk to retrieve the correct materials," Sevodan explained.

Long windows on the far wall of each room had curtains made of flower petals. The structure smelled like welded metal and flowers, giving it a new-spaceship-yet-wild smell. The floor was bare, but Sevodan explained, "We intend to make paneling once we secure wood. It is built to accommodate future enhancements."

Levort shouted, his voice echoing off the walls, "This is amazing, Sevodan!"

The group finished the tour of their new shelter and enjoyed the sunset on Bloom. Sevodan showed them some fun tricks they could do, bouncing themselves together into various shapes while Piper and Floem enjoyed more wine they had brought from Dive. Vobsii casually drank Mubb while Levort tried to get his taste for the fermented algae with a lot of coughing.

TWENTY-SIX

A quarter cycle, Fleet Standard, passed.

Bayfo Niall needed a lead. He had been hopping worlds nonstop in all his waking hours. He had seen the skies of a thousand planets, each stranger than the last, but he had not run into Levort Aatra since his close encounter on Grotrane. Each failure put him in deeper danger. Bayfo knew Gulna might consider him a threat if he couldn't deliver Levort.

Bayfo knew too much.

Alas, Bayfo also knew too little.

Wolil never explained the gateslinger to Bayfo. Having always been a quick study, he had gotten far on experimentation alone. But he was still flying blind. Bayfo planned to change that, so he took a risk and convinced Gulna to let him visit Wolil's prison cell in the Yawning Lock.

The lift brought Bayfo down into the depths of Fernomare, the small world near Tayoxe's star used as Gulna's deepest, darkest prison. Captain Tegarl Myrs greeted him in the guard shack upon his arrival. She had been briefed and gave him access to the rest of the Lock.

A robotic jailor named Abnat guided Bayfo's path. It was a dumb mechanical thing designed to do its job without mercy. It brought Bayfo down many layers in the cylindrical prison pit. Each cell contained a frost wall to prevent the prisoners from seeing and conversing with each other.

Bayfo had no idea why Gulna kept Beyonders alive. His treatment of them was baffling. Still, they were Bayfo's ticket to the life he always dreamed of. They were his pathway to saving his friend from a dangerous cult—or a similar fate in the Yawning Lock.

Abnat came to a cell. The wall facing Bayfo was ice blue and cold to the touch, as were the cells flanking it. Bayfo turned to the robot and nodded his head. The robot's inner workings clicked and whirred, and the iced wall melted away, revealing Wolil. She sat against the far wall with her arms on the floor.

Wolil shook her head as if she had been sleeping. She blinked her large eyes and whispered, "Wha… What?"

"I have some questions for you, Beyonder," Bayfo said, standing outside the crisscrossed cell bars that had replaced the ice wall.

"Oh. It's you," Wolil sighed.

Bayfo unholstered the gateslinger and showed it to Wolil. "I need to know what the second trigger does."

Wolil smiled and said, "Why not hand it to me so I can show you?"

"There's no time for these games. Just tell me what the second trigger does," Bayfo demanded. His tone grew hurried and frustrated.

"Or *what*? You'll shoot me?" Wolil guffawed. "Please do. I'm getting really tired of this dreadful place."

Bayfo shook his head and looked at Abnat. The robot nodded and moved to the next cell over. Wolil perked up and cocked a brow. The robot whirred internally, and the ice wall of the other cell melted.

Another Beyonder was inside the cell, curled into a fetal position. Like Wolil, he had four arms, was mostly nude, and had green and blue skin. He moved slowly, as if recovering from shell shock, and turned to Bayfo. He quickly shrunk away toward the back wall. "No, no! I already told you what I know!"

"Quiet. I'm not here for whatever you're babbling about," Bayfo said. "Your name is Reedor, correct?"

"Y-yes."

"Reedor! I've been looking for you!" Wolil shouted as she slammed against the cell bars.

"Wolil?" Reedor whispered. "Oh no... They trapped you here too."

"Quiet now, you two," Bayfo warned them. He patted the smitegun in his holster.

Wolil sneered at Bayfo, her eyes crunched with worry. "What are you doing?"

Bayfo ignored her question. He held the gateslinger in front of Reedor and asked, "Can you tell me how this works?"

Reedor's breaths became short, and his eyes darted from Bayfo to the gateslinger to Wolil. He shook his head in quick, uneven movements.

Bayfo twirled the device in his hand and asked, "What if I promised to free you?"

Wolil asked again, "What are you doing?"

"Promise?" Reedor whimpered.

"Reedor!" Wolil shouted.

Reedor ignored her plea.

"I promise to free you if you teach me about this device." Bayfo stopped twirling the gateslinger and held it still. "I don't even need much. I only need to know what the second trigger does."

Wolil slammed her fist against her cell bars. "He's lying, Reedor! Don't fall for it!"

Bayfo shouted, "You had your chance! Reedor can benefit from your hesitation."

Reedor cautiously shuffled toward the cell bars. He looked the device up and down and said, "Is-is it linked?"

Bayfo smiled. "You tell me?"

"Reedor! Don't!" Wolil slammed her hand against the cells again. Abnat slid over to Wolil's cell with a sickening speed and jolted the bars with electricity. Wolil was thrown against the back wall of her cell. She gritted her teeth and crushed her eyelids together to push down the pain that rattled through her bones.

"It-it looks linked," Reedor said, stuttering in fear. "If it's linked, that means the second trigger can do two things."

"Please..." Wolil begged through her pain.

"Go on." Bayfo had Abnat approach Reedor's cell and unlock the door.

Reedor stepped out of the cell and smiled. He started shaking with joy. He took a moment to contain himself. Reedor pointed at the gateslinger and explained, "The second trigger is the Wide setting. It's used to go to specific places. Since your tool is linked with another, it can portal to the same worlds the other has visited."

"How?" Bayfo was practically drooling at this information.

Reedor pointed at the various symbols on the device. "Slide that symbol up. It means History in our language. From there, the other marks will change. Each one is the name of the planet the linked device has visited. You can change which planet you want to see by pushing them toward the front of the tool."

Bayfo did as instructed and watched the symbols change. He still couldn't read the words the Beyonders had given each world, but his pool of possible leads went from millions to hundreds. Bayfo's eyes lit up at this revelation.

Wolil whimpered, "Reedor, no."

Reedor ignored Wolil and looked Bayfo in the eyes. "Am I free?"

"Yes. Have your freedom." Bayfo pulled his smitegun from its holster and shot Reedor in the chest. The bang of the gun echoed off the cylindrical prison. The Beyonder stumbled back as green blood oozed from the wound on his chest. He locked eyes with Wolil, his last moments filled with the realization of what he had done. Reedor took a couple steps back before silently falling over the railing into the abyss below.

Wolil curled into a ball and wept.

Bayfo holstered his smitegun and nodded to Abnat. Wolil's cell frosted back over, sealing the Beyonder away until he needed to interrogate her again. Bayfo pointed his gateslinger and squeezed the second trigger. He laughed and walked forward into the *lesser* unknown.

"I'll save you, Lev."

TWENTY-SEVEN

Levort returned from another portal walk in the early morning hours on Bloom. The fresh hit of wildflowers and pure air smacked him in the senses every time he came back. Bloom was becoming the first stable home he ever knew. It retained a comfort Levort had never felt in his one hammock escape pod on Consonance Hub.

But it wasn't enough.

The Beyond was out there, somewhere far off in space, waiting to be reached. Wolil had told Levort beautiful things about that hidden sector of space—the impossible technologies, the brilliant minds that thrived there—but they weren't the reason he yearned to reach it. Levort knew if he remained in the Below, Bayfo would be searching for him. When once he hoped to see his old friend again, now he dreaded what might happen if they were to have another encounter. If he could reach the Beyond, he'd be free, and Bayfo couldn't hunt him anymore. If Bayfo found him first…

Levort shouldered his sack full of foraged supplies from the forested world he'd returned from. Piper Cridhe sat outside one of the structures Sevodan built, sipping a hot cup of something caffeinated that they had discovered on a different world outside of Lodespace. She waved Levort over, and he approached and sat next to her. They watched the sunrise as Piper poured another hot cup for him.

"How was the trip?" Piper asked.

"No dice," Levort sighed and accepted the mug of hot liquid, watching the steam swirl into the air. "It feels like we'll never find someone who can decipher this Beyonder tablet."

"Have you ever thought that we might not need to?"

Levort finished his sip. "What do you mean?"

"Look around, Lev. Bloom is a paradise. You built it with Vobsii and Floem. This is a homestead the original human pioneers would be jealous of." Piper waved her hand in grand gestures before returning her palm to the warmth of her cup.

Levort looked around. Over the past quarter cycle, they had obtained more mouths to feed. Alien races, both familiar and strange, dotted the floral landscape. Floem was great at finding people from all over Lodespace and elsewhere who wanted to reach the Beyond. Resluni, Alberryans, Kurikoids, Fluctans, Marothallans, and some new races thrilled to be part of something larger helped where they could. Some tended gardens, others milled lumber and helped Sevodan build. Everyone they'd recruited helped maintain and build, and no one was required to stay if they decided to leave. None had left. There was a warmth in the air, a friendliness of gathered star travelers. The new residents of Bloom were officially a colony.

Still, none were able to decipher the Beyonder tablet.

"It would be better in the Beyond," Levort stated.

"What would be?" Piper asked. "The horizon? The people? The friends?"

"We'd all be safer. What Wolil spoke about the Beyond was amazing."

"Amazing, sure. Unbelievable, maybe. Impossible, probably. Safer, *unclear*. You told us you didn't get to know Wolil well," Piper mentioned.

"Well, no. But look at everything we've obtained because of her. I can't accept that she was part of some dangerous cult when so much good has come from the technology she's given us." Levort shook his head. "The Beyond is real—and it's out there. If we can get someone to read this tablet, we can get there."

"We're with you. All the way," Piper said. "I only hope you are happy. Life is short. Make sure you appreciate what you have." She looked into her steaming cup.

Levort placed a hand on Piper's shoulder and said, "I am happy. You guys are my family at this point. I've never been in a place with so much love and friendship."

Piper smiled.

"That is why I want to take us to the Beyond. I want the best for us all." Levort looked back toward the horizon, removing his hand from Piper's shoulder.

Piper nodded. "Okay, Lev."

"Thanks for the wake-up juice." Levort stood back up.

"Thanks for the company," Piper smiled.

Levort tucked the Beyonder tablet into his cloak and walked toward the portal yard. Piper cocked her head and asked, "Already leaving again?"

Levort turned and walked backward as he answered, "Not going to find someone who can read this thing sitting around here."

Piper shouted, "Just be careful out there."

Levort approached the *Tumbleweed* and found Floem tightening straps on her exploring kit. Vobsii sat in the chair facing the yard, rifle laid across his lap and gateslinger in the cup holder.

"Let's go together this time," Floem said.

Levort looked at the empty portal yard, then back to Floem. "We cover more ground separately."

"Yeah, but I'm getting lonely, stumbling around strange worlds all by myself. We'll split up after this first one today," Floem bargained.

"Okay, let's do it." Levort smiled. "Vobsii, would you be so kind?"

Vobsii grabbed the gateslinger from the cup holder. "Allow me to get the door." He squeezed the Random trigger, and a light zipped out from the device and slapped into an oval in the yard.

Floem stabbed the jump-phone antenna into the ground and held the other piece in her hand. "All set?" Floem asked.

"Yep. Let's go," Levort said.

Together they stepped through the portal.

TWENTY-EIGHT

Levort's boot sank into the sand. It was hot and dry in this new world, and the sun beat down through a blanketing gray sky. All around the portal were vast wastes, except in one direction, where a grouping of green spheres nested off in the distance.

Floem skipped out from the portal behind Levort and bent over herself. "Woah, this place is a scorcher!"

"Are you going to be all right?" Levort asked with concern. "I can handle this alone if you'd rather go through another one." Even though he was worried about Floem's health, Levort was unwilling to give up a world that could hold a tablet reader. His prospector's gut wouldn't allow him to pass up even the potential of a win.

"I'm good. Check it." Floem smirked and pulled a cord on the side of her flight suit. It rapidly inflated, making her look like she'd been stuffed in a balloon suit. Cool water raced through the suit, keeping her leaves from drying up and burning. A small amount of mist perforated her in spurts. "Got this baby on Aquain."

"I didn't realize you'd been to Aquain." Levort also realized he was losing track of which worlds he and his friends were hopping to on their jaunts.

"Yep. The Fluctans sell the best stuff for us Alberryans. Almost bought one of those flitskippers too. Seems like a fun way to get around."

They began their trudge through the desert. The gleaming coral-colored sand made their progress slow and labored. Although they were scarce, every plant in the desert was orb-shaped and green.

As the travelers surmounted the lip of a dune, they witnessed an expanse of creatures meandering about. They were quadrupedal, with tufts of fur that cast out hot steam. The animals were tall, with stalk-shaped legs and long snouts they used to suck in the sand. Near the base of their snouts, sand spewed sideways as they filtered the needed nutrients and discarded whatever their body couldn't use. One of the beasts noticed Levort and Floem and grunted.

"H-hey beastie!" Floem smiled and gave it a little wave.

The creature wailed, alerting the rest. The herd retreated into one pile of animals as something quickly approached their position. It was a shadow that zipped between the tall legs of the beasts until it emerged from their grouping and raced toward Floem and Levort.

The approaching creature was covered in quills and had four legs that terminated in paws with singular spiked talons. A long tail trailed behind it with a needle-sharp stinger protruding from its end. It roared as it bounded their way.

"RUN!" Levort shouted, but he only had enough time to push Floem to the side as the beast tackled him, pinning him to the ground. It bared its red fangs at Levort and roared in his face. Floem stood up and was about to launch herself at the beast when a loud, sharp crack of thunder cut through the desert air.

The beast snarled, but it didn't bite. It backed off of Levort and allowed him to stand. They heard a whistle and noticed a figure standing atop a green orb in the distance. The figure appeared to be holding a long weapon, and its body was covered in wispy sashes. Another figure emerged next to the first and watched from a distance.

"What do we do?" Floem asked in a hushed tone. Levort kept his eyes on the quilled monster that growled inches from his face and shrugged nervously. Floem shouted, "Hey, over there! We're friendly! Please call off your big scary monster!"

"*Floem!*" Levort said.

"What?" Floem asked. "Did you wanna pet it?"

The quilled beast growled. There was a moment of quiet before another whistle, a different tone, echoed their way. The beast nudged Levort, forcing him to stand up. It snarled, persuading Levort and Floem to walk ahead of it around the herd. They approached the tall green orbs and discovered they were large, bush-shaped plants with a leafy surface so thick they could be stood upon. Two strangers looked down from above, their clothing swaying in the desert wind.

"That's close enough," the taller of the two strangers said. "What are you?"

"That's a little rude," Floem mumbled.

"We're friends." Levort churned his hands as he looked for the right words but didn't have them available. "It's a little complicated to explain."

"You've come a long way," the stranger said. "From a portal?"

Floem and Levort looked at each other and then back to the tall stranger. Levort answered, "Yeah, actually. How did you know that?"

The stranger said, "We denied the Voyalten Web. So tell me how you took a portal here."

Floem answered, "We have a tool. It's called a gateslinger. It makes pocket portals we can travel through. But it's a technology we don't fully understand. We're looking for someone who—"

"You are looking for a Beyonder?" the shorter stranger asked.

Levort took an excited step forward. "Are you Beyonders? How do you know about them?"

The strangers looked at each other for a moment. The taller one nodded, and the shorter one kicked a rope ladder down for Levort and Floem to climb up. They scaled the rope quickly, leaving the quilled beast to tend to its flock. Once they reached the top of the tall bushy sphere, the strangers eyed them from a distance. Levort's feet sank into the bushy surface, though Floem's kept her stable with tiny root extensions on her toes.

The strangers' feet acted more like hands, gripping the stronger branches of the bush's outer shell. When they walked, their toes seemed to find places to grip instinctually. The tall stranger crouched and observed while the shorter, possibly younger, stranger stood with a long rifle gripped in his hands.

The crouching stranger introduced himself. "I am Anduln Yrein. This is my son, Kurnult. You already met our herding Wilnrex. We are shepherds."

"I'm Levort Aatra, and this is Floem Zeu Uubog," Levort said, trying to find his balance on the bush. "How do you know about the Beyonders?"

Kurnult answered, strafing to the right to observe Levort and Floem. "We can tell you are speaking the truth about your portals. We can also tell you know nothing of Orist, the world you currently stand on." Kurnult's eyes darted down to Levort's wobbling feet. "Allow us to enlighten you, Levort and Floem. Here on Orist, we are witnesses of the Sight. It shows us the hidden aura underneath all visible things. That is how we know you are not liars, and it is how we know what you seek."

"I feel like you've given this speech before," Floem mentioned.

Kurnult looked to his father.

"Correct," Anduln said. He removed the cloth from his head and tied it to his arm to keep the wind from carrying it off. The Oristan had a snubbed snout with a wet nose. A mane of fur surrounded his scalp and chin, and three sizeable, sliced-pupil eyes watched Levort and Floem. Large, pointed ears sat on his head, with earrings made of dark metals glinting off the gray sky. His fur was patchy and gray, with a few scars to prove that shepherding on Orist required a tough shepherd. "I explained it to the Voyalten that built the portal when I declined their Web."

Kurnult gestured over his shoulder to the giant rock formation in the distance. Far off in the distance was the gigantic frame for a Voyalten Portal. It wiggled in the heat distortion in the air as it stood tall against the gray sky.

"How long ago was that?" Levort asked.

Anduln bobbed his head from side to side and said, "Earlier this sunrise."

"*Today?*" Floem spat the word. "The Voyalten *just* made it here?"

"The Voyalten Decider left after I made the decision," Anduln said.

"Are you the leader of this area?" Levort asked.

Kurnult interrupted, his voice quiet and grave, "We are the only two Oristans left."

Levort and Floem didn't know what to say. Their shock silenced them. Anduln explained further, "Our world was struck by an asteroid a few cycles back. Many died in the impact, and more died after. Over time, an illness spread, and beasts became more emboldened by the lack of our people. We were already few in number, and one by one, we vanished. Orist is returning to its raw state, and we are the last two witnesses of the Sight."

Floem asked, "Why didn't you link to the Voyalten Web? It sounds like they arrived just in time."

Kurnult, still wearing his cloth over his face, looked away. Anduln noticed, and sorrow came to his eyes. The older Oristan said, "For what purpose? We open the gates, and strangers like you take over our world? Or we leave, abandon our only home, and leave our herd to die. No. Our people are fading the way the Sight intends us to."

"How very sad…" Floem said quietly.

Levort looked at Kurnult. As the desert breeze lapped at his sashes, the young Oristan stared longingly toward the Voyalten Portal frame. Kurnult couldn't look at his father, who was dooming him to vanish with the rest of their people instead of offering him a chance to live.

Levort was reminded of his own parents, who sold him to the Fessenog Fleet and died shortly afterward. He remembered his pain and anger, the same feelings he would never drop. Levort asked Kurnult, "Did you agree to this?"

Anduln stood and snarled, his sharp fangs bared. "You ask my son nothing!"

Kurnult turned to face his father, his three eyes narrowed. He pulled the cloth from his face, revealing deep blue fur with black stripes and blazing red eyes. "I did not sign up to fade away on this dead world!"

"*Kurnult!*" Anduln stamped his foot against the branches.

Levort and Floem remained silent as the father and son stared lasers into each other. Kurnult shouldered his long rifle and pointed at his father. "The Sight has now gifted us two chances to escape this slow death, and you squander it! You see their reaction to the information of the Voyalten. The chances against two portals off-world arriving this day are astronomical. The Sight wants us to leave!"

"You interpret its will incorrectly. We are being tested!" Anduln shouted. "This is our world! Our ghosts should remain within it. I will not abandon Orist. I refuse!"

"Why must I be part of your annihilation?" Kurnult roared.

"Enough!" Anduln shouted again. "Leave now, strangers, or I will see you brought down before me!"

Kurnult roared again, then deftly hopped from the bush top and out of view. Levort and Floem said nothing, not wanting to test Anduln's threat. The Oristan had nothing to lose.

Levort and Floem climbed down the rope ladder and came face to face with the Wilnrex. It growled and followed them back the way they had come. Floem spoke in hushed tones to Levort as they trudged back through the sand. "What a terrible fate."

"I feel worse for Kurnult. He's a victim of his father's zealotry," Levort said.

The portal hung where it had been, wavy in the heat of the desert. Floem and Levort remained silent as they walked toward it, knowing this might be the last time sentient life saw an Oristan. Their world had ended. It was too late for their species.

They approached the portal, and Floem stopped. She turned toward the dune that crowded the horizon. Only the tops of the spherical bush domes peeked above it. Floem sighed and dipped back into the portal to Bloom, taking the jump-phone antenna with her. For a moment, Levort was alone on the strange, dying world. The wind curled the sand into little wisps, and the sound of Anduln's herd was barely audible from this distance.

Levort wondered what happened to a world in this state. Anduln said Orist was returning to its raw form, something without civilization harnessing it. Bloom may have been like this once, before the flowers. There had been no signs of civilization on Bloom, but who knew what cycles of excavation might uncover? Levort didn't know what was lonelier; a world that had a society and lost it, or one that never had it at all.

A figure, hazy in the heat, walked over the dune toward Levort. Levort squinted, trying to figure out if it was Anduln or Kurnult. He hoped it was Kurnult approaching and not his father to shoo him off-world. The silhouette became more defined as the figure approached.

"Wait a minute…" Levort mumbled. Before he could fully make out the figure, a portal appeared before Levort, and Bayfo Niall launched from it, hands first. Levort was tackled to the ground by his old friend, who had locally portalled closer to close the gap between them.

"Not getting away this time!" Bayfo shouted. His face had fully healed, leaving behind only the things time wouldn't forget. His white cloak draped over Levort, like a prospector's kit but altered by enforcer interpretation.

Bayfo struck Levort in the face again. Pain exploded on Levort's cheekbone as the impact came again and again. Levort swung his fist into Bayfo's head and clocked him hard enough to stagger the enforcer. He shoved Bayfo off and tried to sprint for the portal to Bloom. He fell short as Bayfo locally teleported again, grabbing Levort by the ankle and tripping him into the sand.

"Stop this, Bayfo!" Levort shouted and kicked his friend's hand off his ankle. Quickly, another local portal opened in front of Levort, and Bayfo's foot launched through it. He drop-kicked Levort onto his back and stamped a boot down on his chest. Bayfo's use of the gateslinger was advanced. Levort felt a weight of hopeless dread pressing down with Bayfo's boot.

Bayfo shouted, "NO! You need to listen to me! I'm trying to help you! Do you realize how much damage you've caused? People have died because of what you're doing. This Beyonder *drit* needs to end!" There was a deep hurt in his eyes. "You don't know what I've had to go through to save your stupid ass. I've had to…" He hyperventilated for a few breaths. He shook his head. "You're coming with me so we can fix this."

Bayfo shot at the portal closest to him, and it deactivated all his recent local portals in one chain of bursts. One by one, the portals broke out of existence as Bayfo tweaked his gateslinger for the next move.

As the last portal crashed, there was a crack of thunder and a wet thud. Bayfo gasped. He stepped backward off of Levort, and blood pooled out of his chest. Bayfo blinked a few times and looked down at his new wound. He couldn't speak. His eyes fluttered.

"B-Bayfo?" Levort stammered. He looked over his shoulder and barely had time to see Kurnult. His rifle's barrel was bright with the heat of a recent shot. The strong Oristan grabbed Levort by the shoulder and rushed him past Bayfo's body.

Levort pleaded, "No, wait!"

Bayfo fell to his knees as Levort was carried away by Kurnult. The Oristan leapt through the portal with Levort, tumbling into the flowers on Bloom. Levort attempted to scramble back to Orist, but a flash of light crashed into the portal that led there.

The gateway to Bayfo dissolved out of existence.

Levort looked over his shoulder at Vobsii, still holding the gateslinger. Levort's eyes went wide as reality seeped in. "What did you *do?*"

"It looked like you were in danger. I… I just…" Vobsii wasn't sure what he did wrong.

"What happened?" Floem asked. "I thought you were right behind me!"

Piper came running up. "Lev! Are you hurt?"

Levort hadn't realized how much of Bayfo's blood had splashed onto him. "No, it's not…" Levort slammed his fist against the ground and screamed.

Kurnult lifted himself off the ground, his head turning to take in whatever new Sights he now experienced. The Oristan looked at Floem with all three of his eyes and said, "There was another portal walker, like you. The Sight showed me his intentions, and I intervened. He was going to take Levort. I shot him."

Floem and Vobsii exchanged a worried glance. They knew the other portal walker could only be one person. Levort sobbed into the flowers and whimpered questions only he could hear. The crowd that had gathered was silent.

Floem whispered, "Oh no… Bayfo."

TWENTY-NINE

Levort Aatra curled into himself, his head buried in his arms as the breeze brushed back his hair. He wept quietly, allowing the tears to drip into the obscurity of his cloak. The others were kind enough to give him space when he walked off into the wildflower horizon. Levort needed to be alone. The hills beyond their little colony quickly sank into shadow as the short days morphed into a clear starlit night.

"Bayfo…" Levort whispered to the ghost of his friend. "Why did it have to come to this?" He thought of their long time shared together, before the portals, before the problems. When they were just kids. One the son of enforcers, and the other the son of abandoners. Bayfo used to be so quick to stay out of trouble, but Levort had a way of getting him into it anyway. Bayfo would get the worst of it from his father, and Levort would remain forgotten by the ghosts of his parents.

I never considered how much I messed up your life, Levort realized. *You always had my back, and I never stopped to help you.*

Seeing Bayfo with that wound in his chest, bleeding and fading, was too much for Levort to bear. His friend was face down in the desert of a strange dying world. Levort had not yet spoken to Kurnult, the Oristan who had shot Bayfo, since returning to Bloom. He couldn't face him. Levort held no hate for Kurnult—especially not when the Oristan had only been trying to save his life—but he needed time to process what had happened.

A wild breeze kicked at the flowers in the meadow, and petals rode the wind in spiral-shaped clouds. Levort slowly embraced the reality that Bayfo, his best friend, was dead.

Someone approached. Levort didn't bother to look. His eyes remained locked on the playful petals in the waltz of nature. The other presence said nothing, only sat with him in the flowers and observed the stars above. In time, more presences joined around Levort, each sitting near him. Present but respectfully silent. Ready if he needed them.

Eventually, Levort managed to weakly glance to his side to see Floem. She stayed focused on the stars. He felt a warmth in his heart. Levort looked to his other side to see more friends. Vobsii and Piper sat to his right. Less subtle was Sevodan, with three of themselves floating behind the crew. The balloons bounced together as they drifted in the breeze. Levort's grin was mixed with a wince as he felt both warmed by their support and stung by the situation. He hid his face in his arms as his smile shifted to hurt sadness, like a newly built wall with a missing brick.

Levort whispered loud enough for everyone to hear, "Thank you."

THIRTY

K urnult the Oristan stood near the *Tumbleweed*, leaning on his long rifle as if it were a staff. His hood was pulled back, and his three eyes watched as Levort and his friends returned. The patient shepherd had barely moved since arriving on Bloom.

Floem, Vobsii, Piper, and a few members of Sevodan approached Kurnult with welcoming smiles. Levort stopped a few yards short and summoned his strength.

Levort took a deep breath. "Thank you for joining us."

Kurnult bowed and said, "I see you mean it. I am glad. The sorrow within you is immense, and I am sorry it had to be this way. The human who was attacking you meant you great harm."

Levort nodded. "I think you're right." Having someone see through him so naturally felt both reassuring and invasive. The Oristan was only using his born ability to witness the Sight. Although he brought Levort's feelings out into the open, it felt good to have them there.

"But he was a friend to you. I know what it is like to lose close friends." Kurnult looked away. As the last of two Oristans, Levort understood he meant his statement in a more profound way than

Levort could ever feel. He didn't need the Sight to see it on the Oristan's face.

"You are among friends now," Levort said. "We'll have a shelter built for you, and you can tell us what you'd like to do. You're welcome to stay as long as you want. We have a well-maintained farm filled with food from various worlds."

"I thank you all." Kurnult bowed. "What do you call this place?"

Floem smiled. "Bloom. It's sort of our landing place while we search for a way to reach this place called the Beyond."

"Ah, yes. The Beyond." Kurnult nodded. "It is a word I read from your Sight when we first met. I will admit the word confused both my father and me. We originally assumed it had something to do with the Voyalten."

Levort explained, "It's a place we intend to go to. I met a Beyonder named Wolil, and she told me a lot about it. It's reachable with a group like the one we have, but without Wolil's help, we're at a loss for what to do next." Levort pulled the tablet out from his cloak and held it up. "We think this might help, but we can't find anyone who can read it."

Kurnult tilted his head. "You can't read that?"

"Wait... Can *you*?" Levort asked.

Kurnult stepped closer to Levort and accepted the tablet. Immediately, Kurnult turned it around as if he had been handed it upside down. He looked at the Beyonder device with all three eyes, his center eye scanning more quickly than his others. Kurnult smiled, showing his fangs. "You were correct. This tablet holds many secrets. I do not understand some of these words, but I can interpret them for you the same way I speak your language. The Sight provides me the information I need to clarify it."

Vobsii leaned over Levort's shoulder to get a better look at the tablet. He asked, "What is it? A tome? A historical text?"

Kurnult placed his clawed finger on one of the symbols on the tablet's surface and pushed it sideways, revealing more symbols. "Instructions. Schematics. Ingredients. Blueprints on devices I don't fully understand. A replicator? Siphons? Starship parts?"

"So it *is* an instruction manual on how to get to the Beyond! Just like Wolil said!" Levort realized. "If we can find the materials to make these things, we may have a shot at reaching the Beyond!"

"Starship parts!" Floem's smile morphed into a frown when she looked at the *Tumbleweed*. "*Drit*, we really forgot to fix up the old *Tumbler*. Since we landed here, I've been usin' it as my old she-sanctuary."

Vobsii shrugged. "Got all caught up in the portal stuff that we kept putting it off. Didn't need to fly when all we had to do was point our gateslinger and click."

Kurnult offered, "If you would like, I can transcribe these symbols into something we can understand. Perhaps there is a way to fix your vehicle."

The group agreed to take Kurnult up on his offer. The excitement was contagious.

Levort said, "If we had lists, we could find the materials by portal jumping and…" He tried to let his mouth catch up with his rambling mind. He noticed Floem had caught him smiling, glad to see him happy again.

Vobsii unholstered the gateslinger from his belt and held it for Kurnult to see. "I suppose you can read the symbols on this too, then. Right?"

"Yes. But that device is even stranger to me than this tablet. I can transcribe it while I work on the tablet. Is there somewhere I can work?" Kurnult asked.

Floem shouted, "Not a problem! Right this way, the VIP suite!" She leaped onto the ladder of the *Tumbleweed* and scaled it to the hatch, prying it open. A cloud of dust wafted outside, and she coughed. "Sorry, I wasn't expecting visitors."

The friends entered the main room of the *Tumbleweed*. Floem hurriedly cleaned a few things as she walked in. "Skipper! We have guests!" Floem called out to her favorite potted weed. Plants had overtaken most of the room, but Skipper remained stubbornly rooted in its flowerpot—unchanged.

"Your starship is much different than the farming vehicles we used on Orist," Kurnult said. He spread his finger-like toes out on the dusty floor. With one graceful movement, he grabbed a handle on the ceiling and flung himself toward the couch, where his feet gripped the top of the backrest. He perched himself there and put the tablet and gateslinger on the seat. He leaned over himself to peer at them, studying the symbols and deciphering their secrets.

Vobsii blew the dust from a datapad and handed it to Kurnult. Although Kurnult had never seen a datapad before, he quickly understood its purpose, as he had with the Beyonder tablet. Vobsii tried to guide him, "You can use this to write down your transcript—never mind. Looks like you get it. Carry on."

"Don't mind the mess," Floem laughed nervously. Her eyes darting toward all her friends seeing the dirty interior. "I'll clean up the rest."

Levort offered, "We'll do it together."

Floem nodded, "Vobsii. Hit the music!"

Vobsii physically hit the music by bumping his hand against a panel on the wall. The *Tumbleweed* coughed as dust and dirt from Floem's overgrown plants freed itself. The friends got to work, listening to an upbeat tune from their pre-portal hopping days while tidying up the *Tumbleweed*'s interior.

Piper and Floem tended to the overgrown plants, while Levort and Vobsii tossed out some of the heavier objects cluttering the ship. Kurnult focused on his work. His study was unaffected by the music, as he focused entirely on transcribing what the Sight showed him. His left hand flicked at the Beyonder tablet while his right hand wrote down what he was reading.

After some hours, the sun rose again on Bloom.

Levort, Floem, Vobsii, and Piper fell asleep in various positions around the *Tumbleweed*'s interior. The Oristan kept studying in his perched position. The music had ended, and Mubb had been guzzled down. Levort dreamt peacefully, surrounded by his friends.

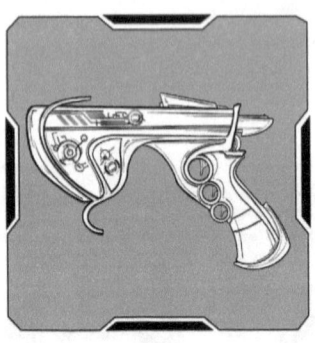

THIRTY-ONE

The days that followed were filled with production. Kurnult steadily deciphered much of the Beyonder tablet's secrets, leaving it up to the rest of the colony to get to work. Sevodan built a sizeable workshop underground, away from the residential area. The remaining colonists were sent out on missions to retrieve the materials needed to construct the unique Curio starships that could reach the Beyond.

The data in the tablet elaborated on what Wolil had told Levort about the Beyond. It also revealed the obstacles they would have to overcome to reach it. As with something as complex as the Beyond, the path there was also tricky.

The Beyond was a sector of space that had been locusformed, which meant the Beyonders had found a way to make the entire sector a survivable atmosphere—void included. This allowed the people living there to do things that seemed impossible in the Below, such as self-teleporting between the planets there without the aid of a gateslinger, defying physics, and even flying. However, the Beyond wasn't without its limitations. The process of locusforming had a side effect, something the Beyonders called "the Barrier."

It was impossible to portal through the Barrier. Going from normal space to locusformed space through a portal resulted in a fatal disconnect in the transferal of atoms between points A and B. It was like trying to mix oil and water. They could not take the easy route and simply launch a portal and walk through it to the Beyond.

The other issue was its location. The Beyond was one hundred cycles away from the outer edge of the Voyalten Web, across a vast empty void. Since the gateslingers strictly only put users in atmospheres they could breathe in, there was nothing viable to teleport to on the normal-space side of the Barrier. Setting up a permanent portal near the Barrier's edge was also dangerous. The *Tumbleweed* proved the risk when Levort, Floem, and Vobsii crashed on Bloom after portalling from Jofnalg's high orbit. Going from zero gravity to the sudden stress of atmospheric gravity destroyed the ship.

To reach the Beyond, the long shot was the *only* shot.

The Curio ships were the solution to all these obstacles. They were explicitly designed to endure the one-hundred-cycle journey across the open void to the Barrier of the Beyond and to pass through it safely. Their hulls were calibrated to neutralize the Barrier wall and slip through, like a key in a lock. Those traveling to the Beyond would rest in slumber in stasis beds that contained more advanced technology than anything built by the Fessenog Fleet.

The schematics in the data tablet detailed the engineering feats required to get the job done right. One choice filled everyone's minds: retrofit the *Tumbleweed* to make it Beyond flight capable? Or build new ships from scratch?

Levort, Vobsii, Floem, Piper, and Kurnult stood outside the *Tumbleweed* in the mid-day sun. Kurnult had an image of the starship they would need to build displayed on the tablet. The others compared it to the neglected *Tumbleweed*.

Vobsii pointed at the old tourist ship. "It'd take a lot of work to make that—" He then pointed at the Curio ship displayed on the tablet. "—into that."

Levort wondered aloud, "But would it take more or less work than building the Beyonder ship from scratch?"

Piper bobbed her head from side to side and offered, "In my experience, tourist ships are only really built to move through the Voyalten Web. Short burst trips from one portal to another and then landing. Thea and I didn't bother buying a new one after our original one cost more to repair. The *Tumbleweed* is a runner. You could probably get her moving pretty quickly if you wanted, but I don't think she can reach the Beyond."

"Shhh!" Floem hushed. "The *Tumbleweed* can *hear* you!"

Vobsii put a large hand on Floem's leafy shoulder and said, "I don't think the *Tumbleweed*'s coming with us. We can get her flight-capable, but not Beyond-capable."

Floem clicked her tongue against the roof of her mouth. "I guess you're right. Skipper's not gonna like this."

Levort huffed, "You could return the ship to its owners—"

Floem cut him off with a cough. "Maybe we'll take her for one last hurrah before we head to the Beyond."

Vobsii added, "Sevodan made ships for the Fleet. They seem willing, and I'm sure they're more than ready to build these new Curio ships."

Kurnult flipped through the tablet to a page about the gateslinger. "I've transcribed the schematics for making more gateslingers. I still need to transcribe the symbols on its surface for you, but from what I understand, the second trigger will bring you to specific locations."

Piper cocked an eyebrow. "So we can freely pop around the universe?"

Kurnult nodded. "The only catch is that there are millions of symbols, each with words I don't fully know how to translate to you. The Sight explains them to me, but even my knowledge is limited. The best course would be to travel and log the symbols as we visit each location."

Levort hadn't even noticed that the symbols had changed between locations. The only time they had removed it from Bloom was to visit Kurika long ago, and he had slung it into his holster and paid it no attention. Before that, he was too busy falling through multiple worlds to take time to study the changing symbols. Levort realized something. "Wait, you said you can't transcribe all of the symbols. But did you manage to figure out some of them?"

Kurnult nodded.

Levort's muscles tightened. "Do you know the symbol for Orist?"

Kurnult inhaled sharply at the mention of his homeworld. His eyes squinted, and he nodded. "I feel it is unwise to return there. For many reasons."

Levort knew of the relationship Kurnult had with his father and knew he couldn't ask Kurnult to go there with him. Still, Bayfo was there, and Levort couldn't leave him in the desert. He had to know what had happened to his friend—even if he had to bury him.

Kurnult sighed and held his hand outward. Levort handed him the gateslinger and watched as Kurnult flicked through its many options with a professionalism none of them had shown before when operating the tool. Eventually, he landed on a symbol that made no sense to Levort but meant everything to Kurnult. The Oristan handed the gateslinger back to Levort.

Vobsii put a hand on the device as Levort held it. "Are you sure you want to go back there?"

Levort looked Vobsii in the eyes. "I have to."

Vobsii sighed and removed his hand. "Then I'll go with you. And we're bringing weapons, just in case."

Levort suddenly couldn't tell what might be worse, finding Bayfo's corpse or finding him alive.

Vobsii grabbed a rifle and handed a smitegun to Levort. To both their surprise, Kurnult stepped forward and joined their side. The Oristan said, "Your Sight has inspired me to do this hard thing. I feel weak, but I must say goodbye to my father." Kurnult shouldered his long shepherd's rifle and stared at the horizon.

Levort pointed the gateslinger forward. "Then let's go."

Levort pulled the second trigger for the first time. The light slapped into a flat shape, and a portal opened. Levort led the way through the mirrored surface, feeling his atoms segment and combine back together on the other side.

Orist looked similar to how they'd left it. The portal had put them relatively close to where it had deposited them before. Levort's eyes darted around, looking for Bayfo's body, face down in the sand. His friend was nowhere to be seen.

Kurnult shouted, "Father!"

Smoke plumed from beyond coral-colored dunes.

"Oh no..." Vobsii whispered. Kurnult dashed over the dune quicker than Levort and Vobsii could move through the thick sand. They raced after the Oristan, mounting the dune's peak to see the bush-domed spheres burning. Kurnult's home was set ablaze.

There was more to the horror. The wilnrex lay unmoving on its side in the sand. The remaining herd animals were either dead or standing around in shocked confusion. Kurnult raced toward the burning homes to find his father lying outside in the sand.

Kurnult's father, Anduln, lay on his back, wheezing. He had inhaled a lot of the smoke and suffered a puncture wound in his torso. Kurnult leaned over him, cradling his father in his arms.

"Kurnult... It's you." Anduln coughed.

"I am here. I will heal you." Kurnult tore off one of his sashes and wrapped it tightly around Anduln's torso. He placed his hand firmly on the wound, applying pressure to stop the bleeding.

Anduln winced in pain. He spoke in broken, hushed words. "The Sight was testing us, but it was I who failed its test."

"Father..." Kurnult's three eyes glistened with tears.

Levort offered, "Let's get him back to the ship. Maybe we can help him."

Kurnult looked over to Levort and weakly shook his head. The Oristan looked back at his father, who smiled through his pain. "You see it. Just as I join the others, the Sight has brought you back to my side."

"I see it," Kurnult said. "I see you."

Anduln coughed and looked at Levort. "A portal walker followed you here. I heard the gunshot from Kurnult's rifle and came to investigate. I watched you vanish." Anduln wheezed and continued, "The portal walker had been gravely injured and slipped into unconsciousness. I took him in and treated his wounds. I was hoping I could have him find you..." Anduln put a hand on his son's mane. "When he finally recovered consciousness, he attacked me. Shot me with some strange weapon. The Sight showed me that he thought I was the one who wounded him so terribly. He burned the houses and killed our animals."

Kurnult gripped his father's hand.

"This is my fault..." Levort's heart sank deep into his soul, and he stepped backward. The horrors Bayfo had brought to Orist were unspeakable. The chase had evolved into a path of destruction. *What other terrors will you commit to find me?*

Anduln coughed, and his breath strained thin. Kurnult leaned over his father and whispered something to him. Anduln whispered something back, and his hand limply fell away from Kurnult's mane.

Vobsii and Levort were respectfully silent. The fire crackled, and the surviving herd animals mewed. Kurnult was the last Oristan in the universe. His father had joined the others as the planet finally returned to its rawest state.

***

Hours passed on the empty world. The fires died out as the wind whispered them to sleep. Kurnult buried his father deep in the dunes. He lowered his head and closed his eyes to whisper his thanks to the Sight.

Levort and Vobsii waited by the portal, hoping Kurnult would join them. In time, the last Oristan came over the dunes and approached them. He shouldered his rifle and carried a satchel filled with the only things he'd take away from his dying homeworld.

"Are you ready?" Levort asked.

Kurnult looked back over the dunes one more time. The sun had set, and the stars were sprinkled through the sky. He began to walk toward the portal but stopped. He looked back over his shoulder, confusion on his face.

"What is it?" Vobsii asked.

Kurnult smiled, then began to laugh.

Levort looked at Vobsii. The Resluni shrugged.

Kurnult slowed his laugh and whispered to the air, "I knew you'd come with me." Without saying another word, the last Oristan stepped through the portal.

All the ghosts of Orist came with him.

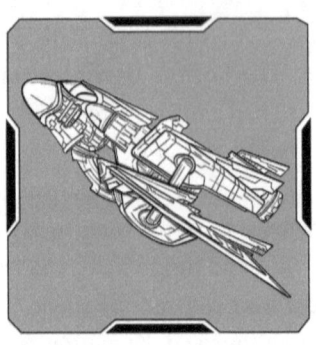

THIRTY-TWO

When Levort, Vobsii, and Kurnult returned from Orist, Kurnult walked in a more relaxed way than he had before their jaunt. He was grinning from ear to ear, revealing a few fangs. It was as if the portal was an excellent therapist.

Piper and Floem stood from their seats and walked over to the returning portal walkers. They noticed the visible happiness in Kurnult's body language, the confused look on Vobsii's face, and the dread in Levort's eyes. Piper asked, "How did it go? Did you find…"

Levort whispered, "We have a problem."

"What's going on here, eh?" Floem looked into Kurnult's eyes. His happiness was infectious.

Kurnult said, "The Sight is with me, and so is all of Orist. I am their vessel."

"Woah," Floem said, revealing her gut reaction.

"We need to talk." Levort looked around. Many colonists were outside, working with Sevodan to prepare for the Curio ship construction. He didn't want to alarm them. This problem was privately their own. "Not here. Let's go inside the *Tumbleweed*, and I'll explain."

They climbed the hatch ladder and entered the newly cleaned tourist ship. Floem and Vobsii sank into the couch. Piper leaned against the wall behind them, and Kurnult took his familiar perch on the backboard of the sofa near Floem. Levort paced the floor in front of the table.

"Bayfo is alive," Levort started.

Floem interjected, "That's good, right?"

Vobsii shook his head.

"Oh…"

Levort continued, "He murdered Kurnult's father and set fire to their home."

Piper cocked an eyebrow and pointed at Kurnult. "Why does he look so happy then?"

Kurnult spread his arms to the sides and conceded, "It is very complicated. Those without the Sight may not understand. But in a way, my father and the rest of the Oristans are part of me now. We can travel the stars and witness the universe together as one. There is nothing to be sad about."

Piper said, "Oh. Well, that sounds nice. I suppose. But Bayfo…"

Levort continued, "Something must have snapped within Bayfo after his injury. I'm worried he will continue to take drastic actions to find me. I'm worried about what could happen if he managed to find us here on Bloom."

Floem exhaled, "No-*va*. I hadn't even thought of that."

Kurnult offered, "I can stand guard. With the Sight, he cannot sneak up on us."

Levort said, "Thank you, Kurnult. But we need you transcribing that tablet if we're ever going to be free of Bayfo. He can't track us to the Beyond. We'll be safe there."

Vobsii asked, "So what's the plan?"

Levort stopped pacing. "We have to play the odds. He's getting better at using the gateslinger than we are. When I encountered him on Orist he outmatched me completely. I could barely understand how he was attacking me, let alone be able to defend myself."

Vobsii took his feet off the table and leaned forward. "Maybe we should prioritize making more gateslingers? We can train with some. Keeping it in that cup holder in the yard probably isn't making us better at using it. If he's going to fight us with portals, we'll have to fight back in kind."

Levort agreed, "I think you're right. Kurnult made the transcription for the replicator. We can start manufacturing some extra gateslingers right away."

Floem asked, "How many should we make? It'd be irresponsible to make too many, right?"

Levort thought for a moment, then smiled. "Make one for everyone. But let them know the dangers of having one. We're not here to restrict anyone's movement. We're here to find the Beyond."

Piper's eyebrows launched skyward. "Everyone? Are you sure about this?"

Levort waved his hand toward his friends. "We all came here on our own, knowing the risks. We all want the same thing—to reach the Beyond. To be safe. To find something new. To satisfy this aching curiosity we all have. The Beyond is so many things and more. We aren't neighbors here on Bloom. We're a team. I trust every part of this team. There's no group of people I trust more."

The friends looked at each other. Concern was evident within their eyes, but Levort's confidence was the heavier motivator. Floem stood up first. "Giving everyone the ability to zip across the universe is a little crazy. It's a good thing we like crazy! This is gonna get wild."

Piper smiled. "It'll definitely be interesting, to say the least."

Vobsii clapped his mighty hands against his knees before standing. "Lots of work to do. But Nova knows we'll do it."

Kurnult grabbed a handle on the ceiling and pulled himself off the backboard of the couch one-handed. "I will get to work right away."

Levort nodded at his friends. "Let's get moving."

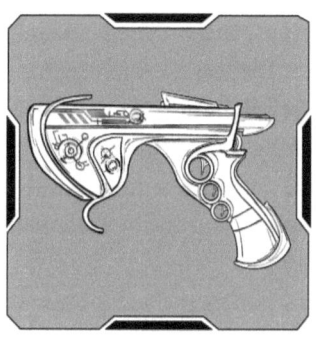

THIRTY-THREE

The replication pool bubbled and boiled. It was an expansive tub, roughly the size of a swimming tank wealthy people used back in Consonance Hub. Machinery surrounded the pool; some mechanical arms dipping into the boiling green and pink liquid and performing multiple tasks.

Levort and his friends weren't sure how it worked, but Sevodan was an expert at operating the controls. The Mulptre had built it perfectly to Kurnult's transcribed schematics from the Beyonder tablet. Slowly, a conveyor belt lifted objects out of the chaotic soup.

The factory was beginning to fill with the skeletons of Beyonder machines. The underground facility had metal-coated walls and a luxurious lighting setup. Sevodan even included a waiting area near the entrance with some amenities. The Mulptre engineer refused to make anything that wasn't aesthetically pleasing to their many eyes.

Where Levort's knowledge had its limits, his friends covered his blind spots. Sevodan understood engineering. Kurnult understood the schematics. Vobsii and Floem understood how to obtain the needed materials and bring more people to their little colony. Piper understood *where* to get those materials with her extensive background as a tourist. Levort brought them all together.

Levort also hoped to be their protector.

Bayfo was dangerous, and his whereabouts had been a mystery in the past quarter cycle. He was Levort's nightmarish shadow. Levort worried about what he might have to do if he crossed paths with his old friend again. Getting to the Beyond was the only way to leave Bayfo in the past. Still, Levort was unsure how much destruction his old friend was causing in his pursuit. *How many lives have been lost? How many more will die?*

One of Sevodan's bodies pushed a lever upward. The conveyor belt brought up the pieces needed to build a gateslinger. It only required assembly. The Mulptre scooped the pieces into a tray and put them on a nearby workbench, where they deftly used several other tools to assemble the portal device. One tentacle soldered cords to microprocessors, and another welded parts of the frame together.

Some unique materials were harnessed to the guts of the gateslinger, things found in specific parts of the universe. These ingredients were the key to unlocking the gateslinger's portal-creating ability—a little sample of the extreme power the Voyalten had used to build their web in the first place. Easy to obtain if you had a tablet that told you where to look.

Before the Beyonders had perfected this technology, it took people from all over the universe to conjure gateslingers into existence. The tablet was a shortcut given to people like Levort to help them seek the Beyond easily. A step-by-step guide. Levort wondered what might have happened if Gulna Kii Fessenog hadn't swept in and destroyed all the tablets he could find. Where would everyone be now?

Sevodan clicked the outer shell into place, and a new gateslinger had been replicated from the original. Unlike the stark gray cover of Levort and Wolil's originals, this one featured a crimson exterior—Sevodan's way of leaving their signature.

Vobsii whispered, "There we have it."

"Excellent work, Sevodan!" Levort commended the Mulptre. He looked to his friends and noticed no one had stepped forward to claim the gateslinger, even though each looked excited to do so. "Who wants it?"

Floem almost spoke up but stopped herself. Her excitement slipped as her eyes squinted, and she winced with thought. Vobsii put a large hand to his whiskers and bobbed his head back and forth with consideration. Piper waved her hand dismissively, silently offering to take a different one. Kurnult looked at them, then to Levort.

"They are worried about the danger," Kurnult said, informed by the Sight.

Floem scoffed. "No! I didn't... I mean... Sure, a little."

Levort took the new gateslinger in his hands. "I understand. It's a lot of responsibility. Just holding one of these like this puts a target on your back. Anyone found with one of these is in serious trouble."

Vobsii nodded. "Up until now, you've been the only one to bring it off Bloom." The Resluni approached Levort and put his hand out. "You've been the only target in our group. Not anymore, buddy. I'll share some of that risk with you."

Levort hadn't thought of it that way. He felt a warmth rush from his heart to his face. The warmth flitted away quickly when the realization of the danger replaced it with ice. "Bayfo is my problem. Hopefully, none of you will ever have to face him."

Vobsii nodded. "Oh, I get it, Lev." He snatched the gateslinger from Levort. "It's a burden, all right." The Resluni inspected the new device with a smile. "But it's also a Zhok of a lot of fun."

Levort laughed as Vobsii slung the red gateslinger into a holster on his belt and walked toward the exit. Floem shouted after him, "Oi! Where are you goin'?"

Vobsii answered over his shoulder, "To play with my new toy outside."

"Don't point it at your face!" She turned toward the pool as Sevodan brought over another finished gateslinger. She took it and thanked the Mulptre, then hurried after Vobsii. "I'm coming too! I got my own toy now!"

A few moments later, Piper approached to receive her gateslinger. She put a hand on Levort's shoulder and said, "I'm sure they'll be fine. They had access to a spaceship for so long. If something was gonna go wrong, it would have gone wrong already." She took her gateslinger and thanked Sevodan.

Levort said, "A little chaos might hide our tracks."

Piper laughed. "Then it seems like Bloom will be hidden forever."

She followed Vobsii and Floem outside.

Kurnult approached next and took one of the devices from Sevodan. The Oristan bowed to the Mulptre, then turned to Levort. "I will explain everything I know outside."

Levort agreed, "Yeah, we better go out there." He turned to Sevodan. "Want to grab a gateslinger for yourselves and meet us top side?"

Sevodan jiggled their balloons. "Thank you for your consideration. We will decline. We have far too much work to enjoy here."

Levort nodded. "The offer is open anytime."

***

Topside in the flower meadow, the new gateslingers were getting their use. Levort emerged into the sunny outdoors to see dozens of portals everywhere, in every direction. He felt the muscles on his shoulders go rigid, and his breath sucked away from his body as anxiety enveloped him. Kurnult must have sensed this and let out a loud whistle he'd used to use to corral his herd.

Floem, Vobsii, and Piper turned toward Kurnult and Levort.

Floem looked at all the stray portals and admitted, "Okay, maybe we went a little overboard."

Vobsii agreed. "We should clean up."

After a few moments of portals bursting all over the yard, the meadow was filled with only flowers and an open sky. Everyone sat in a circle in the meadow. Levort pointed to parts of his device. "Three triggers. The first is local, the second is wide, and the third is random. Kurnult deciphered many of the symbols the Beyonders used for planets we've been to, but there's still a lot of mystery out there."

Kurnult slid his clawed finger over one of the symbols. "This symbol links all of our devices. It allows us to visit worlds we have each previously visited."

Floem said, "Ah! Like a search history on a datapad."

Kurnult agreed. "Yes."

Levort inspected his gateslinger. His had been replicated from Wolil's, so it was a little different from the new Sevodan-made gateslingers. "Link? I didn't know that one. Is mine linked too?"

"No," Kurnult said. "Sevodan attempted to link yours to our new gateslingers, but there was an error. We believe your gateslinger needs maintenance, but we didn't have much time to figure out the issue. Sevodan wanted to fix it after they were done replicating more gateslingers for the colony."

Levort's gateslinger had been with him since Vansparr. It had taken more than a few bumps falling from that world down to Jofnalg, and even more still when the Kurikoids stole it from him in Phiburb. He considered the benefits of having a faulty link on his gateslinger. "If it's all right with you and Sevodan, I'd like to keep mine unlinked. It'll protect you all if Bayfo ever finds me."

Kurnult bowed his head. "A wise precaution."

Vobsii juggled the device as he inspected it from all angles. "Do we have access to the symbols you've deciphered?"

Kurnult nodded. "Sevodan has added a few new features. If you wave your hand over the grip like this, you can set a gesture keycode to give you all the information I have deciphered so far. It will update automatically every time you return to Bloom."

Each of the friends, except Levort, waved their hands over the grip of their devices, and familiar blue holographic screens appeared. They set their passwords, and the screens lit green to tell them it was approved.

"There is one exception." Kurnult put a finger up. "Bloom is not included in any of the databases. For security, we wanted to hide this location from those who pursue us."

The rest looked at each other, again reminded of the dangers of recklessly using the gateslingers. Kurnult continued, "You will need to remember the symbol for Bloom. Keep it secret. It is your lifeline back home." The Oristan used a feature on his datapad to draw light in the air above his device.

Kurnult started with a circle, then traced a delicate line in the center. His drawing became more elaborate until he finished with a symbol that looked vaguely like a blooming flower soaking in sunlight and moonlight from various spheres. Smaller flowered signs flanked the central circle on four sides, with a line connecting each of the extra spheres like an orbit.

Kurnult said, "Study it carefully. There are a few symbols much like it. For instance, see how similar this symbol is?" Kurnult pulled data from a different world and showed similarities to Bloom's. "This is one of Alberrya's garden moons. Notice the angle of the floral designs and the tips of each petal."

Floem added, "I never noticed how similar Bloom was to Hanataba. I haven't really gone there. Our people use it the way humans and Marothallans use cemeteries. Sort of bittersweet, but pretty in its own way."

Levort studied the differences between the similar symbols. He would have to work a little harder to remember. Without access to the altered gateslinger, he couldn't pull up Kurnult's database. Although he could accept a new Sevodan gateslinger, he chose not to. The more he could keep secret from a potential encounter with Bayfo, the better. "Bloom and Hanataba… I see it now. I'm glad you pointed this out because I would have missed it on my own."

Vobsii admired the symbol for Bloom. "It's beautiful. The Beyonders sure have a knack for art. I could think of no better representation of our new homeworld."

Levort tilted his head. "Maybe we could use the symbol as a flag when we finally reach the Beyond. We can show our Below origins."

"All right." Piper stood up. "This is all excellent information, but can we get some practice in? I'm still trying to remember the order of the triggers."

Levort stood up. "Yes, let's establish some rules and test out a few things."

Vobsii stood up. "Rule number one is probably to shut off each portal after you walk through. We no longer need to leave them open if we remember the symbol for Bloom. It'll be like space walking untethered, but we have our lifelines in place anyway."

Levort added, "Yep. Best practice number two is logging the symbol for any random worlds you travel to so Kurnult can add them into the database."

Floem stood and said, "Third rule—*the most important one*—is to have as much fun defying Gulna Kii Fessenog as possible."

THIRTY-FOUR

The *Tumbleweed* blew its loud emergency siren. At once, Levort and Vobsii darted into action. They were on opposite ends of a designated field. A green flag stood atop the starship—their objective flapping in the wind. Over the weeks, this game of capture the flag had become their training for gateslinger use in combat. The two contestants were tasked with returning the flag to their start positions.

Each started the most effective way they could, locally portalling closer to the ship. Once they grew close to each other, the tactics shifted. Levort's local gate spat him out right behind Vobsii. Vobsii—ready for this little trick Levort had pulled before—shot a random portal right in front of Levort's emergence hole.

Levort popped out and found himself waist-deep in a world covered in water. Thinking fast, he toggled the second trigger to send him back to Bloom. He returned at a weird angle, soaking wet from the hips down, and landed on Vobsii as he attempted to grab the flag off the roof of the *Tumbleweed*. Levort rolled backward and sprung to his feet, shooting a portal at the floor under Vobsii. Vobsii screamed as he fell into the sky of another world while Levort grabbed the flag. Levort slid off the side of the *Tumbleweed* and locally portalled safely to the ground, facing his goal.

Vobsii emerged from a portal in front of Levort and grabbed him. Using his great strength, the Resluni hurled the human through the gateway he had just emerged from while pulling the flag out of Levort's hands. Levort was launched into a different world once more—this one filled with floating islands in a pink-hued sky. Portalling back, he returned to Bloom and rolled through the flowers. Getting his bearings, he saw Vobsii locally portalling back to his goal.

One more chance! Levort locally portalled across the field until he emerged directly in front of Vobsii, still on his knees. Vobsii tripped over him and fell to the ground with a thud, kicking up flowers. Levort grabbed the flag and hurled it back through his local portal. It sailed through the field in spurts until it landed near his goal. Vobsii tried to recover and launch another portal but was too slow. Levort dove through his local portals to his goal and slammed the flag into place, ending the game.

Levort took a minute to catch his breath. He remembered a time when moving through portals hurt every atom in his body. Levort had grown a lot since his first trip to Zhok, and his body was now accustomed to zipping around the universe. He no longer felt even a tickle when moving through the gateways.

Vobsii clapped for his opponent and stood up from the ground. Portals hovered in many odd angles over their battlefield, like a hall of mirrors at a carnival in high orbit. Levort and Vobsii walked back toward each other, dissolving the portals they had made as they met in the middle.

"That was good." Levort stuck his hand out for a handshake.

"Yeah, sure. Watch your step." Vobsii shook Levort's hand and playfully shot a random portal at the flowers under the human's feet. Levort screamed as he fell through toward a different world but quickly popped back to Bloom, only a few feet away. Vobsii laughed and deactivated the new portal. "Let's get some Mubb."

Levort inhaled sharply and looked away from Vobsii. His voice was shaky as he said, "You go ahead. I'm going to try a few things out here."

Vobsii crooked an eyebrow at Levort. "It's Bayfo, isn't it?"

Levort didn't respond.

Vobsii said, "You can only prepare so much."

The fire in Levort's chest spread to his limbs. He exhaled through his nose and said, "I have to be better than him. If I can't stop him next time I run into him, I put us all in danger."

Vobsii shook his head. "Lev, you aren't putting us in danger. We know the risks, and we joined you regardless. We can defend ourselves. He's just one guy."

"*Help*!" Piper's voice came from across the field. She had portalled back to Bloom and fell to her knees, leaving her exit gateway open. "Come quick!"

"Piper?" Levort and Vobsii rushed to her side. She had ash on her face and was shivering with pain and fear. "What happened?"

She stammered, "I don't know. I found Erunia through a third trigger portal and... It's bad. Something attacked us."

"Erunia?" Levort removed his prospector's cloak and draped it over Piper. He rubbed his hands on her shoulders to try to stop her shaking. "Calm down, it's okay." He looked at Vobsii. "Can you take care of her?"

"Don't do anything stupid, Lev. Wait right here," Vobsii ordered as he helped Piper to her feet. They hurried off toward the *Tumbleweed* to get Piper checked for injuries.

As soon as they were out of sight, Levort ignored his friend's concern and hurriedly jumped through the portal.

***

The other side of the portal was both familiar and horrific. Erunia's symbol had been unknown until now. This was the world Levort had lived in long ago when he was stranded after visiting Zhok. The town of Eukotall, home to the Erunians that had given Levort shelter for a season, was spewing smoke into the sky.

"Cythemi! Yrelg!" Levort shouted the names of his old hosts. Knowing his way back to Bloom and not wanting to endanger his friends, Levort deactivated Piper's portal and rushed into the burning village.

Erunian bodies with smoking plasma holes littered the town, some with deep wounds cut by a plasma blade. Levort searched for survivors but struggled with the fire and smoke. He could feel the immense heat of the burning buildings without the protection of his prospector's cloak. He was glad he'd retained his gloves and layered pants, at least.

"Can anyone hear me?" Levort desperately called out. "I'm here to help! Is anyone here?"

The sound of roaring fire mixed with the loud boom of thrusters activating. Levort snapped his attention to the sky. The shape of an enforcer mech suit, an EMU, hovered in the smoke. Its bulky frame with sharply pointed robotic arms cast a menacing shadow over Levort.

Before he could fully understand what he was seeing, the EMU rushed him. Levort portalled locally to the side as the mech bashed into the street, creating a cloud of dirt mixed with smoke.

Levort rolled to his feet and felt something bash into his wrist. The sound of the concussion blast deafened him to all other noise for a moment. Levort screamed as the bones in his arm broke, and his gateslinger was flung from his hand. He dove sideways to avoid another heavy concussion blast from the EMU and tumbled into a burning building.

"Enough running! I'm taking you back *today*!" a voice shouted through the megaphone on the EMU. A voice so familiar, Levort felt ice creep through his veins despite the fire raging around him.

"Bayfo..." Levort whispered.

The wall next to Levort exploded as the EMU burst through it. The roof collapsed onto the mech, giving Levort enough time to scramble to his feet and jump through a window. He landed on his side, feeling the broken bones in his wrist. Levort hobbled to his feet and pulled himself around a corner.

Bayfo crashed through the burning building, sending the whole structure toppling into smoke and dust. "Lev! Get out here and face me!"

Levort pulled the smitegun from the holster on his belt and eyed it. He wasn't sure if he could actually shoot at his old friend. He heaved, trying to catch his breath and wincing at the immense pain in his broken arm.

Levort leaned out from the corner to scan his surroundings. He located his gateslinger lying in the street near the side of a burning building. Bayfo slid sideways into view, using the thrusters on the EMU to pilot around the burning buildings until he faced Levort.

Levort, despite his hesitation, fired his smitegun several times at Bayfo. The plasma blasts cracked off the frame of the mech suit, denting the hull and breaking small pieces off the machine. "That's enough!" Bayfo's voice boomed through the megaphone as he rushed Levort.

Levort dashed toward the gateslinger. It was only a few yards away.

Bayfo leaped into the sky and came slamming down on the gateslinger, smashing it into bits under the EMU's heavy metal foot. Levort stumbled to his knees in horror. He was suddenly trapped on Erunia again.

As Bayfo lifted his foot, the remaining pieces of the gateslinger fizzled and popped. The thing that had started this whole adventure was now scrap metal and dust. Levort looked up as Bayfo approached, looming over him. He attempted to lift his smitegun and fire, but Bayfo stopped him with a concussion wave. It emitted from the front of the mech in a wide beam, unlike the pinpoint shot that had broken Levort's arm. The wave shoved Levort into the ground and pressed him there, threatening to break his sternum and collapse his lungs. Levort started to pass out, his eyes drifting, his vision hazy.

The enforcer mech suit opened its pilot hatch to reveal Bayfo Niall. He looked pale and gaunt. His eyes were sunken in deep, bruised pits, and his nose had a lengthy scar. "We're going home now, Lev."

Before Levort passed out, he felt immensely foolish. He had spent so much time training with the gateslinger, only to be surprised when Bayfo actually showed up. He could not have predicted the EMU suit. Levort had been training to fight an unpredictable enemy, only to be undone when they did something unexpected. *You can only prepare so much*, Vobsii's fresh words came to Levort's mind.

Without wasting time, Bayfo extended his EMU's sharply pointed robotic arm and launched a wide portal. Burning Eukotall vanished as it was replaced with the vast crumbling expanse of Tayoxe.

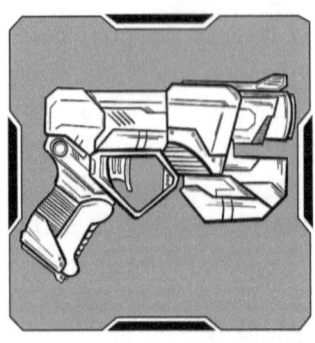

THIRTY-FIVE

Commander Bayfo Niall had finally earned his promotion. With Levort Aatra in tow, he was about to secure his victory. He piloted his enforcer mech unit through the portal back to Tayoxe. His rampant use of the device had made him familiar with a few symbols on its curved surface. Every time he input this symbol and pulled the second trigger, it brought him here.

"Smell that fresh acid air, Lev?" Bayfo spoke to himself. Levort was unconscious from the concussion wave and stored in a holding pod on the back of the EMU. "Ain't it good to be home again, buddy?"

A voice on Bayfo's comm unit said, "Commander Niall, report in."

"It's me," Bayfo acknowledged. "Got a package here for Gulna. I'll be up in a minute."

To accommodate Gulna's personal Beyonder hunter, a system of checks was implemented whenever Bayfo portalled within Tayoxe's atmosphere. In the past, the guns would fire within moments of a portal being activated in their range. Now, a two-minute delay and audio confirmation avoided roasting Bayfo whenever he suddenly returned unannounced.

Bayfo closed his pilot's hatch and allowed it to pressurize before activating the thrusters on the back and legs of the EMU. The lumbering machine bolted into the sky, leaving Tayoxe far below. The rotten atmosphere slowly faded to void black, and soon he was in high orbit above the planet. The Fessenog Fleet eclipsed the stars. Hundreds of ships from hundreds of worlds gathered in one place for glorious trade.

Bayfo sped toward the *Ultimatrion*, Gulna Kii Fessenog's personal ship, the largest in the Fleet. He heard more chatter over his communication channel. "EMU-418, you are in possession of a stolen—"

Bayfo scoffed and mumbled, "Shut up." He piloted the EMU into *Ultimatrion*'s cargo bay. He had assumed going from the vacuum of space to a pressurized environment with artificial gravity would destroy any vehicle, so he avoided it. But now that he was inside the *Ultimatrion*, he was safe to use his portal device to make short work of moving through the ship.

Some workers in the bay yelped in shock as the mech suit threw out a local portal and vanished through a wall. Bayfo hopped through the floors of Gulna's ship with practiced ease until he finally ended up in the boardroom. The directors nearly fell out of their chairs as Bayfo appeared in the center of the room, the EMU's thrusters still smoking from the trip.

Levort Aatra was visible in the transparent detaining pod on the spine of the EMU. The detainer kept him unconscious and unaware of the world around him. The board of directors slowly regained their composure and looked at the man in the glass case. They mumbled things to each other that Bayfo couldn't hear. He didn't care what they had to say about Levort. Bayfo only cared what Gulna thought of this delivery.

Gulna Kii Fessenog once again didn't look surprised, but he did look impressed. As the jets cooled down on the EMU and Bayfo lifted the pilot's hatch, Gulna simply said, "We were wondering where that EMU went."

"I was tired of hitching rides on the prospector shuttles," Bayfo said with a smile as he descended from the mech suit. He gestured to the unconscious human in the detaining pod. "This is Levort Aatra.

He was using Beyonder technology to gather people to an unknown location. I have destroyed his gateslinger and apprehended him."

Gulna looked at Levort with indifference. "Good for you, Commander Niall. Is he dead?"

Bayfo's smile twisted in confusion. "No, still breathing. I have completed my mission in alignment with our agreement that Levort remains unharmed."

Gulna sighed. "If you call this complete, then I suppose you have. But the directors and I continue to see two problems." With a wave of his finger, a group of elite Marothallan enforcers entered the room.

"What is this?" Bayfo demanded.

"You said it yourself, Commander Niall." Gulna placed his hand on the table. "Levort Aatra had been using the Beyonder technology to gather people to an *unknown* location. I would like that location to be *known*. You brought us one head of a monster. We will never solve our issue unless we know where Levort has been taking people. Your knowledge makes you as dangerous as him."

Bayfo snarled. "I did what you asked me to do."

Gulna clicked his tongue to the roof of his mouth and offered, "Partly. How about we make another deal?"

Bayfo's eyes hardened as he waited to hear the offer.

Gulna continued, "You find out where Levort Aatra has been taking people and burn their compound to ashes. Do this, and we'll keep our original promise."

Bayfo shouted, "How in Zhok am I supposed to know you're telling the truth?"

Gulna rolled his eyes. "Use your imagination. The Beyonder threat once eradicated the people of Tayoxe. I was there. I saw it happen. I witnessed the lies of the Beyond and watched as it absorbed the planet. Do you think it is unreasonable for me to alter one deal to ensure it never happens again? I could have you shot with your friend here and hand your gateslinger to someone more loyal. These enforcers behind me are willing to kill to keep the Beyonders from placing a foot in our great fleet."

The elite Marothallans looked bloodthirsty, hoping Bayfo would screw up only so they could have the pleasure of shooting him. This wasn't the way of the enforcers he had grown up with. Something had changed. Perhaps Gulna's fear of the Beyonders had forced him to evolve the enforcers, or maybe they had always been waiting for this shift in attitude toward violence. Bayfo had no idea if Gulna would keep his promises, but he knew if he didn't answer correctly, he and Levort wouldn't leave the boardroom alive.

"I will interrogate Levort Aatra and discover where he has been operating over the past cycle," Bayfo conceded.

"Excellent choice, commander. How about a little reward to entice you?" Gulna smiled. He turned to the elite Marothallan enforcers behind him and briefed, "Lieutenant Ucons and the rest of you. You will now be under Commander Niall's command. Follow his orders and do what he says."

"Yes, sir!" Lieutenant Ucons and the rest of the elites shouted in unquestioning compliance. The enforcers who once salivated for Bayfo's blood suddenly fell in line and saluted. Bayfo looked at his new squadron and felt a rush of pride. He truly was a commander now. Suddenly, this altered deal felt like a new purpose in life.

Gulna continued, "There is a cruiser waiting for you, Commander. The *Shrapnox*. It's yours, as promised, for delivering Levort Aatra. If you wish to keep it, find his friends."

"We won't let you down, sir," Bayfo promised, placing a fist to his chest in salute.

"Good." Gulna smirked. He waved his hand at the EMU resting in the middle of the room. "Remove this EMU from the boardroom, and escort Levort Aatra to your ship. Take him to the Yawning Lock on Fernomare for interrogation and begin your new mission at once."

Bayfo's crew fell in line behind him. Bayfo opened a local portal to move the EMU back to the cargo bay. As he stepped up into the cockpit of the mech suit, he nodded and said, "Yes, sir."

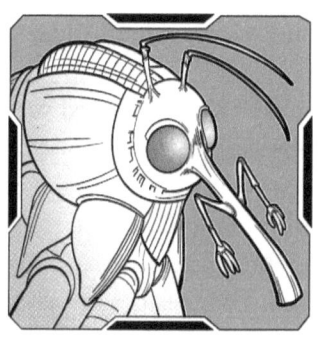

THIRTY-SIX

"What happened here?" Vobsii whispered.

Vobsii, Floem, Piper, and Kurnult stepped into the ashes of Eukotall village. The fires were small now, and smoke clouded the setting sun. They had spent time shouting for Levort, only to be answered with nothing but the breeze.

"Look, here!" Kurnult knelt and beckoned everyone over. The friends huddled over the Oristan's shoulders to get a look at the debris he'd found. The unmistakable shell of a gateslinger lay shattered in the dirt. The massive footprint of an EMU boot outlined it like a crime scene.

"Oh no!" Piper gasped. She stepped away from the crushed gateslinger scrap and held her hand to her face.

"That's not…" Floem muttered and stopped herself.

Vobsii said, "EMU footprint. The Fleet did this. They found him and took him."

Floem kicked the side of a collapsed building. "We weren't here to help him!"

Piper shook her head and asked, "Where did they take Lev?"

Kurnult whispered, "I do not know…"

Vobsii shook his head, and tears rose in his eyes.

Floem came to the Resluni's side and rubbed his shoulders. "We'll find him."

"Someone is coming." Kurnult looked past the ruined buildings to the tree line. Lumbering shapes with black exoskeletons emerged from the stalk tree forest—the Erunians of Eukotall. They approached their ruined village with caution. Some wept, and others fell to the ground in despair. One late-phase Erunian approached.

The Erunian asked, "We heard you calling for Levort. Do you mean Levort Aatra?"

Piper stepped forward and said, "Yes! Do you know where he is?"

Vobsii, Floem, and Kurnult eyed the Erunian with eager anticipation. She looked to the friends and said, "I watched as the enforcer took him. I knew them to be friends once, earlier this cycle."

"Bayfo…" Vobsii growled.

The Erunian continued, "We housed Levort after he arrived on our world. He showed us the portal to Zhok, but it has been gone a long time now."

Floem connected the dots. "You're Cythemi."

"I am. We managed to save some of the people in our village as the enforcer Bayfo burned it down. He asked where Levort was, and we had no idea. Levort vanished the same day the Fleet came to trade. We assumed the enforcers took him back to the Fleet. He didn't like our answer…" Cythemi looked at the ruined village.

Vobsii grunted and kicked the ash at his feet. "He did this to draw Levort out. Who knows how many places he burned in his pursuit?"

Floem spoke softly to the Erunian. "You and your people are welcome to come with us. We have medicine and shelter. We know the symbol for Erunia now, so you can come back anytime."

"The symbol?" Cythemi asked. She turned her head sideways and twitched her antenna.

Kurnult nodded. "We have come a long way in understanding Beyonder technology."

Cythemi looked to her people. They were struck with despair, and their cries filled the approaching night. She nodded. "We will go with you. Let me gather my people. We have special dietary needs that we will need to prepare for."

"We'll help you," Piper offered.

Over the next few hours, late into the night, Vobsii, Floem, Piper, and Kurnult helped the Erunians of Eukotall say goodbye to their village. They repaired what they could, packed whatever survived, and walked solemnly into the portal to Bloom.

Before stepping through the portal, Floem took one last look at the smoldering town. "We're going to find you, Vort. Promise."

THIRTY-SEVEN

"Wake up."

"Wh…what?" Levort mumbled. His face felt numb, and his eyes refused to open properly. He was lying on his stomach on a flat, cold metal surface. His right arm felt like it was pressed between two hot metal pipes.

"Wake up now." The voice was hazy in his ears.

Levort attempted to push himself onto his knees, but the heat in his arm flared into a stab of pain. He yelped and gritted his teeth, then, with a painful grunt, avoided using his injured arm to push himself onto his knees.

The world was confined to a dirty metal box with an open face crisscrossed with bars. Frost dissolved in the room's corners, and heat distorted the figure standing beyond the bars, creating a wavy silhouette. The room's only features were a bed and a toilet.

Levort patted himself to discover he was no longer wearing the clothing he'd traveled to Erunia in, which had been replaced with prison scrubs. He remembered removing his prospector's cloak to drape it over Piper before portalling to Erunia. Metal cuffs were clamped on his wrists, their purpose mysterious.

A thin brace covered Levort's right arm like a sleeve. It started at the metal cuff and ended at his elbow. It had some sort of fiber within it that held his bones in place but allowed him to move his arm and hand, although with sharp discomfort.

"Let me in." The shadow outside was speaking to something else. After a brief moment, the bars slid sideways, and the stranger stepped into the room to reveal themselves as an old friend.

"Bayfo..." Levort whispered.

"Lev." Bayfo Niall gestured to a bipedal robot outside, and the bars slid back into place. He leaned against the wall, wearing a new commander's uniform displayed by higher-ranking enforcers. Bayfo crossed his arms and offered, "Have a seat."

Levort stumbled backward and slumped onto the side of the bed. His vision was still distorted, and his mouth tasted like thick chalk. He muttered, "Where am I?"

"Sorry, bud. That's classified," Bayfo stated coldly.

Levort put a hand to his head and asked, "What's going on?"

Bayfo pushed himself away from the wall and paced as he spoke. "I know you've probably been through a lot. You've been gone most of the cycle. I want you to know I'm doing this to help you."

"Help me?" Levort shook his head. "You don't underst—"

"*Listen!*" Bayfo shouted. "I've been trying to help you for so long, and you have refused to listen! You've been brainwashed by a damn cult, Lev!"

Levort sighed. "Did Gulna Kii Fessenog tell you that?"

Bayfo looked Levort in the eyes. "Yes. He was able to explain it to me because I listened to him. I didn't dive into portals or shoot my best friend to escape the truth." He tapped his chest, where the scar of the wound that Kurnult's father had healed was.

"I didn't do that."

"You let it happen!" Bayfo tightened his fists. "Gulna was there the last time these Beyonder cultists took hold of the system. The people of Tayoxe got sucked up into their delusional beliefs in a paradise far away. It ruined the economy of Lodespace and sent many of the remaining citizens into destitution. Gulna managed to repair it, but it took cycles of work. We are trying to stop that from ever happening again." Bayfo waved his hands in the air as he paced. "But then here you come, portalling around the universe and recruiting people into the Beyonder cult. Don't you see why I had to stop you?"

"It's not a cult. We're only trying—"

"To what? Build a ship that will take you to some paradise that no one else has seen? Let me guess, it involves bringing people to some remote world to work nonstop. Has the ship been built yet? How have you sustained yourselves—stealing from worlds? You don't see how crazy that all sounds?" Bayfo swung his arm in a wide arc.

Levort thought for a moment. What Bayfo was describing was accurate, but skewed. "No one made me do that, Bayfo. I was the one bringing people together. They *wanted* to join me, so we built something. Everyone in our colony—"

"Every cult has its leader, Lev. Someone they would do anything for—even die for."

Levort stood from his bed. "I'm not their leader! I'm just…"

The reality sank in. Levort knew deep down that the others looked to him for guidance. They had pursued the Beyond together, but he was always leading the charge.

Nova, is Bayfo right?

"Fine, tell me about your new friends." Bayfo leaned back against the wall with his arms crossed.

Levort attempted to bring his temper down, but something was off. The way Bayfo was working this argument felt planned. The enforcer was interrogating him, using their old friendship as a whip to lash information out of him.

Bayfo pressed, "Go on. Tell me about the people you left stranded on some random world out in the universe. Your gateslinger is destroyed. You're not getting back to them unless I take you there." Bayfo lifted his own gateslinger out of his holster and limply let it dangle from his finger. Wolil's gateslinger.

He doesn't know we replicated the gateslingers, Levort realized.

"If you tell me where they are," Bayfo continued, "we can go right now and get them back to their homes. We'll only have to ensure they aren't brainwashed, of course. We can't spread this further than it has already gone."

Levort decided to play dumb. "You're right. They are lost."

"*Ulncha-drit!*" Bayfo cursed. "If I could figure out how this damn thing worked, then I'm sure you did too. Don't play stupid with me, Lev. I've known you too long to fall for it." Bayfo slung the gateslinger back into the holster on his belt.

Levort attempted to take control of the interrogation. "How *did* you learn how to use the gateslinger so well?" It was something that had been bugging Levort for some time. Levort got a partial tutorial from Wolil. Still, Bayfo exceeded Levort's skill with the portal-making device, but it had to be more than trial and error.

Bayfo smirked. "I just figured it out."

He's hiding something. Levort could see it on his face. He asked, "Is Wolil here? In this prison?"

Bayfo's smirk shifted into a frown—affirmation that Levort was correct.

She's alive!

Bayfo caught Levort's validation through the change in his expression and shook his head. "Not the case. I had other ways to suss out the information."

Levort squinted. Bayfo's face remained confident. He was either lying, or he really meant it. Levort began to wonder, so he asked, "Exactly how many Beyonders are locked up here?"

Bayfo sighed. "All right, your turn, Abnat," he told the jailor outside. Abnat, the robot, moved near the cell wall and gestured over a panel. The cell opened, and Bayfo traded positions with the mechanical jailor. "I didn't want to get Abnat involved, Lev, but you've given me no choice."

Abnat had a flat triangular head and a small torso with long arms and legs. Multiple lights and lenses on the head constituted a face, and although it showed no menace, Levort knew it had plenty to deal out. It extended an electric baton from its arm. The metal stick vibrated as lightning licked up its length.

The light on Abnat's face blinked yellow, and Levort's arms extended. The cuffs on his wrists magnetically adhered to something in the cell walls. Suddenly, he was lifted off the ground and locked in place, his arms spread out. The pain came next. Abnat thrust the electric baton into Levort's chest. The electricity radiated throughout his body. He screamed out in pain and felt his teeth vibrate. His spine surged and strained so hard, Levort thought it might snap in half. His vision tinged blue, and even the saliva in his mouth lashed him with electrical pain.

After a few seconds of torture, Abnat recoiled the baton back into its arm and deactivated the metal cuffs, allowing Levort to slump to the floor.

Bayfo had stood by and watched impassively, as though his friend's pain had no consequence. He said solemnly, "I'll give you time to cool yourself down before we chat again. If I discover your compound before you reveal it to me, then there is nothing else I can do to help you. Understood?"

Levort moaned with pain, unable to raise his head to acknowledge Bayfo's words. He felt his lungs burn, and his eyes couldn't focus. Everything still had a blue tint.

Abnat stepped out of the cell, and the cell bars slid together. Frost slipped back into the room, and the bars expanded with ice. Levort could still see the hazy shadow of Bayfo and Abnat through the thick blue wall, but he couldn't hear anything. Eventually, they left, leaving only the cold as Levort's company.

Levort carefully lowered himself onto his bedside and buried his head in his hands. He couldn't be sure where his cell was, but he knew it wasn't a space station. Levort now had enough experience on worlds and stations to feel the difference in gravity. Artificial stuff wasn't the same as natural mass-born pull.

"Wolil," he whispered to himself, "you're alive."

***

Time passed, but Levort wasn't exactly sure how much of it was spent. The sleeve that held his broken arm in place eventually came off, and his arm regained its full range of motion.

Confined to his cell, Levort only had time to think and observe. There were a few ways to tell the time in the mysterious prison. The most consistent method was food delivery. It came twice a day, delivered by Abnat via a space in the bars that slid open and closed with each meal. Food consisted of a special broth that kept Levort alive but offered no sustenance. It tasted like *drit* and cleansed his mouth of bacteria, keeping some sort of hygiene routine. Levort would have preferred Mubb.

Abnat's patrol was another clock. Levort manually counted the seconds between Abnat's shadow appearing on the other side of the frost wall. Using Fleet Standard time, the robot jailor came about once every four hours. Still, it was inconsistent, probably depending on whether Abnat had to torture another prisoner or not.

Levort grew to hate the muffled sounds Abnat made as its patrol brought it close to his cell. Sometimes the robot would enter his cell and string him up for another electrical shock. Other times, Abnat would hose Levort down with a deodorizer and chemical spray. It was the only hygiene option offered to him besides the broth that kept his teeth from rotting and falling out. These torture and bathing sessions were inconsistent, keeping Levort on edge whenever he heard Abnat's approach.

After a few bathing sessions, Levort realized that the spray was never cleaned up, yet the floor remained dry. He watched as the chemicals slipped under the cell wall in the corner beneath his bed. After his jailor ended the session and frosted the cell bars over, Levort investigated.

An incredibly thin gap in the metal lined the wall and floor. It sucked away the chemicals and grime, and Levort also assumed it was where his oxygen was coming from. Unsure which planet he was on, Levort couldn't tell if oxygen was pumped in from the prison's exterior or from an oxygen tank that originated off-world.

Even without all the facts, thoughts of potentially utilizing this pipe began to fill Levort's desperate mind.

THIRTY-EIGHT

"Come on, get up." Bayfo's words woke Levort.

Levort turned and looked over his shoulder. He resented Bayfo's cleanliness. Although he had been washed weekly, Levort's hair and bushy beard had grown wild during his imprisonment. Bayfo remained clean-cut and pristine.

Levort grunted and shuffled slowly into a sitting position. How long had it been since he'd seen Bayfo last? It was hard to tell, even with the roughly estimated timeframe Levort managed to keep. Bayfo had been back a few times during Levort's imprisonment, but the time between visits was too hard to track. The interrogations during each visit typically resulted in neither party giving up any new information, then ended with an electrical session with Abnat.

A thin slice of metal he had pried off his bed frame was resting between Levort's metal cuff and the skin on his wrist. He had been scratching away at the corner under his bed for an unknown amount of time, his routine time-tracking interrupted by his hopes of escape. Levort kept the small metal shiv concealed by folding his arms together.

The cell bars slid open, but Bayfo remained outside. "Walk with me."

Levort achingly got to his feet and followed Bayfo outside the cell for the first time during his extended stay. The heat from the prison instantly defrosted his bones, and Levort got a good look at his new residence.

His cell was one of the many inside the deep cylindrical cave pit, near enough to a lava flow to heat the vast space efficiently. Each cell was coated in stasis frost, concealing any way to determine who else was locked up or if the cells even had occupants.

A guard shack overlooked the pit from above, and Levort noticed Captain Tegarl Myrs in residence. He had not seen the Dintuppan enforcer since his life as a fugitive began. She shook her armored crustacean head and moved away from the console she was monitoring. He remembered what she had said about hoping he'd learn the truth about the Beyonders before it was too late.

Has that deadline arrived? Have I learned the truth? What is the truth?

Bayfo nodded to six other enforcers standing nearby, all Marothallans. They acknowledged his silent order and kept their distance. Bayfo leaned over to Levort and whispered, "You weren't the only one making new friends. That's my crew."

"So you're finally a ship commander," Levort said dryly.

"I've been one since I brought you in. I was given command of a cruiser named the *Shrapnox*, and those enforcers work for me. We've been searching for your compound for nearly a cycle together," Bayfo said with pride.

"Wait, that means…" Levort gasped. "A whole cycle has passed?"

"Surprised?" Bayfo huffed. "Makes you wonder how long I can keep you locked up here, doesn't it?"

Levort stopped walking to compartmentalize the panic attack he was battling. He managed to subdue it and then followed up on Bayfo's threat. "Actually, it makes me wonder why you haven't found my colony yet. I bet Gulna admires your lack of results."

Bayfo frowned.

"Why bring me out here?" Levort asked.

"Believe it or not, I'm still trying to help you. And the people like you."

"Then let me go, and I'll be on my way," Levort said with a smile.

He suspected it made him look more rabid than charming, given his current state of dishevelment.

Bayfo shook his head. "I would if you weren't still brainwashed. We still have to break you out of that Beyonder hold first. Gulna knew it would take time, but with every passing moment, the cult grows stronger. You'd save many lives if you told me which symbol on the gateslinger leads to your base of operations."

"Don't you see what's happening?" Levort shouted. "You can't make me believe Gulna Kii Fessenog will let me go after I reveal where my friends are. You don't buy that *drit*, do you?"

Bayfo gripped the handrail tighter. "It's no *drit*. We have a deal. I find your base, and we free everyone from a life stranded on an unknown world. We bring them home—back to Lodespace." He continued walking, turning his back to Levort.

So, he does buy that drit. Levort thought to himself. *Who's really been brainwashed?*

Levort caught up to Bayfo and pleaded, "Gulna is going to have us both executed despite your deal. We know dangerous information. Our lives are a threat to the Fessenog Fleet. Why else would Gulna want to conceal the Beyond so thoroughly?"

Bayfo looked as if he was about to say a few canned responses but stumbled over them and only made a few sounds with his mouth.

"I knew it. Deep down, you know it too," Levort said.

"You know nothing." Bayfo waved a hand over Levort's shoulder.

Unknown to Levort, Abnat had patrolled right into their path. The robot jailor extended its electrical baton and thrust it into Levort's side. Levort screamed and dropped to his knees. His muscles spasmed, and he felt the metal shiv dig into his wrist in its concealment under the metal cuff.

"Take him back to his cell," Bayfo ordered Abnat.

Through the fog of pain that encircled Levort, he considered trying to unsheathe the small metal shiv and stab Bayfo. His hand even went to the cuff and weakly pawed at it, but he didn't have the strength to remove the shiv, much less to overpower both Bayfo and Abnat. Before Levort could stand, Abnat grabbed him by the arm, dragged him back to his open cell, and tossed him limply into the center of the floor.

Bayfo looked down at him as the bars slid closed. "You were right about one thing, buddy. Gulna's patience is running out. Next time we talk, I'll have to start taking more drastic measures if you don't give me the answers I need."

Levort sneered at him.

Bayfo warned, "You better hope I find them before I come back here. Or else the lives that are lost will be on your hands."

Levort knew Bayfo was true to his word. He'd seen the carnage his old friend could reap with only an EMU suit. Levort shuddered at the thought of the destruction Bayfo could cause with his starship.

"We'll talk soon." Bayfo walked away as the stasis frost quickly enveloped the wall.

Levort roared at the top of his lungs in frustration. He scrambled over to the frost wall and banged his fist against it, revealing a trickle of blood. He winced and removed the shiv from its concealment, noticing a cut in his skin.

Has a cycle really passed? Only one cycle? Levort felt like his air had been shut off. His eyes went wide, and sweat dripped from his brow, despite the cold frost of the cell. *How much longer will I be sealed in this tomb? What is this all for anyway? What if Bayfo's right? What if the Beyond is some fantasy invented by a cult? What if I became the perfect mark for an empire of scams? A leader who believes in a lie is a dangerous thing.*

What is real? What is a lie?

THIRTY-NINE

Commander Bayfo Niall stood on the bridge of the *Shrapnox,* manipulating a data table crisscrossed with strange symbols. He knew the gateslinger had names for every planet he visited, and he logged each one as he moved through the universe. The worlds that didn't contain Levort's cult compound were marked in a bright red hue. After creating yet another red symbol, he flicked his hand toward the top of the device and allowed it to scroll through thousands of red marks.

It had been a complete cycle since Bayfo captured Levort and brought him before the board of Fessenog directors. They were gracious enough to spare his life and give him his ship and his crew, but they expected results. Bayfo kept himself looking useful, burning villages on various worlds that contained any hint of Beyonder technology. Gulna appreciated the effort enough to allow it to continue, but for how long was uncertain.

The crew of the *Shrapnox* consisted of Bayfo and his six Marothallan enforcer elites. Bayfo knew they were loyal to the Fessenog Board of Directors and had been hand-picked as the best of the best—devoted to Gulna but not to their commander. He remembered the look in their eyes when Gulna seemed like he was going to request they execute him. He'd never forget the bloodthirsty smiles on their faces. They worked for him, but even after a cycle of working together, Bayfo's trust in them was shallow.

What Levort had said resonated with Bayfo's core. Bayfo knew Gulna wasn't trustworthy, so he had to devise a way to ensure his safety privately. Burning Beyonder presence on worlds inside of Lodespace was one thing, but it wasn't sustainable. Gulna's problem with the Beyond wouldn't end with Levort's compound being destroyed and the cultists executed.

There'd always be more Beyonders to hunt.

Bayfo plotted to keep this operation an ongoing thing, even after his eventual discovery of Levort's compound. He lusted for the respect this new command position gifted him. Becoming Gulna Kii Fessenog's personal blade against the Beyond was a position that any enforcer would envy. He only had to pitch it to Gulna the right way.

The point man of Bayfo's crew, Lieutenant Ucons, approached Bayfo. The dim glow of the data table was barely enough to make his slick black and yellow skin visible among the shadows of the *Shrapnox*. Ucons spoke for the rest of the crew, another facet of their arrangement that Bayfo disliked but allowed—for now. "We're coming up on another check-in, Boss."

Bayfo didn't look up to respond. He resented how often they shirked calling him by his rank. "Boss" felt reductive, like a criminal organization. "We're going to make a few more runs before we check in."

Ucons clicked his sharp teeth together and said, "Not wise. Gulna is expecting a status report."

Now Bayfo looked up. His eyes were fury contained. "Are you questioning my authority?"

Ucons huffed. "Course not, *Commander*." The Marothallan only used the correct title as a stab to the gut. Bayfo could see it on Ucons's amused face. The elites were loyal to Gulna, and Bayfo was Gulna's pet project. They were here because they were ordered to be and nothing more.

Bayfo could feel the lie within that smile like a plasma shot through the chest. He knew he'd have to make these elites fall in line with him, but that would take time. Until then, he had a job to do. Bayfo ordered, "Strap in. We're jumping in five."

Ucons tapped his knuckle against the data table and nodded. He slipped back into the shadows of the ship. Bayfo let his temper simmer before he moved to the bridge of the *Shrapnox*. He plugged his gateslinger into a console with an armature. A new heads-up display replaced the standard ship protocol, allowing Bayfo to adjust the gateslinger's settings from afar. The tracker Gulna had given him to hunt down portals was now part of the ship, and the Fleet engineers had provided the *Shrapnox* with a more refined interface to use for hunting.

The *Shrapnox* could ping for more than a green dot. It could get accurate data readouts of everything on the hemisphere of a planet at once. Within minutes, life signatures, surface structure data, depth scans of anything hidden underground, and signature readouts on anything built by Beyonders were available for him to analyze.

Settings toggled; symbol logged but unknown.

Bayfo checked in over the comm. "This is Commander Niall. I'm heading out."

"Acknowledged. Guns down," Fleet command responded, giving Bayfo a short window to exit Tayoxe's atmosphere safely. Bayfo pulled the trigger on his pilot's console and watched as a portal flung out from the ion cannon mounted on the front of the ship. The ship passed through, and the rough metal wastes of Tayoxe were replaced by a snow-filled sky. There was always some turbulence when moving through the portal in a ship. The instant change in airspeed and gravity slapped the hull. Once stabilized, Bayfo stood from his pilot's chair and approached the data table, allowing the *Shrapnox* to soar through the sky on autopilot while he initiated his scan. His team waited in full gear in the dim light.

Bayfo quietly analyzed his surroundings and shook his head. "I've been here before. This world's name is Golt. There's nothing.... Wait..."

Bayfo was sure Golt would be another pass-through world, but the tracker had picked up multiple portal signatures. He was more shocked than the rest. Bayfo looked at his team. "Let's go hunting."

Ucons and the other Marothallans smiled with murderous intent. They had been waiting for a fight. Bayfo hoped this lead would bear fruit, but it might also satiate his crew enough to gain some of their trust and respect. The team strapped back into their seats while Bayfo took control of the *Shrapnox* from the pilot's chair.

His windscreen showed him a world covered in snow and glacial runoffs, with black-rocked cliffs contrasting the bright white fluff. In the distance, lights ahead created a hazy glob in the sky. The tracker led Bayfo directly toward it.

In the past, Bayfo knew precisely who he was targeting. Levort had been his only prey. Now, his target was unclear. His approach had to be more subtle. This could be Levort's base of operations, or it could be one person from his cult moving around outside of the world the compound was on. Without Lev's gateslinger, Bayfo guessed they must have kept the portals open, which presented him with additional opportunities. Bayfo and his team needed to infiltrate and recover the traveler, then close the portals behind them.

The *Shrapnox* set down in the snowy hills outside the town. It was hidden from the view of any natives that lived there. Bayfo and his squad of Marothallan enforcers exited the ship, each equipped in lighter combat gear to move silently. They wore helmets with night vision-capable goggles, and their suits contained noise-dampening fibers that could change color at will to help camouflage. Each had a modified silent smitegun and rifle, with detainer balloons in case they managed to capture a Beyonder cultist. With a whole colony of cultists at large, they could no longer afford to shoot before questioning.

"Avoid detection until I give the word," Bayfo commanded his crew. "Let's move in." They slipped into the snowy foothills, their black suits shifting to a stark white to make them nearly invisible.

They approached a frontier mining town with hazy lights illuminating the rusty metal walls and heat vents. Metal walkways outlined the upper levels, and a large cliffside with many cave entrances flanked the entire northeast side.

Wolil had called the natives of Golt Xikolings. They were half animal, half plant, with big mushroom-capped heads and feline faces. The town was bustling with Xikolings, each hurrying toward the large open central area. They were too distracted to notice Bayfo and his team slip through the shadows between homes.

Bayfo's team split up and kept quiet, finding ways to flank the town square without being detected. Bayfo was the first to get into position, his gateslinger gripped in one hand and his smitegun clamped tightly in the other. He used the device to teleport around corners and get into places that he'd normally have to expose himself to reach. He found a good spot atop a building, his position masked by smoke from a chimney.

Ucons and the other Marothallans pinged Bayfo as they got into positions. If it hadn't been for Bayfo's HUD on his goggles, he would never have seen them. They were perched around corners and behind various crates and rooftops. With the pieces set, it was time to observe and learn the situation.

A Resluni stood in the city's center, surrounded by eager Xikolings. Directly past the big Resluni was a hovering portal. It shimmered blue and yellow in the warm lamplight of the frontier city.

Bayfo spoke to his team over their shared communication channel: "Portal confirmation. We officially have Beyonder tech on site. That Resluni is our target."

Ucons responded for the whole team, "What's the play? Take him down? If we kill him, we can walk through the portal to the compound."

Bayfo considered this for a moment. There was no way of knowing if this Resluni portal walker was part of Levort's compound, or if he happened to be a new player in this game of company and cult.

"No. Too many Xikolings around him. We don't have a clear shot," Bayfo said. "I'm going to get closer and get the drop on him. When I give the signal, close in and get a stun on him if you can. We'll use him to draw information out of Levort Aatra."

"Affirmative," Ucons acknowledged.

Bayfo scanned the area for the best angle of attack and made his move. He launched a local portal within his concealed position and kept the trigger pulled to influence where it would emerge. Having done this many times over the last two cycles, he had become skilled in getting his emergence portals to go where he wanted them. Upon releasing the trigger, his emergence portal would spit him out behind the Resluni. Bayfo slipped through the portal and came out exactly where he intended to, quickly dissolving the gateway to avoid giving himself away.

The Resluni pulled crates of supplies out from the portal near him. He must have been doing it for a long time because boxes littered the open area around the gateway, and some had been stacked near the buildings. Bayfo crouched behind one of the crates, observing as he waited for the chance to strike.

"In position. Get ready," Bayfo ordered.

"Affirmative," Ucons responded.

Bayfo leaned out from his position behind the crate and pulled the trigger on his gateslinger, cracking out a bolt of light that slapped into the Resluni's portal and caused it to burst.

The Resluni was caught off guard. Bayfo was on top of him instantly, portalling within arm's reach only to swing his smitegun down on thin air.

Bayfo tumbled into the portal on the floor that the Resluni had fallen into. He expected to be dropped onto a different planet, possibly even the world on which Levort's compound was located. To his surprise, he was transported only a few yards away from where he fell, rolling on the floor from an awkward angle.

They made more gateslingers? How? Bayfo realized with horror.

The Resluni was running away, and some other figure was rushing toward him.

"Sir! We have encountered the—" Ucons tried to give an update but was cut off.

The shadow approached Bayfo at a rapid speed and swung something at him. Bayfo rolled to the side and kicked out, catching the shadow in its leg and sending it toppling to the ground. Bayfo deftly swung himself to his feet, and the shadow did the same.

For a moment, Bayfo thought he was seeing the ghost of the creature from the desert world he had been critically injured on. The creature there had healed his wounds, had called its homeworld Orist. Bayfo had killed the beast in a rage, yet the Oristan stood before him. It twirled a long rifle like a staff and swung it at Bayfo's head. He ducked, then countered with a shoulder rush, knocking the Oristan back.

It was chaos after that. Many of the crates in the town square burst open, and aliens emerged from them. Bayfo was surrounded by ballooned Mulptre, creatures he had once watched over who built starships for the Fleet. These Mulptre carried rifles and began firing stun shots.

Bayfo didn't have time to focus on the Mulptre. He dodged another attack from the Oristan by portalling onto an upper metal walkway. Xikolings ran in panic as the ambush turned into a counter-ambush. Bayfo watched an Alberryan crash through a window with one of his enforcers, Rokkis. Rokkis hit the ground, and the Alberryan portalled herself safely to a standing position.

Another portal opened in front of Bayfo. The pursuing Oristan emerged, swinging its rifle in one hand and a stun stick in the other. *How many gateslingers do they have?* Bayfo wondered in panic as he dodged blows from the Oristan.

Bayfo portalled downward and emerged under the walkway he had been standing on. As he exited the portal, one of his other men, Ogna, was thrown into him. Bayfo and Ogna crashed into a residence through the door. As the dust settled, the Resluni that had been their primary target stood in the doorway, fists up.

Ogna rose first and struck the Resluni with a stun stick. The hulking Resluni blocked it with his hefty arm and countered with a vicious right hook, knocking Ogna sideways into the wall, unconscious.

The Resluni shook the arm that had been stunned, trying to get feeling back in it as he approached Bayfo. Bayfo launched a portal close enough to his body to reach an arm through, then set the emergence gate behind the Resluni. He pushed his smitegun through, and Bayfo's arm floated behind the Resluni's head, detached from the rest of himself. He took a shot and missed the Resluni's large head—nearly shooting himself accidently instead. The Resluni grabbed Bayfo's floating arm and pulled him through the portal to throw him back out into the street. Bayfo crashed through the front window and rolled to a stop in the road.

"We need to retreat! We've been played!" Ucons shouted over the comm as Bayfo shook off his dizziness. Being pulled through a portal and thrown through a window completely discombobulated him. In his dancing vision, he watched as the Mulptre balloons carried one of his men off into the sky and hurled him over a rooftop.

The Oristan approached once more. Bayfo shook off his dizziness and prepared to meet it in battle again. This time, he was ready. The Oristan swung its rifle like a club. Bayfo chopped at the ghost's wrist, forcing the phantom to drop the weapon. In one movement, Bayfo pivoted, grabbed the ghost's arm, and portalled downward.

They emerged a few yards away, up in the air. Bayfo crashed down on top of the Oristan with tremendous force, knocking the wind out of his foe. Bayfo smashed his smitegun into its forehead, nearly striking its third eyeball. The Oristan's head cracked against the ground, and it went limp.

Bayfo shouted into his comm, "Move back to the *Shrapnox*!" He pulled the limp phantom over his shoulder and looked back into the fray. Aliens from all over the universe portalled in and out, zipping around at crazy angles and shooting stun bolts. The Resluni emerged from the nearby residence and found Bayfo. Before the Resluni could approach, Bayfo portalled himself across the city's center and out of view, dissolving his portals instantly after emerging from them.

It was quiet outside the city.

Snow fell lazily from above, adding to the fluffy mounds around the frontier city. Bayfo adjusted the limp Oristan on his shoulder as he marched through the snow back to the *Shrapnox*. Once inside, he dropped the strange alien into the brig and sealed it.

Now that he had a good look at the phantom, he could tell it wasn't the same creature he had dispatched on the desert world. This one looked younger, with healthier fur and a thinner frame. "You're going to tell us where Levort's been keeping everyone," Bayfo whispered to the unconscious Oristan in the cell.

Ucons and four other Marothallans boarded the *Shrapnox*. They had been beaten and bruised but not followed. Ucons slammed his fist against the data table and shouted, "It was a trap!"

"They have to be Levort's fellow cultists," Bayfo said. "And by the look of it, they managed to duplicate the gateslingers." He noticed one of his men was missing. "Where's Ogna?"

Ucons stared knives into Bayfo. "He was with *you*."

The last time Bayfo had seen Ogna, the Resluni had punched him so hard he went sideways into a wall. It had taken the Resluni some time to exit the residence. *What did he do to Ogna?* Bayfo wondered.

Bayfo shook his head and approached the data table. It was time to bring the phantom to Levort and see if they could use him as bait. He didn't have time to figure out what happened to Ogna, nor did he really care to put effort into it.

Ucons pulled Bayfo by the shoulder and spun him around. He shouted, "You're gonna leave Ogna behind?"

Bayfo felt his blood race through his body. He slugged Ucons in the face as hard as he could. The Marothallan fell to the floor near the remaining men under Bayfo's command. Bayfo pulled out his smitegun and aimed it at Ucons's head. He had to force himself not to pull the trigger. He had gotten too used to killing anyone who stood in the way of his objective.

Bayfo uttered the words through clenched teeth. "You saw what I saw. The cult is getting stronger, and the gateslingers are becoming impossible to contain. We must get this prisoner to the Yawning Lock and find out where they are building these things before we have another Beyonder event in Lodespace. If you want to try and find Ogna's dead body, you can join him in Zhok!"

Ucons stared at the smitegun in his commander's hand. For a moment, it looked as if Ucons didn't believe Bayfo would pull the trigger. After another few breaths, Ucons's face shifted to terror. He could see it in Bayfo's eyes and knew what Bayfo knew. Commander Bayfo Niall was a killer, and executing a disloyal member of his crew would not even affect his sleep that night. Ucons put his hands up in surrender.

Bayfo slammed the smitegun back into his holsters and ordered his men, "Strap in. We're heading to Fernomare."

FORTY

Floem pointed at the flash of a starship vanishing through a portal in the cold Golt sky. She laughed, "Looks like they left you behind!"

The Marothallan operative named Ogna had a large lump on his head and a look of despair on the rest of his face. He was on his knees with a thick cord tied around his wrists. Vobsii played with the night vision goggles that the operative had traded for a bruise during their fight. Sevodan stripped the rest of the weapons away from Ogna and held them at the ready all around him.

Floem knelt next to Ogna and looked him in the eyes. "What is the protocol for portal hunters? Leave anyone behind who doesn't keep up? How are you supposed to get home? Golt isn't a Lodespace world."

Ogna looked up into the stars and sighed with defeat.

Floem shook her head and stood up. "So, now you enforcers have taken two of my friends, and I only wanna know where I can find them. We've been searching for a cycle but haven't found anyone with the info we could trade for it. Lucky we met you, eh, Ogna?"

"Why would I know?" Ogna tried to bluff, but everyone could see it.

Vobsii pushed the Marothallan with his bulky foot and said, "You were with Bayfo. You know where Levort is."

Ogna spat blood into the snow and cursed. "You know Commander Niall?"

Floem flitted her leafy hands in the air and said, "Ooh, *Commander*. So official!"

Vobsii said, "We know Levort. Levort was Bayfo's friend since they were cubs. Or whatever humans are as not-big."

Ogna stared at the snow with a look of horror in his eyes.

Floem caught it and asked, "Wait, you didn't know Bayfo and Levort were friends?"

Ogna shook his head. "We understood they knew each other, but we were never told they had a history so deep."

Vobsii puffed air through his lips. "Pretty big detail to leave out." He leaned over Ogna and said, "Hey, wait a minute. You don't think your Commander Bayfo Niall set you up to fail, did he?"

Ogna gritted his teeth.

Floem added, "Oh, I think he *does* think that! I think it, too, for what it's worth."

Vobsii continued, "We're all thinkin' it. It's the popular new think to thunk."

Floem snapped her fingers. "Losing track of the path here, Vob." She knelt in front of Ogna again. "If he set you up to fail, why not set him up right back?"

Ogna cursed, "That *konndan drit…*" He silently thought for a moment before saying, "The Fessenog Board of Directors would have me executed if they found out."

Vobsii smiled at Floem, out of Ogna's line of sight. "That's all that's stopping you?"

Ogna stumbled over his words. "Well. Uh. No! It's more… No, I am loyal to the Fleet!"

Floem shook her head. "Nah, come on, buddy. The Fleet hooked you up with a Commander who left you to rot on Golt. They don't care if you leave a really loyal corpse on a random planet in the universe. I'm sure you'll be honored in a weekly message report as a footnote."

Ogna didn't reply, but his face seemed to beg for a solution. It was the moment Floem was waiting for. She winked at Ogna and said, "You tell us where they are keeping Levort and Kurnult, and I'll give you this." She held a red gateslinger in front of the captured Marothallan.

Ogna shook his head. "No deal. If I take that, the Fleet will send Bayfo to kill me."

"We'll handle Bayfo," Vobsii said.

Ogna looked back over his shoulder at the large Resluni, then down at the snow. "I don't want your gateslinger. Just put me back on a Lodespace world."

Floem and Vobsii looked at each other. Floem smiled and slung the gateslinger back into the holster on her hip. "No problem."

Ogna took a few deep breaths, closed his eyes, and said, "The Yawning Lock."

Floem looked to Vobsii, and the Resluni shrugged. "Okay, maybe just a smidge more information."

Ogna sighed in frustration and rattled, "The Yawning Lock is on Fernomare. It's a planet in the same system as Tayoxe, closer to the star. We fly there from Tayoxe because the gateslinger won't take us there—some *drit* about it not being a survivable atmosphere or something. It takes about three Fleet Standard days to travel between it and Tayoxe. The only thing on Fernomare is the subterranean prison."

Floem whistled through her leafy lips. "That's...great. Well, thanks, I guess."

Vobsii patted Ogna on the shoulder. "We'll take it from here. Got a preference for which planet you want to be dropped off on?"

Ogna sighed in relief and considered his options. He smiled when the possibility of being dropped off on any Lodespace world crossed his mind. He said, "I've always wanted to visit—"

"Aquain! See ya!" Vobsii launched a portal under the Marothallan. Ogna screamed as he free-fell into the watery world before splashing down. Vobsii shut the gateway off and laughed.

Floem clicked her tongue and said, "We probably should have untied his hands..."

Vobsii scrunched his snout. "Oh... Right..."

"I mean, he's like a big bad operative enforcer. He can swim with just his legs, I'm sure."

"Yeah, for sure," Vobsii said. "On a planet with almost no dry land…"

They shared a moment of silence.

"So, Fernomare!" Floem changed the subject.

Vobsii was happy to oblige a new conversation. "It's going to be a problem. He said the gateslingers won't take them there. Sounds like Gulna picked it specifically to hide it from Beyonder technology."

Floem scratched at the leaves on her head. "We have a few Curio ships, but Levort told us the Fleet shot Wolil's down shortly after she entered Tayoxe airspace. I wouldn't want to risk the Curios either. The Fleet is probably using trackers to pinpoint portals. A ship wouldn't stand a chance portalling to Tayoxe without permission." Over the cycle Levort had been missing, the colony at Bloom had progressed significantly on the unique Beyonder starships. They had four fully capable Curio ships ready to go.

"Looks like we finally have to fix up the old *Tumbleweed* after all," Vobsii said.

Floem asked Sevodan, "What do you think, pal? We can probably give her a few upgrades while we're at it."

Sevodan and their members grouped together and twiddled their tentacles in anticipation. "We will make the *Tumbleweed* the finest ship to get blown up on Tayoxe."

Floem scrunched her face. "You could have stopped after *the finest ship*."

FORTY-ONE

Levort dug at the metal panel under his bed. He was making slow progress with the help of the shiv made from part of his bed frame. Luckily, there was nothing else to do.

His hand slipped, and the shiv sliced into his finger and clanged to the floor. "*Konndan drit Zhok!*" Levort cursed in frustration and picked up the shiv to throw it at the wall. He almost did it this time. He almost let his rage consume him to the point where he lost his final friend. The small piece of jagged metal had cut him many times during his under-mattress excavation, but it had been the only thing in his life besides Abnat and Bayfo.

The shiv reminded him a lot of Bayfo in some ways.

Levort slipped out from under the bed and sat on the floor, his arms on his knees. Blood dripped from his wounded finger and slid down the crude blade to the floor, where it made a little puddle. Levort's constant questions echoed in his mind.

What is real?
What is a lie?
How long has it been?

The shiv didn't answer.

When he had left his friends to investigate Erunia, they had been working toward the final pieces of the Beyond puzzle. Surely they had built the Curio ships by now, but had they set sail for that far-off place? Was Bloom another empty world with abandoned things like Tayoxe? *If I even made it out of this cell, where would I go?*

The shiv didn't answer.

This time, Levort did throw the shiv at the far wall. It slapped the metal with a clang and then clattered to the floor. Levort's eyes grew wet with tears, and his face contorted in sadness. He pushed his face into his hands, allowing his tears to mix with the blood streaming from his sliced finger.

The stomping of metal feet came muffled through the sheet of frost wall. Levort snapped to attention and scrambled on all fours across the room to the shiv, snatching it up as the frost wall dissipated. Two shadows were silhouetted against the light outside the cell.

One shape was unmistakably Abnat's. Levort had grown too familiar with his mechanical jailor during his stay. The other, he assumed, was Bayfo. To his surprise, Abnat hurled Kurnult into the cell and frosted the bars into a solid sheet of ice.

Kurnult groaned and slowly recovered.

Levort sat against the wall, shiv in hand, legs cupped against his thin chest. His hair and beard were disheveled, and his eyes were wide. His breath held tight. Levort's brain worked overtime to process what was happening.

Kurnult looked around his cell and eventually spotted Levort. All three of his eyes lit up, and a smile came to the Oristan's face. He spoke the first kind words Levort had heard in a cycle of imprisonment: "It is good to see you, old friend."

Levort still wasn't breathing.

"You are bleeding? Have they hurt you?" Kurnult asked, his expression changed from excited recognition to worry. When Levort didn't answer, worry changed to sadness. "What have they done to you?"

Levort finally gasped for air and wailed as he thrust himself at Kurnult. Kurnult embraced him tightly yet carefully. Levort had lost a lot of weight and appeared frail. He sobbed into Kurnult's mane. "It's really you."

"Yes." Kurnult patted Levort on the shoulder.

Levort removed himself from the embrace and slid back against the wall. "But how? Why?"

Kurnult explained, "We have been looking for you since we lost you on Erunia. Cythemi told us that Bayfo had taken you away, but we had no idea to where. We traveled to many worlds and asked about Bayfo and the Fleet, but no one knew anything. Wherever we are, it is a tightly guarded secret."

Levort smiled. "But you know where we are now, yes?"

Kurnult grunted and shook his head.

"Oh…" Levort felt a pang of defeat.

Kurnult continued, "When we couldn't find you, we attempted to draw Bayfo out into a trap. It worked. We continuously visited Golt and exchanged supplies, making sure to always leave the portals on. Vobsii had a tool that could see portals like the Sight."

Levort nodded. "The tracker. I had one too. Sold it for very little hapron."

"Yes," Kurnult confirmed. "We wondered if Bayfo also had a portal tracker. It explained how he kept finding you."

Levort shook his head. "You're right, but there's more to it. I've thought about this for a long time. Remember when we thought my gateslinger's linking ability was broken? It wasn't. My gateslinger was linked to Wolil's, so it errored out when you tried to link the new ones to it. Bayfo had been using Wolil's, so our gateslingers were linked together. It gave him access to all the worlds I visited. We are lucky he hasn't found Bloom, but it's only a matter of time before he does."

Kurnult's three eyebrows lifted. "That is serious. He found us on Golt, and we sprung our trap."

"How did it go?" Levort smiled through his messy beard, his eyes wide and bright with anticipation. This was the most exciting thing to happen during his imprisonment. He had a strange detachment to it, as if it were a story being told to him and not something that actually happened to his friends on his behalf.

Kurnult shrugged. "Bayfo bested me and captured me. Now I am here. I do not know how the others are. Have they also been brought to this place?"

"No…" Levort's bright-eyed anticipation died, and he inhaled deeply to keep himself from throwing a tantrum. He closed his eyes briefly and whispered, "You should have just left for the Beyond."

Kurnult looked offended. "We would never leave you. We had to find you."

Tears welled up in Levort's tired eyes. The words Bayfo had said at the start of his imprisonment echoed in his head. *Every cult has its leader, Lev. Someone they would do anything for—even die for.*

"You should have left!" Levort shouted. "I'm not your leader! You could have saved yourselves. Go to the Beyond, get out of here. I'm nothing—I need nothing!"

Kurnult reared his head back as if he had been slapped.

"We're not a cult. We're not a cult…" Levort mumbled, his face buried in his arms. Despair crept over his shoulders and engulfed him like a blanket of iron weights. He was crushed, facing proof that Bayfo had been right all along. His friends had put him on a pedestal and would do anything for him. He had become their leader, the human who could puppeteer them to steal from anywhere in the universe.

For what?

What is real?

What is a lie?

"We are not a cult," Kurnult agreed, his voice gentle and profound. "They have carved a cavernous wound in you, my friend. I do not need the Sight to see it. They have used our love for you as a weapon to persuade you that you do not deserve it."

Levort shook his head.

Kurnult continued, "You believe we only came to find you because you are our leader. That we couldn't bear to move forward without your influence. Devoted and blind."

Levort nodded.

"That isn't true, my friend," Kurnult said firmly. "And you know it."

Levort looked up from his arms, tears in his eyes. "But how do *you* know?"

"I know because we would have done the same thing for any member of our colony. I know that if I was trapped in this prison, you would have come to save me. You are not my leader, Levort Aatra.

You are my brother." Kurnult's three eyes never left Levort's.

"But I convinced you to be this way," Levort said, his face contorted in pain.

"It took no convincing to befriend me," Kurnult reminded him. "If *convincing* is all it takes to make a cult, I once watched Floem convince Vobsii to chug three jugs of Mubb without stopping to breathe. Does that make her a cult leader? Is Vobsii her worshipper?"

Levort smiled and sniffled. "No, I suppose not."

"The word *cult* is an interesting choice. I have learned that Gulna Kii Fessenog has perpetuated it, lying that the Beyonders are a dangerous cult and should be erased from Lodespace. I am not from Lodespace, but I have now seen both sides. There is an important distinction between what the Beyonders are and what the Fessenog Fleet is."

"What?" Levort asked, his voice strained. "What is the distinction?"

"Intention," Kurnult said.

Levort let the word sink in. He felt like a fist had unclenched from around his heart.

"The Beyonders want nothing but to remove the obstacles that plague the people of Lodespace from reaching the Beyond," Kurnult went on. "Their intention is pure. They gain nothing by allowing everyone to join them. In fact, that takes on a burden. The same burden you have taken upon yourself, Levort Aatra."

"I did?" Levort asked.

"Yes. It is easy to see you care for us. We care for you in return. There is nothing but burden in caring, but it is a welcome price to pay for the people you love."

Levort felt warmed by Kurnult's words. They struck him in his core like a bell being rung. Levort's body vibrated with a heat he had not felt in a cycle. He asked, "What is the Fessenog Fleet's intention?"

"Exploitation," Kurnult answered, his lips curled. "Gulna demands to be worshiped, and he orders devotion of his people. He uses everyone around him to heighten his position, allowing no one but him to gain a thing. Gulna Kii Fessenog builds prisons. He would never risk everything he has to save someone else. He would gladly let them fall beneath him on his path to glory."

Levort stared at nothing in particular. He finally began to answer the questions that had plagued him incessantly during his entire imprisonment.

What is real?

My friends are real. They would risk everything to help me, and I would do the same for them. We don't demand it from each other.

What is a lie?

The labels my enemies use against me are false. I am not something just because someone paints me that way. I know who I am. That is no lie.

For what?

The answer to this one was both simple and complicated.

For the freedom to live the way we want to live. To live fearlessly. To live happily.

Levort's eyes welled up with tears. "Thank you."

"Of course," Kurnult said. "It is good to see you smile."

Levort nodded. His smile faded as he thought about Bloom and the rest of his friends. Bayfo had access to Levort's old list still, no doubt. In time, he would whittle that list down and find Bloom. The clock was ticking, and it had been for a cycle.

"We need to get out of here," Levort stated. "If Bayfo gets to Bloom, it's all over."

Kurnult nodded.

Levort held the shiv up, his old best friend. He was happy to have a real friend locked away with him, but there was still much more bonding to be done with the crude piece of metal. Levort said to Kurnult, "Time to get to work."

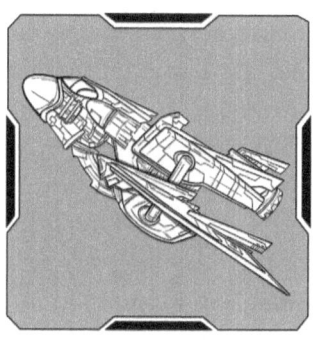

FORTY-TWO

"This better work," Floem said, her voice laced with worry. She wore the prospecting cloak Levort had left behind a cycle ago. On her back was his HAMMER model salvager. It weighed her down more than she liked, but she could manage.

"It...could," Vobsii said. He wore the tight enforcer's uniform they had stolen from the Dintuppan, Captain Tegarl Myrs. His build was similar to the hulky crustacean captain's, but it was a little snug around his midsection.

"Could? Not, *don't worry, Floem! It'll work, surely!*" Floem mocked.

"Sevodan thinks it'll work. I trust them." Vobsii planted his hands on his belt and adjusted his uncomfortable pants.

"But..."

"Sevodan built the scanners the Fleet uses. They had their tentacles up in the Fleet's guts. So they know how it all works. I think we can run with that."

"Yes. I know." Floem smiled. "But this..."

Vobsii regurgitated, "Sevodan knows it'll work. I trust—"

"They are cardboard cutouts, Vobb!" Floem shouted and flailed her arms at the squadron of two-dimensional warships. It was a trick that Sevodan had cooked up. Each of the fourteen flat pieces of sheet metal—not cardboard as Floem had declared—was equipped with the bare bones to trick Fleet scanners into thinking they were a much larger ship. They could fire a weak plasma bolt, mainly to sell the illusion.

"Those are Plan D anyway. Might not even need them. Once we grab Levort, we can come back to Bloom, hop on the Curio ships, and shake it to the Beyond." Vobsii smiled through concerned whiskers.

The Bloom colony had everything they needed—the Curio ships, the symbol of the correct planet to launch from, and the directions for the one-hundred-cycle journey into the vast, deep void. They only lacked the man who brought them all together for this purpose, and an Oristan who carried his people with him.

No one wanted to leave Bloom without Levort and Kurnult.

Floem and Vobsii climbed the ladder of the newly refurbished and updated *Tumbleweed*. Apart from making the ship flight-worthy again, Sevodan had included a few turret guns on its flanks and a long rail gun on its roof. The decoy ships were the distraction, but the *Tumbleweed* was the powerhouse that would do the work. It was no longer a tourist ship. The *Tumbleweed* was ready for a fight.

Piper Cridhe and one of Sevodan's members waited inside. Floem looked around the living room, now devoid of plants and dirt. She had moved all of them outside except for Skipper. It sat, lonely, in a small pot on the copilot's console. The best view in the house.

Floem took a deep breath. "I think we're about ready."

Piper leaned against the wall. "Ready as we'll ever be. I still think we should come up with an actual plan, though."

Vobsii huffed, "We have a plan. Plan D, use the cutouts."

Piper shook her head. "No, we have a list of problems and *one* idea that might work."

Floem thrust a leafy fist into the air and said with confidence, "No plan survives contact with the enemy!"

"That's not an excuse to not plan at all!" Piper argued.

Vobsii shrugged.

Floem dropped the confident pose. "We work the problems in order. Problem one, we need to trick the Fleet into turning a blind eye to our portals so we can get you and Sevodan to Tayoxe in the *Tumbleweed*."

Vobsii nodded. "Don't wanna get the *Tumbleweed* shot down the moment she enters Tayoxe airspace."

Sevodan flicked a tentacle at Vobsii and asked, "You have the leech we gave you?"

Vobsii patted a pocket on his chest. "Safe and sound. Plug this into the Fleet mainframe, and suddenly, portals don't look like portals."

Piper gestured to the costumes they were wearing. "Which invites a few more problems. How to get you two from the surface of Tayoxe to Consonance Hub so you can plug that leech in? We don't have a ship waiting to take you or anything."

Floem waved a hand. "We'll worry about that. You just wait for the all-clear from us. Then it's up to you to go to Fernomare and pick up the boys from the Yawning Lock."

Piper mumbled her worries. "I hope the new railgun is enough firepower for whatever's waiting for us there."

The railgun contained parts Sevodan had stolen from their homeworld, Grotrane. It was supposed to be installed on a new enforcer gunship. Unsure of what waited on Fernomare, they felt a railgun could at least punch a hole in whatever prison Levort and Kurnult were locked away in—if that type of escape was even possible.

Vobsii clapped his hands together. "That's when Plan D starts!"

Piper laughed. "I'm glad you at least gave Plan D room for the unlikely scenario you devise Plans A through C."

Floem smiled. "They aren't gonna know what hit them!"

Piper mumbled, "*We're* not gonna know what hit them either." She gestured to the door and said, "Well, I'll be ready on my end. You two be careful out there. Let's bring Levort and Kurnult back."

Floem said, "You can count on us." She pointed at the spikey weed in the flowerpot. "Yo, Skipper! Listen to Piper. No mutiny on this ship!"

Piper looked over her shoulder at the weed and winked at it.

Sevodan embraced all three friends in their tentacles. "We will load the decoy mini-ships into the cargo bay of the *Tumbleweed* and begin the revolution!"

Piper said through squeezed, muffled lips, "No revolution! We're only getting Levort and Kurnult and leaving for the Beyond! That's it!"

Sevodan released their grip and floated out through the hatch, shouting, "Revolution!"

Vobsii watched them leave and said quietly, "I feel good about this."

***

Floem and Vobsii stretched in the meadow of flowers in the mid-day Bloom sun. The entire colony waited around them. Some sat in the flowers, others watched from balconies of the nearby residences, and others floated, perched, rooted, or slouched. The colony had grown into a full-grown community, filled with people from all over the universe.

The backdrop to this audience were four long Curio ships with emerald-green hulls. Their aesthetic was unique—designed by Beyonders, but built by Belowers. They were angular, with external elements that fit together in the middle, much like flower petals. Each Curio ship harnessed a gateslinger, a tracker, and an entire Beyonder replicator facility, along with the stasis beds needed to house all the colonists of Bloom. Sunlight glinted off their hulls as they waited for the day they would fulfill their purpose. They dreamt of their one-hundred-cycle journey to paradise. Each Curio ship proudly sported the symbol for Bloom on its hull.

Floem walked through her checklist with Vobsii. "Gateslingers?"

"Check." Vobsii patted the gateslinger hidden in a covered holster on his enforcer belt. Floem did the same, revealing it under the flap of Levort's prospector cloak.

"Costume kit stuff?" Floem asked.

"Check." Vobsii stretched and looked himself over. He had a complete enforcer kit strapped to his body, with body armor, a rifle, and a smitegun sidearm. Floem checked all the zippers and pouches on the prospecting cloak and watched as some fabric lit up and displayed various data readouts. She gripped the HAMMER model salvager slung at her side like a longsword.

"Plug-thingy?" Floem snapped her green fingers and pointed at Vobsii.

He patted the pocket on his chest and nodded. "Leech is ready."

Floem slapped her hands on Vobsii's shoulders and shook him. "Then let's do this thing!"

Vobsii threw a fist into the air and turned to face the audience, his other hand gripping Floem's. "We're gonna go get our friends back!"

The audience cheered and threw flower petals, and the sky filled with color, hope, and excitement. Vobsii and Floem turned to each other and nodded.

Floem pointed her gateslinger forward into the open field and said, "Not much longer to wait, Vort! We're on our way!"

FORTY-THREE

Floem and Vobsii dove through the portal and emerged on Tayoxe. They rolled downhill from their portal faster than they could react. Eventually, Vobsii slammed against a mound of junk, and Floem crashed into him, knocking the air out of his lungs and causing the Resluni to gasp violently. Floem shook off her disorientation and looked uphill at their exit portal. She grabbed her gateslinger and shot at it, dissolving it.

The polluted breeze wafted and rolled some garbage around, creating a quiet, tinny noise. Floem waited to see if the Fleet would lance their position from orbit, but nothing happened. She smiled. "*Phew*! We made it!"

"Get off a me!" Vobsii pushed Floem, and she sprung up into a standing position. She dusted off her prospecting cloak and ensured the salvager hadn't cracked in half during the fall. It had definitely banged against her side as she tumbled, and she felt the soreness in her cuticle.

Floem helped Vobsii to his feet. "When we tell everyone about this heroic adventure, we'll leave that part out."

"Right. So…" Vobsii examined their surroundings. "First, we'll need to find a prospecting outpost and hitch a ride to Consonance Hub."

"Any idea where one is from here?" Floem asked.

"Not at all. But looks like we got an acid storm on the way. See over there?" Vobsii jerked his snout toward the horizon. A large mass of dark clouds crackling with lightning threatened to move in their direction. "Let's get to the top of that mound and see if we can get a better look around."

After a short scramble, they reached the top of the nearest junk hill. A hazy brown fog hovered over the garbage expanse, with taller ruined buildings in the distance. Though it was hard to tell what was organized and what was natural abandoned debris, a winding path was noticeably carved into the landscape. It split off into various pockets, outlets of scavenged claims made by previous prospectors.

"There!" Floem pointed toward a clearing in the distance. Closer to the buildings than their position in the wilderness of trash was a little outpost with two shuttles waiting to ferry prospectors to Consonance Hub.

"Good eye, Floem." Vobsii put his fist out toward her, and she bumped it with her own.

Together, they slid down the other side of the junk mound with more control than the first time and landed on the dusty ground. They had slipped into the polluted fog, and Vobsii coughed as he took his first breath. Floem inhaled the dirty air joyfully and exhaled something Vobsii would have preferred to have in his lungs.

The path had high walls of debris on each side, making it feel more like a trench than a sloping valley. The fog obscured their vision so much that the outpost was lost. "Can't believe old Vort used to do this regularly."

"It looks worse here than it did when we visited a while back." Vobsii coughed.

"That was the tourist package. This here's the real-prospecting-deal."

Vobsii pointed ahead. "Wait, what's that?"

Floem strained her eyes to see what Vobsii was pointing at. A shadow was ahead, barely visible in the dirty fog. It was a strange shape, with insectoid legs, thick jagged arms, and a long snout. It skittered into the center of the path ahead and stopped.

Floem whispered, "I don't like this." Vobsii went for his gateslinger, and Floem stayed his hand. "Can't use those until we trick the mainframe with the leech. We got lucky coming here—don't wanna test that luck twice."

The sound of a foot sliding against dirt caused Floem and Vobsii to turn around. Another shadow blocked the path behind them. It was tall and lean, and by the silhouette, Floem guessed it was a Marothallan.

Vobsii whispered, "Bayfo's men?"

Floem tensed up.

The Marothallan shadow spoke with a gravelly voice. "Long way from the outpost, aren't you? State your business."

Floem looked at Vobsii, then adjusted the salvager on her hip and stepped toward the Marothallan shadow. She changed her voice to sound more rugged and mean, "Our business is mind'n our own! Maybe you're in the same business as we are?"

Vobsii sighed.

The shadow laughed. The Marothallan stepped closer and revealed their blue skin and large eyes. The skittering sound announced that the other shadow had come closer too, revealing a Fluctan prospector. He wore goggles and operated its flitskipper like an extension of its own body. Two large robotic arms held a salvager.

"I think you wandered into our—" the Marothallan began.

Floem cut him off, "Wait, are you robbin' us?"

The Fluctan and the Marothallan looked at each other in disbelief at being called out. The Marothallan only said, "Uh. No?"

"Brother. If you're robbin' us, then you gotta say so when we ask. That's the rules!"

The Fluctan turned his head and seemed to be momentarily considering the nonexistent rules. The Marothallan shook his head with frustration. "Fine, you called it. We're robbing you. Hand over yer salvage."

Floem laughed. "Ha! Vents for you! We don't got any!"

The Marothallan clicked his tongue and said, "Pretty sure this vents for *you* more than it vents for me."

Vobsii rolled his eyes and unholstered his smitegun. With a quick flick of his hand, he let loose a stun bolt, striking the Marothallan enforcer in the chest before he could aim his weapon at them. The Marothallan fell onto his back, spasming with the effect of the stun.

A shrill screech came from the Fluctan, and he thrust one of the robotic arms of his flitskipper at Vobsii. Vobsii was thrown sideways against the junk wall with a resounding crash.

"Woah!" Floem shouted. She ducked as the Fluctan swung the flitskipper's other robotic arm at her, narrowly missing the swipe. She kicked out at one of the spider-like legs of the machine underneath the small creature but only hurt her foot in the process.

"*Drit!*" Floem cursed.

The Fluctan struck out at Floem once more, forcing her to dodge around the flitskipper's mechanical appendages. She was backed against the opposite wall of the junk trench, with a massive piece of jagged scrap metal hanging over her. Thinking quickly, Floem grabbed the HAMMER model salvager and activated its plasma cutter. She swung it over her head.

The Fluctan looked up as a giant piece of scrap metal sheared off by Floem's salvager came crashing down. It buried the Fluctan and his flitskipper under rubble and dust. Floem patted her gloved hands together and slammed one foot down on the flitskipper's only exposed arm. She looked into the Fluctan's goggled eyes and said, "Is that enough salvage for you?"

The Fluctan put his flippers up in surrender.

"Think twice before you think about robbin' professionals like us," Floem continued in her falsely aggressive voice.

Vobsii slowly got to his feet, feeling the chest plate on his enforcer gear to ensure it hadn't cracked. "Nova, that thing packs a punch."

Floem said, "Let's get moving."

"Wait." Vobsii approached the still-convulsing Marothallan enforcer. "We can take their data sleeves to get on the shuttle."

Floem's eyes opened wide. "Hadn't considered that!" The Fluctan wore its data sleeve more like a necklace, and Floem had no trouble pilfering it off the slick-skinned creature. Vobsii used a knife to cut the sleeve off the Marothallan's uniform and slid it over his own.

"Before I forget." Vobsii removed the communication device

from the Marothallan's ear and crushed it in his hand. "Let's keep this little exchange a secret, eh?" He patted his huge hand against the Marothallan's shoulder. The Marothallan enforcer's eyes rolled back, and he passed out.

Vobsii dragged the Marothallan enforcer's limp body under an overhang of garbage. Floem asked, "What are you up to, Vobb?"

Vobsii propped the Marothallan upright against the junk and walked over to the Fluctan. "Storm's coming. They gave us their data sleeves. The least we can do is keep them from roastin' to death in the acid rain." He deftly lifted the rubble away from the Fluctan and jerked his head. "Go take care of your buddy."

The Fluctan grumbled. Since his flitskipper had been destroyed, the aquatic prospector was forced to bounce over to the Marothallan on his belly. He plopped himself down and sneered at them.

Floem shook her head, "Hey hey! None of that! *You* tried mugging *us*, remember!"

Vobsii thrust a thumb toward the outpost. "We better get going."

Vobsii and Floem walked away from the crime scene with a spring in their step. Floem laughed. "Now we just have to hope the shuttlemaster doesn't notice I'm not a Fluctan, and you're not a Marothallan!"

Vobsii snapped his fingers. "Easy."

FORTY-FOUR

Floem and Vobsii approached the prospecting outpost. Other groups of prospectors and their enforcer escorts were crowding around the shuttle, attempting to avoid the oncoming acid storm. The wind picked up and blew the polluted fog in great wafts of dirt.

Floem donned the breathing mask that she'd found in a shoulder pouch on her cloak. Vobsii discovered a similar option hidden with a switch on his borrowed enforcer uniform. The masks shielded their lungs from the acrid Tayoxe air and gave them a little more obscurity.

"Uh oh, Vobb." Floem leaned over to her friend. "Shuttlemaster's checking datapads for identification."

"Ours won't work under a close eye," Vobsii grumbled.

"Unless you drop a few kilos and got a way of transforming me into a Fluctan, I'm assuming you're correct," Floem whispered.

Vobsii kept his eyes on the shuttlemaster. "What do we do?"

Floem investigated their surroundings for ideas. The storm was only a few minutes away, and she knew if she could stall the shuttlemaster, they'd eventually have to rush everyone on board to avoid the acid rain. Rushing meant mistakes.

This would be so much easier if we could use the portals, Floem thought in frustration. She and all the colonists on Bloom had grown so accustomed to the gateslingers that they began to rely on portals to fix all their problems. Here, gateslingers were off-limits until they could trick the Fleet's mainframe into ignoring portals. *Think, think, think!*

A duo of Kurikoids, prospector and escort, bumbled down the path toward them. They must have been salvaging until the last moment due to how much loot dangled and clanged from various straps on their gear. They hurried toward the line, waving their hands and shouting pleas to wait.

This could be helpful, but how to use it?

Floem inspected the Dintuppan prospector standing in front of her again and noticed he had a satchel of loot strapped to his back. One item peeked out from the half-unzipped pouch on the back of the bag. It looked like a rusted old trophy that had worn out its placard long ago. Probably an *Employee of the Cycle* award from an ancient Tayoxe workplace.

Ok, let's see if this works.

Floem leaned over to Vobsii and whispered, "Follow my lead."

Vobsii nodded. Floem turned her back to the prospector before her and slipped her hand into the pouch with practiced skill. The trophy in hand, she pushed it into the cuff of her sleeve and kept it concealed.

The Kurikoids approached too quickly to stop. The clanging of the junk they'd salvaged mixed with their panicked croaks. Floem stepped to the side and pulled Vobsii with her as the Kurikoids stumbled and bumped into the Dintuppan at the back of the line. Floem and Vobsii quietly walked around the Kurikoids and took their place back in line behind them, unnoticed. As Floem passed the Kurikoid prospector, she slipped the trophy into an exposed open pocket on their backpack.

The Kurikoid prospector croaked to the Dintuppan, "Apologies-apologies! We-We didn't think we'd make it!"

The Dintuppan prospector growled at the Kurikoids, then placed its crustacean armored claw hand on its satchel. Prospectors were superstitious and wary, and this Dintuppan had immediately patted his satchel for his prize, only to find it had been pilfered. The

Dintuppan spun around, fuming. By Floem's design, the rusted trophy stood out from the other scrap metal the Kurikoids had salvaged. Immediately, the Dintuppan was up in arms.

"You little thieves!" the Dintuppan prospector roared. His enforcer escort, a Resluni, was caught off guard. Before he could react, the Dintuppan prospector slugged the Kurikoid prospector in the face, dropping them to the ground. The Dintuppan retrieved his *Employee of the Cycle* trophy from the unconscious prospector but was struck with a flat sheet of scrap metal from the Kurikoid enforcer.

The Resluni enforcer shoved the Kurikoid enforcer into Vobsii. Vobsii pushed the Kurikoid back with enough force to knock over both enforcer escorts and smash them into the backs of the people next in line.

What ensued was a snowball of brawling prospectors and enforcers. As the bumping and bashing moved down the line, more brawlers joined the fray. Prospectors began openly stealing from one another during the chaos, leading to more hot anger passing between them. The rain began to drizzle down, adding a slippery hot surface to the battlefield. As the clouds started to choke out the light, it was hard to tell who was an enforcer and who was a prospector. It was all flailing bodies and clanging metal salvage.

Floem and Vobsii watched from the sidelines. The acid storm was about to become dangerous. Even the early drizzle was enough to cause burns when exposed too long. Soon everyone would have to make a judgment call and come to their senses. The shuttlemaster desperately tried to regain order.

"That's our ticket!" Floem nudged Vobsii, and they pushed their way through the fighters toward the shuttlemaster.

The shuttlemaster croaked at them, "Just-just get inside! We-we are leaving!"

They scanned their stolen data sleeves into the ship's register, undetected by the shuttlemaster. The shuttlemaster shot her smitegun into the storm clouds and croaked to the rest of the duelists outside, "Stay-stay and die, or get on the shuttle and live! We-we are leaving with or without you *drit*-brains!"

Floem and Vobsii kept their masks on as the brawlers scrambled into the shuttle and sat around them, each sporting new bruises and cuts. None of them wanted to look at each other, which was an added benefit to Floem and Vobsii's situation.

Vobsii leaned over to Floem and whispered, "I think it's gonna be a quiet flight up to Consonance Hub."

***

Levort sawed away at the metal panel under his bed as Kurnult sat on the mattress and kept a lookout for the robotic jailor, Abnat. The panel was bent now, and Levort could almost squeeze his thin frame into whatever lay behind it.

Kurnult had been caring for Levort since his arrival in the mysterious prison. The Oristan had given him all his broth meals, despite Levort's protests, which had allowed him to regain some of his lost strength. He no longer looked like a skeleton with a beard. Levort felt human again.

With another push of his shiv, Levort finished his long-time angular cut into the corner. It was time to see if the effort was worth the risk. He wrapped some cloth he had ripped off his prison scrubs around his fist and reared it back. Levort punched into the cut corner and felt the impact in his knuckles despite the padding. The metal panel bent inward, but not all the way. Levort laughed with insane happiness. Another punch would crunch the metal backward, creating an escape hole.

Kurnult blew out a whistle.

Abnat was behind the frosted cell wall.

Levort dropped his shiv and rolled out from under the bed as the robot defrosted the wall. The cell bars slid open, and at once, Levort and Kurnult were magnetically leashed to the middle of the room with their arms in the air.

Commander Bayfo Niall stepped into the room behind Abnat. Kurnult snarled at him through fanged teeth, and Levort glared at his old friend-turned-nemesis. Bayfo shook his head as he paced around the two prisoners.

"We're getting closer to finding your friends," Bayfo said as he prowled the cell. "That little stunt you pulled on Golt was a mistake." He jabbed his fist into Kurnult's ribs.

Kurnult grunted with the impact but bore the pain silently.

"If you're gonna hit someone, hit me!" Levort shouted.

Bayfo smiled at Levort and unholstered his smitegun. Levort watched with a cold horror in his veins as Bayfo pointed the weapon at Kurnult's chest. He didn't fire, but doing so would not be out of his repertoire.

"Tell me where the compound is, and this all goes away," Bayfo said.

Suddenly, Levort understood why Kurnult had been placed in the cell with him. Bayfo could have stuck Kurnult anywhere in the prison, but instead, he used his friend like a carrot. Kurnult gave Levort hope, and now Bayfo threatened to destroy that hope for good.

"Don't listen to him," Kurnult grunted, staring down at Bayfo with all three eyes.

Bayfo nudged the gun into Kurnult's chest and said, "You have until the count of three."

Levort looked from Kurnult to Bayfo and back again.

"One."

"He is bluffing," Kurnult said.

Levort didn't need the Sight to know that Kurnult was lying. Bayfo wasn't bluffing at all. In fact, Levort was sure Bayfo would enjoy shooting the last Oristan.

"*Two*. Losing my patience," Bayfo said, adjusting his grip on his smitegun.

Levort yelped, "Stop!"

Bayfo smiled. "You're gonna tell me?"

Levort nodded, his defeat weakening him.

"Levort!" Kurnult protested with concern.

Levort stared Bayfo directly in the eyes. "It's called Bloom."

Bayfo slung the smitegun into the holster on his belt and snapped his fingers. Abnat released the magnetic hold on Levort's cuffs, and he dropped to the floor. Bayfo knelt before Levort and said with a vicious smile, "A pretty name for something so evil. But I need more than a name, and you know that. Your friend gets shot in the guts if you don't give me a symbol right now. If I go there and find out you lied to me, he dies. No more counting."

Levort nodded. Bayfo pulled out a datapad from his cloak and gestured to it. "Show me."

With a heavy sigh and eyes full of tears, Levort pushed his finger into the datapad's screen and began tracing out a symbol. Bayfo practically salivated at the sight of the symbol's formation, his long hunt coming to an end.

Levort's hand dropped to the floor when he was finished. Bayfo snatched the datapad and spun it around. Skepticism in his eyes, he pulled out his gateslinger. He sifted through symbols until he found one that matched the symbol Levort had drawn.

"Let's see what we got." Bayfo smiled and pointed the gateslinger at the wall. After it slapped into formation, he leaned his head into it. For a few heartbeats, Bayfo kept his head on the other side of the portal. Eventually, he pulled himself back into the cell and dissolved the portal. "I see why you call it Bloom."

"You got what you wanted. Let us go." Levort didn't look up from the floor.

"Not yet, old friend," Bayfo said. "I'm going to take my men and get on the *Shrapnox*, and we'll find your compound. I'll free you when we're done handling it."

Levort snarled and attempted to lunge at Bayfo, only to be stabbed with Abnat's stun baton. Levort was jolted backward and rolled against the wall of the cell. Bayfo laughed and shook his head. "Prospectors never learn." He gestured to Abnat to seal the cell with frost.

Once the jailors were gone, Kurnult rushed to Levort's side. Levort looked at Kurnult with a dead stare, concern growing on his face. Kurnult shook his head and whispered, "That was not the symbol for Bloom."

Levort shook his head.

"He will discover nothing on Alberrya's moon, Hanataba. Then he will come back," Kurnult elaborated, trying to decipher what the Sight was no doubt showing him already.

Levort nodded. "The hole under the bed is ready. I bought us some time to escape."

"But how much time?" Kurnult asked.

Levort wasn't sure. "Bayfo's shortest interval between visits was about seven orbits. I have a feeling he can't portal his ship here. He has to fly it from a nearby planet or something. I don't think a symbol for *this* planet exists, which is probably why Gulna picked it. Not sure where we are, but it must be inhospitable outside these prison walls."

Kurnult squinted all three of his eyes. "If that is the case, how will we escape without our ability to make portals?"

Levort crunched his face into a weak smile. "Improvise."

FORTY-FIVE

Floem and Vobsii stepped off the shuttle onto Consonance Hub, the heart of the Fessenog Fleet. Having no more use for them, they shed their fake IDs into a nearby trash compactor and took a moment to get their bearings on the busy dock.

"How's that plug thingy doing?" Floem asked as she pulled up some helpful Consonance Hub schematics provided by Sevodan. The Mulptre had been used for cycles to build up the Fleet for Gulna, the best-kept secret of Lodespace. Sevodan had been thrilled to know their forced labor would now be used against their old masters.

Vobsii tapped the leech in his chest pocket and said, "Still resting comfortably. Where to from here?"

Floem looked up at the large sign painted onto the side of the dock to confirm their current location. She sifted through the plans Sevodan provided to find the special access tunnel that would take them to the mainframe. "Sevodan said that Consonance Hub has the long-range scanners the rest of the Fleet uses to pinpoint our portals, so we need to get to the core of this station. Looks like a little trip into the middle district to squeeze into an access tunnel that goes up into the mainframe. Let's hope the engineers who took over after the Mulptre didn't seal up the tunnel."

"Only one way to find out," Vobsii said.

The Alberryan and the Resluni adjusted their disguises. They walked away from the dock into a massive shopping district—the Fleet's lazy attempt to get citizens and visitors to quickly spend their hard-earned hapron immediately upon entry. The bright neon lights and loud sounds of gambling machines lured in people from all over, promising that they, too, could fill their pockets with luxurious trinkets. It was the purpose of Gulna's empire—spend hapron to make hapron. The more hapron you had, the better a person you were, no matter how you earned it.

Hapron made you King of the Below.

"How much hapron did Piper give you?" Vobsii asked.

"We're not shopping! Focus on the mission, Vobb!" Floem nudged him with her elbow.

"What? No, look over there!" Vobsii pointed to a highway tunnel that flanked the sides of the market. Slipcars lined the shopping center, waiting to take riders anywhere they'd like for the right price.

"Good think'n! Beats walking anyway." Floem smiled. They made their way over to the line of taxis and looked inside each. "We don't want an automated one—wouldn't know who was looking in on us. How about… This fella looks nice!"

Floem pointed to a slipcar operated by a Fluctan. Contrary to what Floem had said about him, the slick-snouted driver looked anything but friendly. Knife marks traced around his smooth wet skin detailed a life of fighting, and the sharp teeth protruding from his underbite looked menacing, even as his lips curved into a smile. The Fluctan leaned out his window and said, "Name's Snorkel. Hop in."

Floem nudged Vobsii again and said, "See! Friendly type. Unlike the guys we ran into on Tayoxe."

Snorkel grinned at Vobsii, who remained unconvinced. Regardless, Vobsii followed Floem into the backseat of the slipcar and buckled in. Snorkel leaned over the back of his seat and placed a flipper on the center console. "Where to?"

"Middle district, please!" Floem was bouncing in her seat.

"Right! Get you there quick-like." Snorkel put his eyes on the road. The slipcar grunted as the ignition kicked on, and the car rose a meter off the station's ground. With a few more spurts, the slipcar entered the travel tunnel. "What brings you two to the middle district? I don't take many prospectors down there."

Floem didn't even know what existed in the middle district. They had always kept their trips to Consonance Hub short, pilfering their way through the various dock shopping centers and leaving before anyone caught on.

Vobsii leaned in. "I've convinced my friend here to invest her hapron instead of spending it all at once."

Floem cocked her eyebrow at him, then looked at the rearview mirror to see Snorkel eyeing her. She smiled and said, "What can I say? I live luxuriously!"

Snorkel huffed and smiled. "Wise of you to listen to your friend. An investment in your future is always the smart choice. I m'self am invested in Malxu-Tech. I learned from a friend o' mine that they're in charge of all the little microprocessors and artificial intelligence chips that keep the Fleet in orbit. For Nova's sake, Consonance hub's whole mainframe is built by Malxu tech! Me—being of big intelligents—decided that if the auto slipcars were gonna take mine career froms me, that I'd make a little money off their effort in the pro-sess."

Floem said, "If you can't beat them, join them!"

Snorkel guffawed louder than he should have and said, "Beat them *by* joinin' them, I say!"

Vobsii laughed. "I like this guy."

After a short ride to the middle district, it was time to part ways. Floem paid the fare, almost completely exhausting the little hapron Piper had loaned them. They exited the slipcar and said goodbye to their driver.

"Remember! Malxu-Tech! That's the good 'un!" Snorkel shouted through the window as he piloted the slipcar away to retrieve his next fare.

Vobsii and Floem waved goodbye. Vobsii mumbled, "I feel sorry for the guy. If only he knew what we were up to..."

Floem shrugged. "Whatcha gonna do?"

After a moment of guilt, they turned toward the middle district. This district was taller than the small dock shopping center, with buildings stretching from floor to ceiling. The mainframe hub rested within a sphere in the center of the enormous space, with pillars bisecting it at various angles. Slipcars moved in and out of buildings, almost as if this was its own mini interior-Fleet.

"So, what is this place exactly?" Floem asked.

"Financial district. It's where all the big players from around Lodespace exchange investment stocks and stuff. Basically, the beating heart of the Fleet's economy," Vobsii said as they began walking into the vast district. Aliens from all over the Voyalten Web moved around, each in their own contained world, locked to a comm device or observing a data sleeve on their expensive suits. Floem and Vobsii simultaneously stood out in their clothing yet remained invisible, as no one seemed to care.

A shadow passed overhead as an enforcer mech unit patrolled above. The EMU showed that justice in this district would be firm and quick. Instinctively, Floem and Vobsii slipped themselves near the wall of a nearby building to lower their visibility. The EMU passed around a corner.

Vobsii shook his head. "We have to be careful when we get to the hatch. Right now, we're nobodies, but they will get suspicious when we start messing around with stuff."

"Right," Floem agreed.

They quickened their pace, following the plans Sevodan had provided ahead of the mission. The crowds thinned out as they approached a tall pillar that bisected the central sphere above. Their presence became more visible due to the lack of other bystanders to fill the streets. Eventually, it was only Floem and Vobsii walking around. The evolution from a bustling financial district to almost abandoned walkways was off-putting.

"There!" Floem pointed to a hatch, mostly hidden away in the wall of the giant pillar. To the uninformed, it looked like any other part of the wall, but with Sevodan's intel, the old hatch was a noticeable gateway.

As they approached, they noticed a problem. "*Drit*, it's sealed!" Vobsii cursed.

"Figured as much," Floem said. She looked around to see if anyone was watching and said, "Good thing we brought a key."

"Key? I don't remember a ke—" Vobsii began.

Floem pulled Levort's HAMMER model salvager into her hands. Vobsii smiled but quickly became serious. "Gotta be quick. It's going to make a bright light and a lot of noise. Those EMUs are going to be on us in seconds."

"Ok, I'm ready," Floem said. She activated the plasma cutter on the end of the salvager and quickly punched four holes in each side of the square-shaped hatch. The noise was loud and bright, and an EMU rounded the corner after the last hole was punched.

"Your turn, big guy!" Floem said. She crouched against the side of the wall, watching the patrolling EMU. Vobsii inhaled and threw himself into the wounded hatch door, busting it open and falling into the shaft.

Floem's eyes went wide, and she pulled herself into the hatch right after Vobsii. There he hung, braced against the walls, spread out except for the hand loosely clutching the broken hatch door he had busted through.

"Didn't you know the hatch went both upward toward the mainframe and straight downward toward the outer exterior of Consonance Hub?" Floem asked, reaching toward him. "Pass it here!" She reached around Vobsii and grabbed the dented piece of metal. The sound of the EMU was getting louder outside the hole they had made. She propped the broken hatch door back in its place and hoped for the best.

Floem held her breath as the EMU's jets rumbled the wobbly hatch door. She couldn't see the mech unit itself, only the shadow it cast through the cracks in the dented door. Vobsii struggled to keep himself braced in the shaft and grunted with the exertion.

In time, the EMU moved away from the hatch, and they were in the clear. Vobsii exhaled loudly and allowed his feet to swing down and clang against the shaft wall into some indents that made fine footholds. The indents ran the entire length of the shaft, giving them a ladder.

He laughed. "I forgot this shaft was made for balloons by balloons."

Floem snorted in response. Once they found their footing, Floem said, "Okay, now we have to make the big climb up. Sevodan said if everything goes well, we'll be able to plug in the leech, and they won't notice anything's wrong. They never check the mainframe if it doesn't send up an error."

"After you, I insist," Vobsii said. He followed Floem up the long interior of the shaft to the Fleet mainframe.

FORTY-SIX

"Piper, Sevodan, Skipper—you're up!" Floem's voice crackled through the jump-phone on the *Tumbleweed*.

Piper had her legs up on the pilot's console, sitting next to Skipper's flowerpot. Sevodan had all fourteen of their members floating in the living room. They cheered for Floem and Vobsii's successful journey into the mainframe.

Piper pressed the button to talk. "Good to hear you!"

Floem said, "You're clear to portal to Tayoxe and find our boys!"

Vobsii added, "We're going to snoop around here a little longer. Now that they can't detect our portals, we can move safely. Tell Sevodan they are a genius!"

Sevodan's multiple ballooned bodies bumped and bounced each other in celebration. Their leech had crippled the Fleet's portal scanners. They had filled the cargo bay of the *Tumbleweed* with decoy ships and set the turret guns ready to fire. Unsure of what fight lay ahead, the Mulptre was prepared for anything.

"They heard you!" Piper chuckled. "If things get hairy, jump back to Bloom, and we'll meet you there after we find Levort and Kurnult."

"Signing off for now. Good luck, Piper!" Floem said before the jump-phone cut the transmission.

Piper grabbed the controls on the pilot's console and looked at her co-pilot, Skipper. "It's our turn to shine. Ready?"

Skipper didn't do anything. It remained a weed in a flowerpot, belted to the chair.

Piper smiled and initiated the thrusters on the upgraded tourist ship. "All right, guys. We're having a party, and I'm bringing balloons. Hold onto something back there, Sevodan!"

She could hear the bouncing and bumping of her gas-filled friend in the living room as they curled their tentacles around various holding positions. They shouted, "Ready to launch the revolution!"

Piper laughed. With a jolt, the *Tumbleweed* took to the sky. It kicked up flowers and dust in the meadows of Bloom as it roared off into the sunset. Piper's seat rumbled as the ship rose higher. She remained within the atmosphere to assist with the shift to Tayoxe, not wanting to risk another sudden space-to-planet rupture through portals. With a few more flicks, Piper prepared for the jump.

Piper whispered to the *Tumbleweed*, "All right, baby, hold it together. This will only hurt for a minute." Piper wasn't an ace pilot, but after a few stunt flying classes while touring with her sister, she was the best fit for this part of the plan. She manipulated a gateslinger harnessed into the pilot's console. It had been preset to Tayoxe in advance, and with a pull of the second trigger, a flat portal launched out and engulfed the air in front of her. "Here we go!"

Piper put full power into the *Tumbleweed*'s thrusters and hit the portal. She entered Tayoxe low to the ground and was forced to pull back hard on the flight stick. Although the acid storm had passed, the air was still very turbulent. The *Tumbleweed* blasted its engines at full thrust, melting a mound of scrap unlucky enough to be behind the ship as it portalled in. A rear-facing gateslinger dissolved the portal behind the ship, concealing it from the next wave of prospectors and enforcers that would no doubt visit Tayoxe the following day.

"Climb, baby! Climb!" Piper grunted through gritted teeth as she wrangled the ship. The *Tumbleweed* was moving across the landscape but wasn't ascending yet. She felt a hard bump as the bottom of the ship bashed against a pile of junk, sending an explosion of rubble and salvage into the air. The jostle was enough to alter the *Tumbleweed*'s course, and the ship slowly climbed into the sky. Piper had to roll the ship left to avoid the top of a skyscraper ruin, but it was open polluted air once she passed that.

After more rumbling, the *Tumbleweed* entered a low orbit around Tayoxe, and the weight of gravity once again lifted. Skipper slowly straightened out, and Piper took a few deep breaths to shake off the adrenaline.

Outside her window, the Fleet moved around like insects working in a space hive. No one seemed to notice her arrival, confirming that Floem and Vobsii had accomplished their task. "Good job, guys. I guess Plans A through C weren't needed after all."

She gave Skipper a quick glance. The plant hadn't moved. She then looked over her shoulder and called, "Hey, Sevodan! You all right back there?"

Sevodan cheered with all their members. "Next stop, revolution!"

"No, next stop, Fernomare! Maybe we'll do a revolution some other time." Piper laughed. She looked out the front visor into the open void of space, the auto-shade dimming the star Tayoxe and Fernomare orbited to avoid blinding her. Fernomare rested close to the star, burning its surface in a constant assault of heat and radiation. It was more like Zhok than Zhok was. Piper thought of Kurnult and Levort standing on that scorching surface, like candles burning too hot.

Piper whispered, "Just hold on a little longer, guys. We'll get you home soon." She clicked a few more buttons and switches to prepare the *Tumbleweed* for the long, three-orbit haul to the mysterious prison world.

***

Commander Bayfo Niall slammed his fist down on the data table on the bridge of the *Shrapnox*. Rage shook his body, and his teeth gritted together so hard he thought they'd crumble to dust.

"Sir?" Lieutenant Ucons asked. "Is there something wrong?"

Bayfo turned to Ucons and glared daggers into him with ferocity in his eyes. "What do you see out that window?"

Ucons looked out the window as ordered. "You said this place was called Bloom. It's uncharted, right? Except for the Beyonder compound."

"Does it look familiar to you?" Bayfo asked. Somehow the conversation cut his anger a little. Splashing Ucons with his rage didn't fix the issue, but it felt better than stewing in it alone.

"Uh. Not… No," Ucons mumbled.

"I thought the same thing. It certainly matches a place Levort Aatra would call Bloom. Too bad this place already has a damn name. Hanataba. Ring a bell?"

"That's one of Alberrya's satellites, isn't it?" Ucons answered, wary of what his commander might do if he was incorrect.

"That's right. At first, I didn't recognize it because I'd never been to these garden moons, so the evidence lined up when I poked my head in. But Levort played me. The *Shrapnox*'s scanners don't lie, though. It's reading nothing but plants!" Bayfo took a deep breath and stared at the empty readings on his data table. "We've been set up. This has been a waste of time."

"What's our next move?" Ucons asked.

Bayfo looked at his crew and waved a frustrated hand at them. "What do you think? Strap in. We're heading back to Fernomare to kill Levort's friend. He will learn he can't keep his friends safe from me forever."

Ucons nodded, then asked, "Sir, have you considered Levort Aatra might be a dead end? He's been no use to our hunt in a cycle. There might be other ways we can find his compound without him."

Bayfo wanted to tell Ucons to shut the Zhok up, but what the enforcer said resonated with him more than he wanted to admit. Bayfo had known, deep down in his heart, that Levort was the kind of guy who would never betray his friends. Even this act of misdirection was admirable. As much as Bayfo didn't want to admit it, he knew this hunt would never proceed with Levort's interference.

Part of Bayfo wanted to become friends with Levort again.

The other part of Bayfo remembered being shot in the chest and dragged across thousands of worlds hunting a friend who wouldn't listen to reason.

Strategically, it makes more sense to kill Levort and get the information from the Oristan.

Bayfo looked away from Ucons and stepped toward the pilot's chair. "We're portalling to Tayoxe. From there, we'll head straight to Fernomare. When we arrive, I'll decide how to deal with Lev."

FORTY-SEVEN

Piper jolted awake. After three orbits soaring through the void from Tayoxe, the *Tumbleweed* was finally approaching its destination. Beeping on the pilot's console signified a new notification. She grunted and stretched her arms wide, blinking away the sleepiness that had overtaken her. The console read, ENTERING FERNOMARE SPACE. Piper looked over to Skipper, her copilot weed in a flowerpot. "Why didn't you wake me?"

Sevodan floated a member toward the cockpit and asked, "Are we there yet?"

Piper smiled. "Yes, *this time*, we are actually there. You can stop asking now."

The Mulptre wriggled their tentacles and moved back into the living room area of the *Tumbleweed* to rejoin the rest of their members. Piper activated the long-range scanner to see what they were up against.

"Ok, seems like we have some problems," Piper mumbled. She counted four AS cannons—anti-starship guns—clustered in a single area on the other side of the planet from their current angle in orbit.

Fernomare's surface was scorching hot and uninhabitable. It was a barren wasteland of flat superheated stone with no atmosphere to give it breathable air. Fernomare resembled an old cannonball from fairy tales Piper's mother used to tell her. The star that warmed Fernomare, Tayoxe, and the Fessenog Fleet loomed everywhere on the horizon, fighting her sun shield's dampening effect. Skipper probably loved it.

Piper pushed the button to speak over the communication channel. They were all within the same star system, providing only a slight delay. "Floem, Vobsii, you guys hear me?"

Floem answered a few seconds later. "Yeah, we're here. You make it to Fernomare?"

"Yes. We are on approach to the Yawning Lock. How is that mainframe looking?"

When Vobsii answered, it sounded like he was chewing on something. "Still blindfolded. You should be able to sneak in, no problem."

"What are you eating?" Piper asked. She was a little jealous. She had only eaten reheated, pre-prepped food during the travel to Fernomare.

Floem snorted and said, "We got bored waiting in the mainframe, so we ordered some exotic human food. *Pete-zah*. I even tried some. It doesn't beat sunlight and water, but it's pretty damn close."

Piper imagined Floem and Vobsii sitting in the mainframe of the Fessenog Fleet, dangling their legs over a catwalk and eating an overly cheesy pizza. Her stomach growled. She shook off the daydream and said, "Looks like we have some AS guns mounted outside an access door. Turns out Plan D will come in handy."

"That is why we plan," Floem stated severely. "Meticulously. No leaf left unpruned."

Piper rolled her eyes. She looked over her shoulder and asked, "You ready back there, Sevodan?"

Sevodan and their other ballooned members each grabbed a remote and headset and placed them on their faces. "We are ready for the fight!"

Piper leaned into her pilot's seat and looked over at Skipper. "I know you're ready. You don't have to say it."

Skipper didn't respond.

"All right! Let's hit it! Plan D engage!" Piper shouted. She punched the throttle and cut altitude to soar closer to Fernomare's flat scorched surface. After a few moments of high thrust approach, the anti-starship guns focused on the *Tumbleweed*. "They are engaging. Deploy the decoy fighters!"

Piper pulled a lever on the console above her head, and the cargo bay dropped out the fourteen decoy mini-ship fighters. Each decoy mini-ship was made of a few thrusters, a flat metal cutout with a painting of a warship on its front, two wings, a plasma gun, and a leech. Instead of tricking the guns into ignoring the mini-ships, it fooled them into thinking each mini-ship was a significant threat. Even if a gunner spotted one visually, the metal cutout would hopefully do enough to throw them off.

The attack needed to be quick, however. Too long, and the AS gunners would catch wind of their scheme. Sevodan rolled the decoys into formation around the *Tumbleweed* and began firing for effect. The AS guns started firing on the approaching false squadron of warships. Piper toggled the comm to hear what the AS gunners were saying, using a hack provided by Sevodan.

"Where the Zhok did these guys come from!" a gunner cried out in panic, the sound of the giant anti-starship cannon firing in the background.

"I've never seen warships move that fast!"

"They're everywhere! Keep firing!"

"Fleet, this is Yawning Lock actual. We are under attack from an unknown warband. I repeat—"

Piper rolled the *Tumbleweed* to dodge a plasma bolt. She clenched her teeth. "They know we're here now. The Fleet's been alerted." With a flick of her fingers on the joystick, the rail gun rotated into position on top of the *Tumbleweed*. It was the only weapon they had with enough firepower to damage the AS cannons. The decoy ships were only good enough to distract.

A mini-ship exploded on the *Tumbleweed*'s starboard side. One of Sevodan's members cheerfully removed their headset and tossed it to the floor. Wasting no time, the Mulptre floated over to the port side of the ship and strapped themselves into a turret gun seat. There were only two manual turret guns on the *Tumbleweed*. Whichever member's mini-ship died first got dibs, and each member was undoubtedly excited to dish out the revolution Sevodan insisted on.

Piper roared toward the closest AS cannon, firing off a blast from the powerful rail gun. The *Tumbleweed* lurched as the gun fired, and the powerful bolt smashed into the AS gun's thin midsection, causing a massive explosion and sending the top crashing down onto the section below, resulting in a secondary explosion.

Piper hollered an excited battle cry and pumped her fist into the air. She quickly looked over to Skipper and laughed, then rolled the *Tumbleweed* to the side and cut into a U-turn to get a better angle on the remaining three guns.

Another voice came over the Fernomare comm channel. "Yawning Lock actual. This is the *Shrapnox*. I am here to assist."

As the *Tumbleweed* completed its U-turn, Piper saw the approaching cruiser. It had a black hull with a red underbelly. It was slick, sharp-edged, covered in guns, and outmatched her upgraded tourist ship in every way.

"*Drit...*" Piper felt sweat bead on her forehead. "We have a problem." Another one of Sevodan's members threw their remote control to the floor, announcing the death of another mini-ship as the *Shrapnox* blew it out of the sky. Piper looked over her shoulder and shouted, "Grab that other turret! We have a real fight now!"

Sevodan's idle member strapped into the last remaining open turret gun station. The *Tumbleweed* was now ready to fire the railgun and the two turret guns on the port and starboard sides of the hull. Twelve decoy ships zipped around the sortie area, distracting the guns but not the pilot of the *Shrapnox*. It blew more of them out of the sky as it directly approached the *Tumbleweed*, heading at it straight on.

Piper fired the rail gun, forcing the *Shrapnox* to barrel roll to the port side. Sevodan fired at its underbelly as it rolled past, hitting it directly but not causing much damage. The cruiser's hull was thick and ready for war.

"*Drit*, he's gettin' behind us!" Piper shouted. "Keep firing on him!"

The two turret guns pivoted to fire backward and keep the *Shrapnox* occupied with dodging. The rail gun was in a fixed position, only able to fire ahead, so that is what Piper did. She pulled the trigger and fired at another AS gun, hitting it precisely as it fired on one of the decoy mini-ships. The explosion was a massive blue inferno of fire and fragmented scrap metal. Two more mini-ships were shredded in the chaos of the fireball. Piper flew through it, forcing the *Shrapnox* to pivot around it and lose momentum.

Seven mini-ships remained of the original fourteen. Sevodan floated their idle members to any open windows to try and keep an eye on the *Shrapnox*. The *Tumbleweed* shook from the damage it had taken flying through the explosion. Piper could feel the ship shudder, cut by a thousand tiny fragments of debris, and a cloud of thin smoke was tracing their wake.

"Two AS cannons left!" Piper shouted through her teeth. The *Tumbleweed* shook with the direct hit from one of the *Shrapnox*'s guns. "He's got a lock on us!"

Sevodan crashed a mini-ship into the front of the *Shrapnox*, blinding the pilot as the metal cutout jammed itself into the nose, temporarily blocking visuals through the windshield. Piper threw the *Tumbleweed* into a port-side U-turn, and the *Shrapnox* rolled to release the blindfold. It began its pursuit again, firing out of its side cannons as it tried to join the *Tumbleweed* in its about-face. The long distance between the starships made a chaotic firing pattern. Still, a few shots cracked against the side of the *Tumbleweed*, impacting the port side wing and turret gun.

"Hull breach!" Sevodan shouted. They floated below deck to repair what they could while Piper focused on the remaining AS cannons. One gun down. Six more mini-ships left. Piper lined herself up to hit both remaining anti-starship guns. She brought herself so low to the ground that the surface threatened to scratch the *Tumbleweed*'s belly. Blasts of scorched stone kicked up around the *Tumbleweed* as the *Shrapnox* fired on it.

Sevodan fired back with the remaining turret gun, striking it multiple times. They then diverted the remaining decoy mini-ships into the *Shrapnox*'s path, smashing them into its hull and causing the pilot to lose some of their pursuit's momentum in the chaos.

"This ought to throw him off!" Piper shouted. She grabbed the gateslinger and squeezed the top trigger. Two local portals launched out, and Piper slipped through, giving herself some distance from the *Shrapnox* and moving in closer to the AS guns. The movement within the same atmosphere didn't harm the *Tumbleweed* and gave her room to think. She immediately deactivated the portals behind her and fired the rail gun twice in succession, feeling the lurch of the gun firing like a slipcar crash.

The last remaining anti-starship cannons exploded into fire and metal, crashing down upon themselves. Piper navigated through the mess of debris and fire, dodging pieces of giant shrapnel as they came smashing into the ground around her. As she cleared the farthest explosion, the *Shrapnox* exited a portal directly in front of her flight path.

"NO!" Piper screamed as she pulled the flight stick upward and back. The *Tumbleweed* bashed into the top of the *Shrapnox* and began to roll forward. Piper struggled to orient herself as the ship spun wildly. On the verge of passing out from the intensity of the rolling, Piper felt something overtake her in the chair, followed by the *Tumbleweed* regaining its balance. Sevodan had grabbed the flight stick. One member surrounded Piper with tentacles, and another floated above Skipper in the co-pilot seat.

"Piper, you must get into the prison and save Levort and Kurnult," Sevodan said, unstrapping her from the pilot's seat.

"We need to get through that hangar door." Piper stood and allowed the Mulptre to take control of the *Tumbleweed*. She looked out the windscreen to see the giant metal square indented in Fernomare's flat surface.

It might take more than a railgun to punch through that. Piper realized with despair.

Another of Sevodan's members handed her a spacesuit and a backpack full of gateslingers. They said, "We will get you close enough to locally portal through it. Once you enter, you can find Levort and Kurnult and portal back to Bloom."

"What about you?" Piper asked.

"We will join you back on Bloom after we distract the *Shrapnox*." Sevodan brought the *Tumbleweed* around to face the *Shrapnox* again. "Portal downward when we give you the signal!"

Piper kissed Sevodan on the side of their balloon and said, "Thank you, friend."

Sevodan focused on thrusting toward the *Shrapnox* and firing the rail gun.

Piper rushed through the living room and down into the cargo hold, the lowest part of the ship, where two more of Sevodan's members waited. Piper slammed the spacesuit helmet on and pulled the rest of the suit over her body. She ensured the backpack full of gateslingers was tightly strapped to her back behind her life support. The space suit would only keep her alive in the extreme heat of Fernomare's surface for about three minutes.

The *Tumbleweed* rumbled with the impact of another shot, tossing Piper to the side. She grasped a nearby railing and held herself steady.

"Get ready!" Sevodan shouted, grasping the railing next to her. Their other member in the cargo hold burst as a plasma shot punched through the hull.

"Sevodan!" Piper shouted.

"Go now!" Sevodan pushed Piper into the middle of the room.

Without hesitating, Piper pulled the top trigger and fell through the portal. She emerged, freefalling into the open sky of Fernomare. The *Tumbleweed* zoomed away from her, the *Shrapnox* close behind. Piper was thrown sideways by the jet-black cruiser's close range and sheer speed, sending her tumbling as her ears filled with the roar of its engines.

Piper screamed, disoriented and falling through the scorching sky. She thrust her arms and legs out and managed to stabilize herself. The destroyed AS guns burned around her, casting pillars of smoke into the atmosphere. The giant hangar door raced toward her as she plummeted toward it without a parachute. She steadied the gateslinger in both hands and waited for the right moment.

Too early, and she'd emerge locally and smack into the hangar doors. Too late and, well, same thing.

Piper made her best guess and pulled the top trigger of the gateslinger, casting a mirrored surface in front of her. As she raced toward the portal, she watched the *Tumbleweed* soar into the

Fernomare sky in the reflection on its surface. A moment before she passed through the portal, the *Tumbleweed* exploded with the impact of the *Shrapnox*'s plasma guns. The jet-black cruiser vaulted through the fire and smoke that was once the *Tumbleweed* as Piper slipped through the portal and out of sight.

FORTY-EIGHT

Piper exited the portal, still in a freefall. She had made it through the hangar doors and into a large interior room. In the few breaths she was still falling, she noticed a group of enforcers waiting to greet her, guns ready and aimed. She launched another portal and fell through the floor, away from the welcoming committee, emerging on a vacant floor below them. Quickly she launched another local portal angled to the side to avoid hitting the ground directly.

Piper rolled across the floor until she smashed into a wall. She felt the breath leave her body, and she gasped for air. Piper removed her helmet and threw it to the metal ground away from her. She inhaled deeply, struggling to regain her breath and feeling every bump and bruise from her rolls through the portals.

"Hurry! I heard something down here!" The voice of a Dintuppan enforcer captain echoed from the floor above. The welcoming committee would be on her in seconds.

"*Drit*!" Piper looked around and saw she was on a ring-shaped metal catwalk lined with frosted prison cell walls. She pushed herself to a stand and portalled into the closest cell.

Piper emerged in front of an inmate with purple skin and four arms. As she entered the room and deactivated the portal behind her, the creature fell backward in shock. Piper took a moment to catch her breath and immediately gasped and fell backward as well when she realized she was standing before a Tayoxan Beyonder.

"You're… You're…" Piper stammered.

The Beyonder put their hands up in confusion and shook their head, wholly stupefied and concerned about the mysterious human who teleported into their holding cell. "I don't know—Please don't hurt me!"

Piper took a deep breath and shook off the shock of seeing a Beyonder in person. Before she could explain herself, she noticed the Beyonder looking at the frosted cell wall behind her. Muffled voices came from the other side, and shadows rushed past.

"She went this way!"

"Find her!"

Piper hoped the welcoming committee didn't start checking the prisoner cells. The colonists of Bloom had been training for cycles with the gateslingers, and it created a new mindset within them to think of using portals for almost everything. These prison guards had not done the same thing. They would have checked the cells first if they had.

The shadows moved away, and Piper sighed with relief. She put a reassuring hand outward to her new cellmate and whispered, "We don't have much time. At some point, they will check the cells to find me."

The Beyonder squinted at her and asked, "Who *are* you?"

Piper smiled. "Oh. Right! My name is Piper Cridhe. What's your name?"

"Sciolin," the Beyonder answered. "You're not working for Gulna Kii Fessenog, are you?"

"No, pretty much the opposite of that," Piper said, holding back a hysterical chuckle. *Keep it together.* "I came here looking for my friends, but it seems like there's more I can do than that." She rummaged in her backpack and felt her heart drop.

There were too many gateslingers. Sevodan had packed enough for all their members and more as redundancies, but they were all accounted for inside Piper's backpack. Every single one. She panicked.

You kept at least one, right? Tell me you kept one, Sevodan!

She felt something soft within the bag and stopped rummaging for a moment.

A crushed flowerpot, loose dirt, and a small weed were inside the bag.

"Oh, Sevodan..." Piper whispered as she carefully piled the dirt around Skipper's roots to keep the plant alive. The Mulptre had snuck her co-pilot into the backpack before sending her to the cargo bay. "You knew..."

The sound of the welcoming committee pounded around the catwalk outside, their search relentless. Piper grabbed one of the gateslingers from the bag, careful not to jostle Skipper too much. Piper steeled herself for the moment. She wouldn't let Sevodan's great sacrifice be in vain. She held the gateslinger out for the Beyonder. *Revolution it is!*

Piper stated, "You know what this is."

The Beyonder put a hand to her mouth, and tears shone in her large black eyes. She nodded. "It has been a long time since I've held one."

Piper put the gateslinger in the Beyonder's hand and said, "Can you help me find my friends?"

The Beyonder accepted the device and nodded. "I will try."

***

Levort and Kurnult heard the commotion outside. Their cell was in total disarray. The bed was moved to give them better access to the escape hole they had been carving at. They finally knew what was on the other side of the wall—a water drainage pipe, big enough for each of them to squeeze through. It was unclear where it would lead, but it was better than staying in the cell and waiting for Bayfo to return.

Levort was on his belly inside the pipe. He was crammed uncomfortably and about to start moving down the drain when the sounds outside their cell halted their escape. "You don't think it's—"

Kurnult was still within the cell, kneeling outside the escape hole. He whispered, "Abnat shouldn't be back for hours."

The sound of footsteps and rustling raced up to their cell. Kurnult grabbed the bed and shoved it back into position, resetting the scene as the frosted wall evaporated and revealed Captain Tegarl Myrs and a group of enforcer guards.

Levort wasn't sure what was happening. He was facing the wrong way and could only hear the sound of water babbling past him. He kept quiet. The raised voice of the Dintuppan captain barely bypassed the sound of dirty water. "Where is he?"

Kurnult said something, but Levort couldn't hear it. Another voice of a Kurikoid came through, "They took him!"

Levort whispered to himself, "They? What is happening?"

Captain Myrs got angry. "Grab him! They'll have to pry him out of our hands if they come back!"

There was a scuffle, and the bed moved in the fighting. Levort tried to hurry back into the cell, shoving himself backward in the pipe and pushing against the current. He emerged from the dented hole as the cell wall frosted over.

"Kurnult?" Levort whispered, his eyes wide and his mouth sagging open in shock. "No, no, no!" He pushed himself back into the room and scrambled out from under the bed. "*Kurnult!*"

Levort slammed his fist against the frosted cell wall and slunk to the floor. *What in Zhok was all that about?*

Light flashed against the frosted cell wall, followed by footsteps. For a moment, Levort thought the guards were returning to take him, but the footsteps weren't coming from the other side of the wall.

"Lev!"

Levort's eyes went wide. Slowly, he turned his head to see where the voice had come from. He felt the breath evacuate his lungs. He couldn't believe it.

Piper Cridhe stood within his cell. She wore a spacesuit, carried a backpack, and had tears in her eyes. She took deep breaths, as if she had been running for a long time. With her was a Tayoxan Beyonder holding a red gateslinger.

Levort practically flew across the room and embraced her tightly. She returned his hold, hugging him so firmly that he thought he might pass out, but he didn't care. Levort sobbed into her shoulder, allowing his disheveled hair and beard to soak in his tears.

"We're here to save you and Kurnult," Piper whispered.

"Kurnult!" Levort pushed himself out of the embrace and held Piper's shoulders. "The guards took him. I don't know—" He looked at the Beyonder, then at Piper.

Piper cursed. "*Drit*. They must have known we'd come for you. Why didn't they take you too?"

Levort gestured to his wet clothes. "We were breaking out. We broke a panel under the bed, and I was inside when they came in. They must have assumed you got me out."

Piper nodded. "We watched them come this way, but we were too busy keeping hidden to see where they took Kurnult. My guess is the guard shack on the top floor. They wanted to funnel me into a trap when I first arrived. Now they have bait."

Levort started to weigh the situation. "Where's everyone else? They didn't find them, did they?"

"Vobsii and Floem are sitting in the Fessenog Fleet mainframe," Piper explained. "They disabled the Fleet's ability to track our portals on Tayoxe. Sevodan…"

As she bit her lip, Levort felt his muscles go weak. "Oh no…"

Piper took a deep breath to steel herself. "A ship called the *Shrapnox* took out the *Tumbleweed*. Sevodan was piloting it at the time. They had me portal out and enter the prison while they distracted it."

"The *Shrapnox*…" Levort remembered the name of that ship. "Bayfo."

"Zhok, that means he's here somewhere. I'm sure he's going to be down here soon," Piper said, checking her gateslinger. "We should get back to Bloom."

"Wait." Levort looked at the Beyonder. Thoughts started to come to his mind. A plan—a *crazy* plan—began to grow. The Beyonder stared back at Levort, her eyes glowing with thoughts of revenge. She had been here for far more cycles than he had.

The Beyonder wanted the same thing he wanted.

"I don't like it. What's that look on your face?" Piper asked.

Levort's heart beat like an engine burning full throttle. His mind raced with ideas. He asked, "You can get back to Bloom, right?"

"Well yeah. The original plan was to portal back, get on the Curio ships, and leave for the Beyond," Piper explained, then she smiled. She was ready for whatever Levort had in mind. "What's the plan now?"

Levort looked at the Beyonder. He didn't need to say anything. They were both thinking the same thing. He turned to Piper and asked, "Can you get me my gear? I have an idea."

Piper launched a portal against the cell wall. "What are we doing?"

"First, we're going to free everyone in this prison," Levort said. "Then we're going to free *everyone* from the Fessenog Fleet."

FORTY-NINE

Wolil woke up when the bright light entered her cell. She weakly pushed herself off the floor and turned to see what it was.

"Is that…" She squinted, unsure of what she was looking at. There wasn't only one person in her cell. There were many. A bright shimmering oval silhouetted her visitors, and it took time for her eyes to adjust. First, she noticed a human wearing a cloak, his hand outstretched to help her up. Then she saw others like her. The native people of Tayoxe—or, as they called themselves now, Beyonders.

"Nova, take me," Wolil whispered as she took the human's hand.

"I had a feeling you were in here with me," the human said.

Wolil wobbled to her feet and took another look at the man in the cloak. She had to think back—cycles back—to recognize this man. The disheveled beard and hair didn't help her memory. But then she smiled and said, "Levort Aatra. It looks like you figured out how to use the gateslinger."

Levort smiled and embraced her. When he removed himself, he said, "We're freeing everyone. We have a little colony set up on a place we call Bloom. You'll be safe there."

Wolil patted him on the shoulder. She looked at the other Beyonders and recognized them all. "Sciolin. Geuba. Qaxu…"

These were the faces of Beyonders that had gone missing, the Tayoxans she had sent out to investigate the Below who had never returned. The exact people she had come back to Lodespace to find. "This was all my fault..."

Sciolin shook her head. "The only one we blame is Gulna Kii Fessenog."

Levort added, "There are others who were locked up here too. They are waiting on Bloom."

Wolil looked at the human. Tears welled up in her eyes, and she couldn't speak. She had no words to express how thankful she was. Her joy mixed suddenly with rage. She snarled and took a step back. "Damn Gulna! He can't get away with this."

Sciolin nodded. "He is a greater foe than we have ever faced before. Organized, ruthless, efficient, and well-equipped. We were all taken down within moments of entering Tayoxe airspace. The response time can mean only one thing."

Wolil spat the words: "He's using our technology against us. Bold of him. Maybe stupid."

"It's now his blind spot," Levort said. "My friends disabled his ability to track our portals. Tayoxe is open ground."

Wolil's heart skipped a beat. "Is that so? How did they pull that off?"

Levort shrugged. "I have creative friends."

Wolil smiled. "Indeed." She looked to the other Beyonders. "If we can move around Tayoxe freely... Has Gulna discovered the armory?"

Levort leaned in. "Excuse me? The what?"

Sciolin turned her head and raised her eyebrows. "We'd have to check."

"An armory? On Tayoxe?" Levort let out a low whistle. "A hidden armory would have been the score of eons when I was a prospector. Even one functional ship would have set me up for life in the Fleet."

Wolil cocked an eyebrow. "And now?"

Levort twirled the gateslinger on his finger. "Now, I've got a better life in mind."

Wolil shared heated glances with her fellow Beyonders. She could feel it in the dank cell air. She had dreamt of this moment for cycles, never thinking she'd actually be able to release her wrath on the Fleet. "It's time for Gulna to pay for what he's done to Lodespace."

The Beyonders smiled and bumped their many arms with each other.

Levort stepped to the side and gave the Beyonders access to the portal to Bloom. "You all go on ahead. We have plenty of gateslingers you can use. I have something I need to do here."

The other Beyonders stepped through the portal to Bloom, but Wolil hesitated. She asked Levort, "You're staying behind?"

Levort nodded. "My friend is being held captive in the guard shack. I have to save him."

"Bayfo Niall?" Wolil spat the name. "He's no friend."

Levort shook his head. "Not him. But he's waiting for me too. I need to settle this."

Wolil stared at the human. She couldn't decide if his bravery outweighed his foolishness, but she knew his loyalty was heavier than both. "You're one of us now, Levort Aatra." She smiled.

"Thank you. For everything." Levort bowed to Wolil as she stepped through the portal.

FIFTY

Commander Bayfo Niall marched through the door into the guard shack on the top level of the Yawning Lock. His Marothallan crew followed him a close step behind. They filled the room so quickly that they startled Captain Myrs and her fellow prison guards.

"Where is he?" Bayfo asked. He didn't need to elaborate.

Captain Tegarl Myrs had once been in command of Bayfo Niall, but ever since the incident with the portals, she had been exiled to work prison duty in the Yawning Lock with three other Kurikoid guards. Here, she could be forgotten about and keep the secrets she knew. The vocation was as good as imprisonment, minus the mistreatment by the patrolling robotic jailor.

Captain Myrs stammered, "He. We. I mean. We aren't…"

Bayfo unholstered his smitegun and kept it palmed. "I'm going to ask again, Captain Myrs. Where is Levort Aatra? I destroyed a ship with portal technology built into it, and I know they will try to find him. You better come up with a more suitable answer than *we don't know* if you want to keep your head on your shoulders."

Captain Myrs exchanged worried glances with her Kurikoid wardens. They had the Oristan named Kurnult tied up on his knees in the back of the shack. Even with her back turned to him, Myrs could feel the blades he sent into Bayfo with his three stern eyes. Myrs told Bayfo, "We entered Aatra's cell like you ordered, but he wasn't there. His cellmate was, though. We've brought him here in case Levort comes back to grab him. He'll have to get past us."

Bayfo snarled back at Kurnult. His second in command, Ucons, leaned into Bayfo's ear and whispered, "Levort Aatra could be anywhere by now."

Bayfo appeared to consider that Ucons might be correct in his assessment. If it were Myrs, she would have ditched the Yawning Lock and never returned. But she suspected Bayfo knew Levort Aatra better than that. If the prisoner hadn't given up his friends in a full cycle, he wouldn't abandon one now.

"No, he's here," Bayfo said with a sneer. He was certain. "I'm sure of it. Everyone split up and start checking cells."

Bayfo smiled at Kurnult, knowing Myrs's bait was too good for Levort to pass up. Myrs hid a sigh of relief. "If Levort wouldn't leave this Oristan behind, he must have a portal somewhere in this prison," she suggested, hoping to steer even clearer of Bayfo's ire. "Otherwise, he'd have to trek here from Tayoxe."

The commander shot Myrs a glare that indicated he'd already thought that through, then exited the guard shack with his crew of Marothallan enforcers. Myrs exhaled slowly, then pointed her smitegun at Kurnult.

"You're not going anywhere," she told him.

***

Bayfo and his enforcers stepped down the stairs onto the first rung of the prison and fanned out, some taking the lower floors. Abnat joined them and began defrosting the cell walls.

After the first cell opened, Ucons shouted, "Sir, there's a portal here!"

Bayfo's head snapped toward Ucons. "Check it!"

Ucons gripped his enforcer rifle and slipped through the portal. He returned a moment after stepping through and announced, "It leads to another empty cell."

One of Bayfo's other crew members, Rokkis, shouted from a lower rung, "Empty here too! But we have another portal."

"Come on, check the portals!" Bayfo was getting frustrated.

Rokkis mimicked Ucons's action, stepping through the portal and returning. "Same here. Leads to another empty cell."

"How many empty cells are there?" Bayfo shouted in anger.

Abnat responded, "All cells should be occupied."

Bayfo slammed his fist against the panel on the nearest cell. The frosted cell wall evaporated, revealing an empty cell with a portal hanging inside. He did as his men had, leaning his head inside the portal to discover the interior of another empty cell. "Damn it! Open them all!" Bayfo pulled his head back in and shouted up to the guard shack.

A moment later, all the frosted walls evaporated, revealing an entirely empty prison free of prisoners, except one.

Levort Aatra stepped out of a cell on the lowest floor and looked up at Bayfo Niall. He wore his old prospector's cloak and held two objects. One was a smitegun, and the other was a red gateslinger.

Bayfo didn't know how to respond at first. For a moment, the air hung still and hot. Bayfo stared down at Levort, and Levort looked upward at him, an old friend turned prey. Bayfo's shock turned to concern. Levort didn't look weak and scared like he had for the cycles Bayfo had been hunting him. Levort Aatra stood with the confidence of a man who was done running. Bayfo felt a bead of sweat race down his brow.

The sound of banging and bashing caused the moment to break.

Inside the guard shack, a Resluni and an Alberryan threw Captain Myrs and her Kurikoid wardens against the walls. A gunshot went off, lighting the room with a flash of plasma. Bayfo shouted to his closest man, Suvall, "Get in there! Don't let them escape!"

Suvall rushed up the stairs to the guard shack and was met with plasma shots. The Marothallan enforcer pushed himself against the doorframe and leaned in to fire on the intruders. Portals opened inside the guard shack, creating a kaleidoscope of mirrors and lights. The Alberryan grabbed Kurnult and jumped through one of them before it dissolved.

Suvall wasn't quick enough to stop their escape. He fired several more times as portals began to break down and vanish in the guard shack, revealing an empty room. Not even Captain Myrs or her Kurikoids remained. Then, a portal opened over Suvall, and the huge Resluni dropped down on him with a crunch. Before Bayfo could lift his smitegun and fire, the Resluni portalled away with Suvall.

"Enough with the tricks!" Bayfo looked back down to see that Levort had vanished from his position. Wasting no more time, Bayfo locally portalled himself to where Levort had been on the lowest rung. He stepped out of the portal to see an empty cell and heard screaming rush past him.

Rokkis plummeted into the chasm in the center of the cell pit. Levort now stood on the railing on the top floor, having switched positions with Bayfo. He stepped off the railing and portalled away. Bayfo roared with frustration and shot the portal in the cell next to him with his gateslinger, causing it to break down and dissolve. He watched as it created a chain reaction of portals shattering in every cell.

Every cell except one.

That's it!

It would be the path to Levort's compound. If he could lure Levort there, this chase would be over. Bayfo teleported his way over to the stray portal and had to dodge the robotic body of Abnat as Levort hurled it at him. Bayfo rolled sideways and watched as the mechanical jailor was blasted to pieces by Levort's smitegun. The jailor attempted to lift itself off the floor as one more plasma bolt struck it in the triangular head and caused it to burst.

Levort shifted his aim to Bayfo and pulled the trigger, striking the floor near his legs. Bayfo scrambled to his feet, surprised that Levort would not hesitate to open fire at him—despite the cycle of imprisonment he had just put his old friend through. Knowing Levort would follow, Bayfo threw himself through the stray portal.

He landed on the other side of the portal on his shoulder and rolled to a stop. Bayfo lifted himself off the dirty ground and readied his smitegun, expecting a world filled with Beyonder cultists. The portal he exited through shattered, separating him from his crew, the *Shrapnox*, the Yawning Lock, and Levort Aatra.

"No..." Bayfo whispered to himself. Mountains of junk and ruined skyscrapers lined the hills and valleys around him. His aim slacked as he realized he wasn't near Levort's Beyonder compound. The Fessenog Fleet was visible high up in the hazy sky, and Consonance Hub looked like an egg-shaped moon.

Commander Bayfo Niall was standing on Tayoxe.

It got eerily quiet. Even the light breeze hushed, and not even the loose pieces of metal rattled in the stillness. Bayfo could hear his heartbeat.

The sound of an in-atmosphere burst echoed across the landscape and jolted the junk-filled hills. A massive portal appeared overhead. A starfighter emerged from it, a design Bayfo was unfamiliar with. It raced out of the portal and toward the Fessenog Fleet high in orbit above. Another portal opened, revealing another strange starfighter, and more portals opened after that.

One hundred starships emerged from portals and raced toward the Fleet above. Bayfo shuddered at the raw awesomeness of the sight. He had no words and no idea what to do.

"It's all coming down."

Bayfo spun around to see Levort Aatra standing behind him a few yards away. The wind had picked back up, fluttering the tails of his prospector cloak. Levort stood tall, ready to fight but in no hurry to start a brawl.

Bayfo straightened himself and gripped his smitegun and gateslinger in his hands. He shouted to his old friend, "I told you it was all too dangerous! You didn't listen! Look what you're doing! There are innocent people up there who will die because of you!"

Levort shook his head. "You don't get it, Bayfo. The Fleet is a prison! We're going to free everyone from Gulna Kii Fessenog's empire of lies."

"You're blind!" Bayfo shouted. "You've traded everything for this wild lie. Now I'm going to have to stop you." He readied himself to pounce.

Levort lowered his head. "If this is how it has to be, let's finish it."

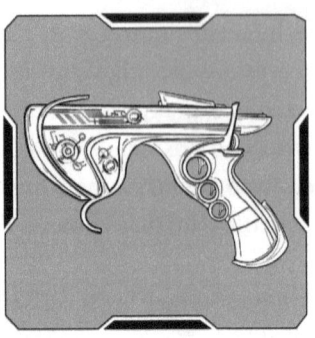

FIFTY-ONE

The vessels of the hidden Tayoxe armory soared into battle, engaging the Fessenog gunships and EMUs head-on. Some of the larger trading vessels smelled danger in the air. They began to thrust toward the giant Voyalten Portal to safety, making room for the starships to battle. The *Ultimatrion* and Consonance Hub remained, trapped by centuries of rest, their thrusters and engines unable to fire to move them to safer space.

Floem and Vobsii hitched a ride with Wolil. Her old Tayoxe warfighter was sleek and similar in design to the Curio ships. These warships had a lot of tricks up their sleeves, tricks not used since the last time the Tayoxe people had to fight off a threat like Gulna Kii Fessenog. Centuries hidden under the great abandoned cities had not worn them down. If anything, it had made them anxious to fight.

Wolil piloted the warfighter into the fray, dodging plasma bolts that zipped past her hull. An enforcer gunship approached, blaring its cannons. Wolil pulled one of the triggers built into the flight stick, and the Tayoxe warfighter portalled sideways. Wolil cut engines and let the void drift them farther away, granting them a clear angle. "Hit them!" she shouted to Vobsii.

"Oh, hohohoho! Been waitin' for this!" Vobsii said with a smile. He grabbed the handles on the turret control and turned the gun toward the enforcer gunship, then slammed his fingers down on the triggers. Using solid beams of light, the turret blasted the gunship into explosive fragments, eviscerating the enemy's hull.

"There we go!" Floem slapped her hand against Vobsii's shoulder.

"Target in sight, on me!" Wolil called out into the comm.

Other Tayoxe warfighters joined their flank as they raced for the blockade guarding the *Ultimatrion*—Gulna's personal squadron of fighters. The battle began in earnest. Tayoxan warfighters strafed and zipped around, using their unique portal technology—technology Gulna had hidden from the Fleet—to outmaneuver the gunships. Explosions rocked Wolil's ship as they pushed their way into the fight. Shrapnel from exploded hulls and other debris floated in the battlefield.

Wolil jerked the flight stick to the port side and let the Tayoxe warship barrel roll away from more incoming fire. Two enforcer mech units engaged their position. Wolil had accidentally rolled into one of the EMUs, allowing it to latch onto their hull.

"*Drit*! We have a clinger! Floem, can you scrape him off?" Wolil shouted.

"On it!" Floem slammed a helmet over her head and grabbed a large rifle with a built-in rail gun. She rushed into the airlock and found a winch cable and a sizeable blinking button. Floem strapped the line to the harness on her spacesuit as the airlock depressurized. She slammed her hand against the button, opening an airlock and giving her a direct view of the EMU crawling on their hull.

Floem leaned out sideways, aimed her rifle, and squeezed the trigger. A beam of light lanced out from the railgun and struck the EMU, obliterating its flank and blowing it open. The enforcer inside tumbled out and fell away from view.

Vobsii fired on the other trailing EMU but struggled to hit it. The mech unit was quick to the chase and almost as fast as the Beyonder ship. Wolil used evasive maneuvers to keep its weapons out of range, but it was closing in quickly. Plasma shots cracked against the hull, striking the metal near Floem's feet. Floem gripped the line on her harness and pushed herself off the hull, allowing it to go taut and swing her around the hull.

The EMU tracked her and shifted its aim.

"Floem!" Vobsii shouted from within, still trying to fire on the EMU but narrowly missing.

"Yeah, I got him!" Floem floated behind the Tayoxan warfighter, closing the distance between it and the EMU. The EMU fired at Floem, narrowly missing her and the line she was attached to.

Floem steadied the railgun in one hand, her feet dangling out into space. A ball of light grew at the end of her rifle. The EMU managed to strike a shot against the airlock her tow line was attached to, causing Floem to bounce and lose her aim. She released the rail gun in the chaos and grabbed the tow line, which luckily remained attached.

"*Drit*! I don't got him!" Floem shouted, holding onto the tow line and regretting her decision. Her rifle slammed into the EMU and ruptured, hitting it hard enough to knock the pilot out of his flight path and into Vobsii's turret fire. The turret blasted the rifle and ignited something inside, creating a tremendous explosion that blew the EMU into pieces.

"Just like I planned!" Floem shouted in triumph. She summoned her strength and pulled herself back to the airlock. Tayoxan warfighters and Fessenog Fleet gunships battled all around them as the *Ultimatrion* grew larger during their approach.

Wolil's voice crackled on the comm, "Floem! Get inside. We're going to portal into the *Ultimatrion*!"

"We're gonna WHAT?" Floem shouted. Her eyes went wide as the master ship of the Fessenog Fleet grew in size. She hustled back across the rest of the hull and slammed the button to close the airlock door.

"Strap in! This is gonna be rough!" Vobsii shouted.

"Normally, this would be a bad idea," Wolil admitted as she pivoted the warship.

"But now it's a good idea! Right?" Floem asked as she strapped herself into a seat.

"Nope! Still pretty bad!" Wolil pulled the top trigger on her flight stick, and a local portal launched out in front of the ship. Floem and Vobsii screamed at the top of their lungs as they entered the portal.

There was a tremendous explosion of sound and light outside the hull, and the occupants of the Tayoxan warfighter tested the limits of the crash seats. Floem felt the spacesuit's chest plate crack as she slammed against the restraints.

The warfighter screamed and crunched as it settled into an abrupt stop within the walls of the *Ultimatrion*, but its interior had remained intact enough. It would never fly again, much less be able to move into a cargo bay from its weird position inside the guts of the *Ultimatrion*.

The warship exhaled, and pressure returned to the interior of the ship. Floem could feel gravity ease off, pulling her down instead of back. She laughed, "We're not dead! Right? Everyone's not-dead?"

Vobsii grunted. "Still kick'n. Think I looked right into the Nova on that one, though."

Wolil unstrapped herself from the pilot's seat. She seemed unaffected by the chaos. "No time to waste. Look out the window."

Their view outside was filled with fire and smoke. Sparks flew, and metal sheared. The warship had abruptly popped into existence inside the *Ultimatrion*, yet it had suffered only minimal internal damage. The *Ultimatrion*, on the other hand, unexpectedly made room for the Tayoxe warship and had bent, blown, and melted anything in its way to accommodate.

Wolil grabbed a rifle and slung it over her shoulder. "Learned that trick accidentally when Gulna shot me down the first time. Tayoxan ships are built well enough to withstand a local portal into a solid object. Not sure if it was intentionally designed that way or not—but *drit*, it works." She shot a local portal through the windshield. "Let's go knock on Gulna's door." She moved through the gateway and appeared outside the warship, crouching on one knee and aiming her rifle ahead to face resistance.

Vobsii smiled and said, "I like hanging out with Wolil."

Floem grabbed another rifle off the wall and said, "Yeah. Same."

***

Explosions in orbit raged against the void.

Down below, Levort and Bayfo crashed into each other on the surface of Tayoxe. It was a battle of portals, plasma shots, and brawling. Levort exited a portal above Bayfo and smashed down on top of him. Bayfo, outweighing the prospector, held himself up and threw Levort off his back. He snapped his smitegun upward and shot, hitting only the sky as a portal appeared and dissolved with deadly efficiency.

Levort leaped out of a portal from Bayfo's side and blasted off a few plasma shots, missing his target by inches. Bayfo portalled sideways and ended up behind Levort, smashing the butt of his smitegun into Levort's cheek and drawing first blood. An explosion high in the sky created a dull boom.

Levort kicked Bayfo in the chest, knocking him backward. Levort, using the distance and Bayfo's unsteady balance to his advantage, charged into Bayfo. Before they both slammed into the ground, Levort shot out a wide portal, and they plummeted through the sky. After a short freefall, they hit the ground in a heap.

Vansparr boiled around them.

Thermal vents blasted steam into the air with high velocity. Bayfo threw Levort into one of the raging surges of water. The pressure was so hot and fast that Levort hit it like a wall and skidded off. It was as if he had fallen out of a moving vehicle. The speed and pressure of the thermal geyser tore through some of his cloak.

Bayfo got to his feet in time to see Levort launch a portal into the spraying geyser. Another portal opened in front of Bayfo, and the geyser erupted into his face. It threw him back, tumbling over himself as if he'd been hit by a slipcar.

Levort terminated his geyser portal and watched the steam dissolve into a thick fog. Bayfo launched himself from inside the mist, catching Levort off guard and smashing him to the ground. Bayfo was in control this time, and he launched another portal, sending them falling into another world.

***

"Join me!" Wolil shouted into the comm. They had made their way deep into the *Ultimatrion*, forcing back the enforcers guarding Gulna and pushing toward the boardroom. Floem and Vobsii were close behind, providing covering fire and picking off any enforcer who strayed too far out into the open.

Plasma bolts whipped back and forth down the hall. Wolil, Floem, and Vobsii were vastly outnumbered, and their cover was losing its integrity. They felt the *Ultimatrion* buck and shudder as more Beyonders portalled into the ship, a series of quakes erupting in succession. Floem could barely aim straight as the Fessenog ship tossed around with the impacts.

Portals opened, and more Beyonders joined their side, filling the hallways with plasma bolts and light beams. Wolil led the charge, pushing farther and farther into the ship.

"How does she know where to go?" Floem asked.

Vobsii shrugged and took another shot down the long hallway. "Dunno! But it's not like I know any better! Keep up with her."

The last of Gulna's personal guards lost his nerve and ran back toward the large door at the end of the hallway. He desperately slammed his hand against the door lock panel, pleading for it to open.

"Hey." Vobsii tapped the last guard on the shoulder. The guard screamed, and as he fumbled, his weapon fell to the floor. He went to reach for it.

"Come on, man. This is embarrassing," Floem said as she slammed her foot down on it. The guard shook with worry.

Wolil approached and jerked her head to the side, telling the guard to get lost. The guard whimpered and took off, running down the hall past the rest of the Beyonders grouping near the door.

"This is it!" Wolil shouted to her comrades. She pulled out her gateslinger. "Gulna and his directors are going to be inside. Get ready!"

Floem and Vobsii aimed their rifles at the door and nodded. Beyonders filled the hall behind them. Wolil looked at her comrades one more time, then nodded. Every Beyonder in the hallway pointed their gateslingers forward and sent out a portal. Floem and Vobsii followed Wolil into the room, popping out on the other side of the wall.

The boardroom was filled with an array of mirrors and lights. The Beyonders quickly stunned the few guards standing in the room. Gulna Kii Fessenog raised a smitegun to fire at Floem, but Vobsii beat him to the draw. He blasted off Gulna's arm from the elbow down.

Gulna screamed and cursed as he gripped the bleeding wound of what was left of his arm. The Beyonders had successfully neutralized all threats in the room. It was silent for the first time since the battle had begun.

Gulna snarled with impatience. "Well, get on with it!" he challenged Wolil.

Wolil approached the boardroom table. The other directors cowered under the ring-shaped desk, shivering and hoping they would somehow escape the Beyonders' wrath. Each of them had a Beyonder pointing a gun at their backs. Wolil didn't say anything at first, allowing Gulna to stew in his regret for a silent moment.

Gulna's impatience got the best of him, and he shouted, "What are you waiting for?"

Wolil touched the table and sighed. "I hate seeing what you've done to my ship."

"Oh, please," Gulna snorted. "It's *my* ship. And you are trespass—"

Wolil cut him off. "When we left the system, you were only some smug brat who worshipped the old bosses. What did you do after we left? Play Pretend Emporer and use our discarded things as your own?"

"I *built* this empire! You could only dream—"

"You built *NOTHING*." Wolil slammed her fist on the table.

Gulna jumped.

"*We* built everything, and you perverted it for your own selfish gains. You didn't make *anything*. You only shoved our inventions into little boxes and called them yours!" Wolil stared down as Gulna cowered, slipping onto one knee and holding his remaining arm up to shield himself.

Wolil turned to the other directors, aliens from all over Lodespace. "And all of you knew this! You came from everywhere and ignored what he had done to benefit from it. None of it mattered as long as it didn't affect you directly."

The other board members were quiet.

"Well, here we are. *Affecting you directly.*" Wolil spat the words. "This was inevitable. You just hoped it would happen after you died fat and rich."

Gulna stood up from the ground and tried to straighten his suit with his remaining arm. He regained his composure while Wolil watched with disgust. "So what?" Gulna countered. "*You* left *us*. We did what we needed to make space profitable for everyone. We brought people together. You come barging in here now, after all this time, to what? Shoot us? What heroes you are, so pious and perfect. You forget that we chose *not* to leave with you."

Gulna's words emboldened the directors.

Malxu weakly shouted, "Yeah-Yeah! He's-He's right!"

"True," Wolil conceded. "You chose not to come with us. You had every right to do that. It was what you did after we left that makes me sick. This is about the choices you denied others."

The Beyonders behind Wolil gripped their weapons tighter. They had spent cycles imprisoned in the Yawning Lock on Fernomare. They knew Wolil's words. They felt them.

Wolil looked at the other directors, then at Gulna. "It wasn't good enough that you ruled this part of the universe. You had to hide what we built from your people, because you knew no one would remain underneath your power if you didn't. So you expanded your empire and forced everyone in Lodespace to remain small. You mislead entire worlds, scared of what might happen if more of them chose to leave for the Beyond. You didn't give them the same choices we gave you. You took that from everyone."

Gulna squinted at Wolil. "I resurrected the empire you Beyonders let die. I built the Fessenog Fleet with my bare hands out of the garbage on hand. I could build fortresses out of mud! You can say all you want, but in the end, you know I did something the universe noticed here. It drives you mad that I didn't need to sail out into the void to accomplish this. Given a chance to do it again, I wouldn't hesitate for an instant."

Wolil and Gulna stared at each other for a moment. The room was quiet. Even the whimpering of the terrified directors had halted. There was nothing more to say.

Vobsii leaned over to Wolil and asked, "What should we do now?"

Wolil smiled. "Give him what he wants."

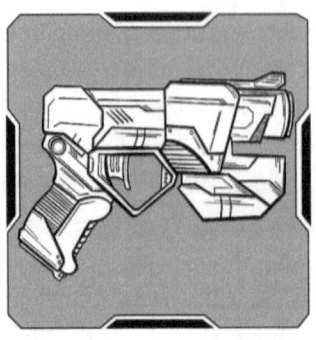

FIFTY-TWO

Levort and Bayfo tumbled through the air and splashed down into an ocean. Aquain engulfed them, stalling their fight as they scrambled to swim to the surface of the watery world. A few Fluctans swimming nearby noticed the strangers' arrival and watched them struggle to the surface.

Bayfo grabbed Levort's leg and pulled him back down before he could take a breath. Levort needed air. His lungs had pushed everything out as they impacted on the water. He was weak and struggling. Desperate, Levort pulled the trigger on his smitegun, and there was a flash of light. Bayfo's scream was muffled by quickly reddening water. Before Levort could take another shot, another portal opened and created suction, ripping both Bayfo and Levort through to another world.

They slipped through the portal and rolled down the side of a mountain foothill. The planet Dintup surrounded them with spires of rock and stone, everything jagged and sharp. The portal spewed water onto the foothill like a waterfall birthed in mid-air. Levort inhaled deeply and struggled to his feet. Bayfo deactivated the portal to stop the water flow and allow himself to stand up. He held his wounded arm and pushed himself to his knees.

Levort noticed his smitegun lying a few yards away from his

position. He pushed toward it and felt the white-hot searing pain of a plasma bolt tear through his leg. He cried out and tripped, his momentum sliding him toward his smitegun. Levort snatched the weapon with one hand and shot a new portal with the gateslinger in his other—all in one movement. Plasma shots cracked against the ground in his wake as he slid downhill through the new portal.

Levort landed on Zhok. His wounded leg lanced his body with a sharp stab as he crashed down onto the eerie crimson misted world. The hazy red star hovering in the permanently overcast sky haunted him still, and he begged the Nova not to let him die on this world. Levort pulled himself behind an outcropping of rocks as Bayfo dropped through the portal.

Bayfo swung his smitegun around, searching for Levort. "Come out and face me!" Bayfo shouted. His left arm was bleeding, staining his white commander's uniform as red as Zhok's surface. Levort was hidden, but not for long. He tore off part of his damaged prospector's cloak and tied it tightly around the wound on his leg. He gritted his teeth as the pain grew dull. His adrenaline masking it for now.

"This can only end one way, Lev! If you can't find reason, I have to stop you before you cause more damage. I didn't want it to be like this!" Bayfo shouted, his words echoing off the nightmare world.

Levort summoned his strength and prepped his next move. He launched a local portal toward Bayfo and dove through it only to be met with Bayfo's knee to his chest. Levort fell to his back but quickly kicked out at Bayfo's leg, sweeping his feet from under him. Bayfo fell to the ground, and Levort was on top of him instantly.

Levort brought the butt of his gateslinger down on Bayfo's head, drawing blood as he bashed him. Bayfo returned the assault and swung his smitegun at Levort's head. It struck Levort hard enough to knock the prospector off. He rolled sideways and launched another portal to catch himself.

Levort landed in a pile of deep snow. Golt wafted with streams of icy mist as the cold wind raked at his body. Any moisture remaining on him from Aquain immediately frosted over, putting a chill into Levort's bones. He got to his feet and tried to find a better position to face Bayfo.

Levort cried out as he tried to stand and run. The pain in his wounded leg came back in force. He couldn't hide. The blood that leaked from him gave his position away, trailing in the snow like a big red arrow. Levort knew he couldn't last much longer. Bayfo was ruthless and clever. He was a killer, and Levort wasn't. Even after all of this, Levort knew he couldn't kill Bayfo. It wasn't in him.

A gunshot.

Levort's back right shoulder exploded with burning pain, and he was thrown forward, face-first into the snow. The wind howled, and the icy cold invaded Levort's body like a flood. He rolled onto his back and looked up into the Golt night sky. The moons had blanketed the snow with light, giving the planet a soft blue glow.

Bayfo approached and stood over Levort. His smitegun exhaled a thin trail of smoke, and he was gasping for air. His wound was also taking its toll. The two old friends were bloody and battered, having fought across the universe and back. Bayfo took a few deep breaths and lifted his smitegun.

"You should have listened to me," Bayfo said as he gripped the weapon.

"I'm sorry." Levort whispered the words through his teeth, his voice quiet, his eyes full of tears.

"Goodbye, Lev." Bayfo sneered.

Bayfo pulled the trigger on his smitegun.

Levort pulled the first trigger on his gateslinger.

A local portal burst into existence between Bayfo and Levort just as Bayfo shot. The plasma bolt flung into Levort's portal shield and emerged behind Bayfo. Bayfo coughed as his own plasma bolt struck him in the back. The deadly laser continued through his body into the portal shield, where it emerged again to hit him a second time.

Bayfo's smitegun dropped into the snow.

Levort deactivated his portal shield and saw Bayfo drifting in place as blood spilled from his wounds. He coughed, and blood spat from his lungs. He looked at Levort, his eyes tearing up with immense regret.

Bayfo whimpered, "*Lev?*"

Levort lunged for Bayfo, catching him before he hit the ground.

In the same movement, Levort portalled downward, and they landed in a meadow on Bloom. Flower petals exploded around them.

Levort held Bayfo in his arms. The flowers they had disturbed drifted down around them in lazy arcs, like slowly moving rain on a half-cloudy day. The warm air eased the frost of Golt away, and the smell of wildflowers was everywhere. It was quiet, except for the ragged breaths of an old friend.

Levort didn't know what to say.

Bayfo looked up at the slowly drifting flower petals. He blinked a few times and whispered, "Where...are we?"

Levort let a stray tear fall from his eye. "This is Bloom."

Bayfo winced and looked to the side. In the distance, the colony dotted the hillside. Residential buildings pocked the flowers, and Curio starships awaited their departure. Everyone was so busy that no one had noticed the prospector and the enforcer fall into their world. The colonists continued their day as if nothing was happening.

Levort didn't notice the others in the distance. His muscles were weak, his wounds searing with burning pain. But his eyes were locked on Bayfo. Nothing else around mattered. It was as if the universe had gone dark, and Bayfo was the only star left—fading rapidly.

"This is...your colony?" Bayfo asked through deep, ragged breaths.

Levort nodded. "Yeah. What do you think of it?"

Bayfo's tears dripped onto the prospector's ripped cloak sleeve. He smiled. "It's nice."

Levort winced. "Thank you."

Bayfo crunched his face together and lifted himself into a sitting position with great effort. He faced away from the colony buildings and looked out into the vast flower-filled horizon. His breathing was ragged, and his face grew pale.

Levort offered, "We need someone to treat your wounds."

"Just...sit with me." Bayfo looked down, his eyes wide, the realization setting in. Levort knew it too. There wasn't much time left. The prospector took a seat next to the enforcer.

Bayfo's breaths became weaker. "Lev, I'm..."

"It's okay."

"I'm...jealous," Bayfo admitted.

Levort shook his head. "What?"

"I have....always been...jealous...of you..."

Levort felt weakened by the response. "Why?"

"I...was never...*content*... I had...everything... You had...nothing..." Bayfo coughed, and his eyes fluttered. "I always...needed more... And I needed you to...have less than me..."

Levort's breath caught. "Is that what this was all about?"

Bayfo didn't answer.

Levort looked at the horizon. The breeze wafted the scent of wildflowers into his nostrils, sending a cool wave through his soul. He whispered, "When I was just a scared kid living in a sorting facility, you were there for me. I will never forget that. You were the big brother I never had—the family that stepped in after my first had abandoned me. Even if you didn't feel it that way, I did." Levort Aatra shook his head. "I wish it wasn't like this. I wish you could have joined us."

Bayfo's tears ceased, and his eyes closed. He sighed his last words. "Me too."

The enforcer's head sagged on his shoulders, and his last breath seeped through his lips. Levort didn't look away from the horizon. He knew Bayfo had passed, but he couldn't bring himself to look at his old friend. Levort told himself that if he didn't look to his side, Bayfo was still there. If he kept his eyes on the flowers, he kept Bayfo alive.

The prospector sat with the enforcer a little longer.

One last time.

FIFTY-THREE

Gulna Kii Fessenog struggled to push himself off the ground with one arm. He felt like he still had both arms, but as he flopped into the mud, he tasted the adjustment to come. The shouts of his fellow board members were cut short as they also flopped face-first into the ground. The steady rain drizzled down on them.

The world onto which Gulna and the rest of the directors were being thrown was filled with ankle-deep mud and small islands of rocks. The sky was gray with a blanket of overcast clouds, and the rain was light but consistent enough to keep everything drenched to the bone. There was no sign of civilization, no flora taller than stray grass, and no Fleet to overlook it all.

To Gulna, this was Zhok.

Malxu, the Kurikoid member of the board of directors, shook the mud off his face and shouted, "You-you can't do this to us! You'll-you'll send us to our deaths!"

Another board member was thrown into the mud from beyond the portal. Wolil stood on the side with the muddy directors and laughed. "On the contrary, Director Malxu! Gulna Kii Fessenog promised to build you a fortress here! The Fleet *we* built wasn't a true test of your rock-hard ingenuity and work ethic. But *this* world?"

Wolil stretched out all four of her arms and took a deep breath of humid air. "This is *your* world to reign in! Time to show us what you've got."

Malxu clapped his hands together and begged, "Please-please! I-I didn't want any part of Gulna's plan to hide the Beyond! I-I—"

Gulna cut him off. "Oh, just shut up, you bulby-eyed coward. They know better."

Malxu's bulbous eyes shifted over to Gulna, and he snarled. "This-this is *your* fault! I-I'll kill you, Gulna!" Malxu lunged at Gulna, who stepped back and watched as the Kurikoid belly-flopped at his feet.

Wolil laughed. "I have a feeling you are all going to do great."

Gulna snarled at Wolil. "It'd be smarter to kill us. I'm going to find you, and when I do, I'll—"

Wolil exhaled loud enough to cut him off. "I invite you to try, Mr. Fessenog. Listen, I have an appointment to run to. Until next time, everyone!" She waved a hand and added, "I wish you all the best of luck in your future endeavors."

"Wolil! I'll find you! Mark my words—*Agh*!" Gulna yelped as Malxu bit him on the ankle. The other nine directors jumped on Gulna, pushing him into the mud and beating him down.

***

Vobsii dusted off his hands after throwing the last director through the portal. Floem sat in Gulna's old seat and played with one of his expensive tablet pens. The Beyonders discussed things well above Floem and Vobsii's knowledge.

Wolil came back through the portal and dissolved it. All eyes were on her. She stepped into the center of the room so they could all get a better look. She asked no one in particular, "*Assurance*, can you give me the comm?"

The room around them lit up with blue holographic light. The wall behind the director's seats opened, revealing a floor-to-ceiling window that showed them the Fleet—a shutter that Gulna had kept shut for hundreds of cycles. The *Ultimatrion* was responding to its true name after a long slumber under Fessenog control.

Holographic heads-up displays floated into space around Wolil, giving her a view of every ship left in orbit around Tayoxe and even a few shuttles left on the abandoned world's surface. She looked at her fellow Beyonders, then to Floem and Vobsii.

"Can you get us in contact with Bloom?" Wolil's voice was strong and gentle at the same time.

"Uh…" Floem blinked and kicked herself into gear. "Yeah. One second." Floem rummaged through the items she had on hand and found the antennas for a jump-phone. She launched a portal to Bloom and tossed one end through it. "Comm's all yours, Wolil."

Wolil nodded. "Thank you." She looked at everyone in the room and told the ship, "*Assurance*. Patch me through."

"Presenting to all local comms," the ship responded in a voice similar to Wolil's.

Wolil inhaled a gentle breath. She was relaxed. It was as if an enormous weight had been removed from the universe, and she was breathing fully for the first time since she began her mission.

"Many of you may not know me. My name is Wolil," she began her speech.

Confused and scared from the battle, the various alien people of Lodespace turned their attention to any screen they could. Wolil's image was displayed on every datapad, city screen, marketing bar, starship bridge, and device with a flat data surface. Many observers had never seen a Tayoxan native before. Most had never heard of the Beyond, nor would they believe it existed. Gulna had been thorough enough to ensure that. But they needed some answers and to know what was next.

"I was once a native of Tayoxe, long ago. Our culture began to expand in all forms of thought. When we heard of other worlds like our own, collectors who uplifted each other, a new way of life was presented to us. We call it the Beyond.

"The battle you witnessed ensued because your former leaders chose to hide all the technology we had invented to achieve our access to the Beyond. So thorough were they that they began to imprison my people in secret, siphoning our knowledge to trickle it to you for hapron.

"We fought not because we wish to force you to go to the Beyond, but to give you the tools we made so you could live how you want.

The Beyond is a choice, but the technology is revolutionary. It should not be kept from you to make more hapron off your misinformation.

"We will not leave this system unguarded and in chaos. We understand that life must continue here and that no one has signed up for this. We are not conquerors. We are here to free you from the restraints Gulna Kii Fessenog and his board of directors placed on you.

"And so here is the new Fleet. We will make our technology available to all who wish to use it. We will hold elections for those who can keep the Fleet running smoothly—without the barrier of lies and exploitation. We will ensure the people are given what they need to live the way they want and open access to all of Lodespace. No longer will you be shackled by fees and licenses. Hapron does not rule you.

"It may not be easy. There will be problems and sacrifices, but there will be a new future when the dust settles. A future of freedom. A future of choices built on intelligence and cooperation instead of misinformation and greed. We have not come to control you, only to give you many paths forward. It will be a future you decide on."

Wolil paused for a moment, then nodded. "We will build something together. For now, sleep soundly. The danger has passed. Let your curiosity stir and think of brighter days ahead. I am Wolil, and Lodespace is now yours."

It was quiet when she finished. This was a giant endeavor, and everyone who heard Wolil's words knew it wouldn't be easy. A hush of reflection overtook everyone, but a wave of curiosity replaced it. With that came hope—even excitement.

Vobsii was the first to say something. "What should we do now?"

Wolil smiled at him. "You should do whatever you like. My people and I will work here, ensuring we aren't leaving Lodespace in disarray. We want these people to be happy, and any of them who wish to join us in the Beyond are welcome. Once we have established a solid direction in Lodespace, we will return to the Beyond, mission accomplished."

Floem smiled. "But we're free to go there now?"

Wolil chuckled and nodded. "Yes. We will handle this."

Floem gave a hurrah, and Vobsii cheered with her. Their excitement was infectious, and suddenly there was a celebration on the bridge of the *Assurance*. Beyonders embraced each other, and friends who had been long-time captives in the Yawning Lock were reunited. Joy was in the air, and excitement for the future of Lodespace was abundant.

After celebrating, Floem and Vobsii said their goodbyes to the Beyonders on the *Assurance*. Wolil was the last to bid them farewell. "Thank you for everything you have done here. We will make sure to visit Bloom before your journey begins. Everyone here wants to thank those who rescued us from the Yawning Lock."

Floem hugged her and turned to Vobsii. "All right, Vobb. Let's head home."

FIFTY-FOUR

It had been a few quarters since the battle for Lodespace. Things had begun to settle, but they would never be the same. In the initial chaos of the power shift, the Fleet's economy had gone extinct. Many desperate people needed assistance to forge a new way of life that didn't rely on the Fleet being the powerhouse hapron generator of the universe. Luckily, it was easy enough to own a gateslinger. With the flick of a trigger, your life could change, and you could keep changing it until it worked how you wanted it to.

With Beyonder technology, the transfer of power was already beginning to stabilize. The tech was so efficient at bringing people together that negotiations and preparations were done much more quickly than had ever been accomplished in a misleading system built on greed.

Things were already on the upswing in Lodespace and would only improve with time. Life was more hopeful. Prospectors no longer had to scavenge for scrap to make a living. Enforcers no longer had to press down on the populace to hide the Beyond. Civilians no longer had to sell everything they owned to afford a license to move around freely.

It certainly helped that the Beyonders were brilliant enough to organize it all.

Those who yearned for the Beyond set out in Curio ships. Their journey would be long, but their yearning for the unknown outweighed their worry. More Curio ships were built to replace the ones that left, and soon it was common to set out for the mysterious zone in space. The path was open to anyone with the curiosity to walk it.

***

Levort Aatra allowed the scent of wildflowers to wash through his body. The wind blew his hair, and he could feel its gentle warmth on his closed eyelids. He still wore his refurbished prospector's cloak. It felt lucky, and he couldn't shake the old superstitions. This cloak had showed him Wolil's ship on Tayoxe and sent him on a path where he found his new friends.

Vobsii, Kurnult, Piper, and Floem—carrying a recently repotted Skipper—approached Levort and plopped down in the flowers beside him. Levort welcomed his friends with a smile and enjoyed the late afternoon sun with them.

Floem sighed. "Beautiful day, isn't it?"

Levort smiled. "Been nice for a little while."

Everyone agreed.

Eventually, Vobsii asked, "So what about today? It being so nice and all."

"*What* about today?" Levort asked.

Floem shoved him playfully, breaking his meditation. "You know what he means! Are we going to the Beyond or not?"

Levort laid on his back and looked up into the cloudless pink sky. "We can go whenever you want."

Vobsii shook his head. "I know. But..."

Levort turned his head to him and said nothing.

Kurnult grinned but remained respectfully silent. The Sight had already informed him of everything he wanted to know.

Floem waved her leafy hands through Skipper's petals, petting them gently. "I think I see why you're hesitant."

Levort raised his eyebrows.

"We built so much here. It seems sort of wasteful to just up and leave it," Floem admitted. She looked at Levort and said, "Vobsii's been saying the same thing too."

"Have not!" Vobsii blurted. "Okay, yeah. Seems wasteful. Sure."

Levort tilted his head a little.

Piper whistled and looked away from the group.

Floem pointed her finger accusingly. "And Piper and Kurnult!"

Piper mocked a *How dare you!* face.

Kurnult shrugged. "It is true."

Floem looked at Skipper and added, "Sevodan would have agreed too."

There was a silence that followed. Levort looked back up into the sky. They were slow to believe it. They had hoped their ballooned friend would show up unexpectedly for some time after the event. But in time, they had to accept the truth. Sevodan sacrificed everything so that their friends could have a better life. The Mulptre had saved every prisoner in the Yawning Lock. The Beyonders never got to know their savior. Levort would forever be grateful for Sevodan's sacrifice.

Levort sat up and put his arms on his knees. "I *do* want to go to the Beyond."

Everyone looked a little slapped.

Until Levort added, "Someday."

They exhaled in unison and nodded to each other.

Piper smiled. "Yes. Someday. Someday sounds good."

Vobbsii looked up into the clear sky and grunted his approval. Kurnult joined his grunting with his own purring.

Floem nodded in agreement. "Yeah, I do too. Someday. Now that the Fleet isn't killing or capturing people to hide it, there's suddenly no rush to go to the Beyond. Curio ships are available anytime, and we can go whenever we feel like it. But…"

Levort added, "It's a long journey."

Kurnult whispered, "One hundred cycles."

"Nothing would be the same if we ever came back," Piper mused.

Vobsii looked down at the flowers. "Bloom might not be *our Bloom* anymore if we did."

Floem squeezed her leafy face and said, "And truth be told, I've always been afraid of commitment."

The journey to the Beyond was like the trip from Tayoxe to

Fernomare, but with a much higher time debt cost. Launching from the closest accessible point in the Voyalten Web would take over one hundred cycles of stasis. Returning to Lodespace would cost another hundred cycles, meaning they would leave everything they knew behind permanently.

Wolil proved the high cost when her people left Tayoxe. When they'd departed, Tayoxe was still a highly advanced civilization. Upon their return, Gulna Kii Fessenog had taken over Lodespace and hidden their existence. Their planet was abandoned and stripped of everything that made it special. No one knew what they might return to if they were to leave again.

Levort laughed.

"What's so funny?" Vobsii asked.

Levort shook his head and said, "We spent all this time trying to reach the Beyond. We solved so many problems and fought so many fights. We had our adventures and our trials and survived them all. We fixed Lodespace and made life so good here…"

Floem nodded in agreement, and Piper smiled and looked over the horizon toward the colony. Kurnult kept all three of his eyes on Levort, and Vobsii took a deep breath of wildflower air. Skipper didn't react in any noticeable way.

Levort said, "It's like we accidentally made our own Beyond. Right here, right where we're sitting." He put a hand up and let it drift. "The Down Below Beyond."

"Made it ourselves." Floem chuckled.

"Homegrown. All natural, Belower made Beyond," Piper jested.

Levort stood up. He looked to the horizon. "Maybe we never needed the Beyond. It's not about the place. It's about accomplishing the goals you set for yourself. We all have our own happiness we work toward, but I think it's important to know when you've found it. I have found it here."

Vobsii stood up and dusted off his pants. "So what do we do now?"

Levort laughed. "Whatever the Zhok we want. The universe is our playground. We'll go to the Beyond when we're ready. For now, let's just be happy with what we have right here."

"I like the sound of that," Piper said.

Kurnult stood and said, "I am glad we all know it now. It was frustrating keeping all of your Sights to myself."

Vobsii laughed.

"Then it's settled!" Floem stood and shoved Levort into the flowers, then dashed off in the opposite direction. The others ran through the flowers, shouting loudly and celebrating their decision. Levort laughed and scrambled to his feet to chase them through the wildflowers of Bloom. Skipper waited patiently on the ground.

In the distance, a Curio ship lifted away from the colony and soared off into the stars.

Levort and his friends had already made their journey. They had found their Beyond, and they embraced it fully.

DRAMATIS PERSONAE
THE MAIN CAST

BAYFO NIALL | LEVORT AATRA | WOLIL

FLOEM ZEU UUBOG | VOBSII ESSAURNTII | PIPER CRIDHE

SEVODAN | KURNULT YREIN | SKIPPER

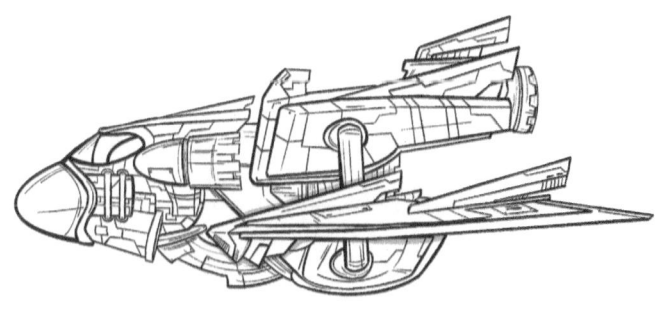

SIDECAST

Cythemi *(Erunian)*
A gentle matriarch of the humble village of Eukotall.

Captain Tegarl Myrs *(Dintuppan)*
A captain of a small squad of enforcers.

Darbles *(Kurikoid)*
A shifty gang leader of the village of Phiburb.

Gulna Kii Fessenog *(Marothallan)*
The founder of the Fessenog Fleet and head of the Fessenog Board of Directors.

Anduln Yrein *(Oristan)*
The oldest surviving Oristan.

Abnat *(Robot)*
A mechanical jailor of the Yawning Lock.

Ucons *(Marothallan)*
The second in command of Gulna's most trusted enforcer elites.

ALIEN RACES

(In alphabetical order)

Alberryan *(origin: Alberrya)*: Highly sought after for starship crews, Alberryans are plant people who can scrub CO_2 and exhale breathable oxygen. They do not die. Instead, they become rooted and turn into a tree.

Dintuppan *(origin: Dintup)*: Crustacean with a humanoid body. Dintuppans are born tough to cope with the mountainous terrain of their homeworld, Dintup.

Erunian *(origin: Erunia)*: Erunians live in four stages and require blood to ingest to grow their form. They have blood sacs under their exoskeleton that they can retract their entire bodies into once they are ready to up-phase. They must do this three times in life, or their internal organs grow too large for their exoskeleton. They are considered parasitic but intelligent enough to have developed a solution for their species in Carbon Farming.

Fluctan *(origin: Aquain)*: Fluctans are best suited to water-filled environments. Outside of water, they use a vehicle called a flitskipper to move around more easily.

Human *(origin: Kamaria)*: After being driven out of their original star system long ago, humanity found a new beginning on Kamaria. They adapt well to most situations and are highly capable of making allies. Still, humans are rare within the Voyalten Web.

Kurikoid *(origin: Kurika)*: Kurikoids have large bulbous eyes and often croak when they speak. They are bred within spawning pools, where they mature into adulthood despite still looking like children until they grow elderly. The lifespan of a Kurikoid is notably short compared to most Lodespace races.

Marothallan *(origin: Marothall)*: The most common civilized lifeform in Lodespace. They replaced the Tayoxans after their mysterious departure from the Voyalten Web.

Mulptre *(origin: Grotrane)*: A hive-mind race of balloon-sacked creatures. Their existence is unknown to most of Lodespace.

Oristan *(origin: Orist)*: Oristans are witnesses to the Sight, a mysterious ability to read the aura of all things.

Resluni *(origin: Marothall)*: Hulking reptiles with tentacle-like whiskers protruding from their snouts. They are often used for manual labor due to their size and strength.

Tayoxan *(origin: Tayoxe)*: The mysterious race that abandoned Tayoxe. Nothing is known about their departure. The Fleet has made sure to hide all knowledge of their existence.

Voyalten *(origin: Faultasma)*: The creators of the Voyalten Portal Web. They are a race of phantoms from a world with no light who discovered ways to travel the universe and create a link between worlds. Not many people have interacted with the Voyalten, but almost everyone has benefitted from their achievements. *To learn more about the Voyalten, read the "Song of Kamaria" trilogy.*

Xikoling *(origin: Golt)*: Creatures that are feline and fungus. They keep warm in their frontier mining towns, forging underground cities in peace off the Voyalten grid.

PLANETS

(In alphabetical order)

LODESPACE WORLDS

Alberrya *(Biome: Forest):* A welcoming world full of meadows and thick forests. A hot spot for starships looking to crew up.

Aquain *(Biome: Ocean):* An ocean world home to sea-dwelling creatures who live in underwater bubble cities. Considered one of the top trading partners to the Fessenog Fleet.

Dintup *(Biome: Mountain):* A world cluttered with mountains that births tough, crustacean-like people. The world is covered in large stone castles dating back to the origins of Lodespace.

Dive (Biome: Canyon): Considered one of the most beautiful worlds on the outer rim of Lodespace. Rivers sliced into canyons gave rise to cliffside cities.

Erunia (Biome: Grassland): Home to phase-changing creatures, both civilized and wild. The Fessenog Fleet extorts the Erunians for their rare luxury food items.

Fernomare (Biome: Inferno): Sister planet to Tayoxe. Not many are aware Fernomare has a prison under its surface called the Yawning Lock.

Fessenog Fleet (Biome: Orbital Trade Hub): The center of trade for all of Lodespace and the most extensive collection of ships that has ever been assembled throughout the Voyalten Web.

Grotrane (Biome: Industrial): Another dirty secret of the Fessenog Fleet. The world is now a series of trenches, mines, and shipyards, and it uses forced labor to build luxury starships.

Jofnalg (Biome: Jungle): A dense jungle world on the outer rim of Lodespace. Often used to export both jungle plants and wildlife to various other planets.

Kurika (Biome: Swamp): A swamp world dotted with large breeding pools and even larger wildlife. Due to the short lifespan of Kurikoids, civilization on Kurika uses medieval age level technology.

Marothall (Biome: City): The whole planet is considered one giant city. Overpopulation led to the birth of the Fessenog Fleet.

Tayoxe (Biome: Abandoned): Once a thriving civilization, Tayoxe has been abandoned by its people. It has been picked apart by the Fessenog Fleet and turned into an acid bowl filled with mountains of junk and refuse.

OUTER-WEB WORLDS

Bloom (Biome: Flower Meadow): A world filled entirely with flowers. There is no lifeform bigger than a common insect on its surface.

Golt (Biome: Tundra): Off-grid mining world covered in snow, ice, and glaciers. The people who live there are half feline and half fungus and dwell underground or in their frontier mining towns.

Orist (Biome: Desert): A dying world consumed by a plague that had left all but two Oristans alive. It is a desert world pocked by small domiciles made of spherical bushes.

Vansparr (Biome: Thermal): A world made of crystal and steam. Underneath Vansparr's boiling surface is a cold interior filled with pools of mineral water capable of healing deep wounds.

Zhok (Biome: Nightmare): Given the same name as the place where bad people go after they die, Zhok is scary to most who observe its surface. It is layered in a thick crimson fog, uneven terrain, and thorny vines.

ACKNOWLEDGMENTS

Down Below Beyond was such a fun novel to write. It's a story about people coming together to achieve something extraordinary. Just like the story of *Down Below Beyond*, it took many people to help bring this book to life.

To my wife, Carrie. She was an expert at nodding her head and pretending like any of the crazy words I was saying made sense. I am fortunate to have her love as my constant guide. She keeps me from drifting too far off into space.

To my kids, Nathan and Adam. They were still forming their personalities when I finished *At the Threshold of the Universe*. Now they are full-fledged humans! They make our days better, and I love watching them grow. I wonder what stories they will tell me in the future. If we're lucky, maybe we will visit *their* worlds one day.

To my mom, who has been my biggest supporter, and not just because she's obligated to be! Her support has always been outstanding, and I am thankful for all the effort she put into her beta reading. It truly has made this work readable.

To my dad, who encouraged me to read *Gateway* by Frederik Pohl my entire life. *Gateway* was a massive inspiration for this novel, and his prodding me to read classic sci-fi literature is what urged me to write my own novels.

To Maria and Jason, for helping me do a little thought experiment that led to the creation of a few alien races included in the book. Getting help with those initial thought exercises is a great way to brainstorm a world. Outside input helps keep it fresh!

To the book bloggers I've met since the *Song of Kamaria*. There are more of you now, and I am so happy to keep crashing into you on the internet! To Scarlett at *Through Novel Time & Distance,* Lorraine at *The Book and Nature Professor,* Andrew at *Andrew's Wizardly Reads,* Adrian at *SFF Addicts Podcast,* Athena at *One Reading Nurse,* Nick at

Wicked Good Books, Alyssa at *Into the Heart Wyld,* Sue at *Sue's Musings,* Justin at *Escapist Book Tours,* Rowena at *Beneath a Thousand Skies,* B-Man at *The Tipsy Trope,* Anj at *A Pocket Full of Tomes,* Isabelle at *The Shaggy Shepherd,* and Elise at *100 Acre Wood Library.* I hope there may be more after the writing of this novel! Thank you so much for reading. You are amazing, and I love reading your reviews.

To my team of freelancers, who brought this novel across the finish line in glorious style! Tom Edwards designed the amazing cover you see on the front, I was floored by it the first time I saw it! Alana Joli Abbott was wonderful to work with as a copy editor, and really knew how to pull out more detail in my characters with little additions to each sentence. Isabelle Wagner is not only a great book reviewer, but she did a fantastic job proofreading this book. It was really fun working with someone who knew and enjoyed my work prior to working together! And of course, what is a novel without its formatting? Lorna Reid is my go-to formatter, and I am always thrilled to work with her. Bravo team! Cheers to a job beautifully done!

To my fellow authors whose works I have also enjoyed. To Jonathan Nevair of *Stellar Instinct,* Peter Hartog and his "Guardian of Empire City" books, G. M. Nair with *Duckett & Dyer: Dicks for Hire,* and many more. I look forward to jumping into more adventures. Thank you for not only supporting me but for introducing me to your worlds as well. Reader, go read those books! They rock!

To my readers, I have no more words, but I will try. You are the lifeblood of these stories. Without readers, words are only ink on a page. Your imagination fuels our worlds, and I hope you enjoyed these stories.

Cheers everyone!
—T. A.

ABOUT THE AUTHOR

T. A. Bruno grew up in a suburb south of Chicago and moved to Los Angeles to pursue a career in the film industry. Since then, he has brought stories to life for over a decade as a previz artist. At home, he is the proud father of two boys and a husband to a wonderful wife. He wrote his first trilogy of novels in the early 2020s: the Song of Kamaria (*In the Orbit of Sirens, On the Winds of Quasars, and At the Threshold of the Universe*).

For more about this book and author, visit:

TABruno.com
Instagram.com/TABrunoAuthor
@TABrunoauthor.bsky.social
Goodreads.com/TABrunoAuthor

www.ingramcontent.com/pod-product-compliance
Lightning Source LLC
LaVergne TN
LVHW091622070526
838199LV00044B/904